Let Me Catch You

KENT DERON

Copyright © 2016 Kent Deron

All rights reserved.

Cover Design by www.thecovercollection.com

Editing by Charlie Winters

This book is a work of fiction. All names, characters, places and events are created from the author's imagination or used fictitiously.

This book contains adult themes intended for a mature audience.

For questions and comments about this book, please contact the author at kentderon@hotmail.com

DEDICATION

To all the other *strange little birds* out there

LET ME CATCH YOU

∞

ACKNOWLEDGMENTS

A huge amount of gratitude to my beta readers: Rob, Gala and Merel. Each of you offered such great feedback and advice for me to move the story forward.

Merel, I wanted to say a super special thank you for your enthusiasm and kindness in helping me. I really am grateful we connected.

Charlie, you have been so generous with your time, knowledge and humour. Thank you for being such a good sort. P.S., your music taste rocks!

To my pals, coffee and nicotine. Where would I be without you? Probably healthy and wealthy and going to bed at a reasonable hour. Still, both of you kept me motivated.

Family and friends, cheers for not stabbing your ears with knitting needles while listening to me go on and on about this tale stuck in my head. I know at times it probably felt as painful as watching holiday slides, so thank you for your patience.

And of course… *you*

PROLOGUE — JANUARY 31 1996

The night rode in on the back of a storm. It brought with it a howling gale saddled with thick grey clouds carrying angry rain that lashed the tiny town of Clifton below. The sea churned with driftwood, shifting heavy boulders along its ocean floor like marbles. But that wasn't all the waters were dumping on the coast this rough night. A sliver of silver moonlight falls on a corpse waiting to be delivered to the shore, its soul having departed its earthly enclosure two days prior.

This rugged New Zealand coast is well acquainted with death having visited its shores on numerous occasions. Since rival tribal wars where victors feasted on the flesh of their enemies, crew trapped in wrecked ships or fun seekers sucked out to sea by rips, grief has been part of the landscape. Some say the land is tapu. A sacred place that should not be ventured, not even approached. All who violate this open themselves up to a form of spiritual justice that can bring about great misfortune, sometimes death.

Dotted along its bluffs sit large pohutukawa trees, some hundreds of years old, the last remaining witnesses to some of these tragedies. Their limbs claw out above the sheer drop they sit atop with their tiny leaves hanging on for dear life. In summer, this Kiwi Christmas tree blossoms the most brilliant bright red, much like the colour of blood spilled through the years on the black sand below.

The strip of land where the town sits, hugs shallow fields gifting it a beach used as a playground by residents and holiday makers with short memories of the dangers that lurk on this shore. A short walk from the swimming beach high cliffs frame the coast where the unsuspecting can be caught in fast raging tides. Their bodies slammed against the cliffs, flesh ripped away by sharp rocks of the reef, eaten by sea creatures eventually caught by fishermen who take the catch home to feed hungry mouths.

Now another has been added to the tidal tally. The broken boy floating three hundred metres from land will be coughed up in the morning. His ragged corpse will lay face up, feet pointing to the sky as a crowd of onlookers inspect the grisly scene of death. His body now an empty shell will be a reminder to one young man of his guilt and involvement in this dark fairy tale. The beach will carry the stench of death, a cruel sweetness like a rank perfume.

This time, the sea will return this son of Clifton, but she won't be so quick to give out the boy's secrets. Shaun Munro will now be laid to the earth and connected to the land. He will be part of Clifton. Something the town folk have never granted the Munro family.

CHAPTER ONE — 2016

STEPHEN

The moment he opened the door to the stranger with green eyes, Stephen knew he could do it. That with the right situation, amount of pressure and booze—for both of them—he could have his way with Inver Murray. The unassuming dark-haired boy from twenty-years ago had grown into a pleasant-looking but awkward creature that reeked of self-doubt.

Stephen hadn't gone that way in a very long time. He was ashamed of that side of himself back then, and for that shame he wound up paying the dearest price anyone ever could. Not now though. Now, he didn't even view it as a *side*. Instead, he just saw it as a fluid movement along some invisible spectrum, one he was able to shift along with greater ease than others.

It wasn't that he particularly wanted to do it; he just wanted to prove a point. The deal he had made with Rusty all those years ago was mute now. Besides, it never included anything that said he couldn't fuck the lazy prick's son.

As much as he had himself to blame for Shaun's death, Rusty too had played a part, and now Stephen would be sure to get retribution, even if it was to be taken out on the dead man's son. He knew this obscure revenge was grasping at straws, but maybe if he did this, it could help alleviate some of his guilt. A guilt which through the years had snowballed into regret for being too scared to walk a path hand in hand with another man.

Stephen had tried praying—asking for forgiveness—but it didn't work. Prayers were nothing more than whispers for help in a burning building, uttered by the desperate and heard by no one.

The plan needed to be executed with careful

precision. A move too soon could deliver days of awkwardness—or worse—scare the hapless, straight Inver off before he finished cleaning up Rusty's house. Stephen had no intention of clearing up after the miserable ginger-haired bastard if he could help it. This dilemma meant it was all about timing.

The shy stranger now staying in Stephen's house lacked any real social skills and seemed desperate to make a good impression. This made him easy pickings. A compliment here, a wandering touch there, and this lad would be eating out the palm of his hand in less than a week.

Inver Murray needed to leave this farm broken and pay for the sins of his father. After all, Stephen had a score to settle.

CHAPTER TWO — 2016

INVER

It was a long way down to the reef below. A sheer drop of sixty feet where the waves crashed over jagged rocks emitting a thunderous blow, sending sea spray high splattering against the grey clay of the cliff. Inver stood a safe distance back from the edge, admiring the deadly drop. He shuddered, acknowledging the relatively small step separating safe ground from a ghastly end. Nature was like people in that way, he thought, danger and beauty settling hand in hand. His musing was cut by a wintery howl blowing in from the Tasman Sea, its bitter nips penetrating the thin threads of the suit he was wearing.

The stunning backdrop was the perfect complement to his host's enormous home with its abundance of rooms and extensive backyard. The section Inver stood in was an overgrown mess of native trees, shrubs and an assortment of citrus plants, all dotted through a yard close to an acre in size. The garden was a leafy oasis framed by miles of dull green farmland that ran inland to the foot of forested ranges. This suburban refuge belonged to his father's former boss, Stephen Davis, who had insisted Inver stay with him when he called three days before breaking the news that Inver's father had died.

Inver spotted a large tree perched precariously on the cliff's edge, shading a track leading down the cliff's face. The tree's trunk looked chipped and carved while its huge roots had broken through the dirt and clay of the cliff leaving them bare hanging above the sea. Any more erosion and the tree would tumble down. Inver contemplated descending the track to the reef below, but the tide was changing and soon the reef would be metres under water. Besides, the track looked far from sturdy. Sure, he was slim for his height of just over six feet, but it wasn't a risk he fancied taking.

Running a hand through his wavy black hair, Inver wished he had gotten a haircut before leaving Auckland. Too long without one was bringing out stubborn curls he had spent years trying to hide. Inver felt uncomfortable in the suit a size too big for him that he'd just worn to Rusty's funeral.

A lifetime of heavy drinking and smoking had finally caught up with Inver's father. The service had been a quick affair, attended by a small handful of stoic Clifton locals, including the pub maid who had poured the dead man's drinks for over three decades.

There were no eulogies—just in and out—well, in Rusty's case, just in and buried. This is what the man would have wanted, everyone said. Rusty hated funerals, especially the ones where people got up spouting bullshit about how wonderful the deceased had been, when in private they probably thought the person was a bastard. This philosophy definitely rang true about the man who theorised such an eloquent sentiment.

It was a relief now to be back at Stephen's, away from the funeral where he had felt like an imposter, shaking hands with his father's friends as each left through the cemetery gates. He may have been the only blood relative Rusty had left, but the truth was they barely knew each other. Life would go on without this man and the difference would be negligible to Inver. He hadn't cried at the news of Rusty's death and it seemed weird that a person could die and not one cheek ever get wet from a tear. Inver wondered whose fault this was, those who didn't feel the emotional impact or the individual who hadn't created enough of one for tears to flow.

Inver turned to make his way back inside the sprawling house. It was an extravagant monster for a farm house, but then this was Clifton. A remote seaside holiday town filled with wealthy commuters and mortgage-free land owners like Stephen Davis.

Before Inver even got two steps through the yard, a woman's voice called out to him.

"Inver, you want a coffee?" It was Kimmy, a friend of Stephen's.

"Yes, please," Inver replied.

The strong wind blowing drowned out his words. Kimmy's head lurched forward and she raised a hand to her ear. Inver ran up to join her on the porch.

"Yes, please. That would be great. Thanks."

"Coming right up then," she said.

A pretty blonde with a svelte figure and pleasant face, Inver suspected Kimmy was a couple years older than his thirty-one years of age. She was introduced as Stephen's *friend* but the way she doted on Stephen in-between lustrous looks told Inver she had lofty ambitions of becoming more than a friend. He had only met her that morning, but she seemed lovely and down-to-earth. She had been the one to make all the funeral arrangements according to Stephen, and Inver was grateful to be spared the humiliation of trying to arrange a service for a man he didn't know.

Inver followed Kimmy through the ranch slider that led into the lounge and dining room area. The vast living area had an expensive-looking grey lounge suite pressed against its cream coloured walls that were decorated with strategically placed photos and fancy bits of pottery.

Kimmy raced up the two steps that climbed to the kitchen where the jug was already boiling. She grabbed some cups from the pantry while Inver took a seat at the long dining table which had eight chairs to choose from.

Footsteps came down the hallway until in the doorway to the kitchen, Stephen appeared. He was still in his black dress pants from the funeral; his white shirt fully unbuttoned leaving his front exposed with its fine dusting of wispy chest hairs. He turned, giving Inver a smile.

"How you holding up, mate?" he asked.

"I'm all good. Just glad it's all done with, to be honest."

Stephen gave him a sympathetic look. "Yeah, I know what you mean. It's no fun burying your parents."

Surely they must know how unaffected by all this I am, Inver thought.

Stephen walked over to the kitchen bench, racking his knuckles on the counter. "So are you making one for me, trouble?"

"Ha, I'll give you trouble, Stephen Davis," Kimmy said. She giggled as she pretended to flick the spoon at his face.

Stephen joined Inver at the table. "You wanna watch that one, Inver," he said, lifting an eyebrow.

"No, Inver, you want to keep an eye on *him*, not me," Kimmy said.

Stephen relaxed back into his chair and swung his black sock-covered feet onto the table, all the while unashamedly scratching at his groin.

Through subtle eyes, Inver perved at Stephen who was busy teasing Kimmy. Even in his early-forties, Stephen Davis was an incredibly handsome man. Inver hadn't seen him for twenty years but he could still make heads turn like he had in the summer of his youth. Specks of grey scattered the sides of his light brown hair and there were more lines on his chiselled face than what Inver remembered, but those eyes were still the same—electric blue ponds that gave this man his x-factor.

Kimmy ambled over with three coffees and joined them at the table. Inver looked inside the white mug at its potent pitch-black liquid. *Good memory.* She had made him a coffee that morning and remembered just how he'd liked it. Black and strong.

"Has your mother emailed you back yet?" Kimmy asked.

"I haven't checked but I'm guessing I probably won't hear back from her 'till she gets home." Inver took a sip on the hot brew, burning his bottom lip. He quickly sucked it down with his tongue, trying to nurse his injured mouth.

"Oh, that's no good, you poor thing," Kimmy cooed.

Kimmy obviously had no idea about his family background. Even if Inver's mum, Donna, hadn't been on a fortnight cruise to the islands, there was no way she would have come to the funeral. She didn't have pleasant memories of her years in Clifton or her now deceased ex-husband. When Donna left with a ten-year-old Inver all those years ago, she vowed never to return.

"So, is there a Mrs Inver back up in Auckland waiting for you to get home?" Kimmy asked.

"Uh, no... no Mrs Inver back home," Inver said, feeling embarrassed. He didn't know why he couldn't just tell them he preferred guys. They probably wouldn't react badly.

Or would they?

A self-conscious Inver always guarded himself against others' views.

Kimmy ran a hand through her hair, smoothing it out. "Well, while you're down here, you can come join me one night at the pub and we can help find you a nice girl," she said.

"Stuff finding him a nice one. You need to find him a downright fucking *dirty* one," Stephen joked.

"That's enough from the cheap seats, thank you." Kimmy whacked Stephen's arm playfully. "Anyway, you always refuse to go drink there, so you won't have a choice in the matter."

"The lad's only in town for a week. Why would he want some girl who sits with her legs crossed, ain't I right, mate?" Stephen gave Inver a sly grin.

Oh god. Inver felt himself begin to blush. It was moments like this he hated having a pale complexion. Any embarrassment could be seen in a split second when his cheeks reddened. Inver quickly changed the subject to safer territory, rambling on about being back in Clifton after all these years.

Kimmy suddenly turned her head sharply, glaring at the kitchen clock. "Anyway boys, would you like me to cook you some dinner?"

"Nar, she's right, Kimbo," Stephen replied. "We can fix something up ourselves."

"Oh, come on, it's no trouble. We can't have poor Inver here putting up with your cooking, considering the day he's just had." Kimmy's eyes honed in on Inver like he was some sort of helpless child.

"What you think, Inver?" Stephen asked. "Fancy a decent meal or you wanna brave my culinary skills?"

Inver looked at Kimmy who sat with an eager smile. "Only if you don't mind. You don't have to go to any trouble just for me."

"Honestly, it's no problem," Kimmy said. She promptly made her way to the kitchen, rummaging in the freezer like she owned the place.

∞

Two hours later, Kimmy served them up a roast chicken, accompanied with crispy potatoes and healthy dollops of vegetables. It was far from the height of sophistication, but it must have been the best meal Inver had eaten for months. Since leaving his job he had lived on food accompanied with poverty—watery tins of baked beans and tasteless two-minute noodles.

At eight o'clock, Kimmy declared she had to get home to get her nightly TV soap fix.

Stephen found her addiction to drama plenty hilarious. "So, what painful shit have you got lined up tonight?"

Kimmy smiled. "Only the classics. Holyoake's, Coronation Street and Emmerdale," she said. "And they're not shit, Stephen. They are a beautiful art form of simmering emotions that are a snapshot in time of a changing society." Kimmy did her best to hold a straight face as she spouted the ridiculous sentence. Inver and Stephen laughed at her mocking summary.

"I'll take your word for it, but personally I'd rather swallow razor blades," Stephen scoffed.

"Maybe one day I'll get my own beautiful soap opera moment. 'Till then I'll live through theirs," Kimmy said.

She gave Stephen and Inver a hug and kiss on her way out, leaving the two men alone in the lounge. Inver sat there feeling awkward, unsure what to say to this man he hadn't seen for two decades. Luckily, the television hogged Stephen's attention, sparing Inver from scraping together any mind-numbing chat he could think of. After an hour of being seated in silence pretending to be interested in whatever it was on the television, he asked Stephen if it was alright to have a shower.

"Yeah, mate. Go for gold. You can use the ensuite; it's got the best pressure. Second on the left. Just grab yaself a towel from the rack behind the door," Stephen said, never taking an eye off the TV screen.

"Thank you." Inver went to his guest room and grabbed a fresh change of clothes; he tucked them under his arm and made his way to the bathroom where he found four towels folded neatly on a glossy metal rack as instructed. Inver turned the nozzle of the shower, sending water erupting from the spout. It hit the shower floor, echoing like a thousand war drums. He pulled his shirt forward and was greeted with a light pong of body odour mixed with stale cologne. Inver stripped out of his clothes and once the room misted, he stepped under the spray to absorb its warmth.

The water felt great tickling his back while freeing his body of dried sweat. Inver ran a finger down his hairy chest before resting it and tapping his taut stomach. He looked down at his wet trimmed pubes and flaccid member, his dark leg hair dribbling beads of water down to his long feet. His own nakedness made him aware how he was standing in the very place which Stephen probably stood nude every morning. The idea that he was naked in the same spot as such a sexy man turned Inver on; he began to wonder if Stephen ever played with himself in the shower.

The perverted thoughts ran thick and fast as Inver picked up a bar of soap sitting in an indented compartment in the wall. He studied the pale pink object in his hand, intrigued that he was holding an item that had been rubbed all over Stephen's body. Slowly and firmly, Inver pressed the soap around his torso, rising it up under his armpits then straight down between his legs, lathering thoroughly, hoping somehow it left traces of Stephen on him. Inver put the soap down and grabbed hold of his stiffening cock. He tugged furiously 'till he felt the full size of his girth between his fingers. With his free hand, he cupped his smooth balls and closed his eyes, imagining Stephen standing there beside him.

As he got lost deeper in the fantasy, he felt himself getting close to shooting. He was about to moan and release his load, but just before he could, the erotic images of Stephen disappeared and were replaced with *that face*: the ever-present resident of his mind who refused to stop haunting him. Inver let go of himself, his body seizing with hurt. He fell back against the shower wall, slowly sliding down under the nozzle's spray and began to cry as a tender breeze enwrapped his aching body.

CHAPTER THREE — NOVEMBER 1995

STEPHEN

The sun shone brilliantly on Stephen and his two mates. *More like mate and associate.* With a hand above his eyes, shielding the sting of the sun, Stephen peered into the distance from the top of the grassy ridge they were perched on, looking south to Mt Taranaki. Its perfect cone shape peak was in full display, not a cloud in sight.

The ridge top where they stood was called Razor's Mile, and it climbed high above the surrounding paddocks of Stephen's family farm. Below them, the hill broke off into smaller ridges leading down to flatter land. From above, the bare ridges looked like veins in an old hand, dry and lumpy, forking out in all directions. Looking down at the steep gradient of the hill, a moment of clarity came over Stephen. *This is probably a stupid idea.* It was no doubt fuelled on by sitting in the sun after drinking one too many beers. *OK, this is definitely a stupid idea.*

An hour before, they'd decided to come up and have a go at grass sledding. Drinking beside the pool in Stephen's backyard had grown boring, and although warm for November, there was no way anyone was jumping in the water. It was Shaun who had spotted an old plastic sale sign leaning against the vine-covered garden shed, giving him the idiotic idea.

"Yeah, I saw a group of guys doing it at the Fitzroy golf course," Shaun informed them.

"Sounds a bit fucking lame to me," Luke said.

"It'll be like that movie, Cool Runnings, mun," Shaun said with a terrible impression of a Jamaican accent.

Luke guzzled the last of his beer. "We can't slide around a back lawn, ya fucking moron," he muttered, throwing his empty can at the bin. The can hit the side with a loud clunk and fell on the patio next to two previous attempts. "Unless…" Luke's voice perked up.

"Unless what?" Stephen asked.

"We go up Razor's Mile." Luke raised his eyebrows.

"Where's that?" Shaun asked, completely oblivious.

Luke and Stephen gave each other a sly grin.

"Come on, we'll show you," Stephen said. "Bring your sled, Rudolph."

Now stood high above the cliff-like ridge, holding the sale sign, Shaun probably wished he hadn't taken them up on the offer. Stephen was grinning ear to ear, waiting to see if the fool would have the balls to go through with it.

Luke stood towering over Shaun, urging him to start this kamikaze grass ride. Next to each other they looked like David and Goliath. Luke—white in winter, red in summer—with a wild mop of brown hair was tall and bulky, every inch the rugby player. Shaun, in comparison, with his creamy gold tan, was slight in stature and an inch away from being considered short.

"Fuck, give me a minute," Shaun demanded. He placed the sign on the ground before seating himself down and wriggling his butt on the makeshift sled.

Stephen could sense Shaun's trepidation, as the associate of the group bought time pretending to line the sled up just right for its grassy trajectory.

"I knew you wouldn't fucking do it, critter," Luke bellowed. "See, he's just a soft cock." Luke spun round and shot Stephen a look, encouraging him to join in with egging Shaun on.

Shaun glared up at the domineering Luke. "Yeah, well I don't see your fat arse sitting here to have a go," he snapped back.

Luke gave Shaun a not-so-playful punch on the shoulder that Shaun laughed off. He rubbed where Luke's fist had landed. Then, without warning, Luke jumped behind him and gave Shaun's back a firm shove.

"Off ya go, bro," Luke sputtered.

Shaun was caught off guard, quickly grabbing each side of the sign and hunching his knees up under his chin, bracing himself for impact. He careened down the hill, soon building up a heart-stopping velocity. Stephen and Luke cheered him on as he gathered speed, hurtling down the hill.

"Fuck yeah!" Luke screamed, fist punching the air.

Shaun was nearly at the bottom when the sled hit a clump of tussock grass, hurling his body into the air. With flailing limbs, he ricocheted the rest of the way down until he landed in a crumpled heap at the foot of the hill.

Luke and Stephen's cheering fell deadly still—frozen in place—staring down at the motionless Shaun. Stephen willed his legs to move and ran straight past Luke, scooting down the hill on his backside to reach Shaun.

Stephen reached their stricken friend in a blitz of panic. "Shaun, man! Shaun, you okay?"

Luke came puffing to a halt beside him, standing with his hands planted atop his head. "Fuck, I think he's dead."

Shaun's eyes were closed, lying flat on his back, his tanned limbs lifelessly spread.

Stephen placed a hand on Shaun's shoulder, giving it a light squeeze. "Shaun?" he asked worryingly. No response. "Shaun?"

"BOO!" Shaun sprung to his feet like a jack-in-the-box, giving Stephen the fright of his life. Stephen tripped backwards, falling on his arse, his heart pounding so hard he thought it would explode in his mouth. Luke and Shaun both keeled over laughing.

Stephen felt a split second of relief, his pulse slowly pacifying as he caught his breath before anger took hold. "That's not fucking funny," he snarled, his eyes shooting Shaun the filthiest look they could muster.

Shaun stopped laughing and his posture went rigid. Once seeing how wild Stephen was, he quickly dressed his face with an apologetic look. "Sorry, man."

Stephen punched the ground with both fists. "Fucking arsehole, I thought you were dead." As soon as he said it, he knew he sounded too upset.

Luke's laughter trailed off. "Settle down, Stevie. He was only joking."

With a scowl still on his face, Stephen felt stupid for not being able to laugh at himself.

Shaun trod in circles, smoothing dust from his earth stained knees. He pulled his long dark brown fringe up from his forehead where it dangled, hiding his equally dark eyes.

He picked up the sale sign and extended it out to Luke, waiting for him to take it. "Guessing you're up next." Shaun flashed Luke a cocky smile.

Luke held his hands out in protest. "Fuck that shit," he said. "It's alright for runts like you, but if one of us went down, we'd keep going 'till we reached the fucking road."

Luke made a good if exaggerated point, Stephen thought.

"Aww, so who's the soft cock now, Luke?" Shaun teased.

"That'd still be you, critter," Luke fired back.

Luke walked over and ruffled Shaun's hair, bringing Shaun's long fringe back down, blocking his vision. *Pfft.* A quick huff of breath restored his vision again.

Shaun went over to Stephen who was still sitting on the ground, simmering in anger. Shaun's lips curled into a guilty smile. "I'm sorry, Stephen." He extended out his hand. "Thanks for coming to check on me." Shaun's eyes shimmered with genuine remorse.

Stephen studied Shaun's hand before gripping it and hoisting himself to his feet.

"At least I know who to rely on in an emergency," Shaun said, "unlike someone." He jokingly pointed a finger at Luke.

Stephen looked down at his watch. *2:45 p.m.* "Look guys, I gotta get back to the house anyway. Delphi said she'd be calling after three-thirty."

They both stared at him, unsure if they had heard him right.

"Gotcha self a new prospect, Casanova?" Luke said with more than a tinge of jealousy.

"Is that Delphi Savage?" Shaun asked.

"Sure is," Stephen declared with some pride.

Luke's eyes widened. "Oh man, you know I've always had a thing for her." He sounded like a child who had had their toy stolen.

Stephen grinned. "All's fair in love and war 'till the pants are down, mate." This would only rile up his friend's jealousy more, which Stephen got a kick out of.

He had bumped into Delphi the day before at the general store when she nearly ran him over by accident with her trolley. This near-collision sprung up a conversation started by her endless apologising. They'd not seen each other since last summer's semester break and she somehow looked even better than he remembered. Luke had been madly in love with her growing up, but she had been on Stephen's wish list too, just not to the same degree.

Stephen knew though, that he suffered from—and revelled in—a well-earned reputation for working his way through the local girls. As a result, Delphi had always stayed politely out of his reach, keeping a safe distance, never daring to succumb to being another notch on his well-adorned belt of conquests.

He was more than a little vain. At five-feet-eleven, he had a slender but well-built physique, brown-blond hair, blue eyes and an attractive smile that masked his usually less-than-pure intentions. The day before had gone so well though that numbers were exchanged and it got Stephen thinking that the previously impossible was now entirely possible.

"Give us that." Luke grabbed the sale sign from Shaun and threw it across the paddock like an overgrown Frisbee. "She probably won't even call, bro."

Stephen ignored Luke's attempt to burst his ego as they began walking back to the house. "Nar, she will," he said in a confident tone, bordering on smug.

"I'm so jealous! I'd give her the ride of her life if I were you," Shaun blurted out.

That'd be the day.

"As if you'd fucking know how, virgin," Luke said hotly, putting Shaun in his place at the bottom of their pecking order.

"Piss off! I'm not a virgin," Shaun protested.

Shaun was always fending off this accusation, a little too defensively, Stephen thought.

"Sorry, Shaun, but fucking your mum and sister don't count," Luke said.

"Eww, what the fuck?" Shaun flipped Luke the finger.

"Yeah, my mistake, even your mum would turn you down and that ain't like her," Luke replied, raising two fingers in response.

"Dick," Shaun muttered feebly.

Stephen tried to ignore the sore point, but it was true. Shaun's mum had more than a little reputation around town for being easy pickings. She wasn't known as *Desperate Debbie* for nothing.

Stephen turned to Luke. "So do you know when Troy's back home?"

"He said he was gonna stay a bit with Clare and her folks, then come up next week."

Troy was Luke and Stephen's other good mate. Together they were a tight trio. Troy had been dating Clare for four years and as a result wasn't as socially available, but he still did his best to fit in time with the boys each summer.

"Lucky shit, gets to come home and swan back off to university in a few months," Stephen said enviously. He had just finished his own pointless arts degree and was back in Clifton permanently; ready to begin work on the family farm. Being the only son of a sixth generation farming family came with expectations and he had returned home to fulfil them.

"Cheer up, Stevie. It ain't all bad here," Luke said.

"True, but we're barely in our twenties and already becoming our parents. You and me farmers and Troy on his way to being a lawyer like his dad," Stephen replied.

Luke grinned at the depressing observation. "I'm not sure that philosophy is one-hundred percent correct, mate."

"What ya mean?" Stephen asked.

"Well, Shaun's a grease monkey, not a dealer or a whore."

They both burst out laughing.

Shaun sighed dramatically for effect. "Just cos my mum doesn't have tits down to her knees like yours both do doesn't make her a whore." Shaun gave them both a condescending smile before pretending to walk like he was tripping over heavy boobs. "You guys must get tired of helping them up all the time," he joked.

Luke laughed while Stephen just rolled his eyes at their social cling-on, who through years of sticking like shit to a blanket had become tolerated more than accepted.

Shaun was a year younger and a Munro, which meant nothing good in these parts. Growing up here, before Stephen and the other wealthy kids left for boarding school, they never gave the try-hard clown the time of day. Luckily for Shaun, his relevance had increased in recent years, due to his ability to deliver them a steady supply of pot and booze during summer breaks, thanks to his mother's contacts and vices.

Shaun, not one to keep quiet, continued talking nonstop the whole way back through the dry paddocks. Anything and everything from what were Stephen and Luke doing that night or dribbling on about what car he was fixing up at Bob's Panel n Paint, where he worked.

Does he ever shut up?

As if Luke had read Stephen's mind, he blurted out, "Fuck, man. Give your mouth a rest."

Stephen laughed, hoping Shaun would get the hint to zip it.

Shaun walked on unfazed by their bluntness. "I can't help being so interesting."

"No, Shaun. You're confusing *interesting* with bullshit," Luke flung back.

Shaun ignored the jab, instead turning his attention to kicking a small rock like a soccer ball as they walked along.

"Well, only about six weeks now 'till my fight," Luke crowed.

"Oh yeah, how do you think you'll do?" Stephen asked.

Luke blinked at him like he had asked a stupid question. "I'll win of course," he said confidently. "I could be competing in Sydney come 2000 at this rate."

Luke-the-monstrosity-with-muscles was good at boxing, no word about it, but he wasn't *Olympics* good. Boxing had been his newly acquired sporting obsession after accepting the reality he would never represent New Zealand in Rugby or Cricket. Luke was always training hard at something, chasing a dream of sporting glory, the closest thing Kiwis could hope to achieving superstardom.

As Luke continued on pumping up his sporting prowess, Stephen zoned out. The walk back to the house was dragging, and the sun was packing a ruthless punch as it always did in New Zealand, compliments of a sapped ozone hole. Stephen scratched his back and felt it was clammy from sweat. His mind wandered to the idea of taking Delphi to the beach for a swim. Any excuse seeing her in a bikini. *Or less.*

The sexy images he conjured up quickly had an effect on his body, bringing on a semi. He reached down pretending to scratch himself in an effort to reposition his cock firmly to the side, hiding his state of arousal.

Once back at the house, Luke and Shaun piled into Luke's silver Ute. Luke wound down his window, calling out to Stephen before he had a chance to go inside

"Oi, would you be up for a hunt when Troy gets back?" Luke asked.

Stephen walked back towards the Ute and stood beside the driver's side. "Yeah, could do. We haven't been out the three of us in ages."

Shaun sat like an impatient child in the passenger's seat, fiddling with the hem of his shorts before asking, "Can I come? I've never been hunting."

Luke laughed. "And you probably shouldn't start. You'll just be a fucking burden."

"Nar, I could help carry your guys' stuff or something," Shaun said, sounding a little too desperate.

Stephen popped his head in the window and leered across. "Okay, but no playing dead on the ground this time or I promise I'll shoot."

Luke started the engine. "It's okay, Shaun. You can play dead as much as you like. Stephen would miss anyway."

"Funny guy," Stephen groaned. "Anyway, give me a call when Troy's back and yeah, we'll arrange it." He slapped the side of the Ute and stepped away, watching them drive off before going inside to wait for his phone call. Maybe being home wasn't going to be so bad after all.

CHAPTER FOUR — 1995

STEPHEN

The back tyres skidded over the metal road, flicking a haze of dust trailing the car's path. The old green Telstar had seen better days, but it still managed to zip round the bends with the agility of a trapeze artist.

Stephen's sweaty hands gripped the steering wheel, his sight set dead ahead, racing to his destination. He was running late again. His mother insisted this was a habit he'd acquired since coming into the world nearly three weeks overdue. The added wait for her bundle of joy probably compounded her disappointment when she discovered he was not the daughter she had wanted to compliment the first born son. Fate, of course, had known what they had not.

Troy had arrived back in town the night before and they had all agreed to meet up at Luke's place on Wairua Road to go hunting. Luke had his own house on the family farm, just a few kilometres down the road from his parents. Luke's family, the Bridgemans, owned the craggy wet paddocks Wairua Road winded through, reaching far inland to the isolated hinterland which was all bush-clad hills, filled to the brim with goats and pigs. Not the cream of farming crop but still a sizable station worth holding onto, 'cos as Stephen's dad would often say, "They ain't making any more land."

Like a lot of the guys around here, Luke took his shooting seriously. This instilled in him a competitive streak that could make him difficult to bear when it came to any hunting trip. Stephen preferred the hunt of girls at the beach, the one where flirting was the weapon and sex the bullet. Of the three of them, Stephen knew he was the weakest at hunting. This made Shaun's debut appearance a blessing in disguise since he would likely get the bulk of the mocking—a treatment he was more than accustomed to.

Stephen changed gears as he rounded the last bend before driving into Luke's property. Luke's Ute, dusty and covered in crap, sat parked next to Troy's near new Holden Commodore. Shaun didn't have a car and relied on the mercy of the others to pick his arse up, hence his less than frequent appearances with the group. Stephen assumed it must have been Troy's mercy that filled the role of taxi today.

In front of the house, Luke and Troy were decked out in bush shirts, shorts, and gaiters above their boots. They were knelt down, assorting their weapons on the ground. Shaun stood idly behind them in a red singlet with his arms folded, watching them dissect their killing instruments. Stephen honked the horn and parked up next to Troy's car. Stepping out of the vehicle, his nostrils were immediately hit with a grassy pong from the freshly mowed lawn. He fetched his gear from the trunk and made his way over to join everyone.

"It finally decides to arrive," Luke bellowed from his crouched position.

Troy waved and walked over to Stephen, gripping his hand in a firm shake. "Good to see you, man."

"Yeah. Shit, it's been months since we all caught up," Stephen said. Troy looked exactly the same. Sandy hair with skin so pale the guy could probably hide in a milk bottle. "How's Clare? I'm amazed she let you out to play." Stephen enjoyed giving Troy this ritualistic ribbing.

Troy laughed. "Yeah, she's good. She's coming up in a few days, so I'm off the leash 'till then." He smiled, showing off his ridiculously straight teeth. The smile probably hid the fact he was already missing her. ==Troy adored Clare and was content to be on a leash.==

"Well, we better get a move on since arsehole here has put us an hour behind," Luke blurted.

Stephen rolled his eyes at the exaggeration to his tardiness.

Shaun strolled over to stand with Stephen and Troy. "Did Delphi end up calling you?" he asked.

"Uh, yeah she did." Stephen was surprised by the question since this was week-old news.

"Yep, he ain't half stopped going on about for days,"

Luke said as he packed his rifle in its case and placed it in the back of his Ute.

"Fuck off, I have," Stephen hollered back.

"So... what happened?" Shaun asked, in little more than a whisper. His brown eyes pinged with curiosity.

"Well, nothing yet," Stephen said. "We're meeting up tomorrow night."

Shaun raised his hands up and crossed his fingers. "Good luck."

Troy slapped Stephen on the shoulder. "You don't need luck, do you, mate? Just lots of booze so she has no idea who she's with."

Shaun snorted, trying to hold in a laugh.

"Thanks for the faith, guys," Stephen said, his words loaded with contempt.

Luke started the Ute, revving it loudly, letting them know to hurry up. "Come on, fellas."

They grabbed their stuff and put it in the back. As they jumped in their seats, Luke wasted no time in zooming off through a side gate on the property which led to a dirt track. Stephen knew this track well like he did all the ones on Luke's farm. This particular path led high up into the hills around the farm where vast forest kept the paddocks at bay. As kids, the bush here had served as the ultimate playground. Tangled trees and shallow creeks had been their kingdom where they'd spent hours exploring. Once they'd grown out of the antics of climbing trees and playing hide 'n seek, these hills had become their killing fields.

The further the road went, the bumpier it became, shaking Stephen's bladder and bringing on a desperate need to pee. The track continued through the paddocks until bush framed both sides of their path. Tree limbs dangled inward like monster claws, grabbing for the road, casting thick shadows which left only shreds of daylight. The Ute continued chugging along in the shade, 'till eventually they came to a large circular clearing signalling the end of the road.

As soon as Luke turned the engine off, Stephen jumped out of the Ute as quick as he could, racing toward the trees to unzip his pants and take a slash. He was so lost in the physical relief of letting out what felt like an ocean, he hadn't heard Luke sneak up behind him until it was too late. Luke grabbed him by the hips and jolted his body, sending dribbles of pee splashing over Stephen's fingers and shoes.

"Fuck sake, Luke," Stephen fumed, flicking his hands clean. He looked down at his pants to see dark piss stains streaking down his legs. All three of his mates were busy laughing their heads off at his misfortune. He zipped up and wiped his hands on the grass, casting them a look so shitty it didn't need spoken subtitles.

Luke clasped his hands behind his head, trying to catch his breath from laughing so hard. "Calm down, bro. I was only taking the piss." The three of them roared again with hysterical laughter.

Stephen held his death stare, not the slightest bit in the mood to laugh at himself. He stropped back over to the group and grabbed his rifle and backpack out of the Ute. He bided his time, fiddling with the zips on the bag, not yet ready to talk to his mates. While he sulked, Troy and Luke paired off in a huddle, discussing their plans for the hunt like it was a secret mission. Out the corner of his eye, Stephen saw Shaun approaching him. This pairing suddenly reeked of being pre-planned.

Shaun stopped a couple metres away, sensing Stephen's need for space. "Did you want me to carry anything?" he asked cautiously.

"No, it's fine. I've got it," Stephen snapped. He snatched the backpack up and slung it over his shoulder.

"Okay, so, do I just follow you?"

"Looks like it," Stephen huffed, "wait here." He walked over to Luke and Troy who were still huddled on the other side of the Ute.

"Aren't we all going as a group?" he asked.

"Nar, we figured we'd take the north ridge and let you guys have the valley. We'll meet back here at three o'clock," Luke said, running his hands down his front, trying to avoid looking Stephen in the eyes.

"For fuck's sake." Stephen turned around making sure Shaun wasn't within hearing shot. He lowered his voice and continued, "Why do I get lumbered with numb nuts? You're the one who invited him."

"Cos he's more at your level," Luke said with a smearing of sarcasm.

Stephen unleashed a frosty eye roll and shook his head.

"Oh, come on, Stevie. We wanna go up the north ridge and he'll just hold us up. So, if you take him down the valley, that'd be a big help." Luke did his best to sound like the situation was accidental.

Stephen sighed, his breath coming out hot and vexed.

"Shaun's lucky he's with such a patient sort," Troy teased.

"Good one," Stephen groaned.

Luke lowered his head and whispered in a gravelly voice. "Look, he's lining me up a tinny for tomorrow night, so if you can babysit him today, I'll split it with you."

Stephen bit his lip, thinking it over. He could do with some weed for his Friday night, maybe share it with Delphi? He finally nodded. "Okay, just this once. But if he slips off a cliff, I ain't responsible."

Luke grinned. "Well, try not to push him too hard then," he said, "but I'll understand if you do."

"Fuck, since when did you two become so nice to your mates?" Troy asked.

Luke shot Troy a crooked smile. "Hey, that's just rude. You don't call a Munro a mate, Troy."

The three of them sniggered.

"What are youse laughing at?" Shaun called out, seemingly unaware.

"Nothing, mate, just giving Stephen shit about his date with Delphi," Luke called back.

"Trueness," Shaun replied, none the wiser.

"Moron," Luke mouthed to Stephen and Troy.

Troy tapped Luke on the shoulder. "Shall we make a move?"

"Yeah, may as well." Luke looked at Stephen. "Right, Stevie boy, we're off. Take good care of the little critter." He gave Stephen a wink and with that he and Troy disappeared into the bush, leaving Stephen standing there feeling resentful for being left to deal with the burden of Shaun.

Stephen took a deep breath, imagining he was inhaling the wealth of patience needed to see the day through. When he turned around, he saw Shaun wandering across the grassy clearing with a sense of direction in his stride. Stephen moved around the vehicle to get a better look at where he could possibly be headed. In the centre of the clearing were three rusty metal drums. Shaun kicked the side of the one closest to him; it bellowed a loud clunking echo through the air. The idiot then leaned over, reaching his hand deep inside the drum.

"Shaun, don't!" Stephen yelled.

Shaun spun around. "What?"

"Don't put your hand in there in case they go off!" Inside the drums was where Luke stored claw-like traps to catch possums and feral cats—barbaric contraptions, capable of severing a hand.

Shaun ignored the warning and went ahead inspecting the drum anyway.

What did I say, idiot?!

Shaun dug his hand in, pulling out one of the traps and made a hell of a racket as it rattled up the sides. "Fuck, this is a meaty weapon." He raised the trap high in the air, looking up at it almost hypnotised by its capabilities.

Stephen marched over to him. "Yeah, well, best you just put it back."

Shaun dropped it back in the bin, causing another loud echo of noise. Stephen wondered how he would get through the next few hours without ripping the guy's head off. He set off, making his way to the trees with Shaun quickly following behind.

"Hold up," Shaun called out.

"What now?" Stephen growled, spinning around to find Shaun hunched over tying his shoe laces up.

"Reckon we'll get anything?"

"Not if we stay here all day."

"Sorry, man." Shaun's face was locked with concentration as he tied the last of his laces. "Ready." Shaun sprung to his feet. "Can you believe it? All these years here and it's my first time out hunting."

Stephen looked at his assigned helper in his red singlet, camo shorts and flimsy canvas sneakers. "Funnily enough, I can," he mumbled.

∞

The pair trampled through the woods, beads of perspiration dripping from their faces as the merciless sun streamed through gaps in the trees. Sticky wet air made it feel like breathing under a cooking sea. Korus on unfurling silver fern frons decorated the waist-high foliage they waded through, Stephen occasionally letting a punga leaf launch back to whack Shaun under the guise of accidental. The forest with its tall, native trees and strangling vines had been alive with bird song and wonder, but after two hours it had become a tiring slog against nature which had left Stephen with a sore foot. The constant buzz and bites of insects irritated Stephen's hands and face almost as much as Shaun's trivial and constant nattering.

A cool rippling creek was a welcome sight. Stephen tore off his boots and peeled away his sweat-sodden socks to discover the source of his sore foot was a bright red blister. He dipped his feet in the cool water, feeling instant relief.

Stephen glanced over his shoulder and saw Shaun shirtless, unbuttoning his shorts. "What are you doing, nutter?"

"Going for a swim," Shaun answered, surprised at the question before stripping his shorts away to stand before Stephen in a pair of cheap-looking white briefs.

Stephen shook his head and laughed. "Suit yourself." He leaned back on his elbows, leaving his feet to dangle in the water while he watched the clueless Munro tiptoe to the edge of the creek. Shaun peered over, inspecting its depth. His body looked like it could do with cooling off, his olive skin glistening and his leg hair sleek from all of the sweat.

"I hope there's no taniwhas," Shaun said, turning to flash Stephen a grin.

Stephen found himself wishing there were such things as taniwhas, a water monster to drag the painful Munro away and leave him in peace and quiet.

Shaun teetered on the edge, gazing into the creek. "Looks cold," he said before loudly declaring, "fuck it." He jumped high in the air, tucking his knees up under his chin before bombing the water, sending a big splash that drenched Stephen's legs.

Stephen grumbled pointless profanity at his dopey sidekick who was under the water and couldn't hear a word. Shaun emerged from the surface, spouting water out of his mouth like a fountain. He relaxed into the creek, floating on his back, watching Stephen watch him. A scar on his eyebrow appeared more prominent as he wiped water from his face.

It was now quiet apart from the rippling of the creek, a blissful and rare peace with such noisy company. Stephen wondered how Luke and Troy were getting on, surely they wouldn't be far off returning to the Ute, no doubt crowing with stories of what they had tracked down and killed. Stephen would return with little to show for his efforts other than a blister and mosquito bites.

Shaun's voice disrupted his thoughts. "All we need is a beer and we'd be set."

Stephen nodded. "I reckon."

"And like one of those fishing rod holders with a space for the can so we can catch us a feed," Shaun said.

Stephen smiled. He knew they would catch fuck all in this creek. "Actually, that would be really cool. I've been meaning to get one of those for ages."

Shaun rambled on about how he could make one when Stephen saw movement out of the corner of his eye. He put a finger to his lips, signalling for Shaun to be quiet. Instinct told him there was opportunity nearby.

Further down the river, standing on some rocks, was a shaggy brown and white goat feeding on grassy reeds. Stephen quietly slunk to his belly and fetched his rifle tentatively. He lined up the barrel and looked through the gauge, eyeing up the target. The goat froze with a piece of grass in its mouth as if it could sense the danger it was in. Stephen tightened his jaw and placed his finger on the trigger, giving it a gentle squeeze. *Ping.*

At first, Stephen assumed he had missed. The goat stood there with a dumbfounded look on its face, a piece of grass still in its mouth. Gradually, the goat lost its footing, scrambling on the rocks before collapsing on its side.

Stephen yelped a cry of victory, picked up his bag and ran barefoot towards the stricken animal. He slid down the riverbank onto the rocks where the goat lay bleeding. The animal heaved, gasping for breath, its feet thrusting about before finally giving in to the bullet's full effect.

Clumsy footsteps came from behind; Stephen craned his neck upward to find Shaun scrambling down the bank having followed in pursuit. Shaun carefully walked over loose stones to join Stephen knelt over his prize.

"Shit," Shaun muttered, staring at the dying animal.

Stephen rummaged through his bag and grabbed out a knife. He clutched the goat by the horns and placed the blade to its throat, slicing deeply, severing life and misery. Blood gushed out its neck, pouring little red rivers, running down the rocks into the creek.

In the distance, Stephen heard the faint yahooing of Luke and Troy, coming to inspect the war cry he had just bellowed. *Fucking idiots shouldn't be in our area.* Stephen wiped the blade clean and was about to begin gloating when he looked over his shoulder and saw Shaun standing a few feet away with wet eyes.

He's not, is he?

Shaun sniffed and rubbed an eye before turning away in a desperate attempt to hide his face.

"Don't let them see you like that or they'll give you shit for weeks," Stephen warned him.

Shaun nodded and wiped the tears from his face.

Normally, this would be the type of thing Stephen would have great joy in passing on to the others. But it didn't seem right to use this against him, the weakest member of their group.

CHAPTER FIVE — 2016

INVER

Stephen had insisted there was no hurry in cleaning Rusty's place up. Inver was grateful; not many landlords would be quite so accommodating. Then again, Rusty had worked for Stephen's parents before Stephen had inherited the farm—all up twenty-five years—so maybe that had extended some loyalty to be passed on.

Mind you, the little Inver *did* know about his father, thanks to the few memories of his own and stories from his mother, was that the man suffered from a severe case of being a lazy sod. Rusty would sooner light a smoke and have a beer than lift a finger. Inver's mother would joke that Rusty's hands would be the softest of any farmer going, having not been exposed to a hard day's work in their life.

Inver stood looking out the Davis family home's large lounge windows towards the horizon of blue sea. Concrete grey clouds hung ominously in the sky, deliberating whether or not to rain. Knowing Inver's luck, the sky would open up and bucket down the moment he stepped foot outside. He was trying to put off as long as possible the chore of leaving Stephen's warm house to go clean up his father's mess.

A loud beep came out of Inver's pants pocket. He hurriedly dug a hand in retrieving his phone, a rush of excitement ringing through him—someone was actually thinking of him.

Battery dying. Great.

He should have known better than to think it would be a text message. His days of having countless friends contacting him were well gone, not to mention the fact he was at least an hour's drive away from getting any sort of reception. This forgotten corner of New Zealand with its rugged coastline and enclosing hills worked as a barrier to modern technology, one of the few places the twenty-first century had yet to penetrate with cell phone coverage.

Reluctantly leaving the luxury of the Davis homestead, Inver walked down the flower-fringed driveway 'till he came to a fork in the road. If he continued straight ahead, he would end up on the main highway that led into Clifton. Turning right put him on a muddy track that would take him to his childhood home. He turned right begrudgingly.

The walk to Rusty's wasn't an overly long one, but far enough away so not to corrupt the image of the Davis family home. Sporadically placed pine trees loomed over the dirt track, cutting through lush green fields filled with curious cattle.

Inver carried a yellow bucket and a mop tucked under his arm. Inside the bucket held a variety of cleaning products: bleach, spray 'n wipe, toilet cleaner and a bunch of toxic heavy-duty agents. Inver was physically ready—even if not mentally—for the onslaught of cleaning.

Treading carefully along the track, Inver did his best to avoid stepping in any solidified cow pats or drenching his shoes in dirty mud ponds. A few minutes into the hazardous walk, the old house came into view. The dilapidated two-bedroom weatherboard home was in desperate need of a facelift, its white paint peeling and its corrugated iron roof rusted to within an inch of its life. It certainly hadn't seen a lick of maintenance since Inver's mum dragged the pair of them away in the middle of a crisp night in 1996.

The only new item in the scene was Rusty's red Ford Mondeo parked in the lean to carport, likely the only thing the man owned of any value. Inver went and took a closer look at the sparkling car, sizing up how much he could sell it for. Any windfall of cash from Rusty's death would be a great help to Inver, who was definitely residing in poverty-peak since fleeing his job and *that face*.

After inspecting the car, he went to the front door, put down the bucket and mop and fumbled for the keys jingling in his pocket. It seemed pointless the place being locked; the lower panel of the door was covered with a flimsy piece of cardboard nursing a broken sheet of glass. Anybody stupid enough to rob the place would be doing Inver a favour. After twisting the tiny key every which way he could, the lock finally clicked open and Inver pushed forward, stepping inside a memory.

A musty, dank smell swarmed across Inver's face. He coughed and raised a hand to cover his nose. "Sheesh, Rusty, you could have cleaned if you knew I was coming," he joked to himself.

The entrance went straight into the kitchen where he placed down his cleaning products and leaned the mop against the kitchen bench. Inver ran a finger along its grimy surface, leaving his fingerprint covered in a sticky grey residue.

The ice blue walls snowed the kitchen under a chilly impression, one which even a hot summer's day would struggle to melt. A cruddy dining table stood at the end of the bench, its surface smudged with numerous tanned rings from spilt morning coffees.

The very dead living room came immediately off the kitchen. The poorly decorated room had a scungy lounge suite pressed against the walls and an old box television set with bunny ears sitting in the corner. Stacks of old newspapers were dotted through the lounge like dusty columns amongst a sea of beer cans littering the rotting carpet. In front of an arm chair was a cardboard box acting as a coffee table, an overflowing ashtray sitting in its drooping, flimsy centre. Inver imagined his father sitting there, half-cut, ashing away his filterless roll-your-owns—adding to a haze of smoke that climbed up the walls, tainting the ceilings an even darker cancerous yellow.

Inver should have expected the workload before him. When he had asked Stephen how the place was, Stephen had replied with a sly grin, "Let's just say, you'll be kept busy a while."

That was the understatement of the century.

While Stephen had insisted he could stay with him as long as he liked, Inver had hoped to swoop in and piss off in a couple of days, but thanks to Rusty's filthy habits, he would be here all bloody week.

Why am I so surprised?

Rusty had always been a grubby man. He would walk inside from a day's work and sit down for dinner in his shit-stained overalls usually eliciting a moan of disapproval from Inver's mum that would always go ignored. Even on the rare treat when they would go into New Plymouth for KFC—the Murray family equivalent of fine dining—Rusty would be dressed like a pauper. He would sit there, hunched over the bucket of chicken, feasting like a ravenous castaway before slurping up potato and gravy like a milkshake. The other customers would give disgusted looks at the Murray family patriarch. Rusty just didn't care and would loudly declare, "Fuck 'em all." It used to make Inver giggle hearing this while his mother looked like she wanted to crawl under the table and hide from all the judgemental glares.

Fuck 'em all was Rusty's response to most things in life. Why didn't you vote, Rusty? "Fuck 'em all." The All Blacks losing a rugby match? "Fuck 'em all." Even coughing his guts out on a cigarette. "Fuck 'em all". The man fucked 'em all right through life with his don't-give-a-shit attitude, something Inver wished he had inherited. Instead, he always worried what others thought of him to the crippling point.

THUD, THUD, THUD. The loud knocking at the front door echoed through the toxic house with pulsating urgency. Inver raced to the door, expecting an emergency, ripping it open to find an old man in a trench coat, holding a large envelope between his dirty fingers. The old man's hair was buried under a leopard print beanie, his floppy cauliflower ears sticking out the sides, granting him the look of a simpleton.

"Who the fuck are you?" the old man said, staring up at Inver who towered over his short height.

Inver was taken aback. Not some sweet old man at all, just a cantankerous old shit. "I'm Inver Murray," he answered, extending a hand out to the frowning old man.

"Who the fuck is Inver Murray when he's at home?"

"I'm Rusty's son… I'm here cleaning his house up." Inver took a deep breath trying to compose himself. "He died, you know," he added, hoping to inflict some guilt.

"Yeah, I know that already." The old man had no time for hollow condolences. "Well, where's Stephen? I thought he was meant to be cleaning up the place."

"I don't know where Stephen is. Somewhere else on the farm I imagine." Inver waited for the old man to walk off in a huff, but he wasn't budging. "Have you tried Stephen's actual house?"

The old man's face crinkled with anger. "Do I look like a spring fucking chicken, boy? You think I've got the energy to be waltzing all the way over there?"

"Sorry, but who are you?"

"Eddie Tucker, I live next door."

Next door, in the middle of farmlands, didn't really narrow it down for Inver. His face must have given away his confusion.

"*That* house, ya bleedin idiot." Eddie pointed in the distance toward the main road with a bony finger, its black nail caked in filth. Inver stuck his head forward, looking to where he pointed and saw a tiny tin-roofed house planted near the edge of the road, surrounded by a wiry hedge.

Eddie shoved the envelope under Inver's nose. "Be sure to give this to Stephen and tell him Eddie will be back."

Inver took hold of the envelope which felt as angry as the piqued pensioner.

"And don't you be opening it 'till you give it to him, you hear me?" Eddie hissed in a cold breath before storming off up the dirt track as fast as a *spring chicken*.

CHAPTER SIX — 1995

STEPHEN

Most of the year, Clifton had fuck all going for it. Summer was the exception when the population would swell with townies throughout the region coming to camp at Clifton for their Christmas holidays. It was now early December—the official start of summer—but it would be another two weeks 'till the beach would begin to fill with tourists.

The horde of visiting families always included a healthy sample of girls keen to go home with stories of a summer romance. Local lads were more than happy to oblige and feign interest if it meant they got something out of it. Last year, Stephen had deceived his way through five such summer memories.

The next few months, after each girl had gone home, Stephen wound up receiving mail from all of them, saying how much of a good time they'd had and how he just *must* come and visit them. Stephen never replied, dashing their hopes by ignoring them. After two or three unanswered letters, they'd gotten the message.

Tonight though, he wasn't relying on imported holiday talent. Instead, he was meeting Clifton's finest, Delphi Savage. She had called three hours earlier confirming she was still keen to *catch up*. Her particular choice of words did not go unnoticed by Stephen during the brief conversation. Despite this, he had high hopes it would become a date of sorts the longer she was in his company. He had assumed getting Delphi to meet up in the first place would be the main challenge. With this part taken care of, everything else would fall into place.

Stephen spent far too long perusing through his options of what to wear. His wardrobe was an expensive well-fed beast thanks to inheriting his mother's penchant for buying the best threads. Twice yearly trips to Sydney were mere excuses to bring back fashion which seemed immune to New Zealand's shores. Admittedly, he would have been just as happy in old pants and a baggy T-shirt like he wore around the farm, but when it came to what he wore when leaving the property, if it didn't have a label, it just wasn't viable.

In the end, Stephen settled on a pair of black jeans with gold stitching and a short sleeve grey shirt with a small tag alluding to its brand, *26 Red*. He picked up his cologne and sprayed some at the base of his neck before dabbing some gently behind his ears, letting his skin capture the mild scent and create an essence that was truly his own. He slipped on his chunky black Doc Marten boots, laced them up tight and marched out to the living room.

His parents were out for the night; his father had already gone to the pub and his mum was in New Plymouth for a pottery class she taught every Friday. Stephen knew neither would be home for hours, so he just had to think of a way to convince Delphi to come back here. Even if his parents were home, the house was so big he could easily bring someone back if he wished. It wasn't as if they'd notice, and if they did, he doubted they'd care. Stephen pat his sweaty palms on his legs, surprised by his own nerves, as he fetched his keys hanging up in the kitchen and went to begin his Friday night.

∞

Delphi's family lived on a lifestyle block just the other side of Clifton. Like Troy, she was only back for the summer before heading back to university and continuing her studies, unlike Stephen, free of expectations.

An intricate colour-coded, bumpy, cobbled driveway led to her two-story Lockwood home surrounded by pretty gardens which competed against that of his own family each year in the Garden Trail Festival.

After knocking twice at the door, Stephen was greeted by Delphi's father, a conservative-looking man with greying-brown hair and glasses.

"You must be Stephen," he said, holding out his hand.

Stephen gripped Mr Savage's hand, giving it a firm shake. "Yes. Stephen Davis. I'm here to pick Delphi up." A slight moment of embarrassment rushed over him for stating the obvious.

"I'm sorry, but Delphi is still getting ready," Mr Savage said, "I think she wants to make sure she looks perfect just for you." The subtle scorn in his voice told Stephen the man had a sense of humour despite his uptight appearance.

"Daaaad, shut up," snarled a voice from up the stairs.

Mr Savage looked towards the stairs behind him. "Looks like I've been told off. Come in, Stephen."

Delphi's father guided him into the lounge where Stephen got to spend a further ten minutes of awkward small talk, waiting for his *catch up*.

Delphi finally emerged dressed in a short skirt and tight-hugging sweater. She gave Stephen a quick smile before flicking her silky brown hair that contained streaks of blonde. Stephen eyed her bronzed legs before quickly looking her in the eyes, returning the smile.

"Sorry for keeping you waiting," Delphi said, she grabbed him by the hand, letting him know they were bolting. "We better go. We're gonna be so late."

Late for what?

Delphi went up to her father. "I shouldn't be out all night," she said and pecked her father on the cheek.

"Nice meeting you, Mr Savage." The words had barely left his lips as Delphi hauled him out of the room toward the front door.

She promptly dropped his hand once they were outside. "Sorry for leaving you alone with him," she whispered, "and I wasn't trying to be perfect *just* for you."

"Well, you do," Stephen said, "look perfect, that is."

Delphi coughed up a smile.

As soon as she hopped in the car, her perfume snuck around the air, burying itself into Stephen's nose. He watched her as she adjusted the seat forward to accommodate for her short height. She was tiny and every inch of her stunning; if Stephen had his way, he'd have to be careful not to break her.

He had never seriously dated anyone before and the idea of it seemed foreign to him, but if anyone could make him not stray, it would be Delphi.

"So, where are we going?" Delphi asked, looking in the sun visor mirror, checking her face.

"I was thinking we could go down to the beach and maybe later if you want we could go back to —"

"Seriously, Stephen? Down to the motor camp?" She said it like he had committed an atrocity. "Like, don't get me wrong, I love hanging out down there and seeing the others, but if I was gonna do that, I would have gone there with Jade and the girls." Delphi sighed, a cross look locked across her face.

Stephen struggled to change into fourth gear and the car choked and jolted. "Well, nar, I meant like we can park up at the south end and you know… go down to the cove," he said in a voice filled with hope.

Delphi laughed. "Oh, come on, you don't think we're making a trip to Cherry Lane, do you?" She tapped his shoulder playfully, the look on her face softening. "I like your determination though," she said with a big smile, making him feel small.

"I can stop and get gas at the junction and go into New Plymouth… dinner… a club?" he said, scrambling to salvage some control.

"Now *that's* more like it," Delphi answered, returning to look at her reflection in the mirror. She pursed her pink lips like she was entertaining a thought. "You know what? Let's go to the beach."

Stephen went into fifth with ease, his greedy knuckles white as they squeezed the gear stick. "Really?" he blurted with a little too much glee in his voice.

"Yes, really, but not to the cove, I mean just to the campground. It'll be good to catch up with everyone. I've not actually hung out there since I got back."

Stephen was pissed off with Delphi for toying with him, exerting her power, but then kind of relieved at not having to waste money on a night out in town. It was still early—anything could happen.

"Sounds good to me," Stephen said. He gave her a smile and drove towards the beach. He leaned a hand over to rub her knee.

Delphi swatted his hand away and giggled. "Easy tiger."

∞

With the sun still up, they drove through town where a jumble of cars were parked outside the pub. Patrons spilled out the front doors and onto the pavement in a messy fashion. In Clifton, like any good town, you didn't need any better excuse to hit the piss than it being the weekend. Stephen and his mates tended to avoid drinking at the local watering hole, not wanting to party in the same bar as their fathers. Instead, Fridays and Saturdays were a choice between drinking at the beach or driving to New Plymouth for a night out.

Stephen turned the car down the road leading to the domain, knowing at the beach waiting for him would be Luke and Troy, and further belittling. He had confidently told them not to expect to see him any time before 10:00 p.m., straight after he had struck Delphi off his cock's to-do list. The bastards were going to have a field day. Stephen parked the car up and took a deep breath, bracing himself for the reaction to his premature appearance.

Sure enough, as he walked along the sand with Delphi—a healthy distance from his side—he saw his mates sitting around a bonfire, their faces flashing with sly grins as they watched his approach.

Delphi squealed when she recognised Jade Niemand standing by the fire, promptly ditching Stephen and rushing over to her friend who led Delphi away to chat with two other girls that formed part of the Clifton clique of wealthy daughters.

Stephen joined Luke and Troy who were sitting on a long hunk of driftwood doubling as a pew. The look on Stephen's face told them things weren't going to plan.

"I told ya she was onto you, mate," Luke said, smiling at him.

"So it would seem," Stephen replied, sounding raw.

Troy's hand disappeared into a box of beer at his feet. He fetched a bottle out before handing it to Stephen. "At least you sort of got a date, unlike someone I could mention."

Luke shuffled on the log, knowing Troy was referring to him. "See that?" he said, pointing at the group of girls gathered around Delphi. "That's an ocean of opportunity right there. I could have my pick tonight. So hey, I'm just keeping my options open for now."

"More like a puddle of pity," Troy said.

Stephen chuckled. "Hear, hear."

"O, ye wankers of little faith," Luke said smirking. He climbed down from the log and lay on his side, closer to the fire.

"I'll give you that, Luke. You're a glass half-full type of guy." Stephen nodded, "Which is just as well, 'cos at least you'll have something to drink when you luck out."

"Piss off," Luke snorted before guzzling back on his drink.

A tap on Stephen's shoulder nearly made him spill his beer; he spun around to see who the culprit was. It was Shaun. Barefoot in shorts and a singlet, he was standing with Megan Dombroski, his regular drinking-buddy-come-drunken-pashing-partner. Shaun had a cheesy grin on his face while Megan stood there indifferently, hands on her wide hips, not even trying to hide the fact she would rather be somewhere else.

Shaun leapt over the log in the gap between Stephen and Troy, hurtling around to face them. "What you guys up to?" he asked, his grin wide and radiating excitement.

Luke piped up from his sandy spot. "I'm taking a wild guess here, Shaun, but I think they're sitting on a log having a beer."

Stephen felt like cringing on Shaun's behalf for being so easy to mock. Shaun though, ignored the statement and walked over to Luke where the pair talked in hushed voices.

Troy turned to Megan. "Hey, Megan, how's your night going?" he asked politely.

"All good," she replied coolly. She waddled around the log and went to sit down on the sand across from them.

"Delphi and the others are over there," Stephen offered, hoping she would get the hint and leave.

Megan spun her head around looking at the girls gossiping in a huddle. "That's nice," she grumbled and faced the boys again.

Megan wasn't on the inner with Delphi's lot just like Shaun wasn't with Stephen and his mates. The difference was, Megan didn't give a shit. She had no desire to be part of what she openly referred to as the "snob squad." Her disdain was generous and extended to Stephen and his friends too.

Stephen would bump into Megan each summer break at the same parties, where she would usually be dancing alone, all tit and no rhythm. She grated him nearly as much as Shaun did. Stephen preferred his friends to be like his clothes—equipped with a label that proved they were worth something.

Stephen watched Shaun discretely grab something out of his pocket which he handed to Luke. *The tinny.* Stephen wondered when he would get his half as promised; he sure as hell had earnt it from being left alone to put up with Shaun that day. After some more muted whisperings with Luke, Shaun wandered back towards Stephen and Troy.

"Mind if I have one?" Shaun asked, motioning to the box of beer beside Troy's feet. Troy was reluctant at first, resembling something of a gatekeeper in charge of keeping enemies out. Luke gave a thumbs-up and Troy dug a bottle out, handing it to Shaun.

With the beer in his hand, Shaun went and sat beside Megan, sharing the bottle between them. Sure enough, it didn't take long for him to start hogging the conversation, telling everyone about his day at work and how much trouble he and his boss had fixing up some customer's car. His face was animated as he kept leaping up, telling the story in his naturally booming voice.

Stephen had to give Shaun credit. As draining as he could be, he certainly was lively. Everyone watched as Shaun jumped up and down, pretending to swing an axe into a car bonnet, his pantomime antics fuelled on by having the attention of his peers. The light of the fire illuminated Shaun's lithe figure and cast a glow over his golden legs with their down of fine leg hair. Stephen caught himself wishing he had olive skin like that.

"Anyway, how come you were so late? I thought you

weren't gonna turn up," Luke said, interrupting Shaun's story. The weak link in the social chain must have failed to deliver at the requested hour.

"Yeah, Lydia was being a bitch, refusing to look after Josie 'till I agreed to pay her twenty bucks," Shaun replied. He sat himself back down on the sand and folded his legs like a school kid.

Luke laughed. "Fuck, you're a sucker. You should have just ditched and not paid her anything. It ain't your fucking kid."

"True." Shaun grabbed the beer from Megan and gulped down a big mouthful like he was trying to drown a reaction. He began fidgeting with his legs as if rubbing out invisible creases.

Stephen knew enough that the parenting of six-year-old Josie had fallen mostly to Shaun and his sister, Lydia. Their mum, Debbie, had better things to do, like spending her wages from her job at the general store, downing vodkas at the pub before going down on her latest catch.

At thirty-seven years-old, she was still one of the best-looking women in town. Shaun must've known they all thought his mum was hot and wanted to shag her. Stephen imagined Shaun worried mostly by the fact they probably stood a chance after she'd had a few drinks. Because, despite Shaun's desperate attempts to be one of their mates, he seldom used the trump card of inviting them back to his place for free booze and an audience with Desperate Debbie.

"How's it going with you know who?" Shaun asked, looking at Stephen.

"Too early to tell," Stephen mumbled quietly.

"I wouldn't say it's too early, mate. I'd say you've already lucked out," Luke said with some glee.

"Nar, Stephen's got the deal sealed, I reckon," Shaun said.

"Thanks, Shaun," Stephen said, surprised by the supportive comment.

A big grin spread across Shaun's face. "Yeah, so when you leave, can I have your share of the booze?"

Troy and Luke laughed at the false praise.

"Hmmm, let me think," Stephen said, tilting his head thoughtfully. "How about narrr," he said and joined in with the laughing.

"What's so funny?" called a voice. It was Delphi leading the girls back to join everyone around the fire.

"That would be Megan's face," Luke answered, taking a cheap shot at the guest who couldn't stand them.

Megan rolled her eyes, unfazed by Luke's rudeness. "Yeah, well, not half as funny as your small cock," she replied, gathering a roar of laughter from the group.

Troy threw Megan a beer. "That deserves a drink."

"Thank you, Troy." Megan greedily started on the bottle.

Stephen flashed a stern look Troy's way that went unnoticed. *Don't encourage them to stay.* Troy was too polite sometimes.

Delphi and her giggly followers sat together on a separate chunk of driftwood farther away from the fire. Perched in a tight row, squawking amongst themselves, they resembled sparrows on a powerline. Stephen glared across at her, offended she hadn't chosen to sit beside him. He soothed his ego by reminding himself the night was still young. It wasn't even dark yet. With a little patience, he could still turn the *catch up* into a date.

∞

Three hours into the evening and the booze continued to flow, creating a social cohesion amongst the group which felt familiar and comforting. Stephen was well ahead of everyone else on the beer count, an achievement he usually accomplished in such gatherings.

His enthusiasm had morphed into thinning patience as he brooded over Delphi's frigid tactics. *She should have come sat with me hours ago.* He was about to swallow some of his pride and make a move over to his *catch up* when a woman's shrill laughter pierced his ears. Stephen looked down the beach and saw the shadowy outline of four figures approaching as the laughter grew louder.

Shaun with his back to the approaching posse knew exactly whose voice the laugh belonged to.

"Fuck sake," he muttered, shaking his head. He got to his feet and turned around. "Shit, Mum, I can't escape you, can I?" he joked.

"Is that you, Shaun?" the woman's voice called back.

"Yeah, unless you got another son you don't know about."

Debbie ran frantically towards the glow of the fire, carrying her shoes in her hand. She wrapped her drunken, flailing limbs around her son, squeezing him tight and smothering his cheek with a kiss. "My baby."

Shaun stepped out of her embrace, rubbing his cheek free from her lipstick. "Thanks for sharing the war paint."

Debbie surveyed the group sitting around the fire with a wobbly nod of her head. "Nice night for it. How's everyone doing?" she asked.

"Good, thank you, Mrs Munro," Delphi replied with a tinge of superiority.

"Oh, come on now, call me Debbie. All Shaun's mates do, don't you, boys?"

"That we do, Debbie," Luke said with a flirtatious wink.

Debbie's slim figure was fitted tight in a black dress, her dark-blonde hair stacked high. Despite possessing appealing petite features, she carried a coarseness about her which politer people would label as being down-to-earth. Her slurring voice and swaying balance told Stephen she had had as much, if not more, than him to drink on this balmy evening.

Shaun put his arm around his mum's shoulder, trying to steady her balance, motioning toward the three figures still approaching. "Who's with you?"

"Oh, you guys know George, right? She's back in town for her mum's birthday. She played tonight at the pub with her band."

George, aka Georgina Pike, was a few years older than Stephen and his crew. She lived in New Plymouth where, to the best of his knowledge, she did nothing much but walk around town with an air of importance, proclaiming to be a musician.

George came into sight with two male companions. She was easily spotted with her peroxide blonde hair that looked like a mess of feathers, her bony figure framing a plasticky-fixed leather skirt and a raggedy white top as she dawdled along in knee-high black boots. Stephen assumed it was a half-arsed homage to her idol Courtney Love, but rather than look like a grunge rag doll, she looked more voodoo doll. Smeared makeup covered her blotchy face that looked worn and punctured. Definitely a junkie; no doubt an accidental trait picked up in pursuit of an image.

George's smoky voice called across the fire, "How's everyone doing?" she asked. She stood beside Debbie in a slightly less wayward state.

Megan stood to her feet and went over to give George a hug. "Hey, girl. I've not seen you in forever."

George reluctantly accepted the embrace. "Yeah, been a while, huh... I didn't know you hung out with this lot." The loud and awkward observation was quickly followed with, "You got a spare smoke?"

Megan shook her head.

George stared at everyone sitting down, her eyes begging for a cigarette. Stephen grabbed his packet out of his pocket and opened it up for her. George staggered forward and greedily plucked three out. "Thanks, man."

The two men with George appeared equally musician-like, both closer to thirty than twenty. One tall and lanky with a shaved head, dressed head-to-toe in black, the other a good-looking Maori guy sporting dreadlocks that dangled out from a Rastafarian beanie. Stephen didn't appreciate the competition.

"Shaun, this is Dion." Debbie grabbed the hand of the bald lanky one. "Dion, this is my boy Shaun and his friends Troy, Stephen, Megan aaaaand Luuuuke," Debbie slurred as she shakily pointed her finger at each of them, failing to carry on to Delphi's crew.

Shaun extended a hand out to the solar panel bean pole. "Nice to meet you, man."

Dion pretended not to see and grunted some indecipherable response.

"Is Lydia looking after Josie?" Debbie asked.

"Yeah, Mum. I'll go home and check on them soon."

"No need. Stay here with your friends. Lydia will be fine. Enjoy your night. That's what I'm doing," Debbie said, giggling like a woman half her age. She let go of Shaun's hand and leaned into Dion's shoulder, her pink painted nails dragging across his chest like she was about to purr. "We're just going for a walk. Me and George are just showing the boys the,"—Debbie clasped a hand to her mouth as she hiccupped—"the beach." With her shoes under her arm, she tugged on Dion's hand, leading him past the fire and through the small gathering to the other side. "You coming, George?"

"Nar, youse go," George said, flashing Debbie a wink. "Don't eat him alive though, Debs." George burst out laughing with her dreadlocked sidekick. "Same goes for you too, Dion. Even if she asks you to." She turned to Shaun, smiling. "Fuck, your mum's a hard case."

"Yeah, hard out," Shaun mumbled.

Stephen felt embarrassed on Shaun's behalf but figured he must be used to it the way he calmly sat back down and continued fidgeting with his legs.

George and her dreadlocked sidekick made their way over to the girls whose seat still had plenty of room for bums to sit on. Stephen watched through jealous eyes as Dreadlocks effortlessly struck up a conversation with Delphi in no time, laughing at her unfunny jokes all whilst working his magic very subtly. Stephen hadn't said a single word to this guy, but he already knew he hated him.

It didn't take long before the pair excused themselves for a walk in the same direction as Debbie and Dion. Stephen's stomach twisted in knots, knowing what the pair were about to get up to—that he had all but lost his *catch up*. The only thing Delphi was going to be catching up with tonight was this prick's cock. Stephen didn't want to give her the pleasure of seeing him pissed off, so he bit his tongue, trying not to choke on the taste of humble pie.

He picked up pace with his drinking, trying to ignore her betrayal but the booze only heightened the emotion of being burned. Stephen knew when he got this drunk it usually led to one of two things—fucking or fighting—and with Delphi gone, it was pointing to the latter.

He sat there feeling sorry for himself while the others kept on with their happy ramblings. Stephen couldn't decide which of the conversations being had irked him the most. Luke's harping on about his training regime and upcoming boxing match, Megan with her fat paws rubbing Shaun's shoulders, greedily waiting for him to finish rolling a joint while she whispered sweet nothings in his ear, or Jade and the other girls asking George all about her band and if she would be doing another gig at the pub anytime soon. Stephen was about to choose a winner amongst the nominees for most irritating when Troy shot to his feet, waving his drink in the air excitedly, grinning from ear to ear.

"I was meant to be keeping this a secret, but I'm way too excited not to say anything," Troy said.

Everyone stopped talking amongst themselves and looked up at the pasty Troy, the fire's glow bringing out the soft spread of faded freckles on his face.

"Me and Clare are engaged," Troy announced as everybody started to clap. "But the best news is," he paused for effect, "I'm gonna be a dad!"

The group erupted with cheers and a loud "WOOP" came from Shaun.

"Congrats, man." Luke stood up and fist-tapped Troy's hand.

"You'll be such a good dad, Troy," squealed Jade.

"I think news like that should give him the honour of first toke aye, Shaun," George said in a raspy voice as she clutched a bottle of Jim Beam she had fished out of her bag.

"I reckon," Shaun agreed, handing the joint over to Troy.

"Thanks, man." Troy sparked it up, inhaling deeply before spluttering his guts out. He swatted the air with his hand, shooing away the smoke, before passing the joint to Luke for it to begin the rounds.

"So, do you want a boy or a girl?" Megan asked as she wrapped an arm around Shaun.

"I don't care aye. I'll be happy either way," Troy said with a visible glow.

Stephen sniggered at the proud father-to-be.

Troy gave Stephen a concerned look. "What's up?"

"Nothing," Stephen said before sniggering again.

"Nar, come on. What is it?" Troy demanded.

Don't do it, don't do it. Stephen could feel the alcohol take hold, ignoring the inner voice telling him to shut his mouth. "I just think it's fucked up that you're celebrating your life being over, that's all." Everybody's eyes locked in on him in disbelief. Stephen wasn't fussed. "Seems like Clare got what she wanted, aye." He cocked his head to the side, letting out a burp that tasted of beer.

"What the fuck are you on about?" Troy asked, sounding equally annoyed as confused.

"You heard me," Stephen replied full of gusto.

"You wanna watch what you say, mate." Troy's voice warbled in anger.

Luke and George started to laugh, entertained by the brewing drama. Everybody else sat silently with gaping mouths, sensing the tension. Troy didn't do angry, but it was clear for all to see, he was about to.

Stephen staggered to his feet, waving his bottle around. "Well, fuck, I'm sorry that I'm the only one here who cares enough about you to be honest and tell you you've gone and fucked your life up," he said, doing his best to fake serious empathy.

"You've got a fucking nerve, Stephen," Troy heaved the words out through gritted teeth, his fists clenched at his sides. "I actually love Clare and our baby. So stop being a stupid arsehole just 'cos Delphi up and ditched you for someone else. Just fucking handle it, man."

"Oi, guys, let's all calm down," Shaun interrupted.

Stephen flashed Shaun a filthy look. "Why don't you fuck off, Shaun? Nobody wants you here. You were only invited to supply the weed."

Nobody said anything. They all knew it was true.

Stephen shifted his gaze back to Troy. "And *me* the stupid arsehole? I ain't the one who's in love with some baby you never met who could just be a miscarriage waiting to happen," Stephen narrowed his eyes. "Maybe that's why Clare told you to keep your mouth shut, moron."

BAM!

Troy's fist came hard and fast out of nowhere, viciously hitting Stephen in the face. Its impact threw Stephen off balance, tripping him over the log. Gripped in slow motion, he felt his body fall backwards as he watched his boots dangle in the air above him before he felt the hard thump of the sand on his back. The coldness of his beer shocked his skin as it spilled all over his front, saturating his shirt. Stephen lay there half-conscious, his cheek burning from the punch, barely registering what had just happened.

He could hear Luke and George laughing their arses off and one of the girls saying, "Oh my god, is he okay?" Another muttered, "Good job, Troy. He's such a dick."

Troy leapt over the log, his feet landing inches away from Stephen's face. "I should fucking deck you."

"You already have," called out another voice, followed with fits of laughter.

Stephen half expected Troy to start laying into him and kick him in the guts.

Shaun appeared over the log, grabbing Troy by the arm and holding him back. "Leave it, Troy. He's drunk. He doesn't mean it."

Troy threw Shaun's hands off him, lowering his head to spit right in Stephen's face before storming off into the dark, mumbling abuse.

Stephen gingerly raised a hand to his face, wiping away the gooey saliva. He looked up at Shaun and gave him a goofy smile. "I sure showed him."

"Yeah, not exactly, buddy," Shaun said. He reached down and helped Stephen to his feet. "I think it's time you call it a night, yeah?" He hooked one of Stephen's arms over his shoulders and led him back around the driftwood to the fire. "I'm gonna take this one home." Shaun heaved Stephen up who kept drooping toward the ground.

"Good idea. Take him away before Troy comes back to finish the job," George said.

"Nar, I'm good. I can take myself back," Stephen slurred, wrestling a hand into his pocket to yield his keys.

"Yeah, I don't think so," Shaun said, grabbing Stephen's wrist to rip them out of the pocket.

"Want me to come?" Megan asked eagerly.

"Nar, she's right," Shaun replied, "I should manage." He hauled Stephen along in laboured steps. "See you all next time." He gave the group a quick wave. "Good catching up with you, George."

"You too, mate," George shot back.

Shaun continued lugging the drunken dead weight of Stephen home as everybody talked excitedly about the drama they had just witnessed.

"See, Stevie? You did get lucky, mate," Luke shouted before bursting out laughing.

CHAPTER SEVEN — 1995

STEPHEN

They wandered up from the beach at a snail's pace, bypassing Stephen's car and heading straight to Shaun's house. Stephen was so drunk he didn't pay much attention and the fraction of a second that he did, he just didn't care. At the back of his mind was a sober segment of the brain that was aware if Shaun drove him home in the car then Shaun had no way of getting himself back.

Shaun lived at home with Debbie and his two sisters. It was only a few blocks away from the beach so the walk wasn't far, but Stephen had to practically be dragged the whole way. Consequently, it took a good twenty minutes before Shaun finally got them outside the rundown, yellow beach batch he called home.

Shaun led them up some rotten-looking steps to the front door of the house. He leaned Stephen against the wall of the front porch. "You all good to stand?" he asked.

Stephen nodded, his eyes flickering in a drunken daze.

Shaun turned the handle quietly and stepped inside with Stephen following in heavy staggered stomps behind him. Through blurred vision, Stephen could see they were in the small home's lounge, a hideous room trapped in a 70s time warp with its brown and yellow carpet. The walls were plastered with family photos while too many pot plants dotted the sides of the room for Stephen's liking.

Shaun helped plonk him down onto a soft lumpy couch and asked if he would like a feed. Stephen shook his head and zoned out while Shaun disappeared out of the room. From somewhere down the hallway, a door creaked open, followed by the splashing sound of Shaun taking a piss. The noisy flush of the toilet retrieved Stephen from passing out; he opened his eyes to find Shaun followed into the room by his sister Lydia.

"What the fuck's wrong with his face?" Lydia squawked.

"Nothing," Shaun replied defensively.

"Doesn't look like nothing," she said.

"Yeah, well, doesn't look like any of your business either." Shaun stepped between her and Stephen, motioning with a pointed finger for her to leave the room.

"Whatever, dick," Lydia said, rolling her eyes.

Stephen gave Lydia a silly smile and waved hello.

"Hey Stephen, are you okay?" Lydia asked, batting her pretty brown eyes, a feature she shared with her older brother. Lydia was fifteen, but could easily be mistaken as the older sibling with her curvy figure.

"I'm good." Stephen gave Lydia a droopy thumbs-up. "I just got into a fight is all."

She smiled. "It looks more like you got into a hiding."

Stephen shrugged, far too wasted to get the joke.

"Did you get Josie to bed alright?" Shaun asked, suddenly sounding concerned.

"Yes, Shaun. Shit, I'm not useless," Lydia snapped.

"Cool." Shaun cocked his head to the side and looked down at Stephen. "Well, I think I'll go put this one to bed."

"Yeah, he looks like he could do with a sleep," Lydia said.

Shaun retrieved a twenty dollar note from his pocket and handed it to his sister. "Thanks for babysitting."

Lydia's eyes glowed excitedly, quickly grabbing the green note and letting out a dramatic sigh. "Well, it shouldn't be you or me doing it anyway. It should be Mum's job."

"You know how she is though," he said warmly. Shaun stepped in front of Stephen who was still slumped on the couch. "Come on you." He put a hand out for Stephen to grab and led him down the hallway towards his bedroom.

Shaun's room was tiny, barely more than a closet with a skinny single bed squeezed into the cramped space. Stephen sat down unceremoniously onto the mattress, looking around the claustrophobic room, taking in its posters of cars and bands pinned to the walls. Next to the bedside table was a small black stereo nestled into the corner of the room beside a skinny CD rack which curved like a wave in its centre.

Shaun perched down in front of the stereo, scanning through the variety of CDs. "Do you like —"

"Whatever, man. You choose," Stephen said abruptly. He yanked his boots off and threw them beside a pile of Shaun's clothes at the foot of the bed.

Shaun opened the disc tray and slipped in a CD. Music soon seeped out, playing quietly in the background. It took a while for Stephen to recognise the music, but the Irish singing voice soon gave it away—The Cranberries.

"You're gonna have a shitty as hangover in the morning," Shaun said sympathetically.

"You reckon?" Stephen rubbed his head as if it were about to hit.

"Yeah, not to mention a sore face."

"Is it bad?"

Shaun scooted over and knelt in front of him, tenderly touching Stephen's chin as he lifted his face into the light for a better look. "Hmm, I think you'll live. Maybe just a black eye for a couple days."

"Fuck my life," Stephen exhaled and lay back slouched against the wall. "I'll have to call Troy tomorrow and apologise. I didn't mean to be such a cock."

"Didn't you?" Shaun asked surprised.

Stephen's lips curled into a devilish grin. "Yeah, okay. I probably did mean to be a cock, but you know what I mean."

"I know. Alcohol can do that, aye." Shaun pat Stephen's knee as he sat up on the bed beside him.

Stephen covered his face in shame, remembering what he'd said to Troy, his voice bleeding out a shameful groan. "Fuck, yeah, I'll definitely give him a call." He unclasped his hands from his face. "Do you think he'll be good about it?"

"Yeah, you guys are mates and I think he would have calmed down a lot by then. So yeah, you'll be fine." Shaun smiled. "No one ever hates you for long, Stephen."

Shit.

Stephen remembered the vile words he'd spat at Shaun back at the beach. Guilt was attacking him from all angles in his drunken emotional state. In a whisper of a voice, he uttered, "I'm sorry about what I said to you too." He looked Shaun in the eyes. "You know I didn't mean it."

"It's all good," Shaun said, brushing it off like it meant nothing. "I know I'm sorta on the outer with you lot..." Shaun's voice trailed off like he was unsure of what to say.

Stephen draped an arm around Shaun's shoulder. "Seriously, I didn't mean it," he said. "I dunno about the others, but I don't hang 'round you just for pot." Stephen shook a finger in Shaun's face, emphasising his apologetic point.

"Yeah..." Shaun said, sounding like he didn't believe him. He looked down at his feet and began fumbling with his shorts, ironing out those invisible creases again.

"No, Shaun, look at me."

Shaun tilted his head to face him.

"I really didn't mean it. I was a fuckwit and I'm sorry," Stephen said. "Now, repeat after me. Stephen, you're a fuckwit."

Shaun laughed at Stephen's self-deprecating reference. "Stephen Davis, you're a fuckwit."

"Good." Stephen huffed, feeling better seeing Shaun smiling. He swung his legs up onto the bed and lay back on top of a thin red quilt, resting his head on a lone straggly pillow. "All good if I crash?" He had no intention of fighting off the need for sleep any longer.

Shaun stood up, looking down at his groggy guest. "Yeah, man, not a problem. Did you need another blanket?"

"Nar, I'm fine." Stephen leaned forward and unbuttoned the top two buttons of his shirt, pulling it over his head before throwing it to the end of the bed. Letting out a boozy breath, he lay back down and inspected his pale chest which still waited to acquire its summer tan. He tapped his fingers down his small island of chest hair that fed thinly down to a wispy trail below his navel, stopping just short of his pubes. Stephen proceeded to unhook his belt and unzipped his jeans, tugging them down over his deceptively smooth inner thighs, but as the pants went lower, the true hairiness of his legs was revealed. He nearly managed to get the jeans entirely off 'till they became snagged around his ankles, rendering him helpless and thrashing about like a fish in a bucket.

"You need some help there?" Shaun asked with a half-smile on his face.

Stephen looked down at his imprisoned feet. "Yes, please."

Shaun leaned across the bed, grabbing Stephen one hairy calf at a time as he yanked each leg free from the black jeans. Stephen felt exhausted; he laid back, his body left only in red silk boxers and black socks. He heard Shaun chuckling at the end of the bed.

Stephen lifted his head off the pillow. "What's so funny?"

"You might want to readjust yourself. You're, umm... compromising your modesty."

Stephen wondered what the hell Shaun was on about. He fumbled a hand over his crotch 'till he groped the problem. One of his balls had slipped through the leg hole of his boxers, giving Shaun an eyeful. He quickly adjusted the glaring flash and laid his hands behind his head, letting out a soft laugh. "Sorry you had to see that."

Shaun pointed to Stephen's feet. "Socks off too?"

Stephen nodded.

Shaun peeled his socks off for him, dropping them onto the floor. He returned his hand and ran a thumb along the sole of one of Stephen's size ten feet.

"Tickles," Stephen mumbled with his eyes closed.

Shaun wrestled the blanket out from under Stephen and pulled it up over him, tucking the end snugly around his bare shoulders. The music suddenly stopped playing and the light switched off, darkening the room.

Stephen heard Shaun's footsteps near the edge of the bed, followed by a soft warm peck on his cheek. "Good night, buddy. You're not as bad as you think," Shaun whispered.

Stephen smiled in his mind at what he thought a sweet gesture. He heard Shaun exit the room and close the door, leaving him to pass out within seconds.

CHAPTER EIGHT — 1995

STEPHEN

Stephen felt rancid, his mouth crying out for water. He sat up in Shaun's rickety bed and with a big yawn swung his feet onto the floor, scrunching the carpet with his toes. He looked beside the bed, hoping to find a glass of water to quench his thirst.

Fuck sake.

The bedside table was bare of fluids. All it had was a small black lamp and a chunky looking leather covered book, which on closer inspection turned out to be a bible. Stephen scoured the room for his clothes 'till he found them bundled at the foot of the bed.

Once dressed, he made his way out to the lounge where he found Shaun sprawled out half-naked on the couch, snoring his head off. He tiptoed quietly into the kitchen and hunted for a glass. On the sink bench, he found a white dishrack with clean dishes wedged in rows. Stephen groaned to himself at the Munro's lack of a dishwasher. *It's 1995, for fuck's sake.*

He grabbed the biggest clean glass there was and downed two full glasses of water from the tap. His mouth was still a field of prickles, but he had to get a move on. A quick getaway was in order before everyone woke up; he had no intention of hanging around Shaun any longer than he had to.

A voice startled him. "Big night, was it?"

Stephen spun round and saw it was Debbie. She stood in the kitchen doorway, draped in a blue dressing gown, her blonde hair bunched messily from a pillow's imprint. "Ooh, look at that shiner. What happened to you?" she asked, reminding Stephen of something he would rather forget.

Stephen dabbed his fingers around his sore eye. "A big night, like you said," he said sheepishly.

Debbie chuckled. "Say no more. I know them nights all too well." She sauntered to the kitchen bench and grabbed the kettle. "Did you fancy a coffee before you head off?"

"No, thank you. I probably should head back home." Stephen whispered, trying not to wake Shaun in the next room.

Debbie looked around the kitchen with dozy concern, wondering why Stephen was keeping his voice so low. She stared at the wall separating the lounge and kitchen as if she had x-ray vision. "Oh, don't worry about sleepy head in there. Trust me, he could sleep through a house demolition, my boy," Debbie said.

Stephen inched towards the door. "Tell Shaun thanks for the bed."

Debbie nodded. "Well, look after yourself, Stephen, and watch out for them doors as I like to call them."

∞

By the time Stephen got home, he found the house to be dead quiet, giving him the privacy to make a call to Troy and apologise for his drunken spectacle. Standing next to the cordless phone, shame pulsated through his body as he conjured up the courage to dial Troy's number. Stephen took an internal sigh before dialling.

After three rings, Troy's voice came down the line fresh and friendly, "Hello."

"Troy, it's Stephen." He paused, waiting for a tirade of abuse. "I just wanted to say I'm really sorry about last night."

Laughter came through the line. "All's forgotten, mate. I know what you're like when you've had a few."

"Yeah, I'm a royal prick."

"The royalist." A brief moment of silence. "How's your face? I'm sorry for lashing out but, yeah, I guess you really pissed me off."

"I think I'll survive, just," Stephen said jokingly.

"Good to hear, mate, good to hear."

"Troy, congratulations. Seriously, I am actually really happy for you," Stephen said, trying his best to muster some enthusiasm.

"Cheers, man." Troy sounded genuinely pleased. "You'll get to be Uncle Stephen and look after the tyke on weekends I've decided."

Stephen laughed. "Sorry, but I really don't think I'm babysitter material."

"Nar, you'll be all good," Troy said. A voice in the background seemed to be asking Troy a question. "Hey, sorry, Stephen, but I gotta go. Clare's just arrived, and we got lots to talk about as you could imagine."

"Yeah, of course, no worries. Say hi to Clare from me."

"Cool, will do. And thanks for calling. I appreciate it."

Stephen felt relieved that Troy let him off the hook so lightly. Had it been anyone else, Stephen wasn't so sure a pardon would have come quite so easily. He considered making another call, this time to Delphi. He cringed, wondering if she had heard about his less-than-stellar performance last night. In the end, he fought the urge to call, his pride winning out over his cock. *Fuck it. She can ring me.* His mental bravado was based more on hope than any real confidence.

Stephen set about fixing himself a feed from the kitchen. He figured if he was gonna mope about in a woeful mood all day then he could at least gift his taste buds some happiness. He was busy spreading dollops of creamy butter on soft, white bread when he heard a muffled groan coming from one of the bedrooms. He stopped what he was doing and followed the source of the noise. When he rounded the corner to the hallway, he saw Ricky's bedroom door slightly ajar. He knew right away what he would find in there. Stephen continued with heavy stomps to give warning of his approach. He tapped on the door and waited two seconds before pushing it open.

"Mum…"

His mother was seated on the edge of Ricky's still unmade bed, hugging a pillow to her face, inhaling what was left of her dead son's smell. She quickly placed the pillow on her slender lap and wiped tears away from her crystal blue eyes.

"You okay, Mum?" He knew she wasn't. She never was if she was in there, but he also knew what her answer would be.

"Oh, I'm fine," she said, shaking the trembling emotion out of her voice. "I'm just being silly." She stroked her faded blonde-near-grey hair before putting the pillow back onto the bed. "It's coming up to Christmas and, well… I guess it makes me miss him," she said with a pained sigh. Her eyes focused on Stephen's face and her maternal instinct kicked in. "What happened to you?" She stood up hastily, crossing the room and immediately fussed over him. "Who did this to you?" she demanded, her voice returning to its usual crisp, prim delivery.

"It's nothing, Mum. We just got a bit rowdy last night is all."

She looked into his eyes, not sure whether to believe the story. "Yes, well you should be more careful." Her sternness quickly faded and her face softened. She ushered Stephen out of the room and together they made their way back to the kitchen where he finished off preparing his snack.

"Do you know what field Dad's working on today?" Stephen asked with a mouthful of food.

His mother pulled a face at his bad habit. "I think he's in Wonderland."

Stephen nodded. Wonderland was their nickname for an old forgotten part of the farm that housed the original Davis family home built at the turn of the century, now little more than rotting kindling.

"Stephen, you know we don't expect you to start working 'till the new year," his mother said. "Go out and enjoy your last summer break. You'll have plenty of time to help out soon enough."

"I know but I feel like a twat not helping out even just a little." His parents were stupidly generous and had insisted he not start working full-time until January, letting him have one last student summer.

"Your father has Rusty with him to help, so I'm sure you're not needed, love."

"I thought Rusty had the day off."

His mother smiled. "He does, but he's decided to work 'cos Inver has chicken pox and Rusty's never had them, so I think he's living in fear of catching them." She chuckled. "Mind you, it's a terrible thing a grown-up catching those. It can nearly kill you. I'm so glad both you boys caught them, even though it was a nightmare nursing you both. Poor Donna though, looking after an itchy toe rag."

Stephen nodded along to her spiel as he downed his cheese sandwich. "Well, guess that means he won't be bothering us anytime soon," Stephen said with a mouth full of food, resulting in another disapproving look from his mother.

"He's not that bad, Stephen," she said with a shake of her head. "He's just a little boy."

Little Inver was a pain. The kid had no siblings to play with so he would follow Stephen around the farm like a bad smell any chance he got. He wasn't even a cute annoying like some kids were. He was just *awkward* annoying.

"Well, this little boy's off to get changed," Stephen declared. He put his plate down, gave his mum a smile and marched off to his room. Walking through the hallway, he saw they'd forgotten to close the door of Ricky's bedroom; he pulled it shut knowing his mum liked to keep the shrine sealed off as if she was keeping a memory fresh. Stephen scanned his dead brother's room with its walls covered in 80s posters of bikini-clad babes—the rooms shelves were decorated with numerous sparkling trophies from Ricky's Motor Cross racing, one of the many things Ricky had been better at than his cocky kid brother.

Stephen hated coming in here, it always reminded him of the night their lives had changed forever. A two in the morning knock at the door was never going to bring good news. Stephen was home for midterm break when it happened and had been the one to open the door to the policemen who informed the family that Ricky had died in a car accident. Stephen would never forget the sound of his mother's sharp breath before she exhaled countless tears while his father shook his head, insisting to the police it must all be a 'terrible mistake.'

Ricky received the grim honour of being the only one to perish in the crash. The other three passengers had managed to crawl out unscathed of the upturned vehicle after it had failed to make a bend and rolled down a hill, landing upside-down in a boggy creek. Ricky had been thrown out of the vehicle and trapped beneath the car's final resting place, where his life slowly seeped out of him in the lonely dark.

Stephen's big brother had helped add life to the house. He was fun and easy going, the type of guy everyone would call 'a good cunt,' whereas Stephen was sullen and moody. This striking difference between the brothers made Ricky the family favourite by a country mile. Now, the favourite had been reduced to little more than a statistic: an ominous reminder in the form of a plain white cross, warning motorists to slow down.

Ricky had been five years older and, unlike most big brothers, he didn't swipe Stephen away. If anything, he encouraged a friendship. He'd been the one to teach Stephen to drive, ruining their dad's beautiful green paddocks in the process, gave him his first smoke and passed on dirty advice like some wise elder.

Stephen didn't remember crying much at all, he just got on with life—school, dating, growing up. Ricky's death hit during the long wave of puberty and, in a sad way, his brother dying just felt like one of many changes. Stephen knew this made him a bad person, but he accepted it.

Now he was a year older than what Ricky had been when he died and it felt weird knowing that from here on out whatever he experienced was new territory for either brother. It seemed wrong to Stephen for him to be the first one reaching milestones like his twenty-first three months earlier.

Had his parents been younger, Stephen was sure they'd have tried for another child, but they had been very late at starting a family as it was. He and his brother were called double miracles, considering the barren barriers his folks had faced in nearly twenty years of marriage before having children.

Prior to Ricky's death, Stephen had been free to dream up whatever he wanted to be. But now his fate was decided. He would stay here in Clifton, working alongside his father and one day inherit what should have been Ricky's responsibility. He hadn't dared challenge this in fear of his parents feeling like they'd lost both their sons.

As Stephen walked away from Ricky's bedroom, he had a flashback to the funeral where his mum had sobbed over her dead son and planted a kiss on his cold forehead. The image jogged his mind when Stephen remembered passing out in Shaun's bed and the warm kiss he had planted on *his* cheek.

What the fuck was that about?

He dismissed it as a drunken moment but he couldn't shake it from the back of his mind. His cheek burned where Shaun's lips had pecked and something between a shudder and a tingle gripped his body.

CHAPTER NINE — 2016

INVER

The sea was retreating in on itself, the low tide exposing scatterings of small rocks digging into the wet black sand, sticking out like tiny headstones. Inver ran along in his running gear of black shorts and a red nylon T-shirt, his feet flirting with the water's edge. He leapt in the air each time a wave came too close to his sneakers, landing back down and leaving a large footprint on the ground. He had his mp3 earphones in blocking out the world, an old school Nirvana track blasting his eardrums.

Becoming fed up with hours of cleaning, leaving him with stinging hands from chemicals and red knees from being on the ground for all the wrong reasons, Inver had gone into Clifton and parked at the domain beach park for a run. Running was free, and it had been his one escape the past six months since he could no longer afford to pay good money for the luxury of running in one spot on a treadmill.

Assuming the tide went out far enough, he figured he could make it all the way to the reef hidden below Stephen's backyard. The view from above had been enticing, and he wanted to spend time exploring the drowned life in rock pools, discovering what might be hiding under the slithery clumps of seaweed—an adventure of sorts which he hadn't done since being a small kid.

The beach was practically deserted, spare a man with his young son, trying to fly a bright yellow kite in the gusty winds. It didn't take much for it to take off. One throw from the man's arm saw the kite picked up by the wind and swoop high as it tugged tightly at the stretched out string.

Continuing along the beach, Inver came to Rapanui Creek, a shallow sandy stream which fed inland to a small cove with a lagoon the locals coined Cherry Lane, on account of the amount that had been popped there through the years. He leapt over the stream in one huge bounce, landing heavily and filling his socks with gritty specs of sand that became instantly irritating. He made his way towards the entrance of the cove, walking around the corner to the lagoon's sandy edge tucked behind the cliff. On the other side of the eerily still water hunched scaly flax bushes and tall crooked trees sucking the light from the small indent, providing privacy for horny couples to get up to all sorts in nature's shadows. It was only once he walked as far as the lagoon allowed that he spotted it: a gaping black hole in the wet grey clay of the cliff. Its entrance was a high arch about twelve feet off the ground and its width generous. He couldn't see how far the cave went in, but its darkness looked like a hungry mouth wanting to devour him. It was a distinctly creepy spot for its intended purpose, he thought.

Drawn around the cave's edges were small carvings, declarations of love and insults etched into the clay. JASE AND LISA 4 EVA 98, SHANE R IS A DICK, KB 4 FM. There were large patterns and lines sprawled above the entrance, each adding to the facade's peculiar spirit. Inver ran his finger along the words, intrigued by some of the decades-old markings. He stayed there a good ten minutes, studying them like an archaeologist lost in translation of caveman hieroglyphics. Once he had had enough admiring love legacies from days gone by, he jogged his way back to the beach, continuing on to the reef.

The closer he got to his destination, the more chunks of rock jutted out of the ground, some as big as cars. Their surfaces covered in a drowned wet green moss making them fuzzy to the touch. Eventually, the sand was completely gone, lost to jagged, sharp rocks carpeting the terrain. Inver tread carefully over the hazardous surface, slowly making his way to the backdrop of Stephen's property. Staring straight up at the steep cliff, he felt dizzy as he honed in on the bare roots of the tree that appeared to dangle even more precariously from below. Inver saw washed out steps which formed the bottom of the track leading up to the house. It was odd to think—if it wasn't so dangerous—he could have got to this same point in under a minute, rather than the twenty-five minute slog his body had just endured.

The reef stretched as far out as the tide allowed, its edges thrashed by loud thumping waves. The salty smell of the sea was delicious to someone who was more used to the stench of greasy food fumes fused with sweaty city streets.

Inver found his way to one of the numerous rock pools inhabiting the area. With fingers frozen to the bone, he peeked under rocks where he found starfish, kinas and the occasional undersized paua. By now, his shoes and socks were so overloaded with sand he decided to trudge straight through the knee-deep pools. As he plunged his foot into the water's icy flow, he was brutally reminded of winter's grip on the land. He waded through the shock of it and by the time he was in the middle of the rock pool, his legs were numb to the cold as he swished through golden brown clumps of seaweed.

This was heaven, no soul around, no one to judge him for his juvenile escape. If only he could take a piece of this serenity home with him. Inver raised his arms up and yahooed to the sky, scaring stiff a pair of seagulls that had been watching him carefully with beady eyes. He breathed in, basking in a rare moment of freedom. Then it touched him...

A slick, quick motion that licked above his ankle. Inver stood there rigid, unsure if he was imagining what he had just felt. *I'm going crazy.*

Hesitant to move, his heart pumped hard and heavy as he took a deep breath, trying to calm down when the water rippled beside him and spread a hideous black cloud that enveloped his legs. "What the —"

Inver screamed for his life as the same hideous touch brushed his skin, this time clinging firmer to his leg, its fingers wrapping around him. His arms flailed helplessly as he lost his footing, falling backwards into the cold water of the rock pool and became submerged in darkness.

Kimmy roared in laughter. "Oh my god," she said before taking a sip of her Pinot Gris from a stemless glass. "An octopus!" She found it hilarious Inver had come back soaked to the bone after his inky dousing. "Well, I must say I've never heard of anyone before get beat up by an octopus."

Stephen sat beside her with a wide smile. "Oh, come on, Kimmy, it wasn't a fair fight, was it? Inver here's only got two arms the octopus has eight."

Inver laughed at the healthy mocking. "Yeah, I think if I go back down there, I'll be going with a spear."

"That's the spirit, mate," Stephen said, his blue eyes honed in on Inver.

"Such a beautiful night isn't it?" Kimmy said. She was wrapped up in an overgrown white cardigan she hugged around herself tightly.

"Sure is," Stephen agreed. He clicked the top off a beer he'd just fetched himself from the fridge. In old ripped jeans and a baggy white shirt stained with dried paint, he still managed to look stylish.

Inver looked up at the sky. It was a beautiful night like they'd said despite the cold nip in the air. In the city, the constant orange glow of street lights fought off any glimpse of a naked universe. Not here though—here, the Milky Way put on a raw performance with its streak of stars.

"Guess who I bumped into the other day?" Kimmy quizzed with exaggerated excitement.

Stephen didn't say anything even though it was aimed at him.

"Who?" Inver asked, filling the quiet air.

"I met one of Stephen's old bestest buddies," she patted Stephen's leg encouraging him to join in.

Stephen's face crinkled with surprise. "Who you talking about?"

"Oh, just someone who knows alllll about you." Kimmy dangled the words like bait.

Stephen scratched his head. "I'm a bit rusty on my psychic abilities, so you might have to just tell me."

"Luke Bridgeman," Kimmy said. "He told me you and him were best friends growing up."

Stephen shuffled in his seat. "Oh, yep, and what is it he's supposed to know all about me?"

"I dunno, he just said he knew all about you from being friends for so long," Kimmy replied.

"Good for him," Stephen said, sounding annoyed.

"He said to tell you 'bullshit,'" she said, looking confused by the message. "What's that about?"

Stephen hesitated. "I've not the foggiest idea."

Inver could tell by Stephen's tone and the way his body slunk back in the chair, he was prickly. Kimmy, however, seemed oblivious. Either that, or she enjoyed rattling him.

"So, why'd you two stop being mates?" she asked.

"Sometimes you just drift apart, you know," Stephen said with a coy look on his face. "We were young, he was a dick, and I wasn't." Stephen flashed Kimmy a big smile, rescuing the conversation from turning sour.

"Something tells me you were the biggest dick of all, Stephen Davis," Kimmy said.

"Only where it counts." Stephen looked at Inver and arched an eyebrow.

Inver smiled nervously.

"I swear men never grow up past the age of fifteen," Kimmy groaned. "You'll end up a dirty old man at this rate." She followed her contradiction up with a playful slap to Stephen's leg.

Old man.

"Shoot, I forgot. I was meant to give you something," Inver said, suddenly remembering Eddie's envelope he had left in his room. "I'll just go grab it." Inver raced to his room returning with the envelope. "Your neighbour turned up at Rusty's and said to give you this."

"Old Eddie Tucker," Stephen said, sighing in annoyance at the name. "Real nice bloke, ain't he?"

"Yeah, he was quite… stroppy, you could say," Inver said, doing his best to sound diplomatic.

"I can only imagine." Stephen studied the envelope before opening it carefully like he half expected anthrax to puff out of it. He pulled out what appeared to be photos. Stephen scanned through them slowly and began shaking his head.

"What is it?" Kimmy asked.

Stephen slid them across the table to her so she could look for herself.

Kimmy gasped as she went through them. "Oh my

god. The man's not right in the head."

"Well, considering what he thinks I've done, I guess not," Stephen grumbled.

Inver took the photos from Kimmy, curious as to what the big mystery was. At first, he mistook them for adorable pet photos, two Dobermans asleep side by side. His stomach dropped when he realised they weren't actually sleeping but laid out in a burial pit. Written on the last photo was an ominous message.

What will your grave look like

"Why would he send you photos of dead dogs?" Inver asked, scratching at his unruly hair, puzzled by the threatening epitaph.

"Ask Kimmy," Stephen said bluntly.

Kimmy looked nervously at Stephen before facing Inver. "Last week those not-so-darling dogs broke into Stephen's yard and found their way to the chook pen. They ripped those poor chickens to shreds." Kimmy took a sip of her glass before continuing, "Stephen wasn't going to do anything about it, so I rang the council and told them about what those bastard dogs did." She looked back at Stephen. "I promise I was only trying to help."

"I know you were, but I did say I'd take care of it," Stephen said with a frown before hijacking the tale. "So yeah, the dog rangers turn up to investigate and those two yappers with a temper like their owners bit one of the rangers on the arse. Well, that was all it took, and both were taken away to be put down."

"Whoa…" Inver said.

"The old bastard's a pain, but I didn't want that to happen," Stephen said.

"Well, I think we should call the police. He can't be going 'round handing out death threats," Kimmy insisted.

"No, Kimmy, this is my business. I'll deal with it," Stephen snapped. "Look what happened when you last tried to help." He pointed at the photos.

Kimmy's voice broke into a sob. "I'm sorry, okay? I told you I was only trying to help."

Stephen wrapped an arm around his friend, reeling her in. Kimmy buried her face into his chest and let out a muffled cry.

Inver watched through envious eyes as Stephen consoled Kimmy. He wished Stephen's strong arms were wrapped around him instead, burying him in protection from *that face*.

∞

After another delicious dinner, Inver retreated to his room leaving Kimmy and Stephen to hang out alone. He rummaged through his bag, looking for the Richard Laymon book he had packed away. His hand dug through the bundled mess of clean and dirty clothes 'till finally, he felt the smooth surface of the book cover. He fished it out and lay down on the bed. He had managed to get through three chapters when he heard Kimmy make her way down the hall, go outside and jump into her car. The bright glow of her headlights shone through the green curtains in the room, casting oblong shadows that leaked down the walls.

Inver went to immerse himself back in the story about deadly rain falling on a town, creating bloodthirsty maniacs, when he heard a light tapping at his door.

Inver sat up, trying to appear alert. "Hello?" The door came forward with a light creak as fingers latched around its side, opening it slowly.

Stephen poked his head in the room. "It's safe now, Inver. You can come out."

"Oh, no, I wasn't hiding. I just thought I'd let you hang out with Kimmy alone for a bit," Inver spat the words out speedily, worried he had come across rude for being in his room.

"I know, mate. I'm only kidding," Stephen said. "Anyway, I came to ask if you fancied joining me for a drink?" Stephen waggled his eyebrows like there was fun to be had.

Inver looked at his book and then back at his host. Stephen's blue eyes encouraged him to say yes. "Yeah, sounds good." Inver placed the book down on the bed and followed Stephen back to the lounge.

As soon as Inver walked through the doors to the

dining and kitchen area, he was taken aback by the dimness and heat. The fireplace was stoked full of wood burning away, casting an orange glow which provided the only light. Stephen went straight to the bottom drawer of a dining cabinet and pulled out a bottle of whisky. Its golden brown glistened in the amber glow as he carried it over.

"I figured you and me can have the good stuff now she's gone." Stephen placed the bottle down on the table. "If I opened this with Kimmy around, it wouldn't last bloody long."

Stephen collected two glasses and a bottle of coke from the kitchen that he clunked down beside the unopened bottle of whisky. He twisted its top off and poured an abundance of the drink in both glasses.

"Whoa, that is gonna knock me for a six," Inver said, running a hand through his messy hair.

Stephen chuckled as he topped the concoctions up with a dash of coke. "Live a little, Inver. Besides, we got plenty of catching up to do. I've not had a chance to sit down and hear about your life yet." He passed a full glass to Inver, the fizzy coke crackled as it mingled with the whisky.

It was true; they hadn't had a chance to catch up yet—not properly, anyway. However, it still seemed strange to Inver. Yes, they were both adults now; yet while growing up here, Stephen had never given him the time of day as a kid—usually just a disinterested grunt or half-hearted wave if they ever actually came into contact. In fact, Inver always assumed Stephen had plain disliked the pesky child he had been.

"Cheers," Stephen said raising his glass, all the while eyeing Inver.

"Nostrovia." Inver clinked his glass against Stephen's, returning his stare. They went and sat on the couch in the lounge, the sound of flames licking against the glass door of the fireplace giving the room a cosy vibe. Under the dim fiery glow, Stephen looked almost identical to how he had in the 90s, the soft light flattering his face with the succulence of youth.

Inver sniffed the whisky drink in his hand. "I can certainly smell the alcohol."

Stephen gulped back a large mouthful, swallowing it

down like water. "It gets easier the emptier the glass gets, trust me."

Inver took a tentative sip, the booze oozing down his throat before it slowly burned nicely in his stomach. He placed his glass down on the smooth bench of the coffee table at their feet. "It's actually quite good," Inver said, nodding his head.

"Yeah, it's not cheap nasty shit. It's good for you. It'll put hairs on your chest."

"Ha, I already got plenty of those." Inver tugged at his shirt collar, showing Stephen a healthy crop of chest hair.

"Let me see. Lift your shirt up," Stephen asked.

Inver followed the instruction, raising his shirt high to his collar bone, baring his pale torso.

Stephen leaned across unexpectedly and ran a hand through Inver's nest of chest hair, pulling gently as he did so. "Shit, you do too." His smoky breath wafted across. "But plenty of room for one more I think." He raked his fingers slowly back across Inver's chest before slumping back on the couch, continuing with his drink.

Inver dropped his shirt back down, feeling amazed, almost honoured that Stephen had touched him. Normally, Inver would have pounced on this as a flirtatious move but thanks to *that face* he knew better now than to imagine hope and confuse it with reality. Even though *that face* was two hundred miles away, he could still feel its eyes burning on him, refusing to let him go.

"So, how's your mum? What's she doing now?" Stephen asked as he kicked his shoes off.

"Well, when we got to Auckland, she got a job as a secretary for this construction company and after a few years ended up the payroll clerk. She still works there."

"She must like it then?"

"Yeah, I think so," Inver said nodding.

"Good on her. I'm glad she did well. Wouldn't have been easy down here with old rust bucket."

"True, I think she was glad to give us a new start."

Stephen stared at Inver, his lip curled up before he let out a soft laugh.

Inver frowned at the random response. "What's so funny?"

"You just look so much like her it's crazy."

"I hope that's a good thing?" Inver knew it was.

"Definitely a good thing. Fuck, you could have ended up like your old man."

"What? A dead redhead?"

Stephen laughed, slapping Inver on the shoulder. "Kimmy said you're a funny bugger."

Inver took the compliments and washed them down with the rest of his drink. "So, when did you take over the farm?"

"Mum died of a heart attack not long after you and your mum left town, then dad went in 2002 thanks to liver cancer, but 'cos of him being so sick I was pretty much running the place a year earlier."

"Oh… sorry to hear they went so quickly," Inver said, suddenly feeling stupid for asking.

Stephen stared into his nearly empty glass. "It was a long time ago," he said solemnly. "Anyway, I think it's time for round two." He stood up holding his hand out to take Inver's glass. Inver quickly sculled down the rest of his drink before handing it across.

Stephen swiftly returned with two full glasses even more potent than the first. They talked their way through twenty years of catching up, swapping memories and jokes. It was nice to have company again after going so long without any. The fact it was such attractive company didn't hurt either, Inver thought.

After two hours of walking down memory lane, Stephen stared up at the clock and declared it was time he called it a night. At first, Inver thought the night had been cut short, that Stephen was robbing him of the rarity of company and then he remembered Stephen would be up at 4:30 a.m. to start work, so he'd actually been more than generous with his time.

Inver stretched his arms out and yawned more for show, stumbling to his feet before making his way to bed.

"Wait a moment," Stephen slurred.

Inver turned around to find Stephen walking towards him with open arms that quickly wrapped around him tightly. The strong embrace felt so good, Stephen's warm body pressing against him, his hands latching around Inver's back, making him feel protected.

"I'm so sorry about your dad," Stephen whispered. "I guess now he knows the secret."

Inver with his hands still at his side, uttered, "What secret?"

Stephen gave him a firm squeeze before loosening the embrace and stepping back to look Inver in the eyes. "I don't know. That's why it's called the secret, I guess. You only know it if you don't come back." On those dangling words, Stephen promptly left the lounge, leaving Inver standing alone.

CHAPTER TEN — 2016

INVER

Inver wasn't a big drinker. He had woken up early to a churning gut that soon led to his mouth watering like it had sprung a leak. He knew exactly what was going to come next. At high speed, he bolted down the hall in just his briefs, rushing to the toilet where he crashed onto his knees and buried his head deep inside the porcelain bowl. Hideous heaves retched up streams of whisky-laced vomit, its rushed exit leaving his throat raw. In that moment, he hadn't cared how intimate he'd gotten with the lavatory. After a good twenty minutes of sporadic spews and spitting out the remaining remnants of poison, he felt better, but far from a hundred percent. He sat on the floor, hunching over the toilet to make sure no more wanted to come up.
"Inver," Stephen called out.
Inver groaned to himself, not wanting Stephen to find him sat in his undies with a chin painted with dried bile.
"Yo, Inver, where are you?" Stephen's voice filtered through the house.
"In here," Inver hollered back.
Footsteps followed his voice 'till the bathroom door swung open where a surprised looking Stephen looked down at his half-naked guest hugging the toilet. "Am I interrupting something?" Stephen stood in the doorway, looking every inch the farmer in his gumboots and Swanndri jacket.
"Nar, I think I'm all done here." Inver croaked as he looked up at Stephen who wore a troubled expression. "Everything okay?"
Stephen sighed. "Nope, quite the fucking opposite to tell the truth."
"What's wrong?"
"Last night, did you hear anything strange coming

from outside?" Stephen threw Inver a towel hanging on the rack beside him.

Inver wiped his face free of mess. "I didn't hear a thing last night. I went out like a light."

"Not the dogs barking? Nothing?" Stephen asked, impatient for an answer.

"No... why?"

Stephen put his hands behind his head, moving his body side to side. "Some fucker has come in and emptied the fucking vat."

"Vat?"

"Where the milk's stored."

"Oh." Inver nodded before realising what this meant. "OH."

Stephen bit his bottom lip with a nod. "Yep, goodbye several thousand fucking dollars." Stephen's arm came down from behind his head to punch the door. "That fucking Eddie."

"You reckon it was him?"

Stephen glared at Inver like he was stupid. "Umm, yeah. I think it's pretty safe to say considering what he thinks of me at the moment." He looked at Inver, his eyes floating down Inver's body like he only just realised Inver's state of dress. "Anyway, I was hoping you could join me in going over and having a chat with the old mutt."

"Shouldn't you just ring the police?"

"I can't prove he did it."

"You can show them the photos. They prove he has motive."

Stephen shook his head. "No, I wanna sort this out. If he has the police turn up, it's only gonna set him off even more." Stephen released a charming smile reinforced by his bright eyes. "Come with me?"

Inver wasn't in the slightest mood to move but he couldn't say no to anyone, let alone a *hot* anyone. "Okay, let me just go get some clothes on." Inver got to his feet in awkward fashion and walked towards his room. In the hallway, he turned back to face Stephen. "Am I meant to be the voice of reason or something?" Inver asked with a weary smile.

"Nar, just means I've got a better shot of escaping if

he decides to bring his gun out."
Inver let out a nervous laugh.
"Yeah, that wasn't a joke," Stephen said.
Oh, great.

∞

Eddie's house, a faded lemon colour with a green tin roof, was less rundown than Rusty's, but reeked of creepy. Inver gasped as they passed the shed on the front lawn when he saw a woman's head with stringy brown hair planted in the window. He only calmed down when he got close enough to see it was actually a mannequin's head and torso in a skimpy red bra. The shed's outside walls were decorated with large machetes and old metal saws, a fiendish rustic charm if ever there was one. With such macabre fixtures, Inver wouldn't have been surprised to be greeted by Uncle Leatherface at the front door.

After Stephen's ominous mention of a gun, Inver had made sure to wear shorts and running shoes just in case a dash for safety was required. When they got to the front steps of the house, Stephen banged loudly on the door. He stood confidently—legs apart and arms akimbo—waiting for the milk pirating pensioner to come outside. After thirty seconds of no response, Stephen banged again even louder.

"Open up, Eddie. I know you're in there," Stephen called.

The shuffling of feet came from inside the house, stopping just before the front door.

"Open the fucking door, Eddie. I need to speak with you about what you've done."

No response.

"Eddie, you can't go emptying my milk vat just to try and prove a point. You've cost me fucking money, ya stupid bastard."

"You shit money for breakfast, so what's that to you?" Eddie spat back from behind the door.

A rustling sound soon followed Eddie's words. Inver looked at Stephen for an answer to the noise. Stephen raised his cute dash-like eyebrows and shrugged, equally clueless to what was going on.

"You can fuck off on the horse you rode in on, Stephen. I've not done anything," Eddie yelled. "But you stole from me the only things I had in this world. You deserve everything ya get and I'll make sure you get it!"

"Come on, Eddie. Open the door and we can talk about this," Stephen said, doing his best to sound calm. He waited for Eddie to oblige but when he didn't respond, Stephen thumped the door with his fist. *Bang, bang, bang.* "Open the fucking door, Eddie!"

Inver felt the rage burning off of Stephen. He was half expecting Stephen to huff and puff and blow the house down.

"You're lucky Mussolini and Stalin aren't here or they'd get ya," Eddie mumbled.

Inver rolled a finger around in circles at his temple. "Crazy," he mouthed.

"The dogs' names," Stephen whispered.

More rustling came from behind the door before the handle turned and Eddie appeared holding a plastic bag. He squinted, switching his vile vision between Stephen and Inver. "In fact, maybe they *are* still here." His hand dug into the bag and picked out brown gunk, flinging it at Stephen, hitting him in the face.

"What the fuck?" Stephen scraped it off his cheek, flicking it onto the ground before sniffing his fingers. "Dog shit! You dirty bastard," Stephen cried. He went to step forward but Eddie threw more shit at him, sending Stephen and Inver running into the yard.

"That's right, piss off, Stephen. Piss off!" Eddie barked.

"Fuck, old man. You're lucky I don't beat you with a ball of your own shit!" Stephen said as another piece torpedoed onto his jacket.

Eddie dropped the bag and disappeared behind the door, reappearing with his gun, shaking it around.

"RUN!" Stephen screamed.

He didn't have to tell Inver twice. He sped past Stephen and ran straight out the gate.

"Yeah, that's right. Run, ya sissies!" Eddie yelled.

Their legs didn't stop moving 'till they were back at Stephen's driveway. Inver hunched over grabbing his knees, puffing hard as his heart slowly found its way back to a regular tempo. He was way too hungover for this.

Stephen skidded to a stop a few seconds behind him, wheezing as he tried to catch his breath. "Fuck, I gotta quit smoking." He tugged at his jacket, inspecting the smears of shit. "The dirty bastard." He bent down and wiped his hands clean on the grass.

"Guess that didn't go to plan," Inver said.

"Ya think?" Stephen grumbled.

"I did say to call the police."

"Thank you, 'voice of reason.'" Stephen kicked the ground, screaming in frustration. "I swear I'm gonna throttle the old prick when I get my hands on him." Stephen stormed on ahead to his house like he was on a mission. "But first, I need a fucking shower."

Inver smiled. "Yeah, you look like shit."

Stephen stopped in his tracks, turned around with a grin on his face. "Cheeky bugger." He walked slowly up to Inver, his arms spread wide. "Gimme a hug, Inver."

Inver sidestepped him and jogged in front laughing. "I'll pass. Thanks."

"Oh, come on. Hug a mate when he's feeling like shit."

Any other situation and Inver would have been in that embrace like a baby to a tit.

"How rude! Anyone would think your shit don't stink," Stephen joked. He dropped his arms and waved a hand in front of his nose, shooing away the smell on his jacket. "Too bad mine fucking does."

.

CHAPTER ELEVEN — 2016

INVER

Stephen still refused to call the police, insisting he had control of the situation. Coming back covered in shit didn't strike Inver as much sense of control but Stephen was adamant he knew what he was doing. After his shower, Stephen had gone back to work and Inver went to tackle day two of the clean-up at Rusty's. He was making progress on the disgusting rooms little by little, going through binning the majority of Rusty's crap. To that point, Inver hadn't discovered any treasure that would gift a wealth of inheritance, but then he knew he had a better chance of winning the lottery.

Just as night began to paint the sky a pale black, Inver returned to the Davis homestead, a strange sense of excitement permeating his bones knowing he had another night of company ahead. When Inver got inside, he walked in on a hysterical performance of Stephen fussing in the kitchen. His host, it seemed, was trying his best to impress Inver with culinary skills the man clearly did not possess. Stephen raced around clumsily between peeling vegetables and tending to boiling pots of water. His confidence far outweighed his ability. After burning the meat in the oven, he accepted his shortcomings, and in a heated huff declared, "Son of a bitch." The wasted meal was scraped from the roasting dish into an empty ice cream container. "I guess the dogs will love it," Stephen grumbled.

Inver sat in the lounge, trying not to laugh at his helpless host, who he suspected usually relied on microwave meals or Kimmy's well-timed visits. Not one to give up, Stephen started from scratch, this time a simpler meal. Within minutes, Stephen's voice called from the kitchen, "Dinner's ready."

Inver sat down at the table, and was greeted by Stephen carrying a plate of baked beans smothered over toast. The toast's edges were a deep black, giving away the charcoal crunch waiting underneath. He cut into the burnt meal and scooped up a crunchy forkful.

"It's actually quite nice," Inver lied between mouthfuls.

Stephen eyed him suspiciously. "You reckon?"

Inver munched his mouthful down, nodding. "Definitely, like really good."

Stephen's lips spread to a questioning grin, extracting a chuckle from Inver and exposing his fib.

"I'm sorry. I did my best to lie. But hey, an A plus for effort," Inver said, giving a thumbs-up.

"Thank you for the high praise, Inver." Stephen smirked, flicking a bean across the table. It splattered against Inver's cheek, plopping down onto his shirt.

Stephen laughed. "Sorry, I didn't know I had such good aim." He rose from his seat and licked his fingers before leaning across the table to touch his hand to Inver's face. "Let me clean you up," he said with a beguiling smile. He rubbed his wet fingers over Inver's bristly cheek in firm slippery circles.

Inver tried not to laugh as he sat there enjoying the feel of being groomed.

Once they finished their meals, Inver collected the plates and went to stack the dishwasher. Stephen stayed seated in the dining room, hitched his feet up on the table and dug into his pocket, emerging with a new packet of cigarettes. He tore the plastic tag off the side, ripping into the packet with greedy fingers. Inver watched Stephen, who carefully eyed up each smoke before finally pulling one out and placing it back inside the packet upside down. Stephen then proceeded to pick out a different cigarette which this time he chose to spark up and breathe in.

Inver stood behind the kitchen bench, admiring the view and strange cigarette ritual. He let his eyes glance over Stephen's toned legs, visually fondling them, trying to get a peek up the leg hole of his shorts. Unfortunately, the shadows from the material were too dark to make out any erection inducing detail. His dick daze was cut short when

Stephen spontaneously shot up from his seat and crossed the dining room floor to the drinking cabinet. He opened one of its intricately carved doors, pulling out a fresh bottle of whisky and two glasses which he took back with him to the table.

"Fancy one?" Stephen asked.

"Yeah, sure. Why not?" Inver replied, more out of politeness than any real thirst.

Stephen poured them each a drink before scurrying over to the unlit fireplace and ramming its black iron box full of chopped wood. Inver grabbed his drink and went to sit on the couch. Sipping on his whisky, he perved at Stephen hunched over the fireplace. The man's shirt rode up his back, exposing the tip of his arse crack and the faintest of tan lines.

Stephen ripped up sheets of newspaper, flicked them into flame with his lighter and threw the paper inside with the wood, triggering a feeble blaze. He switched off the lights and TV, letting Inver hear how close they really were to the sea, its powerful waves noisily permeating the surrounding air. Stephen peeled his shirt off, threw it on the couch beside Inver and settled down on the carpet in front of the fireplace. "Fuck, this is nice," he declared, spreading his legs wide as he backed in closer toward the heat. He laced his fingers 'round his glass before glancing up to meet Inver's gaze.

Inver eyed Stephen's shirtless body with subtle deception. He admired the way the man's tan still held on in winter even if just slightly—his stomach not decked out with abs, but certainly flat and firm—decorated with a light trail of hair leading below his shorts waistband.

"So, how long have you been single for?" Stephen asked, the question striking a random starting point for drink conversation.

Inver scanned his mind all the way back to his last relationship. "Oh, about five years. Maybe six."

Less a relationship, more a convenient *regular* called Andrew, who would take him home at the end of a boozy night in town.

"What was she like?"

"Not bad, I guess," Inver replied, feeling uncomfortable knowing he was about to invent a fictitious heterosexual past.

Stephen scoffed at Inver's lack of sharing. "Come on. I wanna hear the details, man," he said enthusiastically. "Name, age, what's she look like? And most importantly, was she any good in the sack?"

"Uh, her name was Andrea. Twenty-six. Auburn hair, slim... in shape, ya know. And, yeah, good, but bloody noisy," Inver spat out the befuddlement of lies based on the real but short-lived romance with Andrew.

Stephen arched his eyebrows. "Nice, I like it when they're noisy. Means I know I'm doing my job."

"Yeah, exactly," Inver replied, trying not to cringe. *Kimmy was right. We really don't grow up past the age of fifteen.*

"What about you? How long have you been single?"

"Too long, mate."

"So, you and Kimmy? Never been an item?" Inver asked, hoping to steer the conversation away from his own made up exploits.

Stephen laughed and scratched his knee with his free hand. "Nar, that is one port I have not docked in."

"Really?"

"Yes, really," Stephen said, "You sound surprised."

"I just thought there was some chemistry there."

"Yeah maybe, but I'm bad news for good people. Kimmy deserves a good guy, not one who chases anything bad for his health," Stephen said, smiling as he patted his cigarette packet on the floor.

"Maybe it's time you start finding something good for your health then," Inver said, knowing he should take his own advice. *That face*, alluring as it was, had led him to wreck and ruin. Again, Inver felt its invisible eyes hovering over him like *he* was in the room with him.

Stephen's voice cut off his mind's pity party. "Are you packing, mate?"

Inver frowned. "What do you mean?"

Stephen laughed at his guest's naivety. "Do you have a big cock?"

Inver nearly spat his drink out. "Umm..."

Before he could answer any further, Stephen leapt up from the floor. "Wait there," he commanded as he ran past Inver and left the room.

He reappeared shortly afterward, holding something

in his hands. "I wasn't trying to freak you out, I just asked 'cos Kimmy bought these for me but they don't fit right," Stephen explained. "I thought maybe they'd fit you." Stephen held up a pair of expensive looking briefs made of white meshed cotton with an orange waistband. He handed them over to Inver.

"Thank you. They look pricey," Inver said, admiring the odd but generous gift.

"That doesn't matter, does it?"

"No, I guess not. I'd have to try them on and see if they fit."

"Well, go on then. Try them on," Stephen urged.

Inver stood up and started down to his room.

"Just try them on here."

"What? Here?"

"I've got a cock of my own, remember? You ain't gonna shock me," Stephen said nonchalantly.

"That's true." Inver glanced down at Stephen sitting in front of the fire. He felt a blush colour his cheeks at the thought of his bare arse so blatantly on display. He scuffed his shoes off and unbuttoned his pants, willing his dick to stay still and not grow from the homoerotic vibe he was no doubt imagining.

Stephen laughed at Inver's blatant awkwardness and covered his face with his hands. "I won't look. Promise."

Inver lowered his pants to his knees then steadied himself as he pulled his legs up one at a time out of the clingy material. With the pants gone he was left in his tatty blue boxers which had seen better days.

"I can tell you do a lot of running," Stephen said.

Inver looked down to find Stephen staring. "Can you?"

"Yeah, sure can." Stephen leaned forward and grabbed hold of Inver's leg, just below the knee. "Tense it?"

Inver flexed his calf muscle, letting Stephen feel its firmness. Stephen's hand clutched greedily at his furry leg. *Stay down, stay down.* Inver battled with his cock to remain flaccid.

"Yep, definitely good runner's legs." Stephen let go and shuffled back to the fire, waiting for Inver to try on the gift.

Inver kept his eyes down, focusing on his feet. In one swift swoop, he whipped off his boxers, exposing his dick and balls to dangle freely. The warmth of the fire felt great the way it streamed across, warming his exposed skin. He slipped into the fancy briefs and found they hugged close around his crotch and buttocks, an almost perfect fit.

"See, they look good, don't they? How do they feel on?" Stephen asked as he lit another smoke.

"Yeah, they fit really well." Inver glanced down at himself, admiring the way the underwear flattered his privates.

"I probably should have told you first that I wore them around a couple days and forgot to wash them," Stephen said seriously.

Inver felt his cock twitch. "What?"

Stephen laughed. "I'm only kidding, mate."

He wished he wasn't. The thought of wearing something so intimate that had been wrapped around Stephen was a huge turn on. Inver peeled the smooth briefs down his legs, bending down to pick up his boxers and get changed. Once fully clothed, Inver felt like he could relax again. Stephen though, glared at him with a mile-wide smirk on his face.

"What's funny?" Inver asked abruptly.

"Nothing," Stephen said, shaking his head unconvincingly.

Inver frowned, a mix of confusion and intrigue. "Nar, what is it?"

"I can see why Andrea screamed so much." Stephen chuckled.

Inver ran a hand through his hair, releasing an awkward smile. Stephen had an ability to make him feel violated, yet at ease simultaneously.

"You quite a big boy, Inver Murray. I imagine you score yourself a lot of screamers," Stephen said, his lips curling into a deviant grin.

Stephen's odd behaviour made Inver toy with the thought of flirting. Maybe he'd ask Stephen what *his* cock was like? He knew better than to risk it though.

"I see you keep it all tidy down there for the ladies?"

Inver nodded and agreed with a smile. "I do like to

maintain a clean house."

This wasn't right. Inver hadn't been *one of the boys* since high school days. He didn't know what was what in this interaction. Stephen believed he was with like-minded company, two straight guys drinking, talking shit and swapping stories. By letting his guard down, Stephen had granted him access to an exclusive club Inver probably shouldn't have entry to. He took a deep breath and decided it was time to drop the charade. "I should probably tell you I'm —"

A phone blared loudly, cutting Inver off.

"Hold that thought, mate. I'll just grab this."

Inver sat there wondering if the phone ringing was the universe trying to save him from a potentially disastrous reaction.

Stephen returned after ten minutes, his movements carrying an air of excitement. "That was my old mate, Troy. Him and his family are gonna be in town visiting this week."

"You'll enjoy catching up then."

"Yeah, sure will," Stephen said, nestling back in front of the fire. "Anyway, what was it you wanted to tell me?"

Inver gulped back a mouthful of drink. "I can't remember now. Mustn't have been important."

CHAPTER TWELVE — 1995

STEPHEN

Stephen had lain low since his less than stellar drunken performance. Thankfully, the black eye didn't take hold as much as it could have, and within a few days the bruising was all gone. He was reluctant to bump into his mates and get a much-deserved mocking, but he knew he couldn't avoid it forever. Finally, on Thursday he drove in to get some items for his mum from the local mart, and as soon as he stepped outside, Luke's familiar voice came booming from across the street.

"STEVIE!" Luke waved for him to come over.

Stephen chucked the grocery bags in the car and joined his friend who was having a smoke outside Ivy's, a dinky café-come-fish-'n-chip-joint.

Luke squinted his eyes, inspecting Stephen's face. "Fuck, what a pity, I was hoping to see some of that eye shadow Troy gave you." Luke threw his fists up, punching the air towards Stephen's face.

"Sorry to disappoint you," Stephen said, trying to sound good natured. "How did your night pan out in the end?"

"Not too good, man. I tried it on with George the fucking cocktease but… nar, that didn't work." Luke stopped talking to take a drag on his smoke. "Yup, I had to give up before she pulled a Troy on me and knocked me out."

"I wasn't knocked out."

"Hmm, let me think. One hit to the face and you went arse over tit over the log. Yeah, I'd say you were knocked out."

Stephen rolled his eyes at the exaggerated detail.

"Funny, 'cos I would have put money on you to win that battle," Luke said genuinely surprised.

"Yeah, but in my defence, I was pretty fucking legless."

"Better luck next time, Rocky," Luke grinned. "Anyway, you wanna come in and join us?" Luke motioned to the windows of the café.

"Us?"

"Yeah, I've just had lunch with Troy and Clare; hence, the after dinner hit." Luke lifted his smoke up.

Stephen looked back in the café and saw Clare waving back at him. *Fuck. What if Troy told her what I said?*

"I really ought to be getting back," Stephen fibbed.

"Bullshit."

"Nar, like I really —"

"Bullshit."

"Seriously, Luke."

"Bullshit." Luke's eyes glowed, knowing he was irritating Stephen.

"If I come in will you stop with the bullshit ritual?"

"Yep." A wide grin spread across Luke's face. "And remember, I've known you all my life, Stevie boy. I know when you're talking bullshit."

It was true. A lifelong friendship had gifted Luke the uncanny ability to smell Stephen's bullshit a mile away. As a result, Luke had the annoying habit of repeating the word over and over 'till Stephen relented with honesty.

Luke dropped his smoke on the mottled grey pavement and stubbed it out under the heel of his shoe. Stephen followed his giant mate inside the café where the aroma of pies hovered in the air, coming from a hot cabinet overloaded with pastry goods. Stephen made his way to the counter where large frames hung on the wall, displaying black-and-white photos of Clifton's early settler years. Waiting to be served, Stephen studied the images and decided the town didn't appear to have grown much since its pioneering days of horses and muddy paths.

Finally, Jayden Charteris came to serve him. Jayden's mum, Linda, owned the café and forced the greasy-faced teenager to work the counter during summer holidays.

"What can I getcha Stephen?" Jayden asked, full of confidence.

Stephen wasn't particularly fond of Jayden. Behind

the lad's acne and braces was a halfway decent-looking guy; in a few years, he'd likely be unwelcome competition in the Clifton talent pool.

"Just a Coke. Thanks, Jayden."

"Sure thing, man." Jayden fetched him his drink and insisted Stephen could have it for free.

"You sure?" Stephen asked, narrowing his eyes.

"Yeah, bro. On the house," Jayden said, seeming eager to please.

Stephen gave him a nod of the head as thanks. One benefit of having a reputation around town for scoring so many chicks was that the younger guys were desperate to be on his good side, as if somehow his luck would rub off on them. *Fucking idiots.*

With his free drink in hand, Stephen went to join his friends and took a seat beside Luke at the table still scattered with dirty plates. He put his coke down and nearly landed his elbow in some dollops of sour cream smeared into the plastic red tablecloth. This Stephen knew would have come from Luke, who around food, instantly became a pig in a trough. Across the table, Troy was glowing with pride next to Clare, something he always did when he was with her.

Although lovely, Troy's girlfriend was far from beautiful. Her rake-thin body carried a plain face framed by mousy brown hair straight as a sheet of metal. Troy, however, thought she was a goddess and worshiped her as such.

Clare gave Stephen a big smile as he sat down. "It's nice to finally see you, stranger. Where have you been hiding?"

"Just at home. I've been trying to get into the swing of things again being back on the farm."

"Well actually…" Luke began before Troy shot him a stern look, prompting him to shut up. Troy, the good guy that he was, obviously hadn't said a word about last weekend's incident.

Clare looked around the table, confused. "Actually what?"

Luke shuffled uncomfortably in his chair, his mind searching for a new end to his sentence. "He's been busy trying to bag Delphi Savage."

"Oh, really? Well, that explains everything," Clare said

in a giddy voice. "Has Delphi moved back too?"

"No, she's just here for the summer," Stephen replied speedily, not wanting Luke to tell the tale.

Although from New Plymouth, Clare had been dating Troy long enough to become well-versed in the who's who of Clifton locals.

"Remind me, she's the ridiculously pretty one, isn't she?" Clare asked, her words containing a glitch of jealousy.

"Yep, a real knockout," Luke said as he elbowed Stephen under the table.

"Yeah, that's her." Stephen elbowed him back discretely.

"Yep, so she's kept Stevie boy here so busy he's been knocked off his feet," Luke crowed, barely making sense for the sake of a joke.

"How is it going so far?" Clare asked.

Before Stephen could even open his mouth, Luke had to get another jab in. "Well, I think it's safe to say he's fallen flat on his face."

"I didn't land on my face, fool," Stephen said, whacking Luke on the shoulder, sending both of them into fits of laughter.

Clare frowned. "What are you two on about?"

Troy groaned. "Nothing, babe. Luke's just being a dick, as per usual."

Stephen snorted as he tried to hold in a laugh. "Yeah, it's not gone to plan, shall we say."

The door creaked open behind their table, a gust of wind escaping in from the outdoors. Stephen whipped his head around and saw Shaun walk in decked out in his blue work overalls, followed by a skimpily dressed Lydia in a white tank top and tiny denim shorts.

"Oh great, here comes try-hard," Stephen muttered to Luke.

Shaun's eyes lit up when he spotted them all at the table. "How's everyone doing?" Shaun's excited voice was so loud that the whole café could hear him.

"Trying to avoid you, that's what," Luke replied, only half joking.

Shaun gave Luke a *whatever* look before turning to face Clare. "Congrats on the baby."

"Thank you," Clare replied bashfully before nudging Troy. "How many people have you told?" She giggled into his ear.

"Are you hapu?" Lydia blurted bluntly.

Clare's face twitched. "Am I what?"

"Pregnant," Shaun quickly translated.

Clare nodded.

"She's my precious vessel," Troy gushed.

Stephen resisted the urge to cringe.

"Faaaar, you don't look it," Lydia exclaimed.

"Well, it's still early on, so I'd hope not. Otherwise, it just means I'm fat." Clare laughed.

Lydia battered her eyelashes at Luke. "How's your training going, Luke? I saw posters for your fight up at mum's work."

Luke stretched back in the chair, spreading his legs out wide as if his balls needed to breathe. "Yeah, good, aye. It's coming along quite nicely."

"I wish I could come watch the fight, but yeah, the stupid bar wouldn't let me in I bet. I know you'll win though," Lydia rattled on, resembling a teenage groupie. Like her brother, she sure could fucking talk.

Shaun gave his sister a shut-the-fuck-up look. "Calm down, Lydia. It isn't like he's curing cancer."

"Cheers for the support," Luke said with more than a hint of shittiness.

"Nar, bro, I didn't mean to be a downer. It *is* exciting." Shaun backed down knowing he had offended the more dominant male.

"Anyway, how come you're here? Aren't you meant to be at work?" Luke snapped.

"We only had the one car to work on today so Bob let me finish early. I'm lucky he can even give me twenty hours a week considering how dead it is."

Stephen sat quietly watching Shaun's lips' sharp movements, remembering it was those very lips which had planted a kiss on him last weekend.

"Lydia, go check if our order's ready." Shaun handed her a ten-dollar note.

"Why don't you go check?" Lydia bleated.

Shaun gave her a stern look. "Because I'm the one

paying, remember?"

"I thought you only just got here?" Troy asked.

"We did but we ordered by phone," Shaun said. "When I got home from work, hunger-guts here insisted she was starving and needed to eat pronto." He shot his sister a sarcastic smile.

"No I didn't, dick." Lydia scrunched the note in her hand and huffed her way over to the counter.

"Right, well I gotta go take a slash. Be back soon," Luke said, disappearing to the toilets.

Stephen could see Jayden trying to chat Lydia up at the counter to no avail. The boy talked away with lively body language while Lydia's gaze fixated on Luke walking past to the toilet. Stephen found it strange how girls would ignore a perfectly good-looking guy their own age in favour of an older—usually less attractive—specimen.

Stephen spun 'round in his seat to talk with Troy but found his mate had grown tired of conversation and was back to sucking Clare's face off. He looked up at Shaun who stood there smiling like an idiot. Stephen returned an awkward smile, unsure what to say or what it was Shaun wanted. *Please fuck off.*

Shaun sat down in Luke's empty seat and leaned forward with his elbows on his knees. "Are you busy tomorrow?" he asked quietly.

"Maybe. It depends how much Dad has lined up for me to do," Stephen said. In his mind he heard Luke yell, *bullshit.*

Shaun's face crumpled. "Well, if you get a chance, come and see me at the workshop. I've got something to show you, but yeah, only if you get the time."

"What is it?"

"Just come in. It's a surprise," Shaun said, finishing his words off with a grin.

"Okay, well, I'll see how I go," Stephen said noncommittally.

Lydia stomped over with a large newspaper-wrapped parcel in her hands. "It's ready."

"Right, I better go. And remember, only if you get the time," Shaun said. He stood up just as Luke was returning. "Catch you all later."

Clare retrieved her tongue from Troy's mouth. "Bye, Shaun."

"Good luck for the fight," Lydia chimed in, just before they disappeared out the door.

What surprise does he have to show me?

Shaun and Stephen had never been close. They'd never even hung out on their own. Sure, the guy was fun in a hyper-idiot way, but too much of him could get on your wick real fast. Stephen wasn't even sure who it was Shaun hung out with when not trying to infiltrate their group. Megan or whatever dregs Debbie had visit the house, he assumed. Stephen didn't like surprises. Unless they were wrapped under a Christmas tree, such things weren't usually pleasant.

∞

Throughout the next morning, Stephen found himself wracking his brains to figure out what it could possibly be Shaun wanted to show him. He figured the little weasel probably just wanted help with fixing up a car, or was it all a ploy to plant another kiss on him? He had images of Shaun leaning in, his warm breath wafting over his face before their lips pressed together. *Would he try sticking his tongue in my mouth?*

Stephen held the thought longer than he knew he should before coming to his senses and shaking the idiotic image out of his brain. As much as he resented going in to see Shaun, curiosity had seeped in. When it got to lunchtime and Stephen saw Rusty was going to be joining the family to eat, he decided to bail and see what the surprise was. He would rather take his chances with Shaun than listen to the grotty Rusty masticate his way through a meal.

When he parked up outside the workshop, it looked abandoned with no sign of Bob or Shaun anywhere. The white brick building with its high, grey roof was barren of any cars in the yard and its large, wooden blue door was pulled far across the garage entrance. Stephen was about to drive straight back home when he noticed a smidgen of a gap at the far end of the door. *Someone must still be inside.* He marched over to the building and squeezed his way through the narrow rift where the stench of fibreglass stung his nose. There were two vehicles inside, but no sign of Bob or Shaun anywhere.

"Anybody in here?" he called out.

Shaun's friendly voice answered from the far corner of the shed. "Under here."

Stephen's eyes darted over to the second car. Only then he noticed a pair of blue overall-covered legs bending up, poking out from under the car's frame. The sight made him feel uneasy, as images of Ricky trapped and dying filled his mind.

Shaun was on a creeper, wheeling himself out from under the car. He sat up with a smile, blowing his messy fringe out of his eyes. "Good to see you, I wasn't sure if you'd turn up." He seemed genuinely pleased that Stephen had come to see him.

"Yeah, well, I couldn't go all day not knowing what this big surprise is."

"Oh, you didn't have to come in. Especially it's not much... I just wanted to give you something."

Fuck. Maybe it is a kiss?

Shaun stood up, his slim frame drowning in the oversized overalls. He wiped his grease-stained fingers down his front and walked past Stephen. "Follow me."

"Where's Bob?" Stephen asked, looking anxiously around the workshop.

"He's gone to Hamilton to visit his sister, so it's just me here today. Apparently, I'm trusted enough to be in charge." Shaun spun round and flashed a mischievous grin Stephen's way.

"He'd be a fool," Stephen joked.

They went to a small room off the side of the workspace, tools hanging 'round the walls with outlines in thick black permanent marker, indicating their shape like a baby's learning game. Shaun went straight to a clunky metal filing cabinet and opened the bottom drawer, rummaging through its contents.

"It isn't much, but I remember you saying you didn't have one and would like one." Shaun pulled out a fishing rod with a can holder built into it. "So, I thought I could make you one." He handed it over to Stephen.

Stephen looked down at the gift in his hands, its

polished metal feeling sleek and new. *Not bad.* It wasn't too shabby for being homemade. "You didn't have to do that."

"Nar, I wanted to." Shaun ran his finger along the object's length. "Here, see."

He followed Shaun's finger and saw the words, *to my hunting buddy, Stephen,* engraved down the side.

Stephen raised his eyebrows. "This is really cool. Thank you." He gave Shaun a look of praise.

Shaun scuffed his boot along the concrete floor. He looked like he was about to blush and quickly stared down at his feet. "No worries," he murmured.

Shaun's awkwardness surprised Stephen. He didn't think Shaun was capable of being embarrassed.

Shaun lifted his head. "Hey, um, I was wondering if you would like to come hang out at my place tonight? Mum and Lydia are both going out, so once I put Josie to bed, it'll just be me there pretty much." His voice came out full of promise.

Stephen frowned at the question. "I've already got plans, sorry. I'm going clubbing in New Plymouth with Troy and Clare tonight."

"No worries. Another time, aye?" Shaun walked back towards the vehicle he'd been working on. "If I didn't have to babysit, I'd be so up for joining you guys."

Stephen felt guilty standing there, holding the primitive gift in his hand. Fuck, the least he could do is have a couple drinks with the guy, no harm in that. "Hey, you know what? I will come 'round tonight."

"Nar, you've got plans. We can do it another time."

"Fuck the plans. You know how much it's gonna cost me?" Stephen said. "Between you and me, the wallet's a tad starved. So hey, I'm better off sticking around here anyway." *Bullshit.* Money was never a problem.

Shaun's voice perked up, "Are you sure?"

Stephen nodded.

"Awesome, well come 'round anytime you like after seven. Mum and Lydia should be out by then."

Stephen made his way back to the garage doors. Raising his present up, he turned to face Shaun. "Thanks again and I'll see you tonight."

When he got back in his car, Stephen put his gift on

the passenger seat and instantly hated himself for letting guilt rope him into spending a night with Shaun. How desperate was the guy for mates that he would go out of his way and make this for him? Stephen groaned to himself knowing that in a few hours, he would be left alone socialising with the social dregs of Clifton, Shaun Munro.

CHAPTER THIRTEEN — 1995

STEPHEN

The last shreds of daylight hung in the sky as Stephen pulled up outside Shaun's house. The home's messy front lawn was overgrown and littered with brightly coloured kids' toys, its shabby condition stuck out like dogs' balls along a street of flash homes with perfectly manicured gardens. Considering the type of town Clifton was, Stephen knew this house and its inhabitants would definitely have left a foul impression on neighbours' tastes. For a brief moment, he regretted not parking farther down the street to avoid his car being associated with the Munros.

When Stephen knocked at the door, he could hear movement inside, indicating an active household. The door flung open revealing Lydia on the other side, her face suffocating under a thick layer of makeup.

Stephen stood waiting to be let in, holding bottles of whisky and Coke under his arm. "Hi, is Shaun home?"

Lydia's eyes shifted from Stephen's face to the bottles, eyeing both suspiciously. "Yeah, he's just getting all pretty for you," she said sarcastically.

A hand grabbed Lydia out of the way.

"Hey man, come in," Shaun said. He was shirtless, towel-drying his still-wet hair with one hand. He held the door open with the other, waiting for Stephen to enter.

As Stephen passed by Shaun's raised arm, he could smell spritzes of LYNX clinging to his armpit. Stephen suspected that his slightly earlier than planned arrival had sprung Shaun in the act of trying to impress him. Stephen put the bottles down on the coffee table and went to take his shoes off.

"Don't worry about that. This place ain't no palace," Shaun said. He threw the towel over his head and finished drying his hair before grabbing what looked to be a freshly ironed shirt off the couch and quickly chucked it on.

Lydia leaned against the small archway into the dining room, looking Stephen up and down like she was baffled by his presence. "What are you two doing tonight?"

"Not hanging out with you, that's what," Shaun spat out defensively.

"Calm your tits, Shaun," she snarled before composing herself. "Sorry, Stephen, you'll have to excuse my brother. He's not used to having friends visit."

The joke probably packed a weight of truth, Stephen thought.

Shaun glared at Lydia. "You were meant to be gone ages ago."

Lydia shrugged. "Sorry, am I interrupting a hot date?" Lydia winked at Stephen, making him feel more uncomfortable than he already was from this social slumming.

"Fuck up, Lydia," Shaun grumbled.

Stephen sat down on one of the chairs buried under a white sheet doubling as a couch cover. "We're just having a few drinks. What else is there to do in this shithole?" Stephen said before quickly adding "town" so they didn't think he was referring to their home, which indeed *was* a shithole.

Lydia walked over to Shaun and lunged at his jeans pocket. "I knew it." Her hand dove in trying to pluck out the contents. Shaun wrestled with her wrist but not fast enough to stop her from pulling out a small bag of marijuana.

Lydia squealed in victory. "I knew it! You raided Mum's stash again."

"Um, um, um, ummm," a little voice said. Stephen looked over and saw standing by the dining room entrance was their baby sister Josie picking at her nose before wiping it through her springy brown curls. She was so tiny, she'd snuck up without him noticing. Shaun and Lydia ignored their baby sister and continued bickering.

"I'm so telling Mum," Lydia said, more joking than serious.

Shaun, visibly annoyed with his sister, swiped it back, burying it in his pocket. "Yeah, and I'll tell Mum you've been using her vibrator again."

"Eww. Fuck, you're gross, dick," Lydia huffed and went to sit on the couch.

Shaun smiled at seeing his sister annoyed. "Uh, no, correction. That would make *you* gross."

"Fuck off, homo." Lydia pulled him the fingers. "I don't know why you lot are friends with this egg."

We're not really.

Shaun went and collected his baby sister in his arms. "I thought you were in the room, sneaky rat."

"I was but I'm thirsty."

"Ahh, I see. Well, I'll get you a drink, but you gotta go drink it in your room and watch your movie, okay?" Shaun disappeared to the kitchen with Josie in his arms, leaving Stephen alone in the lounge with Lydia.

The pretty teen sat across from him with her legs crossed, shaking her foot impatiently. Thanks to Debbie, the Munro kids at least had good looks going for them.

"So, where are you off to?" Stephen asked.

"Wouldn't you like to know?" Lydia returned, smiling arrogantly before realising how rude she sounded. "Nowhere, really. Just going down to the beach with my mates. Same old."

Stephen looked at how done up she was. "Really, 'cos you look like you're going on a date."

"I always go out like this," Lydia said protectively.

Shaun bellowed from the other room, "Yeah, she's telling the truth, Stephen. She always goes out looking like a sad whore."

"Very funny, Shaun," Lydia spoke slowly, rolling her eyes. "At least one of us scores, dickweed."

Stephen snorted at their bickering.

Shaun emerged with Josie in one arm, clutching his neck, tucked under his other arm he carried a bottle of Fanta and a big bag of lollies. "I'm just setting Josie up with a movie in the room. Won't be long."

Stephen looked in the corner and realised the TV was missing. Shaun had obviously planned ahead and intended for his baby sister to have a night of Disney vids so they could hang out uninterrupted.

"Lydia, can you grab Stephen a glass from the cabinet?" Shaun called out.

"The cabinet?" Lydia questioned.

Shaun poked his head back around the corner. "Yes, the cabinet," he said in an authoritative voice.

Lydia was about to say no but reluctantly climbed out of her chair, crossing the lounge in snappy steps to a small glass cabinet near the empty space created by the missing television. She came back with a fancy tumbler in her hand that had a faintly blue-tinted bottom. One look at it told Stephen these glasses were meant more for visual admiration than the practical task of drinking out of. He was certainly being treated like a guest of honour.

Stephen filled the glass up and raised it to his lips, glad for the taste and the relief the first sip granted his nerves. He settled back into the chair and waited for Shaun.

Lydia sprung to life at the sound of the telephone ringing. "That'll be for me," she hollered and bolted out of the room.

Stephen sat listening to her voice coming from the kitchen.

"Hey, wow, took you long enough... aha, yip... okay, see you soon."

Yep, definitely a date.

She came back smiling ear to ear. "I gotta go. Stephen, don't get too bored hanging out with my loser brother." She grabbed her coat and sped out the door.

Stephen sat alone analysing the shabby lounge with its too-many pot plants and couch-cover covered couches. A wicker bookshelf stood at the wall beside the glass cabinet, its unceremonious shelves jutted out with creased book spines. Stephen strained his eyes to read their vertical hinges, the same name cropping up on every second book. *Stephen King.* He hadn't picked Debbie to read much of anything other than the trashy Woman's Day mags that sat piled under the coffee table.

Shaun emerged looking pleased with himself. "Right, Josie's all set for a night of movies, so she shouldn't be coming and bothering us... I hope," he said, crossing his fingers. He disappeared to the kitchen and came back with a plastic bottle of ghastly dark liquid and a more common glass than the regal one in Stephen's hand.

"What have you got there?" Stephen pointed at the

bottle.

"It's some homebrew Mum got off Eddie Tucker."

Eddie Tucker, Clifton's token nut case and Stephen's neighbour, who tried making a living selling second-hand goods out his garage and on occasion putrid homebrews like the one Shaun was holding.

"Are you sure you wanna be drinking his rocket fuel? Fuck, it'll probably leave you blind."

Shaun laughed off his concern. "Nar, Mum reckons it's pretty good."

Stephen stared in disbelief at Shaun's trust of Tucker's concoction. "Here, gimme your glass." Stephen motioned for Shaun to hand over his cup. Stephen filled it with his own bought liquor and handed it back. "Have a real drink."

Shaun tilted his head. "Cheers, man."

At first, Stephen struggled to contribute to the conversation, letting Shaun do all the talking but the more the drinks poured, the conversation too spilled out of Stephen with more ease. It didn't take long to stop wondering how much better his night could have been in town with Troy and Clare.

Shaun sat back with his feet tucked under his legs, his white socks brilliantly bright as he fidgeted with them. Stephen enjoyed watching this boy's quirky reflexes, each one like the telling of a new story. Shaun was a bundle of idiosyncrasies that couldn't keep still, even when trying.

Shaun stopped his squirming movements when he realised Stephen was grinning. "What are you smiling at?"

"You just can't keep still, can you?"

Shaun tugged at his feet one last time. "Sorry."

"You don't have to be sorry. It's kind of cool in a weird way."

Shaun raised his eyebrows. "Umm, thanks, I guess."

"Seriously, it's all good. You can't help being spastic," Stephen said, pulling a stupid face and sticking his tongue out.

Shaun laughed. "Fuck you," he replied and hurled a cushion at him.

Stephen was about to missile it right back when Josie appeared in the lounge, dressed in her Minnie Mouse pyjamas.

Shaun turned and smiled at his sister. "What'cha doing, rat?"

"The movie finished," Josie mumbled. She made her way over to Shaun, clambering onto his lap. She nuzzled into his chest as if marking her territory, letting Stephen know Shaun belonged to her first and foremost.

Shaun kissed her head. "Want me to come put the other video on?"

"No, I wanna stay out here with you two."

"Oh, come on, you'll like the next one. It's the Goonies. It's really good." Shaun's voice feigned excitement, trying to get his little sister to buy into it. Josie didn't look sold on the idea. Shaun looked across at Stephen. "Aye, Stephen, the Goonies is an awesome movie, isn't it?"

Stephen was caught off guard and his face contorted into a puzzled look before finally coughing up, "Yeah, it's the best." He tried mimicking the excitement Shaun had shown but failed miserably.

Josie stared blankly at Stephen, unfazed by his testimony before looking back at her brother. "But it's boring on my own."

"What if I got you another bowl of ice cream?"

Josie's face lit up. Shaun's bribery looked set to work. Shaun's eyes zoned in on the near-empty Coke bottle on the coffee table. "But first, you gotta get me another Coke out of the fridge."

Josie nodded. "Okay."

"Be quick. If you don't get it in three seconds, it'll blow up, Inspector Gadget."

Josie squealed and raced off in pursuit of the kitchen. Loudly and slowly, Shaun counted, "ONE... TWO... TWO-and-a-half... two-and-three-quarters."

Josie ran in flustered and shoved the bottle at Shaun as if she really believed in her hands was a dangerous weapon that could explode at any moment.

Shaun rose from the couch and passed it over to Stephen. "Right, well, I'll go get this video on for her."

Josie's face dropped. "Oh, can I just wait five more minutes, Shaun, please?"

Shaun groaned, running a hand through his already-ruffled hair. "Come on, you promised. We don't break our promises, remember?"

Josie jumped up and down. "I will go, but can we do the love letter game first?"

Shaun rolled his eyes in frustration. "Again? Okay, but real quick." He grabbed his sister's hands and looked at Stephen. "I wish Lydia hadn't shown her this."

"What is it?" Stephen asked.

Josie looked at Stephen and said in a serious little voice, "It's magic."

"Is it?" Stephen replied, trying not to laugh and mock her belief.

Josie held her hands out in front of Shaun. "Lydia can do it but Shaun's way better."

Shaun slapped his sister's upturned palms. "Which one hurt the most?"

Josie shook her right hand which Shaun gripped in his hand before pinching each one of her little fingers.

Shaun let a sigh roll out of his mouth. "Yes, Stephen, this is how you find out the letter of your true love's first name." He winked. "But somebody here always wants a different letter."

Josie stared intently at her hands. "No, this time is the really *real* one," she said as she wiggled her pinkie finger, letting her brother know it was the one that felt the pinches the most. Shaun then pinched her finger in three places, waiting for her to say again which part again she felt most.

"The last one."

Shaun looked at his sister with a dopey look on his face. "Are you sure?"

"Yes."

Shaun frowned. "But are you really really sure?" he asked playfully.

"Yes!" Josie giggled, jiggling her hand impatiently.

Shaun rubbed the skin at the end of her finger before looking down at the spot carefully. "Hmm, it looks like an M to me." He looked closer in, studying her finger. "Yep, definitely an M."

"An M?" Josie looked puzzled, trying to summon up a name beginning with M.

"M probably means Mum," Shaun offered.

"Yeah, Mmmum," she emphasised the M, letting it sink in. "Do Stephen now," Josie said in an obvious stalling tactic.

Shaun went to pour himself another drink. "I don't think Stephen wants to play."

Stephen flashed Shaun a grin. "Oh, come on, Shaun, let me know the letter of my true love." He sculled back the last frothy drops of his drink and placed his glass down, holding his hands out in waiting.

Shaun eyed him almost suspiciously. "Okay, if you insist." He grabbed Stephen by the wrists, pulling his hands in closer to begin the same routine he had just performed on his little sister. Josie huddled in excitedly watching for the enchanted spell to be repeated. The magic ritual led to the end of Stephen's index finger on his right hand as the chosen spot. Shaun's slim fingers gently rubbed away, searching for an outline of some mysterious letter.

"I can't really see anything," Shaun said.

Josie leaned in, staring down at the fingerprint like it was an oil painting with hidden meaning. "Look, look," she urged.

Stephen wondered what she could see. "What is it?"

Shaun studied where she pointed. "That's not a letter, Josie. It's just a shape."

"What's the shape?" Stephen asked intrigued.

Shaun hesitated. "It looks like the infinity symbol." He fixed his eyes on Stephen's fingerprint intently before letting go of his hand. "Trust you to be difficult and not have a letter."

"The infinity symbol?" Stephen said, unsure what that was.

"Yeah, you know like a sideways eight." Shaun's finger drew the symbol slowly in the air.

Stephen's eyes glowed with recognition. "Gotcha." He pulled his hand back, studying where Shaun had rubbed, looking for any outline of this forever symbol.

"It looked like two S's hugging," Josie said, looking very serious. "Two S's 'cos his name begins with S." She looked proud of herself for knowing what his name started with.

Stephen looked at this little girl filled with gumption

of her conviction.

"Is that what you think it is?" Shaun asked, humouring her.

"Yes, it has to be letters, not shapes, silly," Josie said, sounding indignant.

"So, I'm looking for a Sally," Stephen said, his face wearing a look of wonder, "or a Susan, Sarah, Stacy—"

"Or a Shaun," Josie chuckled.

Stephen nearly choked on a laugh remembering Shaun's midnight stolen kiss and instantly felt awkward by Josie's innocent joke.

Shaun flashed Stephen a quick look before standing from his seat. "Right, rat, you have a movie to watch if you like it or not."

Josie ran to the room ahead of him squealing, "Don't forget the ice cream."

Shaun stormed off following her. "Yeah, yeah."

Stephen sat staring at his finger, scrutinising for any sign of this mystery shape. "You sure it wasn't a D?"

CHAPTER FOURTEEN — 1995

STEPHEN

Stephen lay on the messy, half-made bed in his airy and spacious bedroom. Dirty clothes strewn across the floor had waited days to be whisked away to the laundry and be washed. He was half-watching a cricket match on the television which sat atop his bedroom drawers as he enjoyed the small breeze coming through the open window, fluttering the pale curtains. The blaring of the phone poisoned his eardrums, disrupting the cricket commentary. He waited for one of his parents to pick the phone up, but the bloody thing kept ringing and ringing. *Fuck sake.* After the eighth ring, he grabbed the remote, switching the tele off and raced to get the phone.

"Hello."

A friendly inviting voice greeted him. "Hi, Stephen."

It took a brief moment to register who it was. "Hey, Shaun. How's it going?"

"I'm great, thanks, and yourself?"

He had never given Shaun his phone number and was surprised he had it. "I didn't know you had this number."

"I didn't, but I used this magical thing called a phone book. You might of heard of it?" Shaun said, laughing at Stephen's suspicion.

Stephen rolled his eyes. "True, didn't think of that. Anyway, what's up?"

"I was just calling to see if you fancied coming 'round tonight. It's just me and Josie again."

Stephen didn't respond as he processed if he actually wanted to go.

Shaun picked up on his apprehension. "It's okay if you're busy, but last weekend was cool and, well… I'm not really doing anything tonight."

The last visit hadn't been as painful as he'd expected, so he bit the bullet. "Yeah, that sounds good," Stephen said, trying to sound excited. "What time did you want me?"

"Anytime you like, Lydia's already out and Mum's off to the pub soon."

"Cool, I'll come 'round in a couple hours then."

As he hung up the phone, Stephen realised he had the strange sensation of looking forward to another night at the Munro house.

∞

When Stephen arrived, he found Shaun hovering over a bubbling pot in the kitchen, tasty fumes of homemade cooking erupting out of it making Stephen's mouth water. He sat at the dining table and watched Shaun potter about tending to dinner. Stephen wished Shaun had said they hadn't eaten yet; he felt rude at his arrival having interrupted their meal.

Shaun grabbed a bowl from the pantry. "Won't be long, I'm just dishing up Josie's dinner." He gave Stephen a sideway glance. "Shit, sorry. I should have asked if you wanted some? It's chicken casserole."

Stephen shook his head.

"Are you sure?"

"Yeah, I'm not hungry." *Bullshit.*

Rather late dinner, Stephen thought, but he waited patiently and sat staring at a brown paper bag on the centre of the table.

Shaun called out to Josie who raced in at lightning speed before disappearing to her room with her bowl filled. Shaun came and sat down with Stephen and pulled a bottle of Johnny Walker from the bag. "I figured it was my turn to shout the good stuff."

"You're a scholar and a gentleman," Stephen said. He was impressed Shaun had bothered to buy a bottle instead of relying on psycho Eddie's homebrew. Once again, he was treated to a fancy tumbler from the cabinet.

As Shaun poured them each a drink, the dim

lightbulb draped the room in a soft yellow while its tendrils of light accentuated the scar across Shaun's eyebrow. Stephen stared at its perfect piercing shape, curious as to how he got such a defining feature.

"What happened to your eyebrow?" Stephen asked.

Shaun stared back at him blankly.

"The scar," Stephen specified.

Shaun ran a finger along its deep mark. "This?"

Stephen nodded.

Shaun took a deep breath about to exhale the story when Josie came barging into the kitchen. "He got it from fighting pirates."

Shaun spun around in his seat and pretended to wield a sword at his sister. "That's right, rat."

Josie giggled at her brother's antics.

Shaun turned back to Stephen and gave him a wink. "Yeah, Stephen. I was fighting off Evil Roger the pirate, you know the one."

Stephen arched his eyebrows, trying not to laugh at the tall tale. "Ohhh, him. I heard he's a real baddy, that guy."

Josie joined them at the table in a hyperactive-state. "Evil Roger nearly cut off Shaun's head, but he missed and so Shaun cut him down both sides of his facccce." She raised her finger pretending to slice down each cheek, emphasising the imagined battle. "Aye, Shaun, aye."

Shaun smiled at her idolisation. "Haven't you got a bedroom you're supposed to be watching movies in?" Josie stood, still not budging. "If you don't, I might have to tickle you 'till you do." He lunged forward, pretending to grab her. With a squeal, she was off back to the bedroom, leaving them in peace.

Stephen reached into his jeans pocket to remove a new packet of cigarettes, ripping off the plastic seal and grabbing one out to plop in his mouth. Busy searching for his lighter, he only half-noticed Shaun's hand swoop in and rip the smoke from his lips.

"Hold up," Shaun said, grabbing the packet from Stephen's hand and squeezing the cigarette back inside upside-down.

Stephen frowned at the oddness of what his eyes were seeing. "What are you doing, dork?"

Shaun patted the smoke in 'till it was snug alongside the other nicotine sticks before handing the packet back. "It's the lucky smoke ritual. Have you never seen that?"

"Can't say I have."

"The first smoke you pull out goes back in upside-down, so you know to save it for last. It's your lucky smoke."

Stephen picked a different smoke out sparking it alight and taking a heavy drag, giving himself a good hit. Shaun scooted a paua shell ashtray across the table for him, putting it within ash-flicking distance. "So, what's so lucky about that last sucker?" Stephen asked.

"Nothing especially. I guess it's just nice to have good luck charms."

"Good to know." Stephen tipped his head back and blew out skinny plumes of white smoke that transformed into rings. Shaun's eyes followed the rings as they grew wider and wider the higher they climbed before fading into nothingness.

"Impressive work, Mr Davis."

"Why, thank you, Mr Munro."

"Mind if I bum a puff?" Shaun asked.

"Go for gold." Stephen handed the smoke across to Shaun who pinched it gently between his fingers near the orange embers.

Shaun took two quick drags before handing the cigarette back. Stephen put it back in his mouth, feeling the tip between his lips a little dampened with his mate's saliva. Shaun's hand darted back toward him and tugged on his shirt. Stephen assumed Shaun was after another puff already.

"Where'd you get these threads from?" Shaun asked, his fingers rubbing the fabric delicately like it was a priceless heirloom. He let go of the shirt as if reluctant to let go of something he could never have.

Stephen looked down at the top he had on. A crisp looking black shirt with stitched gold coloured patterns. Even at a year old, it was one of his favourites. "I got this from a funky little shop in Bondi."

Shaun's expression was blank. Bondi meant nothing to him.

"Sydney," Stephen said.

"Oh, true." Shaun nodded. "It's really cool."

"Yeah, it's one of my favs," Stephen answered before

patting his chest. "It definitely helps having the flash threads in getting the ladies."

"I could do with some of that help," Shaun said, sounding almost melancholic. "But shit, man, that must have cost you a mint." He chased down his comment with a mouthful of his drink.

"Just a few weeks rent." Stephen laughed to himself thinking of the absurd price he had paid for the shirt.

"Crikey." Shaun shook his head like Stephen had committed a crime. "Why waste that sort of money though?"

Because I can.

"There's nothing wrong with liking nice things, Shaun," Stephen said, a little too defensively.

"Nar, man. Sorry. I didn't mean to sound like a dick." Shaun's eyes quickly shone apologetically, as if he were worried Stephen would up and walk out at the slightest criticism. "But you're already such a cool sort, ya know? You don't need a label to prove that."

"I ain't proving anything to anyone," Stephen grumbled, despite Shaun hitting a point of truth. "But it's nice to know you think I'm cool." Stephen raised an eyebrow. "Hang out with me long enough and you might have some of it rub off."

Shit. Don't encourage him. Two visits here is bad enough.

Shaun laughed and grabbed hold of his own attire hanging loosely from his slim frame. "Can't you see? I'm already cool enough."

Stephen stared at the baggy t-shirt Shaun had on and his navy blue nylon pants. *Very uncool.* "Fuck yeah, Shaun, you're rocking it," Stephen said with a piss-taking grin.

"You know it! I rock the flash trash." Shaun leapt to his feet and started busting terrible dance moves.

Stephen laughed at the ridiculous impromptu show. "Maybe not so flash with the dance moves, mate."

Shaun sat back down looking happy with himself for making Stephen laugh. "They might be trash, but I do it in style."

Stephen looked at the grin on Shaun's face. He decided that Shaun suited smiling and he couldn't imagine someone like this ever looking sad. This guy was a bright spark in a dull town.

"What?" Shaun asked, curious as to why Stephen was staring.

"Nothing." Stephen felt odd for getting lost in his mate's smile. He took a scull on his drink before changing the topic. "So, where's Lydia tonight?"

"Probably out slutting," Shaun replied.

"Lucky for some. I wish I was."

Shaun smirked. "That's you most of the time, isn't it?"

Stephen shrugged at the question and pretended to give his crotch a grope. "Not as much as I'd like."

"Yeah, true," Shaun said, emitting a quiet laugh that made him seem nervous. "So, are you and Delphi talking yet?"

The bloody Delphi topic.

"No, not yet."

"I think you can do better anyway."

Stephen nearly choked at the words. "I doubt it. Have you seen her? She's hot, really on to it and interesting… oh, and did I mention HOT?"

"You're all those things too though, so, yeah, you could do better if you wanted."

Stephen felt his neck redden. "Pretty and clever maybe, but I definitely ain't interesting," he said, waiting for Shaun to respond, secretly wanting more compliments for his ego.

"Of course you are—you're a Davis—that's like royalty around here. That alone makes you interesting."

Stephen was amused by the strange observation. Sure, his family were well known around these parts, but he didn't think people would see them as being interesting for the sake of it.

"I guess that would make us cow shit royals then."

Shaun laughed and nodded. "But still royally interesting."

"Cheers, but I think it takes more than that to qualify as being interesting."

"Compared to everyone else round here you're pretty reserved, so who knows what secrets you got lurking." Shaun's eyes glistened in cheeky fashion. "That makes everybody wanna know more about you."

Stephen wondered for a moment if this was true. He always felt other than the way he looked, he was run-of-the-mill boring. "I think you'll find most people in Clifton are dull as dishwater."

"I know what you're saying but, honestly, everybody's interesting in some way." Shaun ran his finger around the rim of his glass, staring into its brown pond of whisky. "You just have to ask the right questions."

Stephen nodded. "Said like a true guru."

"That's me."

"So, slayer of pirates, what questions should I be asking you?"

"If I told you, that would take the fun out of it."

"Oh, come on," Stephen said, encouraging Shaun to share some secrets.

Shaun smiled. "Trust me, there's plenty of questions you could ask. I'm just not sure you'll like all the answers."

CHAPTER FIFTEEN — 1995

STEPHEN

The small radio in the milk shed was turned up as loud as it could go. The Smashing Pumpkins rocked out of its tinny speakers as Billy Corgan spat out a vicious chorus to the band's latest single. Bopping his head in time to the music, Stephen was glad to be helping out on the farm. Despite his parents insisting he should go make the most of his last summer break, he was glad to be kept busy. As Stephen enjoyed the feeling of being useful, he stood waiting for number forty-six to lead the way for afternoon milking.

Forty-six was the head heifer of the bunch. She led the cattle troop with an air of authority her position afforded her with over three hundred cows following her hoof prints, each one treading over the shit and piss of the higher up. Stephen knew following last would be sixty-seven.

Sixty-seven always brought up the rear with one of the farm dogs hot on her heels, yapping away. Stephen went onto autopilot, going about his job while daydreaming in his good mood.

The past week had been a strange one, socially at least. Every night, he had gone around to visit Shaun, who tended to be the only adult home half the time in the Munro house. Shaun, it turned out, was a good sort. He wasn't the lame clown Stephen had imagined him to be all the years before, and he found himself looking forward to their visits. Besides, it was good timing—this new social outlet—thanks to Troy spending every waking minute with Clare, and Luke being swamped with his training for the upcoming match.

Distracted in a world of his own, Stephen hadn't noticed his mother walk up behind him as he was hosing the milk shed down. "Stephen," she called out.

He nearly dropped the hose in shock before turning

around to see his mother trying not to laugh at his fright.

"Gosh, you're easy to scare today."

"So it would seem," Stephen muttered.

"Your father's gone to New Plymouth for supplies and taken the automatic and I need to get to town and grab some stuff for Christmas dinner," she said. "And, well, you know how good I am at driving your car."

Not very good. His mother wasn't the best driver going and certainly not in a manual.

"Do you need me to take you?" Stephen asked.

"If you wouldn't mind, love."

This wasn't a question.

"Sure, let me quickly hose the rest of this and we can go."

Stephen hurriedly washed the last of the muck away before going and changing out of his work gear. When he returned outside, he found his mum sitting in the car waiting, smiling impatiently. "Somebody's keen," he said.

She stared at him, blinking. "No. Women are just more organised, dear."

Stephen gave an obligatory laugh and started the motor, driving them into town. He was relieved when he arrived and managed to get a park right outside the store, a rare occurrence this close to Christmas with the town and its few veins of streets so filled with tourists.

"Did you want to come in?" she asked.

Again, this wasn't a question, but he knew if he played reluctance she would shout him something.

"I was just going to wait here."

"Oh, come on. Come bond with your mother and carry the bags," she joked. She could see Stephen slouching in the driver's seat not ready to budge. "I'll buy you an ice cream?"

He hoped she was joking. "That hasn't worked for years."

"I know. It's a pity because you use to be so easy to bribe," her eyes sparkled. "A packet of cigarettes?"

"Deal," he said in an instant, jumping out the car to follow her inside the small grocery store. Stephen was lumbered with the shopping basket while his mum perused the limited options available to her.

His mother had been fussing for days about Christmas and already had a stockpile of food but it was never enough. Her baby sister Cindy and Cindy's husband Brian were coming down from Auckland with their two children. Stephen was not looking forward to their arrival. Each cousin annoyed him and Uncle Brian was a world-class prick. But they were the only extended family Stephen and his parents had, so his mum made the effort every year even though it stressed her out.

Stephen's mother seized the opportunity of his young hands carrying the basket that very quickly went from mildly full to ligament-tearing. The general-store-come-supermarket was tiny with its five aisles of overpriced goods, but it was the only shop of its kind for close to an hour north or south of Clifton, gifting it a mean monopoly.

In the corner of the frozen aisle, Stephen saw the crazy loon, Eddie Tucker, digging a bony hand in to fetch a bag of ice cubes. The man had a beanie on and was dressed head to toe in army print clothing that looked far too thick for the summer day outside. Eddie lived across the highway from Stephen's family home, his small house like a tiny freehold island surrounded by the Davis family farm, something the man resented for no good reason, other than the fact they had money and he did not.

This riled Stephen when lazy shits would bemoan his family's wealth. Maybe if the idiots tried working as hard as his parents did, they *too* would have something to show for it. Eddie would usually sneer at Stephen or his parents when they drove past his house with its booze-making shed and yard littered with junk. Eddie's contempt didn't stop Stephen's mum being friendly though. "Good afternoon, Edward," his mother said, smiling at the psycho.

Eddie looked up skittery as a rabbit like he had been caught in the act of being up to no good. He probably was. "Yup. Hi, Miriam," he grumbled from behind rotten yellow teeth. He darted off to the rear of the store like he was stalking something in the jungle.

Fucking loony tune.

Stephen switched the basket to his left hand before the right one fell off. He breathed a sigh of relief when his mum declared she was all done, but his relief was short-lived when they bumped into Luke's mother, Irene.

Irene was tall for a woman at nearly six feet with a chirpy face and a thick body which didn't have a bad bone in it. She had an air of tomboy to her that Stephen wondered had been acquired from the sea of testosterone she lived in which included Mr Bridgeman, Luke and his three younger brothers—all growing into bombastic giants like their parents and elder brother.

The two mothers locked in gossip and launched a scathing attack at the shocking price of Christmas which they both insisted was just getting too expensive for them to afford. Stephen tried not rolling his eyes at what was a load of crap. Once the friendly catch up ran its course and with the basket near collapsing under the weight of Christmas food, Stephen and his mum made their way to the counter where Debbie greeted them from behind the till.

"Hello, Miriam… Stephen." Debbie flicked them both a generous smile.

Stephen's mum returned the gesture. Stephen swore he could feel his mother's unease being near Clifton's one and only, *Desperate Debbie*.

"Hey, Debbie," Stephen said and hoisted the basket onto the counter. Debbie reached across to fetch the basket sending a waft of fruity perfume across that smothered Stephen's nose.

Debbie commenced scanning and bagging the items at lightning speed. "Will we be seeing you tonight, Stephen?"

Stephen hesitated. "I think so."

"Always nice to see you," Debbie said, "and I know Shaun enjoys having you 'round."

Stephen's mother seemed distracted from the conversation as she fumbled around in her purse, looking for money.

"Is this for Christmas is it, Miriam… someone making Pavlova?" Debbie asked.

"Sorry, what was that?"

Debbie held up the kiwi fruit. "Pavlova?" she repeated loudly as if Stephen's mother was hard of hearing.

"Oh, yes… yes for the pav."

"Yum. I wish I knew how to bake one but I can't cook for the life of me." Debbie laughed. "Thank god for the kids. Shaun and Lydia are whizzes in the kitchen."

"And a packet of 20 B n H, please," Stephen asked.

Debbie fetched the cigarettes from a large white cylinder case above the till. "When you're over one night, you really should try some of Shaun's cooking. I hear you haven't been brave enough yet," Debbie joked.

"No, nothing like that. I'm just usually full when I come over," Stephen insisted.

She looked at him, her lips pursed. "I can't accuse you of gluttony, but I'm sure you got the other six sins covered, young Stephen."

Stephen smiled and felt himself blush, not embarrassed by the joke, but by being outed as a regular visitor to the Munro household.

"That'll be $82.85, thanks, Miriam."

His mother handed the precise amount of money over. Stephen picked up the bags of shopping and smiled goodbye.

"See you tonight, maybe?" Debbie bellowed as they walked out the doors.

Once back in the car, his mum couldn't wait to question Stephen about the juicy droplet of information Debbie had let slip. "I didn't know you were hanging out at her house."

"I'm friends with her son, Shaun."

"Are you?" She looked at him like he was mad. "I thought he would be a little bit…" she paused, searching for the appropriate word, "*basic* for you to be friends with." This was her politest way of disapproving of him fraternising with a Munro.

She wore a forlorn look upon her face, gazing in no particular direction. "Poor boy," she said with pity in her voice. "I guess he can't help who is mother is though, can he?"

Stephen's mum couldn't help being a snob. It was bred into her and he knew it was in him too.

"Nar, guess not, Mum. Not everyone's as lucky as me," he said, grinning facetiously.

"Yes, and don't you forget that," she returned. She gave him a knowing glance as she pulled the cigarettes out of the bag and placed them on his lap. He tore into them immediately and carefully picked out a lucky smoke in *basic* fashion.

Just as Stephen was about to light his cigarette, they saw Mrs Bridgeman storm out of the store. Stephen's mum opened the car door, concerned for the woman's rushed exit. "Irene, what's wrong?"

Tears streamed down Irene's face. She cast them a pained look and kept running 'till she hopped in her car and drove off like she was being chased.

CHAPTER SIXTEEN — 1995

STEPHEN

Stephen sat on the lounge carpet, leaning his back against the wall in the shade while he stretched his legs into the patch of sun shining through the open ranch slider door. With the phone pressed firmly between his ear and shoulder, he ran a hand through his blond leg hair, surveying the tan which was getting deeper as the summer weeks scorched on.

He was calling Luke for a much overdue catch up. Luke had been missing in action the past couple weeks with all his training whisking him away to the gym in New Plymouth. As soon as Luke answered, he launched into Stephen with a spate of piss-taking attacks.

"Fuck, man. I get busy for a few days and you replace me with that Munro dickhead?" Luke's laughter made Stephen feel defensive.

How does he know?

Until today with his mum finding out, Stephen had kept his dalliance with the Munros on the down low. "How'd you know that?"

"Bro, I have my contacts," Luke said with more than a little arrogance.

Blowhard.

Stephen retaliated with his own subtle dig, knowing something Luke may not. "Is your mum okay?"

"Yeah, why?" Luke answered, his voice sounding confused by the question.

"I saw your mum today at the store in town and, well, she ran out crying. I just wanted to make sure all was good?"

"You did? Are you sure it was her?"

"Yeah, man, definitely your mum."

Luke went quiet. He was many things, Stephen's best friend, and one of them was, secretly, he was a momma's boy at heart. "Who knows? I'll have to ask."

"Don't tell her I said anything?" Stephen covered his face with his hand, knowing Luke would anyway.

"Nar, man, I won't say anything."

"Cheers," Stephen replied.

"So, mate, when are you off to play with your bestest buddy, Shaun?" Luke asked in the most mocking tone he could.

Stephen pulled his legs in to join the rest of his body in the shade. "I might be heading there this evening," Stephen answered. "Did you fancy joining me? I haven't seen you in ages and it'd be good if you came. You know, help make the company less painful." As soon as Stephen said it, he felt bad.

Luke laughed. "As much as I would love to, NOT! I got plans tonight, but I'll come 'round and see you tomorrow, okay?"

"Sounds good."

"Don't have too much fun without me," Luke said before passing on a social warning. "Just remember, bro. If you lie with dogs, you get fleas."

When the conversation had wrapped up, Stephen was disappointed for caring what Luke thought of him. If Luke bothered to get to know Shaun, then he'd see the guy wasn't so bad. He didn't have fleas.

In the past, they had been unnecessarily cruel behind Shaun's back. Stephen knew they probably should have included him more, but every group of mates shared a weak link and surely by now Shaun was used to that role.

Stephen made his way to the bathroom and splashed some cold water on his face to cool down before looking in the mirror to see if he should bother changing. He stared at his reflection, assessing his appearance. Stephen knew he looked good, but if he wanted to, he could look even better. He ran to his bedroom and rummaged through the wardrobe to find something else to wear. He picked out a fresh white T-shirt, one that would help bring out the tan on his arms, its sleeves cut just right so he could show off his biceps. He chose his favourite cologne and dabbed a little on his neck, offering a subtle dash of scent. Stephen laughed to himself when he realised the effort he was making. *This ain't a date.*

∞

Fits of laughter greeted Stephen's ears as he walked up the driveway to Shaun's house, passing the still-uncut lawn and littering of toys. He skipped up the front stairs and entered the lounge, straight away noticing the festive season had arrived at the Munro household.

In the corner of the room, propped against the wall in a blue bucket stood a sad-looking Christmas tree. The pathetic looking branch was covered in mangy gold tinsel with a homemade angel perched precariously at the top. It was the polar opposite of the tree standing ten-feet high in Stephen's home that his mother had decorated so pedantically and with such finesse it could be used in a shop display window.

Stephen followed the ruckus of laughter through the wide arch of the dining room into the kitchen where he found Shaun in cargo pants and a lumberjack grunge flannel shirt, sliding around the lino on his usual foot attire of white socks.

Josie stood at the end of the kitchen, watching her brother skate around like a lunatic on an ice rink. She made a charge across the floor, trying to join in on the makeshift ice skating. Shaun nearly arsed over when he saw Stephen walk in, steadying his balance and brushing his hands against his shorts, trying to look composed while struggling to hide his excitement at Stephen's arrival.

Stephen grinned at the Munro sibling's antics. "So, Nancy Kerrigan, is this your new routine?"

"Nar, I'm way more Team Tonya," Shaun said, narrowing his eyes into an evil glare.

Stephen looked down at Shaun's hands, imagining them swinging a metal pipe. "Yeah, that I'd believe."

Josie ran up and flung her little arms around Stephen's legs. "Stephen, did you see our Christmas tree?" She looked up at him with wide, animated eyes.

Stephen collected her in his arms and sat her on the dining table. "I sure did. I reckon Santa will really like it. But remember, you gotta leave him out a glass of milk."

Josie's face turned puzzled, unaware of the tradition. "Why?"

"Well, he's travelled a long way and might be thirsty."

Shaun was hunched over making a noise in the fridge, clanging beer bottles about before carrying two over to the table and giving one to Stephen.

"I think Santa would prefer a beer and tinny, to be honest," Shaun said as he ripped the cap off his beer.

"Yeah, I don't think a drunk and stoned Santa is a good thing though, Shaun." Stephen worried if they should be talking such crap around a six-year-old, but Josie was obviously used to it, casually hopping down off of the table and disappearing into her room.

Shaun multitasked as he guzzled back his drink and pretty much with one free hand cooked them all dinner. Stephen took Debbie's advice and relented to accepting a plate full of the meal Shaun was making. His agreeing to eat with them seemed to boost Shaun's already good mood.

Debbie had been right. Shaun was pretty good in the kitchen and the meal which had started out as a crappy looking mince stew had soon become a delicious concoction with the aid of spicy ingredients and vegetables Shaun had added.

After they'd finished eating, Stephen helped out by doing the dishes while Shaun put Josie to bed with another video in her room. The kid must nearly be a film critic by now, Stephen thought. While putting the dishes away, he stumbled upon a stash of homebrew on the floor in the pantry, six bottles across and three rows deep. *Debbie won't be running out in a hurry.* On a shelf above, he spotted a pair of kitchen knives, stained black at the ends from their alternative use. This happy-induced home of vices would bring nothing but scorn from his own parents. Stephen and his other mates may have grown up in the same town as Shaun, but their upbringings were worlds apart.

When they finally relocated to the lounge, Shaun brought with him a Coke bottle bong to go with the steady supply of drinks in the fridge. He sparked it up and breathed in as the ghoulish liquid at the bottom bubbled loudly. He passed it over to Stephen who took an equally long hit.

Shaun strolled over to the stereo, rummaging through some CDs on the floor and chucked on some music. He insisted that whenever he was stoned, he had to listen to The Cranberries. "Yeah, it's like super spiritual on another level when I'm high." He came back to the couch and plonked himself down next to Stephen, giving him a winsome smile.

After three songs had played, Stephen became afflicted with the same supposed spiritual vein of the music, no doubt brought on by the light buzz of the pot. Locked in silence, they sat there in a haze of pungent smog that drifted across the room like smoky desert dunes. Across from them, hanging on the wall was a picture Stephen had never taken any particular notice of on previous visits. Written over the image of a waterfall with mossy green stones was a poem.

Let your heart be calm and still, believe this day will bring a gift to lift your spirit and it will.

The language of it resurrected images in his foggy mind of the bible next to Shaun's bed.

"Are you religious?" Stephen blurted out.

"No, why's that?" Shaun answered, sounding confused. "Define religious."

"When I stayed here that night, I saw you had a bible next to your bed."

Shaun sat quietly, struggling for an answer. "I guess you could say I have a belief. Like I'm spiritual, but not churchy." Shaun looked worried by his own words as if he'd given the wrong answer. "Not that I'm against church," he sputtered trying to cover all his bases.

Stephen chuckled at the flustered response. "I ain't judging you, whatever floats your boat." Stephen rested back into the couch, his shoulder nestling alongside Shaun's as he gazed into space, feeling airy. "If you're not churchy, how did you end up with a bible?"

Shaun paused. "Mum got it for me and Lydia."

"I didn't pick your mum as the type to try and bring her flock to the good lord."

Shaun chuckled as he took a gulp of his beer, some of it dribbled down his chin before he quickly wiped it away with his sleeve. "Not exactly," he said before taking a deep breath. "It's kind of a fucked up story."

"I see," Stephen said smiling. "They're the best kinds of stories."

Shaun nodded like he was thinking it over.

"Well," Stephen said, "Tell me." He whacked Shaun on the arm prompting him to hurry up.

"When we were—"

"Nar, man," Stephen butted in, "a story starts with 'once upon a time,' remember?" He wriggled his eyebrows, enjoying the jovial mood he found himself in.

Shaun shook his head laughing. "Okay. *Once* upon a time when my dad still lived with us he use to get a bit… fist happy after drinking and knock Mum about."

Stephen's buzz got sombre in a heartbeat and he now felt like a complete arse. "Sounds like a jerk," he muttered. Stephen only had vague recollections of Mr Munro, ones of him stumbling drunk through town or stoned at the beach fishing. The dude was a tall, solid bloke daubed in grisly tattoos. Nothing like Shaun.

"He was an okay guy, ya know, when he wasn't drinking. Problem *was* that wasn't too often. So I guess you could say he was a jerk," Shaun said honestly. "And yeah, he got worse over time and sometimes he'd even threaten to kill her, like bring his gun out and bail her up pointing it at her."

"Fuck," Stephen muttered in a mere whisper. He wondered if he had unleashed the questions Shaun had warned him about. With trepidation, he asked, "What's that got to do with a bible?"

"Well, whenever they had a fight, Lydia would come sneak into my room and jump into bed with me begging me to go help Mum, but I was usually crying more than her so I wasn't much fucking use," Shaun said, sounding angry with himself. He swigged back on his drink.

"You must've been just a kid yourself though. That's not your fault."

Shaun shrugged. "So one day after one of their fights, Mum gives me this bible and tells me I need to read it with Lydia whenever things got bad and that our prayers would keep us all safe."

It was sad to think his friend's younger self only had bits of paper for protection. *Why didn't she just tell them to ring the police?* Stephen felt angry on Shaun's behalf. "It'd be a better world if that stuff worked."

"What makes you think it didn't work?" Shaun asked surprised.

"Well, I'm guessing he kept hitting her and shit."

"Yeah, but the thing is, Stephen, he never pulled that trigger."

Stephen was dumbfounded at the conviction in Shaun's tone. How could he think some old book and prayers could save a life? "So, you're saying God's real?"

Shaun thought about the question for a moment before finally nodding. "I guess I am." He stared Stephen in the eyes to back up his claim. "Besides, there's another reason I know God is real."

Stephen felt Shaun's words breathe onto his face. "Oh yeah, and what's that?"

"Only God could have made someone as special as you."

Wow...

Stephen's heart picked up pace, and it felt like a small clink of its icy armour had been chipped away. He was left speechless and in that moment he felt compelled to let Shaun know he was special too. Just as his heart commanded his body to act, the front door ripped open and Stephen quickly reeled his face back before he could plant a drunken kiss on his friend.

CHAPTER SEVENTEEN — 1995

STEPHEN

"The fucking bastard," Lydia screamed as she stormed into the lounge, carrying a septic rage that infected the air around her. She strode across the floor with heavy footsteps before planting herself down in an empty chair. She dropped her silver handbag on the floor and leaned forward, burying her face into her hands and erupting into muffled sobs.

Shaun jumped to his feet and went to kneel beside his sister, placing a hand on her shoulder, asking what was wrong.

Lydia raised her head, revealing a face smeared with soggy mascara lines. "He... he..." Her sentence was soon lost to wailing. The rawness of the emotion tumbling out made Stephen feel uncomfortable, like he was intruding on someone's misery.

He scurried off to the kitchen to get another drink as a ruse to avoid getting involved. As he stuck his head in the fridge, scanning for another bottle, the cool air wrapped around his face, offering a pleasant extreme to the humidity draped over the house like a soggy blanket.

Lydia's sobs from the lounge began to settle down. Drink in hand, Stephen went and stood at the archway of the dining room, watching brother console sister from afar.

Shaun let Lydia compose herself until she was ready to tell the tale behind her tears. Stephen hung back, trying to pretend he wasn't there—*wishing* he wasn't there—it was all too fucking awkward. The only blessing he saw from her unexpected arrival was it had stopped him from kissing her brother. *What the fuck was I thinking?* He blamed it on the wacky backy; no way would he ever kiss a guy otherwise.

Finally, Lydia's voice, free of crying, began to tell

Shaun what was wrong. "The guy I've been seeing—"

"I knew it," Shaun interrupted. He stood up, huffing discouragingly, and folded his arms.

Lydia's face contorted with annoyance. "Don't lecture me, Shaun," she said with a sniffled sob.

Shaun quickly realised his arrogance and gave her a sympathetic look, bringing his arms back down to his side. "No, I'm not lecturing. What's wrong?" he asked soothingly. "What did the prick do?"

It was weird to see Shaun be like this with Lydia—the two of them usually only bickered and saved their sibling affection for Josie.

Lydia stared up at the ceiling, her hands clasped together between her knees. "Fuck, this is so embarrassing." She took a deep breath. "He asked me to give him a blow job." She looked at her brother as if asking for permission to continue. Shaun didn't blink an eye. Seeing her brother's calmness, she continued, "I said I wasn't that keen on the idea but he just kept hounding, so I said I'd do it…" Lydia took another deep breath, trying to gain some composure.

Stephen cringed at the overload of personal information. He could tell she was drunk and would probably regret in the morning, not waiting to sober up before coming home and spilling her guts out.

"Anyway, like I was halfway through, you know, doing *it*, and he pulled me off and told me I was crap at it and that if I couldn't suck dick, then we can't date."

Shaun's eyes flickered with fury. "Well, you don't need to be dating a fuckwit like that."

Lydia appeared to ignore the supportive words. "And when I got angry with him, he told me I was just like Mum, nothing but a whore." Lydia's back heaved with each vindictive word.

Shaun stomped back over to the couch, sat down and reached for his beer. "So who is he?"

Lydia didn't respond.

Shaun raised his voice, "Tell me who the little prick is, Lydia."

Lydia shook her head. "You can't do anything, Shaun. He'll give you a hiding."

Shaun erupted with angry laughter. "Fuck off. Which

little tosser are you talking about? Is it that Jayden Charteris dick?"

Lydia shot a look at Stephen who 'till now had hoped he was invisible and couldn't be seen. Her eyes whispered a warning before turning her focus back at Shaun. "It's Luke… Luke Bridgeman."

Stephen thought his jaw would drop to the floor. No wonder Luke had been so tight-lipped about being unavailable all week. The fucking idiot had been boning jailbait.

"Then we call the police and dob him in for fucking little girls." Shaun's outburst sounded absurd. Yes, she was fifteen, but one look at Lydia and it was hardly a *little* girl.

"No, Shaun. No," Lydia said, raising her hands up and waving them in protest. "We're not doing that. I'm not a nark and, well… I'm not exactly an innocent party."

"Yeah, but he shouldn't be fucking touching you." Shaun pounded the table with his fist making an empty bottle fall over. "I'll fucking get him for this."

"I knew I shouldn't of told you," Lydia said, sounding like a damsel in distress.

"No, you definitely should have told me. In fact, you should have told me you were seeing him weeks ago," Shaun said, pulling a face of revulsion. "What the fuck were you doing hooking up with that cunt anyway?" The words fired out like venomous bullets.

The way Shaun said it made it sound like Lydia had betrayed him, like maybe Shaun had never liked Luke even before tonight's bombshell admission. Stephen assumed Shaun had been clamouring to be friends with *all* of them all these years—maybe that wasn't the case.

Lydia said nothing, her lip quivering like she could burst into tears again at any moment.

"No, he fucking needs to pay for this." Shaun followed the threat with a mouthful of his beer.

Stephen finally spoke, "Shaun, he'll deck you if you try to take him on. He's a fucking giant."

Shaun's eyes pounced on him with a look of disgust. "What, so I'm supposed to let him treat my sister like this, am I?" Shaun stood up and started pacing the room. "And yeah, Stephen, I'm not fucking stupid. Sure, he's a big ugly prick but that don't mean a thing."

Stephen didn't argue.

Shaun stood still and ran a hand through his hair, looking down at his crying sister. "I'll fucking kill him."

CHAPTER EIGHTEEN — 2016

STEPHEN

Stephen looked at Inver sitting on the couch in his shorts and t-shirt, completely unaware that tonight he would become another piece of used goods to discard.

Kimmy, unwittingly, was going to be part of the plan. She was due any minute, a surprise social hijacking that would consist of dragging Inver to the pub to help find him a *nice girl*. Kimmy, of course, loved that shit and would try her hardest, but Stephen knew this lad with a reticent charm was not going to score at Clifton Pub with its limited options, especially with his lack of social skills.

Stephen eyed up his guest, sat on the couch reading; his masculine long limbs spread out comfortably, making himself at home. Stephen knew he had lulled him into a false sense of security with hospitality and crumbs of subtle flirts that Inver had swallowed down as innocent compliments.

Other than getting back at Rusty for his role in Shaun's death, the whole payback thing was giving Stephen a taste of his former glory days. Days where he chased girls around town, sleeping with them and claiming them as a conquest. He had always enjoyed a challenge and seducing a straight man would be one mighty fucking accomplishment. The thought gave Stephen a sadistic shiver as he admired Inver's face with its dark stubble accentuating a chiselled jawline. It was then that he noticed it, a tinge of sadness to the boy who had a book opened on his lap, but his mind not on its pages.

"You all good?" Stephen asked.

"Huh?" Inver looked up startled.

"You look sad about something."

Inver stretched out his arms and yawned. "Yeah, I'm fine," he said. "I was just thinking about Rusty."

Stephen nodded. "Guess it takes some getting used to when they go, aye?" Stephen didn't believe him. Inver didn't even refer to the man as Dad and he knew the pair had been about as close as the earth was to the moon.

Inver closed his book shut. "What are your plans for tonight?"

"I think I'll have myself a nice night in alone."

"You will?" Inver replied with a confused shake of his head. "What about me?"

The sound of the front door being opened and slammed shut answered the question for Stephen. Laughter echoed down the hall 'till Kimmy and her best mate Mihi appeared in the kitchen.

"Speak of the devils. Here's your plans for the night," Stephen said.

Inver twisted 'round on the couch and looked at the two women dressed up and ready for their night out. He sat forward on the couch becoming stiff and looking unsure of himself.

Kimmy was in a dainty outfit while Mihi busted at the seams in her tight white top and black pants that suffocated her thunder-thighs. If he hadn't been a social refugee for the past twenty years, Stephen would have loved a night out with them, but that ran the risk of town gossip which could flare up at any moment. He knew it didn't matter how smooth his charms were, his secrets weren't.

Kimmy threw her hands out like a magician about to perform a trick. "Mihi, this is our lovely male escort for the evening, Inver."

"Way to make the man sound like a whore, Kimmy. This ain't rent-a-gent," Stephen said.

"Trust you to let your mind slip in the gutter," she replied.

Kimmy leaned over the couch running a hand down Inver's unshaven face. "Someone's a bit hairy."

"I think you mean manly," Stephen corrected her.

Inver sat like a mannequin as they dissected his appearance.

"We won't have any trouble finding you a lady," Mihi said as she scoped Inver out. "Are you really Rusty's son?"

Inver nodded. He turned 'round, giving Stephen a

look that asked *what the hell is going on?*

"Kimmy and Mihi here are taking you out for the evening to help you find love Clifton-style," Stephen said, giving him a wink.

"But I'm not really—"

"No is not an option. Go get your glad-rags on, stud," Kimmy said. She leaned back over the couch and ruffled Inver's wavy locks. "Don't deprive the girls of those curls."

Inver dutifully disappeared to his room to get changed. The guy was such a push over, Stephen thought. Such a weakness would definitely come in handy later when Inver got home from the pub.

"Cor, I can't believe that came out of Rusty," Mihi exclaimed.

"Well, to be fair it's not like Rusty gave birth to him," Stephen mocked.

Mihi pulled a stupid face at him. "You know what I mean." She began nodding. "Yep, mighty tasty morsel, that one."

"Oh god, at least try not to rape him before we get to the pub," Kimmy groaned.

"I ain't promising nothing. You know this Maori girl is partial to a bit of fine white meat," Mihi said, rubbing her jelly belly before letting rip a loud laugh.

Mihi continued rambling on in disbelief that a creature like Rusty could produce such attractive offspring. Stephen let Mihi carry on with her spiel while he motioned for Kimmy to come over. He discretely slipped a wad of cash in her hand, not wanting Mihi to see. Kimmy tucked it in her purse before narrowing her eyes at Stephen, the creases between her eyebrows deepening. He knew this was her stern look.

"So, what are you doing about Eddie?" Kimmy asked, changing the topic with pushy precision.

"Same thing I told you on the phone. I'm handling it."

"You don't let someone send you a death threat and then empty your vat and not do anything about it."

Stephen sighed, annoyed at her badgering. "He got his own back for the dogs, so I'm sure he'll just leave it be now."

"The man is loopy, Stephen. I swear he's only one voice away from going to town with his gun all Port Arthur styles."

"He's just… eccentric. He ain't dangerous," Stephen said, downplaying the levels of crazy that probably did reside in Eddie's head. "Well, unless the fucker's got a bag full of dog shit in his hand."

"Still, I'd just be careful," Kimmy said, giving him a look of concern.

"What makes you think he did it anyway?" Mihi chimed in.

Kimmy spun 'round. "Who else would it be?"

"This coast has bad things happen, ya know," Mihi said, her jovial tone replaced with a sombre timbre.

"What are you on about?" Stephen asked.

"The land has a lot of history. Some nasty battles took place along here."

"Meaning?" Stephen quizzed, knowing exactly where she was going with this.

"This whole strip of land north of Rapanui Creek is tapu."

"You think everywhere's bloody haunted and tapu," Stephen scoffed.

Mihi shook her head. "No I don't, but I tell ya, not even a handsome billionaire could convince me for some nookie in Cherry Lane. Some places you just don't go," she said. "Shit, I don't even feel safe here at your house half the time."

"Here we go," Stephen said, rolling his eyes.

"Stop it, you're spooking me," Kimmy said, putting a hand over her mouth as if she was half expecting a fright.

"Sorry, girl, but I'm just letting Stephen here know there's more to this world than what we see."

Stephen laughed arrogantly. "Thank you, Mihi, I'll be sure to keep an eye out for the milk ghost."

"What ghost?" Inver asked from the dining room. He hadn't shaved but certainly scrubbed up well in a checked shirt and fresh pair of jeans. His black hair was smoothed back with sticky gel, smothering his conniving curls in place.

"The ghost of your sex life, Inver. It's time you

resurrect it," Stephen joked.

Inver blushed. "Anyway, I guess I'm all ready."

"Come on, give us a twirl, city boy," Mihi teased.

Inver raised his long arms in the air and turned around for them, showing off his outfit.

"Phwoar, nice arse on that one," Mihi roared.

"Mihi," Kimmy said, feigning shock. She gave her friend a playful whack on the arm. "Are you sure you don't want to come with us?" Kimmy asked Stephen.

"Nar, you lot have fun," Stephen said. He rested his feet up on the coffee table, stretching out and putting his hands behind his head. "I think I'll be fine right here."

Kimmy and Mihi raced on ahead, eager to get to the pub early.

Inver went to follow them before turning around to face Stephen, "I'll see ya later then," he said with a meek smile and half-hearted wave.

"Will do, mate, try not to miss me too much."

Inver smiled. "I'll try not to."

"Oh, just so you know, I've got my earplugs ready in case you bring back any screamers," Stephen said with a salacious grin.

The red in Inver's face flared up again, and he scarpered after the girls.

Stephen chuckled to himself. Inver may have a long list of screamers, but tonight *he* would be the one screaming at the end of a cock—he would prove Rusty's belief wrong, that he would never have a *faggot* son like Stephen.

CHAPTER NINETEEN — 2016

INVER

Planted at the end of the tiny strip of shops was Clifton's one and only pub, The Melting Pot. It was an old wooden building sporting a fresh cream paint job with tables and chairs jutting outside its frontage, neatly fenced off with dark green trellis. Its gentrification desperately tried to portray the image that it was both a family friendly café come pub in the evenings. The balancing act didn't help disguise its true purpose of being just another liver-damage den.

It was odd to be venturing out so early with the sun's dusky daze still dangling in the sky. In the city and his days of partying, Inver wouldn't step foot out the door before midnight. Turning up before Cinderella was due home was desperado territory, but then that was in another life when he had a reputation to worry about.

Kimmy led him by the hand through the front doors, past a small side room lined with pokie machines where two sad souls sat feeding their money into the machines, mesmerised by the lights like zombies. They walked past the undead and a row of gigantic potted plants lining the walls, making a beeline to the bar where a familiar face greeted them. It was the old lady from the funeral, the barmaid who had poured Rusty's drinks 'till the day before he died.

"Good to see you girls brought a friend with you tonight," the barmaid said.

She smiled at Inver. "Hello, love." Her voice carried a healthy dose of recognition.

"Hi," Inver replied, returning the smile, at a loss for her name.

"What can I get for you all?" she asked.

Mihi muttered her choice in Kimmy's ear.

"Two vodka red bulls, please, Sheryl," Kimmy said.

"What about you, Inver?" She stared at him, waiting for an answer.

"It's alright. You don't have to pay for mine," Inver answered, wishing this would excuse him from shouting a round he couldn't afford.

"I'm not shouting. Stephen is." Kimmy opened her purse, showing Mihi and Inver the colourful wad of cash.

"Wow." Inver balked at the rainbow of notes.

"Bloody nice of him," Mihi said.

"Yeah, well, you can thank this one for the donation," Kimmy said, pointing to Inver.

"Me?" Inver replied.

"Yep, I'm under strict instructions to make sure 'Little Inver' here has himself a big night."

"He calls me Little Inver?" Inver laughed. "Classic."

"Who cares what he calls ya. Just drink the fool's money," Mihi said.

"Don't tell him I told you he treated. It was meant to be a secret, but yeah, go ahead and order what you like, hun," Kimmy said. "I definitely will be."

Inver looked up at Sheryl who was waiting patiently. "Uh, make it three vodka red bulls, I guess."

"Coming right up," Sheryl said.

With their drinks in hand, they made their way through the bar's messy maze of stools and sticky tables. The place was far from busy, a couple dozen or so people, all standing in small clusters drinking peacefully. It was a mixed bunch in here, Inver thought. It certainly lived up to its name. Being the only place to drink in town meant the different types of locals had no choice but to rub drinking elbows.

The crowd was void of any talent, bar one cute young farmer sat with a scowl on his face that made him look older than his probable 25 years; his blond hair as unruly as Inver's and his dark green coat and baggy pants hanging off his skinny body like excess skin. Inver eyed him discretely as he followed the girls to a quiet corner in the bar.

The scowling stud swigged back his drink; then, as if he could tell someone was visually violating him, swivelled his head around, locking accusing eyes on Inver who gawked back like a deer struck in headlights. Inver quickly diverted his eyes, avoiding an inconvenient outing. He shuddered remembering the damage of the last one, all thanks to chasing *that face*.

∞

They slammed back the drinks one after the other, making the most of Stephen's generosity. Mihi kept the jokes coming thick and fast as Kimmy talked about how much she loved Clifton since moving here three years earlier to start her own business in holistic massage therapy.

It had been so long since Inver had had a night out that he had forgotten how much he missed this. The laughing, the drinks, the comradery of a night out—this was how his life should be. He did his best to fight the voice in his head telling him that in a few days he would be back in his lonely flat with no social prospects.

On the fourth round of drinks, Kimmy led them back to the bar to get some Sambuca shots. Holy trinities, she called them, insisting these drinks would bring good luck. Inver was puzzled by the name and even more so when he watched Sheryl plop three coffee beans into each glass and begin glassware pyrotechnics, setting each one alight. Inver was gobsmacked to see the down-to-earth baby boomer prepare such drinks with millennial city finesse.

When they returned to their table, Inver went to sit down but was thwarted by Kimmy's hand clutching his shirt, raising it up.

"Whoa, nice knickers you got there," she teased.

"You've got good taste," he said, "I really should be thanking you for these."

Kimmy frowned. "What do you mean?"

"They're the pair you bought Stephen that didn't fit him."

Kimmy looked at Inver in confusion. "I never bought them."

"You didn't?" Inver replied with dumbstruck naivety.

"Trust me, if I was to spend as much as they would have cost, it would be on my own wardrobe," she joked.

Why would he say they were from you?

Inver's suspicion was cut off by Mihi who clapped her hands to get his attention. "So, son of Fanta pants, you seen any ladies in here ya wanna get frisky with?"

Inver laughed. "Nice reference." The booze had eased up his nerves more than enough, letting out a mumbled, "Hmm." He spun his head round scanning the bar which was now beginning to fill up. He looked back at Mihi and Kimmy who were waiting for him to single out a potential. "What if I told you that ladies aren't really my thing?" He felt like a rebel sharing the truth with relative strangers.

Kimmy squealed in excitement and leaned forward on her elbows across the table. "I would say fill me in, sweet cheeks."

"That's what she said," Mihi cracked.

Kimmy ignored Mihi's joke and honed her eyes in on Inver like she was about to win a prize. "Are you gay?"

"Yeah, so you're wasting your time finding me a nice girl, I'm afraid."

Kimmy smiled. "That's okay. We can try and find you a hot guy instead."

"You'll have your work cut out for you tryna find a gay dude here," Mihi said.

"They don't have to be gay, do they, Inver? Just like really drunk," Kimmy said, flashing him a wink. "You don't have a boyfriend already, do you?"

Inver shook his head.

"So, what's your type?" Kimmy asked.

"Umm, I dunno."

"Oh, come on, Inver, everybody has a type." Kimmy tapped his arm prodding him to answer.

"Well, what's your type?" Inver replied, trying to divert the inquisition.

"Stephen is her type," Mihi blurted.

"Mihi," Kimmy chuckled.

"Yip, my girl here has a wee crush on Clifton's most eligible bachelor," Mihi said.

Inver grinned at Kimmy. "Do you?"

Kimmy sat back in her seat trying to compose herself. "I use to have a crush on him. Not now."

"Still, you wouldn't say no if he asked," Mihi said.

"It seems unlikely, it would appear he is impervious to my charms," Kimmy answered in a posh voice.

"Maybe he's gay too," Mihi teased, elbowing Inver as she laughed.

"I wish," Inver confessed, a little too loudly.

"See, you *do* have a type," Kimmy cooed.

Inver rolled his eyes. "I think Stephen's everybody's type."

Kimmy sighed. "I think you might be right there." She looked across at Inver studying his face. "You'd be a lot of guys' type too, I imagine."

Inver pointed to himself. "Me?" he said in surprise.

"Yes, you," she said. "You must get a lot of action up in Auckland."

Inver squirmed in his seat. "Not exactly."

"And why not?" Kimmy quizzed.

Inver shrugged. "I guess I'm not really looking."

"Oooo, you do got yaself a husband then," Mihi said, sounding intrigued.

"No, nothing like that." Inver shook his head. "I'm still sort of hung up on someone, so I've not really been looking." *More like obsessed.*

"That's never good," Kimmy commiserated. "An ex?"

Inver's mind pounced on the youthful image of *that face*, a place he knew he shouldn't venture, but talking about him was like taking the lid off a boiling pot that was continually on the verge of bubbling over. "Nar, just someone I used to work with who I thought was the *one* but… nope, he wasn't." Inver laughed trying to downplay the true level of his craziness for being so into a younger former co-worker.

"Well, you know what they say," Mihi said in a perky voice. "The best way to get over someone is to get under somebody else."

Kimmy grinned. "Or do you prefer to be the one getting on top?"

"I think I'll save sharing my mating rituals for another night," Inver said, raising an eyebrow.

Mihi stuck her hand out in front of Kimmy who instinctively knew what this meant. She handed Mihi a fifty-dollar note so she could go get the next round.

When Mihi returned hugging three drinks in her arms, she had a look on her face like she was dying to share a funny joke. "Heads up. Luke's here."

Kimmy groaned.

"Luke?" Inver asked.

"One of blondie here's many admirers and givers of carpet burn," Mihi joked. She took a sip of her drink, then added, "He's a good sort though, is old Lukey boy."

"Yes, but he's a fling that clings," Kimmy said. "You know the ones." She looked at Inver as if he knew from experience what those ones were like. He didn't.

"Just so you're on board, Inver, I told him I'm seeing someone so he would get the hint I ain't looking for love," Kimmy said. "That someone being Stephen."

Mihi sighed. "I told you, this town is too small for lies, girl. You'll get snapped."

"It's not a lie... I see Stephen most days. We just don't date per se." Kimmy replied, her words balanced with good humour. "Besides, it's not like Stephen ever comes here."

Inver wished he had a friend like Kimmy who lived in Auckland, someone to join him on nights out, making up fairy tale stories to men.

"Aww, you a cold-hearted bitch, Kimberly Pritchard," Mihi said, trying to hold back a laugh.

Kimmy rubbed her friend's shoulder. "But you love me anyway."

"You know it," Mihi said. "That's why this is gonna be so fun."

Kimmy's face screwed up. "What are you on about?"

"HEY LUKE!" Mihi shouted across the bar.

"Bloody hell, Mihi," Kimmy spat out in a whisper. Her body jerking like she had just kicked her friend under the table.

"Love you, babes," Mihi said, smiling back at her.

Kimmy quickly smiled and sat upright. "Hey, Luke," she called out, waving in the direction of the bar.

Inver looked over his shoulder and saw a tall bulky man strut his way over to their table.

"I thought I could hear you lot," Luke said. He wore

a black polo shirt, its material wrapped tight around his puffed up chest, sticking out the sleeves were huge hairy forearms.

Mihi smiled at the giant. "And I could smell you coming a mile away, Luke,"

"That'll be my pheromones setting you off again, Mihi."

"You wish, bro," Mihi replied good-naturedly.

Luke stood there towering over the table. His presence was commanding and hogged the air. "So who's this lad you've got suffering through your girly squawking?"

"This is Rusty's son, Inver," Kimmy said.

Luke extended a weather-beaten hand across the table. Spotting the social cue, Inver hovered up from his stool, taking hold of the giant ugly hand that nearly crushed his fingers in its firm grip.

"And the prodigal son returns," Luke said, his eyes summing Inver up.

"Something like that," Inver said feebly as Luke released his grip, letting Inver's hand breathe again. This man obviously had some knowledge of his existence. It was frustrating not being able to place names and faces that knew exactly who he was. It felt like an unfair advantage.

Luke sat down joining them at the table. What had looked like pure muscle soon became apparent to be the start of man boobs and a growing beer gut. The out-of-shape oaf's eyes fed on Kimmy.

"So, how's pretty boy?" he asked.

"You mean Stephen?" Kimmy corrected him.

"Sat at home being a sad sap when I last saw him," Mihi said cheekily.

"Mihi," Kimmy laughed.

"My bad," Mihi whispered like a naughty child.

Luke leaned in closer to the table like he was glad to hear this. "I told you, Kimmy, you can do better than some vain princess. You need to get yourself a real man."

"Oh, Stephen is more than man enough for her I think," Mihi teased.

No doubt Luke would qualify as a *real man*. The guy was testosterone on legs but he was far from an oil painting.

"And whom might you suggest?" Kimmy asked,

seemingly enjoying Luke's flirt.
Luke put his arms behind his head, relaxing back in the seat. "I mean it'd be a stretch but I'm always on hand."
"How considerate of you," Mihi said, blinking.
"Oh, come on now, I'll be helping out a poor lass hung up on a dud root," he chuckled. "And you know I'm the goods."
His cheap shot at Stephen angered Inver. Was Stephen bad in bed? Like it mattered; he was so hot, the guy could just lie there and be the best sex Inver had ever had.
Kimmy batted her eyelids, playing up to Luke's game. "Ain't nothing dud about my man."
"Flat out, you tell him, girl," Mihi said.
Luke sighed like he was about to deliver bad news. "He's a shady one, that Stephen, I would know. Maybe one of these days, he'll trip up over his lies," Luke's cryptic words oozed ominously. "Don't say I didn't warn ya." He stood up and grabbed a packet of smokes from his pocket. "I'm off, ladies and gent. Nice meeting you, mate." Luke gave Inver a friendly glance. "And, Kimmy, my table's just over there if you fancy joining me for a drink later." He shot her a wink and walked back to join a table of men closer to the bar.
"I think him and your *boyfriend* might just have some unresolved issues," Mihi said mockingly.
"Tell me about it," Kimmy muttered.
Inver wondered what lies Luke was referring to. He tugged at the elastic of his underwear and realised he was sitting on one.

CHAPTER TWENTY — 1995
~~Munro Hated~~ STEPHEN

It took less than forty-eight hours and, as promised, Shaun dealt with Luke. Far from killing him, he did, however, exact a particularly cruel revenge. Stephen had heard the story from two different sources, both reciting similar accounts but with differing emotions. One regurgitating second-hand feedback like a news bulletin, the other an eyewitness to the event and perpetrator of the supposed betrayal.

Troy was the second person to divulge the gossip of Luke falling victim to Shaun's wraith. Troy shared what he knew with a mix of shock and humour. "Yeah, he totally crushed him. It's fucking crazy." Troy had laughed before taking on a more serious tone, "But sheesh, I reckon it's pretty sneaky and underhanded. Definitely not the way a guy should deal with stuff."

"Yeah, it's pretty grim," Stephen had replied.

"I don't know what it is Luke's supposed to have done, but I can't see that it warrants this. He sure as shit won't be in the boxing ring anytime soon."

Stephen had sat on the phone just going with the flow of the conversation, coughing up lines of disbelief, pretending like he didn't know a thing about the *crazy* attack, but of course he did. Troy didn't appear to be privy to the motivation for Shaun's lashing out, which confirmed to Stephen that Luke; A, knew he was on the wrong side of the law, and B, he must have been a complete jerk to the girl.

Troy told Stephen, "I'm not getting involved with this one but, shit, I wouldn't want to be Shaun once Luke gets his hands on him." *Hands* being the magic word. Troy was at least being level headed, even if on Team Luke.

It was Shaun's phone call three hours earlier filled with the brutal details of the event that had made Stephen

Awful & Mean

uneasy. Shaun reiterated with great pace and an air of arrogant excitement his triumph over "that tall prick."

"So yeah, I called him up saying that I needed a hand with a vehicle we were working on down at the shop. At first, he was like 'fuck off' pretty much, but I said I'd line him up a tinny for his efforts, so sure enough, that got his greedy arse down there."

"Just a little drug lord, aren't you?" Stephen had teased.

Shaun didn't react, instead rambling on with his tale of vengeance, "Anyway, as if I'd need a hand from that dumb fuck. So he turns up and sees I've got the bonnet up of this car—yeah, must have been a sign it was meant to happen 'cos no shit, it was the same make 'n model as his dad's one—anyway, I ask him if he'd be able to help me inspect the alternator. So he's got his head under the bonnet, hard out inspecting it to see what the matter was and as he lifted his head back, I slammed the bonnet down on the fucker's hands." Shaun laughed wildly.

Stephen had cringed at the thought, a shot of sympathetic pain running through his fingers.

"Fuck, I thought I'd chopped off his fingers when I saw blood pissing out, seriously. Anyway, he pulls his hands out and falls to the ground, screaming 'n shit and I give him a couple good kicks while telling him to stay away from Lydia or I'll dob him in for underage rape."

Stephen had sat on the phone astounded by the brutality of someone he thought was more wimp than fighter.

"Fuck, man, it could have only gone better if it was his cock I'd slammed under the bonnet."

"I hope you know what you're doing, Shaun, 'cos he is gonna come after you for this," Stephen warned him.

"Well, not anytime soon. His hands are puckarooed, man. Fucking puckarooed."

Stephen was torn in his loyalties. He felt sorry for Luke who probably now had two broken hands and possibly cracked ribs, but also sorry for Shaun who was unaware of the shit storm he'd just opened himself up to.

It was chilling to think that the kindest of people could be capable of the greatest cruelty. Shaun, of course, would say he acted in defence of his sister, but Stephen knew it went deeper than that. Shaun was well aware of how the town viewed his family; behind his cheeky smile lay resentment at the town's preconceived notions of his mum and siblings. Smashing Luke's fingers was like smashing a hierarchy designed for those higher up to feel better about themselves compared to people like the Munros who, like number sixty-seven, had to walk a soiled path, even if they did work hard.

CHAPTER TWENTY-ONE — 1995

STEPHEN

"Fuck," Stephen mumbled to himself. He reached over his shoulder, delicately trying to rub a pinched nerve in his back which had been giving him grief since he'd woken up that morning.

It was another beautiful day as he sat on a rustic garden chair in the front yard, waiting for Shaun to come pick him up. Shaun's boss had lent him a vehicle for the day so he could go to New Plymouth and do his Christmas shopping. Still technically on holiday with nothing better to do, Stephen figured he may as well tag along for the ride.

Lydia's spurning had been a gifting of freedom to Shaun, allowing him to venture out more and relinquish some of the babysitting burden. Not that Shaun saw it as a burden at all, Stephen suspected.

Stephen seized the opportunity and dragged Shaun along with him every night, fossicking for any talent at the beach. The campground was now filled to the brim with holidaying tourists flooding its cramped alleys of tents that wafted with the smell of sizzling barbeques.

Stephen would eyeball every hot chick they passed and ask Shaun, "What about her?"—every time met with the same response, "You can do better." The praise was flattering, but the guy was a shit wingman compared to Stephen's usual partners in crime, Luke and Troy. Troy was too tied up with Clare and impending fatherhood to be of any use and Luke had vanished entirely since his bonnet-beating.

The sound of a puttering motor soon came up the long driveway. It was Shaun, driving something that looked more like a shopping trolley than a car, a little white Daihatsu

Charade, designed for cheapskates and grandmothers.

Stephen laughed his arse off as Shaun pulled up outside the house. "You have got to be fucking kidding."

"What?" Shaun said, pretending not to know what Stephen found so funny.

Stephen circled the car, running a finger along its dusty metal. "You're braver than me, mate. I wouldn't be caught dead driving something like this."

Shaun leaned back in the driver's seat and let out an annoyed sigh. "Just as well you aren't the one driving then."

Stephen smirked. "Yeah, but honestly if we pass anyone we know, I'm warning you now I'm hiding under the dashboard."

"And I'm telling you now that if you do, I'll say you're giving me a blow job."

"Ewww. In your dreams, critter."

"Yeah, sorry. That was a low blow," Shaun chuckled.

"Oh, funny guy. Thinks he's a comedian."

Shaun tooted the horn. "Just get your arse in the car, snob."

∞

With the windows wound down, Stephen enjoyed the wind lathering his face, the hour-long journey over the scenic highway filled with tight bends and craggy hills. When they arrived, the small city was choking with long lines of cars desperately searching for a park and streams of people on the pavements all in a mad rush to finish their Christmas shopping.

Shaun gave up on the miracle of finding a car space, so he drove them a few blocks out of the CBD and they walked to the mall in pursuit of toys for Josie and gift vouchers for Lydia and Debbie.

After they exhausted the mall of all its options, they grabbed lunch from a hole in the wall takeaways. Once they'd chowed their way through their greasy feast of burgers and chips, Shaun insisted he only had one last stop to make: the music store.

The small shop was dull and dank from its dim lights and blackened walls of posters. It did, however, carry the best selection in town with its rows upon rows of CDs set out in different genres.

Shaun made a beeline to the bestsellers stand. He picked up the Alanis Morissette album and took it to the counter where a young Goth girl took his cash and chucked the CD in a bag, all without saying a word. Stephen found this the usual customer service experience from music and video store staff who, despite their minimum wage roles, basked in the pretentious glory of working in the 'entertainment industry.'

"Is that for you?" Stephen asked.

"Nar, it's for Lydia. I think she'll enjoy screaming her lungs out to this considering her current situation."

"Watch out, she might start learning to play the harmonica."

Shaun wasn't listening. His attention had been hijacked by a large poster hanging in the window. He dawdled over to it and stared up at the words blazed across its canvas.

BIG DAY OUT 1996 feat Porno for Pyros, Rage Against the Machine, Elastica and many more!

"Fuck. That would be so awesome to go to," Shaun said with a sigh.

It *would* be awesome. Stephen knew from first-hand experience having gone to the last one with Luke, Troy and Clare where they got to see Primal Scream and Ministry.

"Then why don't you go?"

"Um, do you know how much it costs? I'd have to sell a fucking kidney just to get a ticket."

Stephen nodded. "Yep, that's what I like about you, Shaun. You're not prone to exaggeration in the slightest."

Shaun laughed and nudged Stephen with his elbow. They left the shop with Shaun carrying a look of disappointment on his face, resembling a child who didn't get candy bought for him.

∞

After battling their way through the Christmas traffic, they were back at Shaun's place by three o'clock. They tiptoed discretely up the driveway to the front steps, trying not to rustle the plastic bags of goodies. Shaun gingerly poked his head inside the door only to find the house conveniently deserted.

Shaun darted off to his bedroom to hide the presents before returning and switching on the stereo, letting it find a radio frequency to stream music into the quiet room. The sun poured in through the large front windows, casting a glow around his slight silhouette as he lifted his t-shirt up to scratch his flat stomach.

"Did you want a coffee or anything?" he asked.

Stephen shook his head. Shaun disappeared to the kitchen where the sound of a tap running soon followed. Stephen lit up a smoke and waited for him to return.

When Shaun came back in the room, he stood just in front of Stephen, holding a glass of water. "I'm so glad I have the use of my hands." He smiled at his own random comment before gulping back mouthfuls of the water.

Here we go again.

Since his victory over Luke, Shaun took great delight in repeating his tale of glory.

"You're a dangerous man, Shaun Munro."

"The prick deserved it, but I still feel bad for him. No guy should be deprived their wanking hand."

"Yeah, I guess he's gonna have blue balls for a while."

Shaun's eyes danced mischievously. "Nar. Knowing him, he'll probably roll around naked in jelly meat and then get his dog to lick it off."

Stephen grimaced. "Has anyone ever told you you're fucking gross?"

"Of course." Shaun laughed under his breath. "But it means so much more coming from you," he joked. In playful steps, he carried himself over to the couch and flopped down with a grunt beside Stephen, leaning back into the cushions and spreading his legs wide.

Stephen felt Shaun's leg hair brush against his own, creating a tingling of static-like electricity. The tingling sensation was cut short when Shaun shuffled in the seat and the warmth of their knees pressed firmly together. If it was any other guy, Stephen wouldn't have noticed the proximity, but something about Shaun made him aware of any passing touch, especially skin-to-skin.

"So, what are your plans for New Year's?" Shaun asked.

"Same as every other year. Join everyone else down at the beach, I guess. Do my best to start the new year with a bang, if you know what I mean." Stephen grinned at Shaun, trying to drill home the sexual connotation.

"You shouldn't have any trouble doing that," Shaun said, sounding bleak.

Stephen wondered if Shaun's tone stemmed from jealousy that he never got the same level of attention. He wasn't a bad-looking guy by any means, and other than being a Munro, it seemed odd he wouldn't have more female fans.

"What about you? Are you gonna come join us at the beach?" Stephen asked, forgetting that his loose use of the word 'us' included Luke.

"Luke will be there, won't he?"

Stephen hesitated. "Probably."

"That counts me out then." Shaun laughed. "It's okay though. Mum's throwing a party here, so I'll probably just stay in."

"Megan will be at the beach, won't she? I'm sure she'll protect you if you did want to come," Stephen said. He ruffled Shaun's hair, making his long fringe collapse forward which Shaun quickly huffed back in place. "Look, if Luke starts any shit, I'll stand in. He'll probably clobber me too, but what the heck." Stephen squeezed Shaun's shoulder. "You'll be safe with me."

"My hero," Shaun said in a girly voice.

Stephen laughed and bent forward to stub his cigarette out in the ashtray. Smoke kept wafting from its dislodged orange embers so he waved a hand, trying to chase away the choking fumes. Out of nowhere, the pinched nerve in his back flared in sharp pain. "Ahhh fuck." Stephen winced and pressed a hand to the hurt.

"What is it?" Shaun asked, full of concern.

"It's nothing," Stephen muttered. "I slept funny last night and somehow fucked up my shoulder." He turned to show what he meant, but another jolt of pain burned through his shoulder blade. "Fuck sake."

Shaun patted the floor between his legs. "Sit down here. I'll see if I can massage it out."

"I doubt it!" Stephen balked. "You'll probably make it worse, inflictor of pain."

Shaun shook his head. "No I won't. Come on, don't be a wuss."

Stephen pondered the request 'till Shaun patted the carpet again. Stephen relented and scuffled down to the floor, sitting between Shaun's legs.

Shaun moved his feet apart, giving him more room. "Shift back."

Stephen pushed his hands against the worn carpet fibres and scooted backwards. Shaun's hands went straight to his shoulders, starting slowly and lightly before pressing harder, applying more pressure. Stephen hung his head forward, enjoying the soothing touch, not sure if it would help, but it sure did feel good. He hadn't had a massage for a long time and it felt nice the way Shaun's hands carefully kneaded the knots out of his back in such a caring manner. Shaun worked his hand into a fist and starting at the top right shoulder, pressing his knuckles deep into Stephen's skin, slowly working his way down. At the bottom, he repeated the same movement, working his way up Stephen's left side.

"How's that?" Shaun asked.

Stephen, with his eyes closed, sighed with an affirming groan. Shaun's hands concentrated back at his shoulders, his strong thumbs pressing into Stephen's pressure points.

Shaun abruptly moved his hands away. "Take your shirt off."

Stephen opened his eyes, surprised by the request. "Why?"

"It'll just make it easier."

Stephen hesitated, suddenly self-conscious about having a sweaty back from the hot day. He lifted his arms and peeled off his shirt, exposing his tanned shoulders that were crying out to be rubbed some more. "Sorry if I stink."

"You don't stink," Shaun chuckled. "You always smell good."

"Thanks, I guess."

Shaun's healing hands returned to his skin, which Stephen could tell was more damp than he had originally suspected. Shaun though, didn't seem bothered by his sweaty back and continued rubbing. Stephen closed his eyes again, letting himself enjoy the affection. He could only imagine how Luke and Troy would react if they saw this—not well, he suspected. Stephen sat there zoning out, listening to Shaun explain his massage method and how healthy it was to have human touch. He didn't pay much attention to his words, but he was getting lost in the soothing tone of Shaun's voice, it was as if his voice's timbre matched the calming quality of his hands. Stephen wondered if this is what it felt like to be hypnotised.

Shaun's voice rose from the quiet level it had been. "I told you I knew what I was doing."

Stephen worried he would stop, promptly slap his back and say he was finished. He didn't want it to be over, not yet at least. "Yeah, you're good at this."

"You sound surprised."

"Well, I didn't figure the same guy who crushed Luke's fingers would be capable of such healing qualities."

Shaun laughed. His finger movements became deep and slow as he honed in on the sore shoulder. "Well, that's 'cos he's a dick. My hands are only magic for good people… like you."

Stephen had a tinge of guilt. *Why does he think I'm so good? If only he knew the real me.*

"I don't know why you think I'm such a fucking saint when I'm really just an arsehole." He meant what he'd admitted to, but he eagerly wanted to hear Shaun refute this and fuel his ego.

"Yeah, you can be an arsehole," Shaun said flatly.

"Cheers, you're not meant to agree with me, dick," Stephen said, getting a cheeky laugh in return.

Shaun shifted his hands to Stephen's head, his fingers working through the summer kissed hair, scratching his scalp in circular motions, making Stephen feel tired and sleepy.

"You're not an arsehole, Stephen. You're a good person who sometimes does arseholey things."

"I ain't so sure about that." Stephen thought of all the

bad things he'd done—the using and abusing of friends, lovers and strangers. Once he got what he wanted, he would discard people and begin looking for his next fix. "It's nice that you're on my team, Shaun, but you don't know what I'm really like. I can be a real prick."

Shaun worked his fingers down to Stephen's neck, gently scratching up and down. "How so?"

"I know I'm the moody prick of the bunch. I'm an arrogant son of a bitch who thinks he's hot shit and fuck my way through the town like it's going out of fashion."

"Oh, poor Stephen. How horrible that must be to get laid all the time."

"Dork." Stephen playfully shoved an elbow back into Shaun's knee.

"All that means is you're a male and observant."

Stephen took a deep breath, deciding if he should offer up one of his many sins. "I fucked Clare. Troy's Mrs."

Shaun said nothing.

"And she was gonna dump him for me. But as soon as I'd done it, I told her we weren't on." Stephen laughed. "Yip, just said, 'Nar, sorry Clare, it'd be wrong to do that to Troy,' despite what I'd just done."

Shaun stayed quiet, working his fingers back down to Stephen's damp back and shoulders, stroking him with his fingertips. "Is it your baby?"

"Fuck no, this was like six months ago, but it just makes the whole thing really awkward. And like I don't even fancy her, ya know? She's cool and all but I just did it 'cos I knew I could. Like a way of feeling I had something up on a mate." Stephen placed his hands on his inner thighs, grabbing himself hard, regretting telling his number one fan a formerly well-kept secret. The spilling of truth hadn't erased any guilt like he hoped it would. "I'm not a nice person, Shaun. It's important you realise that."

Shaun let out a deliberate sigh like he was thinking of what to say next. His fingers stroked in circles on Stephen's back, sending goose bumps up Stephen's arms that stood their blond hairs on edge. After what felt like aeons, Shaun finally passed his judgement, "Well, I still think you're good."

"Fuck you're stubborn," Stephen said, confused yet relieved.

"You know why you did these things, Stephen?"
Don't you mean do?
"Why..." Stephen murmured. He sensed movement behind him and felt Shaun close to his neck, Shaun's warm breath floating into his ear.

"'Cos you were lonely." Shaun's hands stopped moving.

Stephen tensed up wondering how Shaun could read into such detail about him. "What makes you think that?"

Shaun's palms were pressed flat and firm on his back, penetrating a cryptic energy. "'Cos I was lonely too." Shaun's finger drew slowly below his shoulder blades.

Stephen instantly recognised its path and what it traced: the infinity sign. Two S's meeting, connecting with one another.

"There isn't a piece of you that's bad, no part I wouldn't touch." Shaun's words lingered like a deep confession, as if he had just exposed a piece of himself.

Stephen gulped. He was nervous at where this might be going, his heart thumping wildly in his chest. He was aware of the vibe attached to this territory and, in an instant, the destination was revealed delicately by Shaun's lips kissing him ever so gently on the nape of his neck. Stephen sat there frozen before another kiss landed, this time a little lower on his shoulder. Shaun's mouth slipped out a faint groan as he let his hands roam over Stephen's slick back.

Stephen closed his eyes and uttered in little more than a whisper, "Are you a fag, Shaun?"

Shaun's hands stopped moving, cemented in place by the question. "No," he responded stiffly before sucking in a deep breath. "Well, maybe for *you* I am."

Stephen opened his eyes. "Okay..."

The heat off Shaun was radiating, spawning a potent sexual tension that demanded to be known. He placed a hand on Stephen's bare knee, slowly raising it higher, exploring the flesh of his leg 'till his fingers got to the fabric of Stephen's shorts. His hand stopped moving as if waiting for permission to climb higher.

Stephen looked down at Shaun's slender fingers resting under the hem of his shorts, waiting for Shaun's next move, bracing himself for the impact. With no response interpreted as Stephen agreeing to its path, Shaun's hand slowly disappeared up his shorts. The warmth of his palm glided along Stephen's thigh 'till his fingertips reached his groin, tickling against Stephen's cotton briefs. Shaun's fingers gently squished his balls through the material, evoking a doubtful breath from Stephen who looked down, unsure of what to do. Shaun rested his hand there, familiarising itself near his most private of areas. Time stood still as Stephen struggled with the obscure thought, *he's about to know what I feel like… down there.*

Shaun's knees nuzzled into his side, pressing against his ribs, locking him in. Without warning, he slipped his hand under the briefs and grabbed hold of Stephen's hairy balls, giving them a good squeeze.

Stephen leapt up, completely freaked out by his nuts being cupped in a mate's hands. He twirled 'round to see Shaun backing off, leaning against the couch, his hands up like an outlaw surrendering.

"What the fuck?" Stephen planted a hand on his forehead, not sure where to look.

Shaun's face was riddled with shame.

"Fuck, I'm so sorry." He stood up and took a step towards Stephen.

"No, don't. Just leave it, alright?" Stephen swatted the air, shooing Shaun away.

"Look, I'm so sorry. I'm really sorry. Fuck, I didn't mean to…" Shaun's voice trailed off like he was about to cry.

Stephen picked his shirt up and hastily put it back on. "I gotta go," he said, marching towards the door.

"You don't have to go, I… I don't know what I was thinking."

Stephen spun around, glaring in disgust. "Trust me. I have to go now!"

"Well, at least let me give you a ride home."

"I think I'd rather walk."

"Please don't tell anyone," Shaun pleaded.

"Yeah, whatever," Stephen huffed, opening the door and slamming it behind him.

CHAPTER TWENTY-TWO — 1995

STEPHEN

When Stephen arrived back home, his anger and confusion over what had just happened were forced to take a backseat when he saw his aunt's silver station wagon parked in the driveway. Of all the fucking times they had to arrive, it was the day he was groped by another guy. Once inside, he found everyone sitting in the lounge, soaking up the room's abundance of flashing Christmas lights despite the daytime hour outdoors. His father was busy talking about the farm with his uncle and his mum was nattering away to her sister about her next exotic plan for the garden. His cousins sat planted in front of the TV, watching some kid movie to which their teenage brains would have felt painful viewing no doubt.

"Oh, here he is, my handsome nephew," his aunt greeted him cheerfully. Her face was rosy already from one too many gins. "Come give your Aunt Cindy a hug."

Stephen walked over and let the gravitational pull of her rolling pin arms drag him in and clutch him tight. He hunched down over her shoulder to meet her tiny height. Aunt Cindy was quite the opposite of his sleek meerkat-like mother. Cindy, the younger sister, had a pretty face but sausage-like qualities, being vertically-challenged and waistline-extravagant.

"Hey, Aunt Cindy," Stephen greeted, trying his best to muster a smile.

"I didn't think you could get any better looking from the last time I saw you, but here you are." She admired his face. "You must need a stick to beat off all the girls 'round here."

Guys too, apparently.

"Something like that," he agreed.

His father's cheeky voice blared from the couch, "Only the stick between ya legs, aye, son?"

"Honestly, Graham," his mother snapped, shooting a stern look at her husband, her eyes pointing like rulers in the direction of Stephen's cousins.

"Oh, it's fine, Miriam. I'm sure they hear worse at school," Cindy responded with a giggle.

Uncle Brian, a bald tubby specimen, waddled over and thrust forward a pudgy palm. "Merry Christmas, wonder kid." He shook Stephen's hand enthusiastically. The festive greeting came out as fake as the man's toothy grin.

Stephen hadn't liked Uncle Brian even as a small child and standing in front of the doughy man now, nothing had changed. Uncle Brian's smile was a lip curl away from being a sneer, proving to Stephen the dislike was mutual, even if unspoken.

His cousins, Katie and Danny, lingered in the background. Katie called out in a grating high-pitched voice, "Hey Stephen," while the spectacle-wearing Danny shot Stephen a peace sign. Both cousins were rake thin, not an ounce of fat on them, unlike their parents who were dripping in it. Stephen smiled in their direction, offering a feeble wave of his hand. He reluctantly took a seat in the lounge with his dad and uncle and pretended to get involved in the conversation, but not enough to let his uncle get under his skin.

"So, you're going into the family business, aye, frolicking around on green fields, living the life of the landed gentry," Uncle Brian mocked. Stephen's father roared in laughter, seemingly oblivious to the thinly veiled insult.

"Yeah, something like that." *It's not like I have a fucking choice in the matter, dickhead.*

Stephen fought the urge to roll his eyes; instead, he practised what his mother did so well with people she wasn't fond of—smile and nod. Stephen made a point of going to bed early to avoid further socialising with the Pillich. He felt bad avoiding Aunt Cindy who, despite her overly-huggy hands, was well-meaning.

"You off to bed already, love?" Aunt Cindy asked.

"I am. I'm feeling pretty shattered, to be honest."

Aunt Cindy looked disappointed. "You better make

sure you're up bright and early for Santa then."

"I sure will," he answered, giving a fake smile.

Stephen evacuated to his bedroom where he discovered a camp stretcher made up in the middle of the floor. *Great. I get Danny as a roommate.* He considered going and telling his mum to get rid of it or drag the bloody thing himself to a spare room, but he figured it wasn't worth the hassle of being so rude. It riled him though, a house as big as theirs and they still insisted on shoving the runty Danny in here for cousin bonding.

Stephen stripped down to his briefs and jumped into bed; normally, he would go in starkers, but having a roomie would require at least some modesty. He nestled into his pillow and stewed about the inconvenience of it all. Once done with feeling snotty about having Danny stay in his room, Stephen's overloaded mind wandered to the day's major shock. *Shaun.*

Why did he do it? Why did Shaun have to go and fuck up a perfectly good thing by fancying him? Stephen didn't know why but he felt betrayed, like this was something Shaun should have told him ages ago. Foreboding words echoed in his mind.

You might not like all the answers.

By the time Stephen began to doze off, he could still feel where Shaun's hands had been. No aching shoulder, just tingling warmth across his back and *other* parts he had touched.

∞

Fid, fid, fid.

Stephen opened his eyes to the faintest of sounds. A soft thumping that was almost rhythmic in nature. He rolled onto his side and slowly opened his eyes. The room was owned by the dark, aside from a pale strip of moonlight which streaked across his room.

Fid, fid, fid.

He focused his vision along the strip of light and discovered the root of the noise. Danny was having a sneaky wank. A mound in the horny teen's sleeping bag, furiously shuttling up and down. Stephen felt his gut turn. *Seriously, what the fuck?*

After five years in boarding school, Stephen had witnessed more than his fair share of self-pleasuring disturbances coming from nearby beds but he wasn't in any mood to hear someone whack off in his own bedroom.

Sure, all guys did it. Stephen's worn socks would be the last thing he took off every night, falling to the side of the bed ready to be the first thing he reached for in the morning,—well, second thing—corrupting them as a convenient hiding spot for his semen. Having a roommate meant that this ritual was on hold, but obviously his cousin didn't play by the same rules. However, he remembered being fifteen. At that age, you did whatever you had to do before exploding.

Out of some small respect, he gave his cousin some dignity and closed his eyes, pretending to be asleep 'till he heard Danny gasp and rustle around in the sleeping bag before cleaning up. Stephen waited another five minutes before he dared to move and get up so Danny didn't think he'd been busted busting one out.

Stephen reached a hand out in the dark, rummaging for a pair of jeans and shirt. He plucked from the floor the first ones he could feel and took them out to the hallway where he got dressed. He meandered toward the kitchen where a rich smell of coffee filtered through the air. Stephen's nose chased the scent, its source the magical cure to wake him up.

In the kitchen, he found his father already dressed in overalls, grey woolly socks, and gumboots at his side, ready to hit the land.

"Morning," his dad chirped.

"Morning," Stephen mumbled back, rubbing grits of sleep out of his eyes. He went on autopilot and poured himself a coffee from the pot before joining his father at the table. His dad knew him well enough not to expect much conversation for the first few minutes. Once Stephen had downed half the cup he spoke up, "Bit early, even for us, isn't it?"

Stephen's father nodded. "Sure is, but I was gonna

get a start early so we can get back here and do the Christmas thing."

"Right," Stephen grumbled.

"You sound about how I feel." His father laughed. "Your bloody uncle's hard fucking work, I tell ya."

Stephen was shocked to hear his dad say this. He assumed they got on well. "So you can't stand him either?" Stephen asked excitedly.

"Hey, now I didn't say that, but let's just say the man is a fucking ankle."

Stephen snorted on his coffee, knowing what his father was about to say next, and in unison they both declared, "'Cos he's lower than a cunt." They had to hold their laughter in to avoid waking the whole house up.

Stephen's father got up and put his gumboots on. He walked past Stephen, placing a hand on his shoulder. "Get yourself another coffee and I'll meet you out there."

Stephen nodded and went back to his coffee booster. He reached into his pocket and fetched out his ciggies to compliment his liquid breakfast. When he opened the lid, he discovered one last cancer stick staring back at him. *My lucky smoke.* For some reason though, it didn't look very lucky.

It just looked fucking lonely.

∞

It was a relief when Boxing Day came and—*boom!*—just like that, his aunt and uncle were packed up and off. Stephen spent the afternoon grazing on the leftovers from their Christmas feast which his mum always made far too much for. They would always end up living on it for the next week, sending their usually healthy diets into a sugary freefall.

Stephen was in his room, busy chomping his way through a box of Cadbury chocolates, when his mum appeared in the doorway to hand him the phone. He grabbed the phone from her and returned to his bed offering up a friendly hello, hoping it was Delphi but expecting it to be Luke. Wrong and wrong.

"Hi, Stephen," Shaun's voice came down the line.

Stephen's face went hard as concrete, matching his tone, "Yep."

"Look, I just wanted to say I'm real sorry about the other day." The line went quiet between them as Shaun waited for a response that Stephen was unwilling to give. "I didn't mean for what happened to happen, ya know? I've never had a mate like you before and I don't wanna mess that up."

"Oh, okay, so that was just an accident, your hand grabbing my nuts, was it?"

"No, but yeah… you know what I mean. I'm not like that and I feel really bad for what I did."

"Oh what, so you're not gay now?" Stephen asked as disparagingly as he could.

He heard Shaun take a deep breath.

"I guess I am… gay," Shaun's voice sounded pained admitting this out loud. "But what I meant was I'm not the type of person to try and take advantage of a friend."

"So you are queer, but you've got morals? Well, that's just brilliant." Stephen laughed. "Look, I gotta go. Catch ya round." Stephen hung up the phone, cutting Shaun off just as he was about to speak.

A part of Stephen actually enjoyed Shaun grovelling for his friendship, but another part of him buried beneath his staunch male pride, felt guilty for being emotionally sadistic to someone who it seemed against their better judgement, genuinely cared for him.

CHAPTER TWENTY-THREE — 1995

STEPHEN

Parked up at the beach domain's gravelly car park, Stephen waited for his double date. The steady stream of summer bodies passing his vision on their way to the beach was his sole entertainment as time crawled by at a painfully slow pace. For once it wasn't him who was late; instead, he was waiting on Troy, Clare, and a mystery girl they promised he would like.

Finally, a loud honk of a horn erupted, rescuing him from his prolonged boredom. Stephen craned his neck to discover Troy and Clare pulling up beside him, he quickly scanned the backseat of their car for any sign of the mystery date—it was empty. *Great, a no show.* Just as he started to dread spending an afternoon as the third wheel, a second car pulled up. Out stepped a pretty brunette with caramel coloured skin wearing tiny shorts and a low-cut top. On her head sat a large white sun hat and hanging 'round her neck was a sizable pounamu necklace in the shape of a koru.

Clare went over and grabbed her friend by the hand. Stephen's eyes pounced on her full breasts jiggling in the plunging top as she walked across to be introduced.

"Lexi, this is Stephen. Stephen, this is Lexi," Clare said, grabbing Stephen's hand to place it with Lexi's for a half-arsed shake.

Lexi's eyes sized him up, a small smile spreading across her pouty lips. "Nice to meet you, Stephen."

"Ditto." He smiled back.

He decided that Troy and Clare hadn't done too badly, but then it wasn't as if he was going to turn anyone down. He still hadn't scored since arriving back in town nearly three months earlier, making this his longest dry spell since losing his virginity at fifteen. Times were tough and

Let Me Catch You

expectations low, but Lexi more than surpassed them.

Once the introductions and small talk were done, they all settled on the domain, stretching out on towels under the shade of leafy oak trees. In the distance, screaming kids played on swings and slides that had seen better days, but still served their purpose of play.

Clare and Lexi disappeared to the dairy across from the park to get some sun cream that they'd both 'forgotten' to bring. Stephen knew the ploy that would follow. When they returned with the bottled flirt, Clare squirted a large dollop into Troy's hands so he could rub it into her back. Lexi then grabbed the bottle and asked Stephen to do the same honour for her.

The cream gunged his fingers as he rubbed the sunscreen into her skin in fine thoughtful strokes. Whilst blending it in, he remembered Shaun massaging his back only a few days ago, carrying similar intentions. Stephen rubbed his hands on the grass, trying to get free of the greasy residue the lotion had left. When he pulled his hands back up, they were covered in small green blades, resembling hairy palms.

"Didn't your parents tell you that would make hair grow on your palms?" A rare funny from Troy who normally fed upon the jokes of others rather than serve them up himself.

A shrieking scream seared through the air, emanating from the far side of the park—it came from the playground, under a grove of leafy trees. A short silence soon followed the scream before a loud blubbering of tears cried out.

Troy stood up with a hand over his eyes, peering across the domain, trying to decipher what was happening. "Looks like we got some carnage on the playground." He looked at everyone, encouraging them to be excited. "Shall we go check it out?"

They strolled across the field towards the scene of commotion. When they got closer, Stephen could see two older children fussing over a little girl crying with grazed knees. Her sobs were heavy, a mixture of pain and fright. Stephen was so focused on the caretaking of the fallen that Troy's voice calling out startled him.

"MUNRO!"

Stephen looked over to the big shady trees and saw

standing under them was Shaun with a chubby woman in her late thirties, both of them staring up, appearing to be fascinated by whatever was up the tree. The sight of the perpetrator with wandering hands formed an awkward knot in his stomach. *Be cool Stephen. Be cool.*

The fat woman bellowed up the tree, "Look what you've done!"

Shaun stood beside the woman, unaware his name had been called out. Troy hollered again, this time Shaun turning back, his face painted with distraction. He went to wave at Troy 'till his eyes spotted Stephen. He swiftly dropped his hand and returned to peering up the tree.

What's so fucking fascinating up there?

"Come down and apologise now." The rotund woman spoke sternly, shaking an angry finger up the tree.

Shaun scratched his head, his body language communicating an air of unease next to the stern woman.

Troy barged on ahead and patted Shaun on the back, asking what was going on as the woman kept biffing orders up the tree. When Stephen and the girls reached the shaded scene, he looked up and could see little pink shoes attached to tiny legs dangling from a branch high up in the tree, safely away from what must have been the ballistic mother of the injured child. *Josie.* Stephen smiled at the tiny terror's rebellion.

"Come on, rat, just come down and say sorry. You're not in trouble," Shaun pleaded.

"No," Josie replied stubbornly.

"Get down now and come say sorry to Daphne," the mother said, her fat arms wobbling as she waved a hand up the tree.

"Fuck off," Josie fired back.

The woman's face looked like it would explode while Shaun held his in shame. Everybody else tried their best not to burst out laughing at the ballsy child.

"Whoa, she's a hard shot, Munro," Troy said, "and I thought you were bad."

Shaun looked at him and just shrugged like he had given up reasoning with his baby sister. Shaun kept his focus between Troy and Josie, not daring to look in Stephen's direction.

The woman's face now glowed with spiteful recognition. "Oh, a Munro, I should have known." The family reputation preceded itself. "Get down now before I come up and bring you down myself," she threatened.

Josie began climbing higher, sending branches shuffling under her feet. "Come up and get me then, turkey tits."

"Holy fuck," Clare said, trying to bury her laughter into Troy's shoulder.

The woman seethed with anger. "Right, you nasty little monster." She marched to the trunk of the tree and grabbed for a branch, trying to hoist her hippo-sized bum up the tree.

It was never going to happen and everyone stood back, engrossed in the woman's losing battle. Astonishingly, she got herself up to the first set of branches, but Josie was much higher and this woman would easily snap the branches that high up.

"Fuck off," Josie squealed. The precocious child began biffing leaves and twigs down.

The woman furiously grabbed for another branch before a soft slurping sound came from high up in the leaves. *Plip, plip, plip.* Josie was spitting on the woman, showering her in snotty saliva.

"Arrrggh, you disgusting little shit." The woman dropped from her perch and fell back on the ground with a thud, wiping the spit from her face before wobbling herself to stand upright. She flashed Shaun a furious glare. "You need to teach that kid some manners and control what comes out of her filthy little mouth."

Shaun finally lost his cool, his protective instinct kicking in. "And you should probably control what goes in yours, you fat bitch."

Stephen was taken aback by his hostile response.

"Oh my god," Lexi whispered in excited shock.

The woman waddled back to her daughter and the older kids, dragging them all away from the playground.

"Yeah, Shaun, control your child," Troy joked.

Shaun flashed him a smile before focusing his attention back up the tree. "She's gone now, rat. You can come down." He got no response. "It's safe now, I promise."

The branches began to shake as Josie descended from the tree top, shaking leaves off 'till she finally swung from a lower branch and dropped to her feet. She looked awfully pleased with herself 'till she saw Shaun's disapproval.

She tugged on his arm. "Are you going to tell Mum?"

"No, it's fine," he sighed.

Troy poked him on the shoulder. "So, what you been up to?"

Shaun kept his eyes firmly on Troy, not daring to even peek at Stephen as if doing so would turn him into a pillar of salt. "Well, we were here to play at the park 'till someone sent a little girl flying into space." He glared at Josie who blushed at her guilt.

"Must run in the family this need to inflict grievous bodily harm," Troy said.

"Huh?" Shaun looked confused.

"Luke's hands." Troy wiggled his fingers to emphasize the point.

"Oh yeah, that," Shaun mumbled.

"What possessed you to do something like that?" Troy asked.

Shaun didn't answer straight away. "Ask him." He showed no intention of getting into details.

Josie tugged on Shaun's arm. "Who is Luke?"

"Nobody. Mind your beeswax." He tussled her springy brown curls, sending her sidestepping in giggles.

"Stephen, are you gonna come play Monopoly tonight?" Josie looked at him, eager for an answer.

"Nar, I can't come play tonight, sorry."

"Ohhh, why not?" she whined.

"He's busy, Josie," Shaun growled.

"But it's better when Stephen plays though." She looked at Clare and Lexi and began whispering, "Stephen steals from the bank, but I always catch him."

Lexi flicked Stephen's shoulder. "Do you now?"

"Hey, it's tough being an outlaw."

Lexi rubbed his arm affectionately where she had just hit him. "I bet."

Shaun's eyes relented, finally glancing across at Stephen to watch the obvious flirting going on. He quickly switched his attention back to Troy but not before Stephen caught a glimpse of what he suspected to be raw jealousy in Shaun's eyes.

Josie though, seemed intrigued by the pretty girl on Stephen's arm. "Are you Stephen's girlfriend?"

Lexi was put on the spot. "Umm… no, we're just friends."

"What's your name?" Josie asked with a deadpan look.

"I'm Lexi. You're Josie, right?" Lexi pandered to the little girl's curiosity.

Josie nodded. "You can't be Stephen's girlfriend anyway 'cos your name doesn't start with an S."

"Oh, I see." Lexi laughed, baffled by the statement.

"Yep, the name of Stephen's true love begins with an S. Aye, Shaun?" She looked up at her brother, waiting for him to back her up. He didn't.

Clare and Troy looked at Stephen as if asking him to explain.

Stephen frowned. "It's umm—"

Shaun cut him off. "Right, well we have to make a move anyways. Good catching up with you all," he said as he put a hand behind his sister's back, willing her to move like he needed to be gone pronto.

Josie put her hand up and gave Stephen a high-five as they went past. Shaun kept his eyes low, avoiding direct eye contact; instead he shot a quick sideways glance which Stephen swore he could feel burn on the very area that had been fondled when they were last alone.

With the tree fiasco over, the group made their way back to their nest of towels. "What's with him today? Did he seem a bit strange to you?" Troy asked Stephen.

Stephen ignored the comment. *He's sad. It's in his eyes.*

"Don't you reckon?" Troy prodded.

"Can't say I noticed," Stephen lied, trying not to let guilt attach itself to him.

"You play Monopoly…" Troy said, sounding bemused. "Since when did you two become such good mates?"

Stephen knew that anyone who knew him would find the social pairing humorous. He did his best to not sound defensive. "You were away and Luke was busy, so, yeah, I hung out there a few times." *Like every day 'till he touched my nuts.*

"Trying to bag old Desperate Debbie no doubt," Troy laughed 'till Clare hit him. "Sorry," he quickly muttered.

Stephen shot him a filthy look. He was less worried about what Lexi thought, more annoyed at the joke about a woman he thought didn't deserve an easy jab.

"I think it's time for a swim," Lexi said, trying to diffuse the awkward comment. She stood there with her hands on her hips and looked at Stephen. "Care to join me?"

Stephen gave her a smile. "I didn't bring my togs."

"Just go in your shorts, silly," Lexi replied.

"Or the nuddy. You know you *want* to," Troy said, getting another playful slap from Clare.

Lexi picked up her towel and waited for him to make a move.

"Fuck it, why not?" Stephen stripped off his shirt and chased her onto the beach.

∞

The swim had been refreshing and was his first proper dip in the sea that summer. When he was younger, Stephen would go swimming every chance he got, but once he reached thirteen, he realised the real fun was to be had out of the water—unless, like today, a dunk in the sea led to fun later.

The choppy west coast waves charged over them, making swimming here not dissimilar to being a rag in a washing machine. After some playful tackling and head dunking as excuses to cop a feel, they made their way back to the shore.

As the sunny day petered out, the beach began to empty with campers returning to their nylon pitched castles. Troy and Clare bid farewell so they could drive back to Clare's home in New Plymouth before it got too late.

Stephen and Lexi sat alone in the dark shade of twilight blue, muddling their way through random topics, both waiting for the inevitable tangling of limbs. As he was in the middle of a sentence, talking about his old flatmates from university, Lexi took the initiative, kissing him on the mouth and shutting him up right then and there.

Stephen smiled. "Whoa." He rushed his face back to hers, kissing her sea-tinged lips.

Lexi lay into his body, sending him tumbling back on the sand, bits of grit soiling his hair. Stephen spread his knees open to let Lexi slip between his legs. He unleashed his hands, placing one on the small of her back, pressing her softness into him while the other snaked down and groped her behind. Stephen pressed his mouth against her neck, lashing her with slick licks. He thrust his hips upward and was met with her abdomen grinding against his dick. His *flaccid* dick. Lexi reached a hand down and groped him through his shorts, giving a soft squeeze on his still slack cock. *Fuck this is embarrassing.*

He found himself not able to fully commit to the conquest even though her movements and grinding indicated he had full permission to do so. *Just get hard, fucking do something.* Stephen's mind felt cloudy with barriers. He closed his eyes to try and visualise sexy thoughts to help him along. He had a reputation to upkeep.

With his eyes closed and face being sucked off, his mind's eye drifted to earlier, seeing Shaun in the park. The nervous Munro wearing shorts and a white t-shirt that had accentuated his tanned slim body, emitting a purity that could wash away sin. *Get out of my head, critter!*

WHACK!

Lexi's pounamu necklace busted him in the face.

"Oh my god, I'm so sorry." She reeled away from his body and put a hand to her mouth. "Are you okay?"

Stephen clutched above his eye where the deceptively heavy greenstone had smacked his skull. "Cheers for the free lobotomy." he laughed.

Lexi let go of her mouth and joined in with the laughter. "Maybe it's a sign."

"What do you mean?" he asked.

"I could tell you weren't feeling it."

Yes, you FELT that.

Stephen didn't say anything. He kept rubbing his eye, grateful for the distraction of owning up to his dick's dismal performance.

"Clare did say that you were sorta hung up on someone, so I understand."

Stephen gulped. "Err, what?"

"A Delphi?" Lexi smiled.

Stephen nodded. "Yeah…"

"I know what that's like," Lexi sighed. "How about we call it a night? For what it's worth, I had a good time."

"Yeah, me too."

Lexi shook her head and smiled. "Maybe things would have gone better if my name started with S."

∞

When Stephen got home, he took his shame-riddled body straight to bed. He lay in the dark, trying to block out the noisy cicadas singing songs of summer outside his window. He tossed and turned, closing his eyes which triggered a movie reel in his brain of the day's events. Different scenes blurred past with hectic speed: sexual humiliation, flirty fun and laughs with mates. But the mental picture show got stuck on one scene in particular, one it refused to let him skip. The sight of how sad Shaun had looked seeing him at the domain, almost scared of being near him.

Guilt began filling the room, nuzzling itself deep inside Stephen's chest. He covered his face with his hands and let out a mumbled groan, willing the guilt away, but it wouldn't budge from its firm grip on his feelings. Stephen wondered why he felt especially awful for his rudeness. It wasn't like he was any stranger to doing shitty things to good people. Why should this time be any different?

It's not like I'm into him.

In the back of his mind he could hear the tiny rumblings of a revelation. *Bullshit.*

NEW YEAR'S EVE — 1995

STEPHEN

The bonfire burned brightly as the young crowd sat around basking in its glow, awaiting the roar of a new year to be ushered in. What had started as a small gathering of about nine people had swelled to over fifty and with two hours 'till the clock struck twelve, more would filter in. Yet, on this warm evening humming with a cacophony of celebrations, Stephen felt particularly alone despite the chaos around him.

He realised now that he'd fucked up. He missed his mate terribly. Shaun had told him everybody was interesting in some way and the way Shaun would sit there listening to his bullshit like he was the only person in the world who mattered, showed the guy lived by this statement. Stephen was desperate to make things right.

He hadn't breathed a word about Shaun being gay and how he'd made a move on him. He figured that he could keep a secret, and he didn't want his own sexuality to be incriminated by default. Besides, if Shaun wanted to, he could tell Troy and everyone about how Stephen had slept with Clare, and then all social hell would break loose.

What was most alarming to Stephen was that since the incident, he'd not been able to shake it out of his mind. The way Shaun had kissed his neck and shoulder before his hand wandered up Stephen's leg, exploring his body as it slipped under his shorts, touching him, feeling him… sensing him.

Shaun had been hesitant to come down here for New Year's in the first place and now with him probably thinking Stephen wouldn't stand up for him if Luke turned up, it seemed pretty darn likely he wouldn't show.

Busy feeling sorry for himself, a tap on his shoulder made him jump and nearly fall off the flimsy driftwood he was perched on, Stephen spun 'round and looked up to see Delphi smiling back at him, looking naturally stunning with no effort.

"Mind if I sit?" She had her sweet voice on.

"Help yourself." Stephen shifted along, giving her room.

Delphi patted his knee. "So, what have you been up to?" she asked, sounding a little too interested.

Stephen scratched his head, thinking of an answer. "Same shit, different day, pretty much." He swigged back on his drink.

Delphi laughed like he had said a joke.

"Oh, come on, Stephen. It's been ages since I saw you. Surely something must have happened."

"Nup, not really," he said, shaking his head back and forth.

Four weeks ago, Stephen would have invented a story to keep the stokes of conversation going, but he had since checked out on the idea of staying at Hotel Delphi.

Delphi seemed oblivious to his change of heart and kept up the friendly charade. *Maybe she does like me?*

As he was about to accept there had always been a chance, he looked behind and heard a familiar smoky voice. It was George, standing with the dreadlocks guy, the one who had already stayed overnight in Hotel Delphi.

Stephen knew this trick well. He was being used as jealousy bait.

Stephen, in a still mostly-sober state, stayed seated with Delphi, offering up scraps of conversation that she scooped up like a starving sparrow, all the while turning around flicking her hair to see if the object of her affection had noticed.

The longer she sat beside him, the more obvious it became that her plan was faltering, but she didn't budge. She was no doubt suffering from the same horrible thing she had inflicted on Stephen—the indignant feeling beautiful people rarely experienced, being the recipient of another person's indifference.

As Stephen cracked open drink-number-five with an hour to go until midnight, he felt the burn not just from the fire, but someone's gaze.

Who's staring?

Stephen scanned around the island of people, looking for the source of his feeling of being regarded. Between gaps in the jutting out bits of wood in the fire, he caught a glimpse of Shaun's brooding brown eyes through the flames.

Shaun, seeing that he had been caught staring, quickly turned away. Stephen kept his eyes honed in on him, waiting for his glance to return. He eyed Shaun up head to toe, taking in his gentle frame wearing green cargo pants and a baggy t-shirt. Megan sat next to him, her boobs nearly spilling out of her black top as she spoke to a group of friends on the other side of her.

Shaun didn't appear to be talking to any of them. He sat there hunched over, ironing out those invisible creases, with a grumbly look fastened to his face.

I should go say hi... or is that too obvious? No, do it now... in front of everyone or should I wait? I'll wait.

Stephen's guilt felt even worse after seeing Shaun's rigid posture. This is the boy who should be burning louder and brighter than the fire, but instead... he looked subdued. As much as Stephen wanted to go over and give his peace offering, he felt it would be best to wait a while, hoping that Shaun didn't leave before he was drunk enough to have the courage to do so.

How long has he been sitting there for?

Stephen was disappointed with himself for not noticing Shaun's arrival, as if he had been robbed of something. Still, he felt good knowing Shaun had singled him out and stared, letting Stephen know he was wanted from across the fire.

Delphi had managed to strike up conversation with a girl next to her and gave Stephen's poor ears a break. He used his freedom to just stare back at Shaun, willing Shaun's eyes to wander back to him where they belonged.

Just fucking look, idiot. Look at me.

As if he could hear Stephen's mental command, Shaun turned his face, looking through the licks of flames and held Stephen's gaze for a split second before a shout from across the crowd made them break away.

"That's him! That's the gutless muppet." Luke staggered forward with swinging arms and bandaged hands.

Following immediately behind him were a couple of his boxing mates, both as physically intimidating as their leader. Stephen didn't know them well, but recognised their busted faces from the matches he had been to watch.

"Yeah, you, Munro. Ya prick," Luke said, his words slurring together. "Coz of ewwww, I didn't get to fight in my match, 'cos, uh, yeah, that's right, you slammed a bonnet down on my hands, you sneaky *faggot*!"

The word stung Stephen's ears, it packed more meaning now.

Shaun held his nerve, remaining seated, not saying a word just giving Luke an icy stare. Luke grounded his bare feet into the sand only a few metres away from where Shaun sat. The tension soon reached the heat of the fire.

"That's right. Not so big now, are you?" Luke taunted.

Well, you do have two backup thugs, so I guess not.

Stephen felt a lump rise in his throat, worried what was about to unfold. He knew he didn't have a choice and would have to step in. He had promised Shaun he'd keep him safe, and he intended to do so. Stephen's knuckles went white from clenching his fists so tight. Taking a deep breath, he braced himself for social suicide and a good arse-kicking. Just as he was about to stand up, his moment of martyrdom was stolen.

"You deserved it, you dirty pig," Megan bellowed, antagonising the drunken beast.

She must know.

"The only pig here is you, ya fat bitch." Luke gave her the finger.

"Piss off, Luke. You're too drunk," Megan blustered back.

Shaun got to his feet and stood in front of her. "Yeah, I did it, and I'd break every bone again if I got the chance." He stared back defiantly in the face of an imminent thrashing and then smiled. "Good luck getting to Sydney with those huckery fingers."

Luke's face turned red and his eyes bulged in anger. "Right!" Luke went to charge at him but his mates grabbed hold of his shoulders, holding him back.

Thank fuck for that.

Delphi interjected with a drunken love message. "Settle down both of you. It's New Year's! Just get along, for Christ's sake." She looked over the fire scornfully at Shaun. "And you should apologise for what you've done, Shaun. That's just evil what you did."

You don't know the full story.

Shaun looked at Luke who was huffing and struggling to break free from being held back. He then glanced toward Delphi, who glared at him morosely. "Fuck this," he muttered, walking away from the fire and into the darkness.

Delphi turned to Stephen. "Seriously, I can't believe someone would smash another person's fingers." She looked up to the sky as if searching for an answer. "He's always been a bit fucking mental though, but sheesh, the whole family is."

"You wouldn't fucking know," Stephen snapped. He stood up and went after Shaun.

"Stephen," she huffed.

Stephen ignored her and shoved through the crowd, chasing after a very misunderstood Munro.

He heard Luke call out after him. "For fuck sake, Stevie, don't follow the faggot."

I've got no choice.

Once through the pool of people, Stephen could see Shaun was a good thirty yards ahead of him, storming forward at a fast pace, his arms and legs swinging with anger as he tried escaping into the night.

"Wait!" Stephen yelled out. He jogged to catch up. "Shaun, man, wait for me."

Shaun didn't respond, continuing his clip like a man on a mission.

Stephen picked up the pace 'till he caught up, grabbing him by the shoulder. "Shaun, I said wait."

Shaun spun 'round with a scowl on his face. "What, Stephen?" he hissed. "I'm going home, okay? Just leave me alone." His tone was angry, but his face looked pained.

"But your home's the other way." Stephen pointed.

Shaun started walking away. "Yeah," he muttered, "well, I'm going the long way."

Stephen followed him. "Oh, come on, man. Just stop." He reached for his shoulder again.

Shaun flicked his hand away and turned to face him.

"Look, I said I'm sorry, alright, so please, leave me alone." Shaun clasped his hands together. "Please."

"No... I won't."

Shaun planted a hand on his face and groaned in frustration. "Fuck, man. I already feel so fucking stupid. Please, don't make me feel any worse."

Stephen stared at him blankly.

Shaun sighed. "Look, I promise I won't bother you ever again. I won't see any of you. Just... please don't tell anyone and leave me alone." Shaun's eyes pleaded as much as his words.

"I won't tell anyone," Stephen said calmly, "and I don't want you to stop bothering me."

"What?" Shaun said in confusion.

Stephen reached into the pocket of his jeans and pulled out an envelope. "I got this for you." Stephen held it out, waiting for Shaun to take it. "It's your Christmas present." He waved it in the air, encouraging Shaun to accept it. "Take it."

Shaun looked at Stephen suspiciously. He put out a reluctant hand and took hold of the envelope, just staring at it between his fingers.

Stephen could sense Shaun thought it might be a trick. "Well, open it, dork."

Shaun ripped open the envelope to find a ticket to the Big Day Out. "What, are you for real?"

"Merry Christmas."

"Whoa, these cost a fucking mint," Shaun said. "Thank you." He stared at the ticket in his hand like he was mesmerised. "But I can't take it."

Stephen sighed. "Don't be a dick, Shaun."

"It's not that I don't appreciate it, it's just... I can't get up there and I'm hardly gonna go on my own. You're better off giving it to Troy or Luke." Shaun went to hand it back.

"Look inside again, fool."

Shaun rummaged in the envelope. "There's two?"

"Yeah, you can come with me. We'll go together."

"But you said..." Shaun's voice drifted off.

"Look, forget whatever I said." Stephen stepped towards him. "I'm sorry, okay?" He extended his hand out

Let Me Catch You

and touched Shaun's arm.

Shaun scanned Stephen's face for any hint of a lie.

"I don't think I handled the situation very well and I feel fucking terrible for being such a dick about it." Stephen said as he began rubbing his fingers along Shaun's forearm.

Shaun looked back nervously at him. "Don't fuck with me, Stephen. Seriously, just don't," he said, his voice sounding flustered.

Stephen stared him straight in the eyes. "Honest, I'm not fucking with you."

Shaun cast his eyes down at Stephen's hand still rubbing just below his elbow. Stephen lowered his hand down Shaun's arm 'till their hands met and fingers interlocked. He spread Shaun's fingers apart, placing his index finger to Shaun's thumb and vice versa, replicating *their* symbol, a shape that said more than a thousand words ever could.

"You shouldn't do it if you don't mean it," Shaun's voice trembled.

"Mean what, Shaun?" Stephen bit down on his bottom lip, extending his free hand out and placing it on Shaun's crotch, grabbing him firmly.

Shaun coughed out a quiet gasp.

Stephen kept hold, gripping his mate tightly in his hand, staring into his dark eyes which were torn between pleasure and fright. He felt Shaun's cock twitch and grow firm between his furled fingers.

"Please don't make fun of me," Shaun whispered, "I did say I'm sorry."

Stephen breathed heavily, releasing his grip on Shaun's dick and lunging toward him, causing Shaun to flinch. He grabbed Shaun's shirt, pulling him into his chest and wrapping his arms around him.

Shaun stood frozen, hands at his side, appearing utterly clueless as to what was happening.

Stephen felt the warmth of his friend's body radiating into him as he stared into the distance of the dark end of the beach. He let his hands wander over Shaun's back, willing him to relax.

Finally, Shaun gave in and rested his chin on Stephen's shoulder, his warm breath moistening Stephen's neck.

"Don't ever be sorry for being you," Stephen said, hugging him tight.

Stephen raised a hand up to Shaun's head and began twirling seductive fingers through his dark locks while continuing to stroke his back. He could feel Shaun's heart racing, his body a fever of nerves, worried if this was all a mean trick.

Only a few hundred metres away, revellers continued to party around their blazing fire, while the dark protected Stephen's apologetic moment from prying eyes.

Stephen poured breathy words into Shaun's ear, "You were right, by the way."

"About what?" Shaun asked, his body still stiff in the embrace.

"I was lonely... 'till I found you." Stephen leaned in and licked Shaun's neck, tasting his aftershave. He breathed in its scent before pecking Shaun on the cheek.

Shaun pulled back, looking Stephen straight in the eyes.

"You smell nice," Stephen confessed.

Shaun shook his head before muttering, "Fuck, you're beautiful." He relaxed his body completely and wrapped his hands around Stephen's waist.

"So, does that mean I can kiss you properly?" Stephen asked, raising his eyebrows.

Shaun looked down at the sand with a bashful grin on his face before returning to Stephen's stare. "Yeah, I think so," he said, emitting a soft chuckle. "You fucking better."

Stephen took the lead and placed his lips to Shaun's where they just pressed together. He pushed his tongue forward onto Shaun's bottom lip, letting his mate know to open up. Shaun did as his lips were told, obediently opening his mouth and allowing Stephen in. Stephen darted his tongue inside, wrapping it around Shaun's, tasting a sweet mix of bourbon and candy. Shaun's fringe fell forward, tickling his forehead, but he persevered. Their bodies pressed together as each other's hands pulled the other in closer, wanting more. They kissed hard and heavy for nearly a minute before Stephen retrieved his tongue, biting down gently on Shaun's bottom lip.

Stephen felt the electric current running through Shaun's body and his cock grinding against his own through their clothes. Shaun leaned in to kiss him again, hungry for more, but a noise coming from behind startled them and they let go of each other.

Stephen quickly jumped back, frightened by the thought of being seen like this with another man. They both looked down the beach towards the group of partygoers and saw a shadowy figure plonking towards them.

Thank fuck. Too far away to of seen anything.

Stephen's vision was slightly out of focus and he strained to make out who the approaching figure was.

"Shaun... it's Megan."

Megan was dragging her heavy feet slowly towards them, her head down, huffing as she walked over to the pair.

"Hey, Megan," Shaun's voice called out, cheery as it had ever been.

Now, that's how you're supposed to sound!

"I was worried about you," Megan said. "I came to see if everything's alright." Megan cast Stephen a suspicious glare.

"Yep, everything's fine," Shaun replied.

"That Luke and all his mates are such fuckwits." Her fist curled up as she growled.

Stephen knew she probably meant the 'all' to include him.

"You got that right," Shaun said.

Megan sighed. "I wanna go back to your mum's. It was better there."

"Really?" Shaun sounded surprised.

"Yeah, she had more drinks than they've got here." Megan laughed.

Shaun looked at Stephen who stood with his hands in pockets, desperate to hide his semi-erect cock.

"You wanna come with us?" Shaun asked.

Stephen looked at them both, deliberating what to do. "I better not."

"Oh," Shaun breathed out.

"But look, I'll give you a call tomorrow, yeah?" Stephen said.

Megan stood there with her arms folded, staring at

the sea, impatient to get a move on.

"Okay, I guess I'll hear from you then." Shaun sounded disappointed.

"That you will," Stephen said.

Megan began walking away, Shaun following after her with his head turning back every few seconds to look back at Stephen.

Stephen let out a soft chuckle and waved. Once Shaun and Megan had faded into the night, he sat alone for a few minutes processing the thrilling rush of what had just happened. He was scared by his impulsive behaviour, yet he couldn't wait to do it again.

CHAPTER TWENTY-FIVE — 1996

STEPHEN

Stephen lay fully clothed under his duvet, counting down the minutes 'till the clock struck 12:25 a.m. That was when he would sneak outside and scramble his way down the cliff face of his backyard boundary. Waiting for him at the reef below would be Shaun and a new chapter of their friendship.

The kiss the night before had blurred the lines between mates and tonight was about pushing even further into new territory. Stephen had awoken that morning with little remnants of a hangover. He had managed to finish New Year's Eve on a natural high with the taste of Shaun's mouth lingering on his lips for hours.

After lunch, he phoned Shaun as promised. The conversation proved just as awkward as Stephen had expected, with neither knowing what to really say. They spoke in a bizarre strand of subtle code, never specifically mentioning what had happened the night before, but talked enthusiastically about how they would meet for a catch up. Stephen wasn't entirely sure what a *catch up* between two men involved, but he was curious to find out.

Shaun was the one to suggest they meet down at the beach. This made sense to a point, but being the height of summer, the town still had loads of holidaying tourists, including late night strollers exploring Clifton's seaside stretch of paradise. This gave Stephen an idea, the beach traffic stopping at Cherry Lane and the short bend 'round the coast to the reef below Stephen's house offering the perfect point for them to meet in private. Stephen checked the newspaper for the tides and told Shaun 12:30 a.m. would be low tide: the best time for them to avoid getting drenched by the sea.

Stephen felt bad that all he had to do was sneak out

of his bedroom and stroll through the back garden then climb down the rock face to the reef. Shaun, though, would have to walk from his house to the beach and then trek along the sand for thirty minutes in the dark before making the same spot. Shaun didn't complain. He was more than willing to this plan because he must have known without it the chances of them meeting were slim. Sure, they could hang out at each other's houses, but the risk factor of being caught was too high.

Stephen rustled out from under the duvet and chucked on his sneakers, making his way quietly down the hall while treading softly so not to wake his folks up. He entered the living area and crossed the lounge to the ranch slider door. With the slightest of pulls, he opened it up and slipped outside into the warm night air. He could hear the sea delicately splashing its waves as he zig-zagged through the garden with its fruit trees and exotic flowers. At the cliff face and its tricky vertical track, he placed a careful foot on the first step, grateful for a nearly full moon that shone like a hundred-watt bulb.

Once at the bottom, he scanned the eerily quiet reef. Leaning against a large rock thirty-metres away, he could see Shaun in a white jumper and dark pants. Shaun hadn't spotted him yet and had begun slowly pacing back and forward, muttering to himself. Stephen navigated his way across the rough rocks of the reef, sneaking along with nimble steps.

"Do you need a moment alone with the voices?" Stephen blurted.

Shaun spun round in fright. When he saw it was Stephen, his face cringed in embarrassment. "Fuck, I didn't see you coming." He breathed heavily, calming his scare. "I was just building myself up to you know, umm... talk to you... and just like talk..." Shaun said, tossing out a salad of words.

Stephen went and leaned against the large rock; feet crossed, elbows back, feeling at ease. "So, did you end up having a big night with Megan?"

Shaun laughed. "I've told you, we aren't an item. And no, I left her in the lounge with Mum's lot drinking. I just went to bed pretty much as soon as we got back."

"Tired?"

Shaun tilted his head away. "I wanted to be alone and think about you."

"You don't need to be alone to do that."

Shaun smirked. "I may have done more than just thinking."

Stephen's ego got a thrill at this confession, smiling and sharing his own. "I *thought* about you too... twice."

Shaun chuckled and nodded like he was pleased with himself. His brown eyes looked almost black under the moonlight as he fixed his gaze intensely on Stephen.

Stephen could tell Shaun wanted to say something, but the words were trapped in his timid breath. He appeared fidgety and didn't seem too good at this flirting business. Stephen though, was finding it rather easier than expected—different gender, but same formula.

"You're cute when you're nervous," Stephen offered.

"I'm not cute." Shaun began pacing again. "Okay, maybe I am a little bit," he said giving Stephen a sly grin.

"I knew you were a cocky shit." Stephen walked towards Shaun, stopping right in front of him, putting his hands on Shaun's shoulders to halt his pacing.

Stephen wanted to see what lay beneath his mate's baggy clothes. Shaun's body was new terrain and he was determined to explore it. He had been around a near-naked Shaun before when swimming, but he had never paid much attention to the detail of his body. Not the way he wanted to right *now*. He wanted to see if his mate was naturally tanned all over; was he hairy or smooth? And fuck, he even wanted to know if he was hung.

Stephen moved his hand to the zipper locking Shaun's jumper shut, giving it a firm downward pull 'till it clicked open at the bottom, exposing a red t-shirt. Shaun stood still as if unsure of what to do next. This didn't faze Stephen in the slightest; he pounced on Shaun's hesitation as a form of surrendering and took charge of the moment. He could feel how anxious Shaun was, a sexy potion of longing and curiosity. Stephen took a step back and just stared at his number one fan standing there with his open sweater.

It's show time.

"Take your jumper off."

Shaun flashed an eager grin and pulled his arms out of the jumper, dropping it on the ground.

"And the shirt."

Shaun nodded, emitting a soft chuckle to himself, again quickly removing the article of clothing, leaving his top-half exposed.

Stephen reached his hand out and slowly traced two fingers down Shaun's warm smooth chest 'till he reached the hairy trail below his belly button. He let his fingers rest there, rubbing the furry strip which led down to what he really wanted to see, before gliding his hand back up and circling a finger around one of Shaun's perfect nipples. He gave it a gentle squeeze which made Shaun ripple with a shudder.

"You've got nice nipples."

"Thanks," Shaun whispered as he shivered lightly against the breeze.

Stephen's eyes fixated on Shaun's torso before glaring down at his black trousers. "Now your pants," he ordered.

Shaun gulped, standing inert, hesitant to obey.

Stephen tapped Shaun's shoe with his foot. "The pants," he prompted sternly.

Shaun craned his neck around, scanning the reef for any sign of hidden persons. He looked back at Stephen with brittle confidence.

Stephen stared back at him with impatient eyes that could easily be mistaken as anger.

Shaun relented, scuffing off his shoes and bending down to take off his white socks. His fingers fumbled at his waist 'till the sound of a zipper made Stephen's cock twitch. Shaun slid his pants down his legs and tugged them off his feet, dumping them on the ground with the rest of his clothes.

Barefoot in just tight black briefs, Shaun stood there with his arms folded, trying to hide an almost resentful look on his face.

Stephen raised his eyebrows, giving him a crooked smile.

Shaun knew what it meant. "But..."

Stephen shook his head. "Those off too."

Shaun looked at Stephen, his eyes pleading for mercy. Stephen gave him none. Shaun ran a hand through his hair, not sure of where to look. "Fuck," he muttered in a shaky whisper. With a deep breath, he hunched over and rose his knees up one at a time, freeing his body from the underwear before dropping them to the ground. His face wore a bittersweet look as he stood there naked, laid completely bare, an offering of flesh.

Stephen took in every detail from Shaun's skinny feet to his hairy tanned legs that became smooth above a tan line on his thighs. His snail-trail fed down to a nest of pubes where below, Shaun's cock was hard and pointing high. Stephen envied its perfect shape while feeling simultaneously proud and relieved that Shaun wasn't quite as big as him.

Shaun's body ruptured with nervousness standing so exposed to the elements and prone to judgement.

"Turn around," Stephen ordered. "Slowly," the word crawled out at the speed of its meaning.

Shaun's eyes questioned a still fully-clothed Stephen but yielded anyway, turning around as instructed, exposing his pale arse cheeks that matched the firmness of the rest of his slim and toned physique. Shaun laughed nervously, raising his hands behind his head averting his eyes from Stephen's burning gaze. "Well, now you've seen all of me," he said. "I've got nothing left to hide."

Stephen kept him hanging, enjoying the sight and power he had over someone so hooked on him.

"Am I allowed to see you now?" Shaun asked, his eyes begging for Stephen to capitulate. "Please?" he added feebly.

Stephen tilted his head, smiling. He stepped forward and brushed Shaun's cheek with his thumb.

Shaun's hands were still behind his head, closing his eyes as if he were expecting a punch.

"You're so hot," Stephen whispered, putting Shaun out of his misery. He planted his lips on Shaun's, locking their tongues together. They kissed so hard that Stephen swore he could taste the essence of Shaun, a flavour not dissimilar to forest rain. Nature and wild intermixed, a body not yet tamed.

The kiss chipped away at Shaun's anxiety as his hands dropped down from behind his head and latched onto Stephen's hips to reel him in. Stephen slipped his hand between their bodies and gripped hold of Shaun's cock, squeezing it tight. Shaun gasped in his mouth.

Plying their lips apart, Stephen sucked in a breath of air before ripping his own clothes off as fast as possible, joining Shaun in being bare-arse naked beneath the stars.

Shaun's eyes were immediately drawn to Stephen's cock. He reached out his hand almost warily and wrapped his fingers around it, squeezing firmly as he explored Stephen's girth. Stephen quivered when Shaun's fingers worked their way to the tip, swivelling around in the precum he couldn't stop from dribbling. Shaun's face looked down in disbelief like he'd wondered where it all came from.

Trust me. That's all from you.

Stephen leaned his face into Shaun's neck, reaching around to clutch Shaun's smooth arse cheeks. "Can I fuck you?" he groaned in Shaun's ear.

Shaun pulled back. "What, here?"

"Yes, here." Stephen ran a finger down Shaun's crack, emphasising his internal intent.

"But I've never done this," Shaun professed.

"True, but neither have I."

"No, like I've never done *anything*... with a guy or a chick."

If it hadn't been so dark, Stephen would have sworn Shaun was blushing. "Oh..."

All the virgin teasing was true.

"Lame, I know, but it's just never happened. Like, I wanna do it, and especially with you, but I dunno if I can... well, not here."

Stephen stared into Shaun's apprehensive eyes. "Are you sure? 'Cos seriously, I'm gonna explode soon," Stephen said with the hint of a smirk. This would be his first time with a guy, but it would be Shaun's first time with anyone—the uncharted realm he could claim as the conqueror made him want this even more.

"Sorry... I will let you. I promise. Just... not tonight." Shaun said, sounding more like he was asking for permission.

Stephen knew that with one command Shaun would subserviently bend over the rock, part his cheeks and grit his teeth through the pain, making sure he took every inch of

Stephen's cock just to please him. All he had to do was say.
I have all the power.

Stephen opened his mouth, about to bark a demeaning order when, out of nowhere, a wave of shame came over him for having such ruthless thoughts.

"I understand," Stephen exhaled.

Shaun smiled sympathetically. "Let me make it up to you." He lowered his face and kissed Stephen's small amount of chest hair, slowly working his mouth down, stopping every third peck to bite and suck. Shaun lowered himself 'till his knees rested on the rough rocks of the reef. He pulled his face back, his mouth hovering only inches away from Stephen's cock. He appeared enamoured by it as he just stared in awe before slowly coming forward and softly kissing the precum-covered tip. Stephen's cock jerked at the feel of the light peck from another man's lips. He thought Shaun was about to give him another kiss, but instead he opened wide, seizing Stephen's hard dick inside his mouth and began sucking eagerly.

Stephen held the back of Shaun's head, gripping tufts of his hair, guiding him in the steady rhythm he liked. Shaun's hands roamed up and down the back of his legs, occasionally cupping his balls all the while keeping Stephen deep and wet in his mouth. The sound of slurping and the feel of Shaun's warm tongue was getting Stephen dangerously close; he was about to say stop, but before he could sputter out the words, he groaned loudly as his cock erupted into Shaun's mouth.

Stephen's body shook and shivered from its premature release. He waited for Shaun to spit him out and complain about the taste of what he had just been fed. Instead, he kept his head in place, waiting for Stephen's cock to stop twitching and spurting. Shaun slowly pulled back and, in one big gulp, swallowed the lot. He wiped his lips and stared up at Stephen with a huge grin painted across his face.

Fucking legend!

The lines were more than blurred—they had been obliterated.

CHAPTER TWENTY-SIX — 1996

DEBBIE

The apple never falls far from the tree.
Debbie use to hear this a lot growing up. It was one of many pearls of borrowed wisdom her mother, Rhonda, liked to spew out. The rancid old bag of bones breathed out sayings almost as much as she fired out smoke from her forty-a-day habit. Debbie had never been fond of the woman since leaving the womb; she was a premature baby, and Debbie suspected her baby-self knew well enough to escape the bitter prison that was her mother's body as soon as possible.

Debbie, being the youngest of four children, at fourteen was left alone with the long-divorced Rhonda and a shared air of resentment. In an attempt to escape the old bitch any chance she could, Debbie began sneaking out of the house every night, going off and drinking with a crowd of friends older than herself. Rhonda was so clueless, she didn't even notice her daughter's rebel excursions. Debbie would sneak out once her mother was in bed or passed out with a vodka bottle in her hand, go have her fun, then creep back inside at some ridiculous hour, falling asleep drunk and a little cheaper than when she had left.

Rhonda discovered her secret life by accident and instead of being mad, all she said in a laugh was, "The apple never falls far from the tree. You'll end up like me, you will."

As if.

There was no way Debbie was going to end up like her, yet twenty-three years later, here she was single in Clifton, drinking every day, smoking like a train and being an absentminded mother.

Know it all bitch.

After a couple years though, these nights out led to

the most amazing thing that had ever happened to Debbie. Mitch Munro.

Mitch would be at the same parties, usually talking nonstop. The man was a real live wire who drew her in with his confident charm and she knew she drew him in too. His eyes would always light up whenever she walked in the room and, after some frisky flirting, they soon became an item. The dark-haired Mitch was tall and solid with broad shoulders... and knew how to fight. In Debbie's mind, this made him the perfect protector—in his muscly tattooed arms, she felt tiny and needed.

He told her he had grandiose plans; he would make it *big*. He insisted to Debbie that together they could make a real life. Without much convincing, she packed up her stuff and left the heartless Rhonda and Auckland behind, heading south to Taranaki where Mitch had a mate with some land where he could begin making their 'fortune,' he'd called it. When they arrived, and she saw that this 'fortune' was in the form of cultivating illicit crops of cannabis, she should have known better, but of course, she ignored the voice in her head telling her to leave. Mitch was her king and she his queen. Besides, as Mitch said, if they kept their mouths shut, they'd live the good life and for a while that's exactly what they had.

Far from a fortune, they did amass a comfortable lifestyle, one that was full of drug-induced bliss. Debbie settled into Clifton quickly, making friends with Mitch's customers and running the most social house in town. Parties were frequent and spontaneous events; Debbie loved all the attention she received. Mitch would get wild at the looks men gave her, but it made her feel good, especially knowing he loved her enough to get jealous. Within a year, she was pregnant with Shaun and the years flew by with Lydia, too, coming into the world.

As time went by though, Mitch became less jealous and more abusive. Debbie had always had long gorgeous hair, but in his fits of rage, he would drag her up the hallway by it for her hiding. Mitch, being the *decent* bloke that he was, wouldn't hit her in front of the kids. In an attempt to take this part of the ritual away from the bastard, she'd shaved her hair off in short, buzz-cut styles. When she had come home with the new do, Mitch was disgusted. "Fucking hell, woman, you think I wanna fuck a boy or something?" He soon grew use to it and the rough love continued with shoving, instead of dragging, becoming the violent means of transportation to the bedroom.

The beatings only got worse through the years, and by then, Shaun and Lydia were old enough to be getting affected by it. Of course, a stronger woman would have left, but then that would mean running out on this man and, despite his good moments being few and far between, she stayed.

One night, his abuse took a sinister turn when he rounded her up in the bedroom and drunkenly waved his rifle at her before making her sleep beside the cold metal of the barrel. This became the new fucked-up norm. The kids became terrified of their father. She would hear their crying over the fighting and this ripped her heart out that she couldn't do anything.

The worst moment was one evening, bailed up in the corner of her bedroom, screaming for Mitch to put the gun down when Shaun—no more than eleven—walked in pleading with his dad to stop hurting Mum. Mitch told the boy to fuck off and as he lifted the gun up at Debbie in front of him, Shaun raced across the room and grabbed Mitch by the leg, punching and screaming, begging him to stop. Mitch raised the rifle and slammed the butt of it into Shaun's face, sending the boy dazed to the floor with blood pissing out of his forehead. A scar remains on his eyebrow to this day from the lousy prick's handiwork.

Debbie was ashamed of what she did next. *Nothing.* She didn't leave her man; she stayed like she always did. To prevent another incident of Mitch hurting the kids, she gave Shaun her old bible; she'd had no use for it for a long time and told the boy that if there was ever any trouble, "Just read this to your sister and pray. I promise this means nothing bad will happen." This had been a lie. The alternative would have been telling the kids to ring 111, but Debbie knew that would mean Mitch could leave her and it wasn't a risk she was willing to take.

As Debbie now sat drinking in the lounge, lost in memories, guilt cut her raw for never leaving such a monster. Instead, it was Mitch who'd abandoned her, fleeing to

Australia after hearing the cops were coming to bust him. They'd flown in with choppers and sprayed the weed, turning up at the house for Mitch only to find he'd disappeared, leaving Debbie six months pregnant and facing charges of possession. She had managed to lay the blame on Mitch and got off lightly, but since then she hadn't met another Mitch—another man to be her king.

After a year of feeling sorry for herself and the snobby wives in town looking down on her, Debbie decided she would live her life how she wanted and on her own terms. Still in great shape, she grew her hair back, and with the help of a little makeup, could still make men drool.

It wasn't the judging eyes of wealthy locals that annoyed her so much, it was more the fact no one treated her or her kids as being part of the community. It was as if these people thought if you didn't have shit loads of cash or owned acres of land, you were excluded from having some sort of connection to this place they all called home.

But Debbie knew they were wrong. You didn't need a lot of something to feel connected to it. Just one metre, one moment or one look was sometimes all it took to get attached to something or someone.

So while the rich bastards and their wives would crow about in town with their oversized dick-extension vehicles, beautiful jewellery, and their kids' bullshit achievements, she kept herself in shape. They could have all of that. Debbie knew she had her own power, the power of being able to make the wives feel helpless in holding onto their men from straying into her bed or anywhere she pleased.

Once a man had strayed, they dared not cross her unless they wanted their secrets exposed with a spray of perfume on a pillow or their clothes, leaving behind the scent of betrayal. This mean streak she had inherited from the best, her mum.

The apple never falls far from the tree.

Recently, her mother's old saying had been lurking in her mind a lot as she observed her son. The past few months she noticed her overly chatty boy who could be a pain in the arse with his nonstop banter—the only trait he had acquired from his father, whereas Lydia was practically Mitch with tits—had become much more subdued at home. Shaun had lost his appetite; he would cook for everyone, then not have any dinner for himself, insisting he wasn't hungry. It was like he was running on some invisible fuel. Debbie knew this behaviour well. She knew the fuel he was running on.

Shaun was in love.

She dared not ask because he would likely tell her to mind her own business as he and Lydia often did. This quiet behaviour went on for quite some time, until finally he had begun to get visits from Stephen Davis. It wasn't obvious at first, but Debbie began to notice each time the handsome cow cocky with those baby blues turned up, Shaun would behave a little differently. He pandered to Stephen, fetching him anything under the bloody sun; that is, after asking him if he would like anything from under the bloody sun.

One night when Debbie was slunk in her chair, half-cut, she saw the way Shaun brought Stephen his drink and the way her son's hand rested a little too long on his mate's shoulder. A caring glint in his eyes whenever he looked at Stephen, a look that contained one of life's cruel contradictions—blissful, pained longing.

Yep, Shaun was in love, and it was with Stephen Davis.

Debbie didn't care that his love was for another man. You were free to do what you like in her books. It wasn't like she could judge anyone, especially with all the dumb shit she had done over the years, but she did worry for her boy. That life was a hard one and especially when you're crushing after the type of guy Stephen was.

She didn't have a problem with Stephen. In fact, he was polite to her and friendly to the kids, but she knew all too well guys like Stephen Davis. She'd fucked enough of them to know they looked down on people like her and her family, and they sure as shit didn't stick around.

Debbie figured it would be a crush that would pass once Shaun realised Stephen was probably only visiting for pot, but just that week she'd gotten one hell of a surprise to see how wrong she was. Now when Stephen would visit, there was an air of electric to him, and when he would stand up to go grab them each a drink, it was *his* affectionate hand resting a little too long on her son's shoulder.

This was a shared queer feeling and not one Debbie

would have picked. In a way, despite Shaun being a larrikin mechanic type, he had always had a vibe… somehow different from other lads his age. *But Stephen?* Stephen came as a shock. The guy had a reputation around town for sure, screwing his way through the ladies, breaking girls' hearts and virtues in one go. Had he not been born with a cock, his name would surely be covered in more dirt than Debbie's.

 This pairing scared her. Pretty boys like Stephen attracted everybody, with their deep layers of beauty and allure, but the truth was guys like that only had depths of bullshit you could drown in if you weren't careful. Shaun, like her, was attracted to the same kind of man. One who posed such promise, yet was bad for your health.

 Of her three children, Shaun was the softest. His strength of kindness, which had been such a big help with raising his sisters, was also his weakness.

 When he was about to turn ten, he had planned himself a big birthday party, one with a superhero theme and had spent weeks coming up with ideas and games. He even designed his own invites which he then handed out at school. When the big day finally arrived, Debbie had a Superman cake all ready and the house all done up in colourful streamers and banners. Shaun sat in the lounge, waiting patiently, but not *one* of those shitty kids ever arrived. Not fucking one.

 Her little man who had been so excited about turning ten and thinking all his friends would turn up was left devastated. Debbie was furious. She knew why they weren't there, but how do you explain that to a child? She wanted to go 'round to every one of the cunting parents' houses and scream blue murder at them, but she resisted, knowing it would only drag the Munro name through the mud even more.

 When it got an hour past the start time, she saw Shaun wiping tears from his eyes, realising no one was coming. Debbie, as absent drunk mother as she was, unlike Rhonda, did give a shit, so she found Mitch's wallet and took two-hundred dollars without asking. She loaded Shaun and Lydia in the car and drove them to Rainbows End amusement park in Auckland and let them spend the afternoon riding on anything they wanted. The beating Mitch gave her for taking the money had been worth seeing her boy happy again, but Shaun had never really learned that these people weren't his friends.

Even when those same kids pissed off to boarding school, he would bend over backwards to hang out with them on summer breaks when they came home and desperately clambered to be their mate. Shaun was blind to the fact they didn't think of him as a mate; they didn't even view him as their equal.

Shaun saw the best in everyone and took pity on the wounded, he always had. Debbie used to have this empathy, but she gave it away when she'd learned it could infect you and leave your heart bleeding. Her son was just like her and this worried Debbie to no end, knowing he was destined to make the same mistakes. With a sense of repulsion, maybe Rhonda was right after all.

The apple never falls far from the tree.

CHAPTER TWENTY-SEVEN — 1996

STEPHEN

Night time rendezvouses governed by the tide had become a surreptitious adventure. Stephen would scramble down the cliff's dicey track at some ridiculous hour every night where he would find Shaun waiting for him at the reef. The hour always changed according to the pull of the moon, but their attendance was consistent.

They would waste no time in ditching their clothes, exploring each other's bodies with greedy hands and hungry mouths, learning every inch in dedicated detail. Afterwards, Shaun would roll them a joint and they'd sit talking, swapping intimate stories. The committing of unspeakable acts gifted them freedom to talk openly. Nothing was off limits. Dreams, hopes, past shames and supposed sins. Each would sit there listening to the other's seaside sermon until they would bid farewell with a kiss, leaving before the sea rushed to shore, washing away their spilled secrets and burying the rocks they got their rocks off on.

Stephen's days were spent working, sprinkled with afternoon naps to catch the hours he was losing in the middle of the night. He knew he should have been way more tired than he was, but Shaun had become his fuel.

It was hard now, sitting in the same room as Shaun, holding back the urge to just lean over and kiss or touch him. There was a thrilling perversion in knowing what Shaun looked like under his clothes, which way his cock hung, the smoothness of his chest and arse. Knowing that if he grabbed the arch of Shaun's foot he would squirm erotically or how licking his left nipple caused him to shiver and moan.

Normally, Stephen would walk around shirtless during summer, but Shaun's penchant for biting—especially when he was about to cum—had left Stephen's chest covered in purple love bites. Stephen had to insist Shaun not sink his sharp teeth into his neck. Days of being a school boy wearing hickeys like a war medal were well over. Still, he enjoyed this secret they shared, that underneath their clothes lay signs of ownership—ravished flesh that marked the other's territory.

They would hand each other items for no good reason other than to sneak a touch of the other's hand or an affectionate pat on the shoulders or back. One time they were very nearly busted when Lydia barged into Shaun's room unannounced. They had been lying on the bed together, hands entwined, kissing when the door had flung open. With lightning reflexes, they quickly pretended to be wrestling and goofing around. Lydia didn't even blink, completely unaware; she just called them dorks and, after grabbing one of Shaun's CDs, walked straight back out. When alone again, Stephen had broken into a cold sweat while Shaun just laughed about the close call.

The thrill of getting caught seemed to excite Shaun, whereas it terrified Stephen. He had no desire to leave the light of the accepted and step into the shadow of an outcast. He was trapped in a bubble of lust for Shaun and, provided no one knew their bubble existed, there was no way it was going to pop.

∞

They made their first public appearance as friends together when Stephen invited Shaun along to have lunch with Troy and Clare. Shaun kept a watchful eye over his shoulder, waiting for a pissed off Luke to turn up but, thankfully, he never did. Stephen had hoped Luke would calm down and be glad he only had broken fingers and not a criminal charge, but he doubted Luke would see it that way.

The café was relatively empty as they sat beside each other across from Troy and Clare who were leaving that weekend to go to Auckland. Troy had one last year of study and Clare was going with him to set up home before they began playing the happy family.

Troy waffled on about the new house his parents had

bought for him, Clare and the baby. "Yeah, it's a good street, aye, and not too far from campus."

Stephen felt Shaun's leg pressing against his, causing a stir in his pants.

Clare chimed in, "You'll have to come up and see it once we're settled in."

Stephen nodded along dutifully to the conversation, trying to control a semi hard-on under the table. The next thing Stephen knew, Shaun's hand was touching his knee.

Troy prodded Stephen's shoulder. "Go on, mate, wrangle a weekend off from your folks and come stay."

Shaun's hand moved up past Stephen's knee, colliding with his crotch in a firm grope. Stephen coughed and sputtered on his food. Shaun quickly moved his hand away.

"Are you okay?" Clare asked.

"Ha, yeah, just went down the wrong way," Stephen fibbed.

Shaun flashed the clueless couple a smile. "He needs to be more careful when he swallows."

After the lunch, Stephen bailed Shaun up in the car. "What the fuck were you thinking?"

The smirk on Shaun's face signalled he knew exactly what Stephen was getting at. "That you're just way too hot not to touch?" he said, giving Stephen's knee a light squeeze.

Stephen rolled his eyes. "Fuck sake, Shaun, we could've been busted."

"We weren't though, were we?" Shaun replied calmly.

"That's not the point."

"Sorry," Shaun mumbled. "I forgot you're meant to be ashamed of me."

Stephen instantly felt bad for losing his cool. "I'm not ashamed of you, nothing like that. I just... just don't want us to be found out. This is between us. Just discrete fun. Nobody's business but ours." Stephen flashed him one of his disarming smiles.

Shaun's eyes caught the smile. "I guess that's good to know," he said indifferently.

"What?"

"Oh nothing, but I was gonna ask what we were, you and me. But I didn't want to sound like a chick." Shaun laughed, suddenly sounding jovial.

Stephen stared at him, sceptical of what looked like a fake smile.

Shaun put his seatbelt on and fidgeted with his invisible leg creases. "Nothing wrong with fun, aye? Shit, fun is good, 'cos fun is fun," Shaun continued, sounding like a man trying to convince himself.

Perhaps this made sense. The past few weeks, Stephen had been struggling with what all of this made him. Shaun already knew what he was, so his battle was trying to work out what *they* were. Stephen hadn't even begun to process that. He wasn't sure he even wanted to because as soon as he did, he was potentially going to let Shaun down or—maybe worse—let himself down by shattering his own idea of who he thought he was.

Stephen sighed, breathing in the awkward vibe in the car. "Look, you're not JUST fun. If you were just fun, we wouldn't be meeting every night, would we? You know what I mean."

Shaun looked at him with discernible confusion. "Yeah, I know what you mean."

Fuck sake.

Since Ricky's death, his future had been so mapped out. Farm, wife, kids, Clifton for life. Shaun had stirred something in him that could change this plan, but the problem was he couldn't change the plan. The plan was the plan. He dropped Shaun off home and was left to stew alone in a car stained with guilt.

CHAPTER TWENTY-EIGHT — 1996

STEPHEN

Stephen had lied to Shaun that he was headed straight home. Instead, he was off to see Luke, who had fortunately cancelled on the lunch with Troy and Clare. Otherwise, Shaun's attendance would have been a no-go for sure.

Stephen pulled up outside Luke's house, juggling in his mind how he could convince Luke to call a truce with Shaun and bury the hatchet. The front yard looked parched, patches of powdery dirt tainting its lawn which screamed out for rain and relief from the effects of a long, hot summer. He knocked on the door, calling out three times. After no response, he peered through the lounge window and found no sign of Luke being home.

Stephen got back in his car and continued up the road to Luke's parents' place. Luke's mum, Irene, was outside the house, knelt over and weeding her colourful flower garden. Her trunk-like legs were exposed in a knee-length dress, lumpy varicose veins worming up their sides. When she saw Stephen approach, she stood up, brushing dirt and weed bits off the front of her dress and greeted him with a huge smile.

He hadn't seen her since her dramatic exit from the grocery store when she zoomed off in peril. Stephen felt incredibly awkward, wishing he had not witnessed a friend's mother so emotional. He smiled back at her and waved.

"Hello, stranger," she beamed. Stephen knew that neither of them would mention the meltdown outside the shop.

"Hi, Mrs B."

"Are you looking for my firstborn pride-and-joy?" she joked.

"That I am." Stephen smiled.

"He's 'round back in the workshop, I think." Irene

wiped a garden glove-covered hand across her brow. "Anyway, how come we haven't seen you in so long?"

Growing up, he and Luke had practically been part of the furniture at each other's houses. Even after Luke moved down the road when the Bridgemans' last worker left, Stephen still came here frequently, usually assisting Luke with raiding the Bridgeman family fridge and pantry to pile up Luke's own desolate food stocks down the road.

"Just busy, I guess," Stephen responded.

"You been up to no good?"

"Absolutely."

"Glad to hear it, so you bloody should be," Irene said. "Hopefully, you can go out there and cheer moody arse up. He's been so miserable since the accident."

"The accident?" Stephen asked, frowning.

"You know, when the bloody oaf came off the bike and broke his hands," Irene shook her head.

"True, of course." Stephen nodded, realising Luke was at least wise enough to keep it secret why he had broken hands.

"When you see him, please tell the lazy sod to get back to work, would you?"

"Will do, Mrs B." Stephen laughed and continued on towards the front door. The Bridgemans' home wasn't the flashiest with its deceptively plain appearance and random extensions, but the house was a lively one with three teenage sons still living at home. Once inside, Stephen found two of Luke's brothers in the lounge, playing on their Sega Mega Drive. It appeared Sonic and Tails were on a mission of some sort. The burly brothers both looked up and spoke in unison—"Hey Stephen"—before looking straight back at the screen, elbowing one another in a fruitless bid to put the other off. Stephen raised his eyebrows as a quick hello, and continued through the lounge, making his way to the kitchen where he went through a side door to the 'workshop,' otherwise known as Luke's old bedroom.

He opened the door and walked straight into a hanging red mass. Stunned, Stephen rubbed his face from the soft hit and saw he'd collided with one of Luke's punching bags.

The room smelt repugnant with a heavy stale stench,

one that reminded Stephen of his school days and the gym locker room. Corrugated iron walls and cobwebbed wooden beams gave away the room's original purpose as Mr Bridgeman's man shed. The fact Luke had never frozen to death while sleeping in there growing up was a miracle. Stephen manoeuvred around the punching bag and dumbbells on the concrete floor, finding Luke sitting on a tatty brown couch, his hands no longer in plaster.

"Hey, mate," Stephen greeted his pal in a cheery tone.

Luke looked up, surprised to see him. "Oh, hey, man," he muttered back.

"You got your hands back."

Luke held his hands out staring at them, slowly curling his fingers. "Yeah, came off last week. Fuck, it's good to be able to do shit again."

"I bet." Stephen looked around the room, taking in its walls covered in Playboy spreads. Pamela Anderson took centre stage above an old television set. "How come you not at your place?"

"Mum's cooking, bro." Luke smiled.

Stephen laughed. "I should've known."

"How was Troy and Clare?"

"Yeah, good, aye. How come you didn't make it?"

Luke shrugged. "Couldn't be arsed."

"One of those days, aye?"

"You could say that." Luke stood up and went to a small fridge in the corner of the room, its outer case spray-painted black. He fetched out a beer and held it up. "You want one?"

"Not for me, thanks."

Luke opened his drink and sat back down, spreading his solid limbs over the couch. "So, what about you, Stevie boy? I ain't seen you in ages. Don't s'pose you got a secret underage Mrs too?" Luke cocked an eyebrow as he sucked back on his drink.

"Nar, nothing quite so illegal. Just settling back into work." Stephen felt uneasy knowing that his beautiful lie was the reason for his mates slow-to-mend fingers.

Stephen pulled up an old wooden chair beside the couch and sat with his legs astride leaning forward, resting his chin on the seat's back. The summer had certainly seen a cooling in their friendship, first with Luke's secret affair and now with Stephen having his own. It took a while for the conversation to flow naturally as Stephen wondered how best to bring up the subject of Shaun. It turned out he didn't have to. Luke did it for him.

"Are you still hanging out with that Munro fuckwit?" Luke's tone sounded resentful.

"Uh, yeah, seen him about a couple times when I've come into town."

Luke stared blankly ahead at the glossy image of Pam Anderson on the wall. "Well, next time you see the little faggot, tell him he's a dead man." Luke looked down at his hands and slowly squeezed his fists before retracting them in a wince of pain. "Once these are fully right, I'm gonna get the cunt."

Stephen's stomach somersaulted, wanting to scream at Luke, to tell him to back off and not speak badly about someone he cared about. He resisted the urge to defend Shaun so recklessly, knowing this would only make Luke suspicious or think he was crazy.

Stephen bit down on his lip. "Look, don't you think it's best you just drop it? Lydia was underage and, fuck, you don't want them to press charges."

"Come on, man. You and me both know it's far from rape, other than her age. Fuck, look who her mother is," Luke laughed callously. "Nar, the way I see it, Lydia wouldn't let them make a fuss. She doesn't want a rep," Luke said, hitting the nail on the head.

"Seriously though, what the fuck were you thinking, man?" Stephen returned. Luke frowned at him like it was a stupid question. "Okay, yeah, I get that you were thinking with the little fella, but why be such a prick to her?"

Luke huffed as he leaned back into the couch. "This is rich coming from Mr-fuck-n-chuck."

Stephen didn't respond. Luke was right. Stephen was a hypocrite if he lectured anyone on bedside manners.

"Look, Stevie, she's just like her mother, a convenient place for a guy to stick their cock. And sure, it was fun while it lasted, but I got my reasons for ending it the way I did."

Oh, like not giving a satisfactory blowjob?

"And as for Shaun, trust me, I'll fucking end him."

"Oh, come on. You were mates before this."

"What are you on? He's just a scabby prick who supplied us with pot." Luke looked at Stephen, waiting for mutual confirmation. "He ain't one of us."

Stephen shook his head. "He isn't that bad. He's just a bit try-hard and he was only trying to protect his sister." Stephen could see this meant nothing to Luke. "You'd do the same for your brothers."

Luke scoffed at the suggestion. "Fuck off I would. They're big and ugly enough to fight their own battles, just like Lydia is." Luke pulled a crude smile. "Nope, trust me. That little weasel has it coming and it's gonna be a hell of a lot worse than broken fingers when I'm done with him." Luke turned away and angrily sculled on his beer. "I'll be following that little fucker and when he least expects it, I'll fucking be there."

Luke was talking big, but he was also crystal clear with his intentions, his words chilling Stephen to the bone.

CHAPTER TWENTY-NINE — 2016

STEPHEN

Stephen smiled at the sight before him. Inver, completely wet through from rain and barely able to stand from being so drunk. An hour earlier, the skies had opened up and heaved a torrential rain that still hadn't quit. Unfortunately for Inver, he had been dropped off during this downpour and his short walk to the house had left him looking like a drowned rat with his dark curls matted down his face.

Kimmy had more than done her part by getting the lad shit-faced and delivering him home courtesy of a kind sober driver. Now it was up to Stephen to take the revenge to the next level and seal the deal.

He fought the small piece inside of him that gnawed in guilt. Inver was a nice guy. Having him around had made the house more alive and it had been nice to have the company, but that couldn't stand in the way of proving Rusty wrong that he was immune from creating a gay son. Well, Inver may not be gay, Stephen thought, but he will certainly have done gay shit by the end of tonight and no doubt go home to Auckland riddled with shame.

In a rambling of drunken excitement, Inver tried to tell Stephen how much fun he had had as he stood on the lounge carpet, dripping water from his soggy clothes. Inver hugged his arms across his chest; he was frozen, but so drunk he didn't seem to notice how badly his body craved warmth.

"Did you want me to light the fire up?" Stephen asked.

"Ye-ye-yes, please," Inver replied with chattering teeth.

Stephen knelt down and threw a couple bits of wood into the fire, landing on top of dull red embers of pinecones.

The clunky bits of wood behaved stubbornly and were slow at catching alight as Inver sat hugging his knees, shivering under a blanket of wet material.

Stephen left Inver sitting alone in front of the fire while he went and fetched a clean towel and the clothes horse from the airing cupboard. He returned to the lounge where he assembled the clothes horse while Inver watched with curious eyes.

Stephen held the towel up. "Right you, we need to get you dry before you freeze to death."

Inver put a wobbly arm out, trying to take the towel from him.

Stephen shook his head. "Let me."

Inver dropped his hand.

Stephen flicked his chin up. "Arms up."

Inver's hands shot up and he wiggled his long slim fingers. Stephen leaned down and clutched at Inver's waist, grabbing the bottom of his shirt. It peeled off slowly, clinging to Inver's skin before getting stuck 'round his head as he thrashed about laughing at Stephen trying to free him from it.

"Hold still," Stephen grumbled, and with one firm tug it came up over his head freeing Inver's outstretched arms.

Inver ran a hand through his wet curls as he flashed Stephen a cheesy grin. "I think you nearly tore my head off."

"Sorry." Stephen picked up the towel and planted it on Inver's head, his hands working in deft movements through the towel, drying Inver's hair and the nape of his neck.

"That's nice," Inver mumbled from underneath.

Stephen stood back, inspecting Inver's now fuzzy hair. "Wow, I think someone definitely needs a haircut."

"I know, right?" Inver agreed.

"Stand up."

Inver got to his feet in clumsy fashion, swaying slightly. Stephen wiped his guest's pale chest and stomach down before going behind him and doing the same to his damp back. He grabbed Inver by the wrist and raised his arm up gently, dabbing the towel over the black hair in his armpits before gliding down to Inver's hip. Stephen could smell the rain on Inver's skin, a strange freshness which he had to resist the urge to lick and taste.

He repeated the same drying technique down the other side of Inver's torso before coming back and standing in front of him.

Inver had a look of caution in his eyes as he saw Stephen's hands coming towards him, going for the belt of his jeans. Stephen loosened the belt, pulling it slowly, its leather length snaking its way through the loops of Inver's jeans 'till it was off and flung to the floor.

"Now the legs," Stephen said with steely demand.

Inver appeared nervous as he swallowed a dry lump behind his saturated lips. He took his shoes off and went to undo his jeans, but Stephen grabbed his hand to stop him.

Stephen smiled. "I'll take care of that." His fingers grabbed hold of the cold metal zip, the sound of it coming down making Stephen aware he was going to enjoy this more than he had originally thought. The jeans opened up to show Inver was wearing the briefs he had given him the night before. Stephen crouched down and pulled the wet denim down the length of Inver's hairy legs, Stephen's face only a matter of inches from his guest's bulge. Inver raised his feet for Stephen to dispose of the pants and wet socks.

"I think you've seen me naked more this week than anyone has all year," Inver joked, trying to tone down the undeniable vibe in the room.

"I thought a good-looking guy like you would have them lined up." Stephen said, working the towel up in-between Inver's thighs, purposely brushing his hand ever-so-briefly against Inver's smooth balls.

"Not exactly," Inver returned on a sigh.

Stephen planted his hand on Inver's arse cheek, pressing, guiding his drunken guest to spin 'round. Inver shuffled his feet, turning around for him, letting Stephen have a full rear view. Stephen took a breath that came out as a low growl as he admired Inver's toned back and firm arse cheeks. He wiped the remaining raindrops from Inver's body, starting at the lad's broad shoulders and working his way down to the arch of his back before gliding the towel over his arse crack, resisting the urge to press a finger in. "All done," Stephen declared.

Inver sat back down in front of the fire while Stephen hung the wet clothes to dry on the clothes horse. The room had begun to heat up nicely, offering a stark contrast to the cold, rainy night outside. Stephen went and sat on the arm of the couch, his elbows hitched on his knees, leaning forward, basking in the sight of awkwardness he had created.

Inver sat with bent knees, his hands placed in front of his crotch, trying to provide himself some modesty. The poor guy didn't know where to look. Stephen was fine with the silence, leering across at Inver, inspecting his body.

The last time Stephen had done this was very different terrain, Inver offering longer limbs and a hairy chest, one which Stephen took a moment to wonder about. *How would it feel to rub against my own?*

Inver stared up at Stephen like he was studying him in return. "I wish I looked more like you," he blurted out.

Stephen was taken aback by the odd compliment. "You do?"

"Yeah, you could have anyone you wanted, probably. That'd be nice to feel." Inver hugged his legs into his chest, resting his chin on his knees.

Stephen laughed. "Twenty years ago maybe, but not now. Now I'm just a mere mortal like the rest." Stephen didn't understand why this guy couldn't see what he had going for him. "You're young and handsome with a big dick, so I don't think you've got anything to worry about." Stephen chose his words carefully, veering Inver to where he wanted him.

"Thanks, but probably only one of those things is true."

"And which one might that be?" Stephen raised his eyebrows.

Inver laughed. "Ha, the last one."

"Which was?" Stephen wanted to hear him say it.

"I've got a big dick."

Inver was ripe for the picking.

"Show me then," Stephen said.

"Sorry?"

"Your dick. Show me."

"But you've seen it." Inver frowned, confused by the request.

"Not properly."

Inver shuffled uncomfortably, looking at Stephen

who stared back with driven intent in his eyes. Inver released a nervy chuckle. "Okay then." He removed his hands that were clasped over his knees and spread his legs apart. He shook his head and muttered, "Fuck, this is embarrassing."

Sheesh. He was bigger than Stephen had thought and the embarrassment wasn't just from showing Stephen his cock.

"I've got wood. I think it's from the carpet," Inver said defensively. His dick stuck out semi-erect. He appeared to become relaxed and left his legs wide and open, allowing Stephen to stare at his handsome prick. Inver looked like he wanted to say something, but put a hand to his mouth before the words could escape.

"What is it?" Stephen asked.

"Umm, I was gonna say that you can touch it if you like?" Inver shot a hand across his mouth like he couldn't believe he had just said the words out loud.

Stephen laughed at the drunken offering, surprised to be invited so freely. Inver's desperate need to impress was making this all too easy.

"Shit, sorry. I'm just so drunk," Inver said. He closed his legs.

Stephen said nothing. He stood up and walked over to Inver, bent down and placed a hand on his drunken guest's ankle. He glided his hand up Inver's hairiness, pressing firmly with his fingers as he did so. Inver spread his legs apart again, granting access to his cock which Stephen didn't hesitate to take hold of; he squeezed it in his hand, feeling it pulse between his curled fingers. He reached lower and cupped Inver's nuts, enjoying the feel of his smooth, shaved balls before returning his hand to Inver's shaft, feeling it grow in girth.

Nothing needed to be said. Inver was at the point needed to be broken. Stephen was about to go fetch his supplies in the drawer next to his bed when Inver spoke, "I'm so bloody confused." The words came out in slips and slurs between his lips and, out of nowhere, he began to cry in dramatic, drunken heaves. "Sorry, I don't know what's wrong with me."

Stephen let go of him. "It's alright, mate. You're just really, really, super-fucking really drunk." Stephen chuckled, hoping the light-heartedness would be soothing.

Inver looked at him, his face droopy from the booze. "I always fuck things up. I don't mean to and I just get stuff wrong. I'm wrong," he sobbed.

Stephen was shell-shocked by the annihilation of drunken emotion. He put an arm around Inver's shoulder, attempting to calm him down. "It's okay, you're okay."

"I'm really not," Inver snivelled. "I'm so hung up on this guy. I just can't get him outta my head."

Guy?

"I wish... I wish I could meet someone like you. You're so nice to me," Inver cried.

You're gay?

If Stephen could see ghosts, he bet right now Rusty would be standing beside him, pointing and laughing.

Inver tore at his hair as if he were trying to rip the problems out of his mind. "I wish you could fix me," he said in a muffled sob. Inver's bloodshot eyes zoned in on Stephen. "Can you fix me, Stephen?"

The desperate question tore at Stephen's conscience, ripping at his vengeful motivation. Inver buried his head into Stephen's shoulder, crying uncontrollably. Stephen could feel the aching coming from inside this mess of a young man and thanks to Stephen's plan to get Inver wildly drunk, the mess was now spilling out of him.

There was no way he could go through with what he had planned. You can't break someone who's already broken.

Stephen cradled Inver in his arms, letting his shoulder absorb the drunken tears. This wasn't the enemy, this was a kindred spirit.

CHAPTER THIRTY — 1996

STEPHEN

The guilt of telling Shaun he was just fun had plagued Stephen's mind all day. Of course, in the moment, Shaun had dismissed it away like an afterthought, but Stephen knew him better than that now. He knew that his summary of what they were would have cut Shaun deeply. Shaun tried so hard to be liked that this just felt like another incident of him trying to reflect what he thought others wanted, but what Stephen *really* wanted was for Shaun to be happy.

Stephen knew he held all the power between them, but he worried if he were to show his heart's hand then that power would slip away and put them both on equal terms, a proposition he found terrifying. This concern though clashed with another fear, the one that if he wasn't honest soon, then Shaun's adulation may evaporate.

Stephen wasn't sure how to say what he wanted to say, or what it even was he needed to say. Sometimes feelings can't be put into words adequately. After pacing in his room for a good hour, a solution finally struck him; Stephen knew what he had to do.

They weren't scheduled to meet for another two hours, but he chased the eureka-moment with excited initiative, packed a duffel bag with supplies for the evening, and crept outside to start his car up. A pitiful turn of the key coughed the engine to life with a harsh groan, choking out a blaze of fumes to poison the quiet country air. Stephen sat hunched over in the driver's seat, clutching at the wheel, waiting to see if the noise had woken his parents up. He felt like a naughty kid again, a ridiculous, skittish fear coursing through his adult veins, worried that he was about to be busted for being up to no good. When no lights from inside the house came flickering on, he put his foot down on the pedal and ever-so-gently rolled out of the driveway toward town.

Driving along, a nervous smile tainted Stephen's lips, knowing he was about to surrender his position of power and embrace the dangers of vulnerability.

∞

Stephen sat waiting amidst the flax bushes lining the narrow dirt path which led from the campground down to the beach. The night air was warm and only added to the heat buzzing in his loins from the anticipation of Shaun's arrival. He'd been waiting for the past twenty minutes since he'd finished arranging everything and he knew Shaun would be due to pass at any moment. The beach was deserted being a Monday night, and provided no impromptu party sprung up or roaming pisshead trotted along the beach, then privacy was all but guaranteed.

Stephen's ears pricked up at the sound of sneakers scuffing along the track. He looked out from behind the flax leaves and saw Shaun coming toward him at a brisk pace in jeans and a dark hoodie. Just as Shaun went to walk straight past his hiding spot, Stephen launched a hand out, gripping his fingers around Shaun's ankle.

Shaun yelped and jumped high in the air, kicking in all directions.

Stephen stood up and began laughing. "Oh man, that was priceless."

Shaun was bent over, gasping for breath. "You nearly gave me a flaming heart attack."

Stephen nodded his head from side-to-side and sniffed loudly.

"What are you doing?" Shaun asked.

"Just making sure you didn't shit your pants." Stephen erupted with laughter again.

"Dick," Shaun chuckled and gave Stephen a light whack on the shoulder.

Stephen finally composed himself enough to greet Shaun properly, stepping over to him and leaning in to give him a kiss. Shaun's hands stayed buried in the front pocket of his jumper, Stephen reaching in and grabbing them out to place one to his cheek. "Your hands are cold." He pressed Shaun's hands together and blew his warm breath on them before kissing each one.

"You're in a good mood," Shaun said. "How come you're here?"

Stephen returned Shaun's hands and began walking ahead through the flax-lined path toward the beach. He turned around and waved for Shaun to follow him. "Well, come on. I'll show you why."

"Sounds interesting. What is it?" Shaun quizzed as he caught up to walk beside him.

"You'll just have to wait and see."

Once their feet hit the sand, they continued along the beach 'till they came to Rapanui Creek, leading to Cherry Lane. They leapt over the stream and Shaun went to continue on to the reef, Stephen grabbing his hand and yanking him back.

"Nope, this way tonight." Stephen led Shaun into the shelter of the cove. The shadowy figures of trees loomed high across the other side of the lagoon that crept through the indentation of the cliff.

"Why are we coming here?" Shaun asked.

"Why not?" Stephen said. He raised his arms up and spun around. "The night belongs to us."

He grabbed Shaun's hand and dragged him farther into the shelter of the cove, leading to the small cave carved out from years of a pounding sea. A lit torch sat on a tartan blanket laid out on the sand.

"You wanna do it here? In Cherry Lane?" Shaun asked, sounding completely baffled.

Stephen squeezed Shaun's hand. "This is where couples come, isn't it?" He narrowed his eyes, giving Shaun a seductive look.

Shaun stared back, unsure what to make of Stephen's electric mood.

Stephen went and fetched the torch before making his way back to where Shaun was standing. "Ya know, earlier today in the car… I didn't mean it when I said you were just fun. You mean way more to me than just that." Stephen stepped behind him and locked his arms around Shaun's waist, resting his head on his shoulder. He pointed the torch up and shone its light on the face of the cliff where the sprawlings of couples' declarations of love were etched into its grey clay. He raised the light high above the entrance to the cave. There, large and prominently displayed, was the infinity symbol. ∞ "So, this is for you, for us," Stephen whispered in his ear.

"Whoa," Shaun murmured, his eyes fixated on Stephen's carved confession. "Like whoa, that is so fucking cool," his voice strummed in elation.

Stephen felt almost euphoric hearing Shaun so happy. Shaun turned around to face Stephen. "Are we a couple now?" he asked gingerly.

Stephen sighed before offering a softening look. "We are whatever you want us to be." As the words came out, he felt the invisible pendulum of power swing to neutral ground.

Shaun placed his hands on Stephen's hips. "So, that means I can call you my boyfriend?"

Stephen rolled his eyes back playfully, pretending to be thinking of an answer. "Hmm, that depends."

Shaun's hands slowly started to climb up Stephen's sides, his fingers tickling more intensely the higher they reached, waiting for an answer. When Shaun's fingers reached his armpits, Stephen began squirming uncontrollably and laughing. "Okay, okay, yes, yes, I'm your boyfriend."

Shaun glowed with a smile and his hands retreated, letting Stephen recover from the tickling torment.

Stephen took a deep breath. "As long as you'll be mine."

Shaun said nothing, leaning in and signing their covenant union with a kiss.

Stephen led Shaun over to the blanket where his green duffel bag lay. He opened it up and showed Shaun the treasures available to them; cans of bourbon, ciggies, soft drinks, bags of lollies and chocolates. All the good things in life that cruelly fuck over your health.

Stephen motioned for Shaun to rummage through the bag. "Choose your poison wisely."

Shaun browsed through the bag's contents before bringing his focus back to Stephen. He reached a hand out and tugged on Stephen's belt. "You're the only poison I want right now."

Instinct followed and they tumbled together onto the blanket, a mess of shifting hands roaming each other's bodies. They puffed ardently as they rid themselves of their pesky clothes.

Shaun lay down on his back, spread out fully naked, staring up at Stephen with a blend of fragility and resolve in his eyes, a beautiful collision of emotions. Stephen studied his lover's slender body; he loved how hard Shaun's cock looked, knowing it throbbed only for him. He lowered himself atop of Shaun, pressing their bodies together as he held Shaun's hands down, pinning him to the blanket. Shaun's dick burned against his abdomen, aching to be touched. Stephen opened his mouth and pressed his lips down on Shaun's nipple, licking up over his olive-skinned chest to his neck where Stephen glided his wet tongue over Shaun's Adam's apple to the tip of his chin, biting down and emitting a low growl.

Shaun squirmed beneath him, adjusting his legs to wrap around Stephen's rump, pressing down, bringing him in hard. Shaun wriggled further up the blanket 'till Stephen's cock slid down past Shaun's balls and rested between his crack.

Is he ready?

Shaun's breath bled out hot and heavy. "You wanna?"

Stephen knew exactly what this meant but he wanted to hear Shaun utter the words.

"Wanna what?" Stephen replied.

"Fuck me." Shaun grabbed hold of Stephen's cock, pressing it against his hole, his expression serious and his eyes focused solely on Stephen. "I want to feel you inside me."

Stephen cocked an eyebrow. "That can be arranged."

Local logic would have you believe losing your virginity made you a man, yet being gay made you somehow less of one. If true, then Stephen was about to embark on the strangest of contradictions by making a man of Shaun while somehow simultaneously, they both became *less* of one.

Stephen reached over the top of Shaun to rummage through the duffel bag where beneath the treats was a well-hidden stash of rubbers and lube. He flashed Shaun a grin as he held up what was in his hand.

Shaun laughed. "Somebody was presumptuous."

"Just thinking ahead," Stephen said, giving Shaun's thigh a squeeze.

Shaun, still flat on his back, laid waiting for Stephen to lead the way. In expert fashion, Stephen slid the condom on with ease, spurting a dollop of lube into his open palm and slathering it along his shielded shaft before rubbing the residue between Shaun's arse cheeks. Its cold sticky touch made the virgin Munro flinch and heave in shock. Stephen shuffled forward on his knees, guiding his cock to Shaun's point of entry. He looked down at Shaun whose eyes gleamed back at him, his body shaking slightly, waiting for impact.

"Ready?" Stephen asked.

Shaun nodded, taking hold of Stephen's hips, digging his blunt nails into the skin, no doubt hoping this could allow him some say in the rhythm of passion. Stephen grabbed hold of Shaun's ankles, hoisted them up and rested them on his shoulders. He glanced down at the tip of his cock aching to get inside Shaun. He didn't rush; instead, he savoured the moment, knowing he was only inches away from doing something that could never be undone.

Holy shit, I'm actually about to fuck another guy!

The fear and adrenaline were colossal but un-fucking-believably exciting. He took a deep breath and with the slightest of shoves, Stephen crossed another line when the tip of his cock pushed through first-time-friction, placing him two inches inside Shaun's arsehole.

Shaun immediately tensed up. "Hold up, hold up," he said in a panicked tone.

"Did you want me to stop?"

"No," Shaun said adamantly. "I want you inside me just... try to go slow."

Stephen attempted again with an even lighter push. He managed to get another inch inside and instantly felt Shaun's arse wrap around him. Stephen felt his cock twitch and swell from the hugging tightness of Shaun's hole enveloping the buried part of him. Shaun's face was painted in pain, but it was clear to see he wanted this so bad he resisted the urge to say stop. Stephen stayed still and leaned forward, letting his weight and gravity do the work, but to no avail, the gentle approach just wasn't allowing him to get any further in. Without warning, he gave a small shove, forcing his cock in Shaun's arse a little further.

"Fuck," Shaun cried out, punching the ground with his fist.

"Sorry," Stephen said guiltily, freezing in place. "Did you need me to stop?"

"No, don't stop," Shaun grimaced.

Stephen admired Shaun's determination; there was nothing but trust in his dark eyes, a knowing look that acknowledged the risk he was taking by gifting his body so freely and allowing another man power over his pleasure.

Stephen lowered Shaun's ankles and looked down at his cock, now wedged just over halfway inside Shaun. Stephen rolled his tongue around in his mouth to slurp up saliva before bowing his head forward and slowly dribbling out a thick white stream of spit, landing on his exposed shaft. He rubbed it in, making sure he was wet as possible. Stephen retrieved Shaun's ankles and kissed the sole of one of his feet before giving it a wee love nip; he then placed Shaun's feet back over his shoulders to resume.

He looked down at Shaun giving him a kissing look with his eyes; then, with firm guidance, he pushed his cock further in. Shaun let go of Stephen's hips and scrunched the blanket between his fingers, heaving a wounded breath that penetrated the quiet night air. Stephen grunted and gave another swift push, feeling his cock being strangled by Shaun's virgin hole. He placed his hands under Shaun's arse and lifted him up before leaning forward and fully impaling him. Shaun gasped in reaction to Stephen's balls pressed against his arse cheeks... to being so fully entered.

"You feel that?" Stephen asked.

"Yes," Shaun muttered.

"That is you with every inch of me inside you," Stephen taunted, proud of himself.

"Fucking oath," Shaun half-laughed before wincing in pain.

Stephen stared down at his conquest, his member fully inside this beautiful guy who grit his teeth through sexual suffering just for him.

Stephen leaned in and kissed Shaun on the cheek. "Guess who isn't a virgin anymore?"

Shaun smiled, lowering his feet from Stephen's shoulders. Wrapping his legs behind Stephen's arse, Shaun pressed with his heels to make sure Stephen stayed deep inside him. Shaun grabbed Stephen by his hair, pulling his face in 'till their mouths met and tongued him deeply. They stayed lip-locked for what felt like ages, tongues wrapped together, breathing in each other's moist air.

Stephen finally retrieved his tongue and moved his mouth across to nibble and lick Shaun's earlobe, whispering words of encouragement in his ear before diving his tongue straight in. Shaun gripped hold of Stephen's firm biceps, squeezing them possessively. Stephen flexed his muscles, letting Shaun know how strong his arms were—these arms that would always protect him.

Body to body, Stephen ignited his rhythm, slowly withdrawing his dick from the tightness of Shaun's arse before each time going straight back in balls deep. He started slow, gradually building up pace as the pair went back to kissing and feeding groans into each other's mouths. Shaun's hairy legs grazed Stephen's sides, reminding Stephen that the pleasure he was giving—the pleasure he was receiving—was entirely male.

Shaun's cock, hot and firm, rubbed between their stomachs, squished in the middle of their bodies' magnetic pull for one another. There was no more lid on the rush of passion. Stephen had free reign to plough, so he upped his game and began moving his cock side-to-side, making sure each stab made Shaun a bit looser. Stephen thrust with hard intent, desperate for Shaun to never forget this night and how he let Stephen deep inside him. He needed Shaun to remember exactly who he belonged to—that he was his and his only.

All mine.

Stephen ripped his face free from Shaun's and began grunting with every fuck motion he gave. Shaun became noisy with no mouth to keep him from moaning. Stephen yelped in hurt when Shaun suddenly sank his sharp teeth in just below the dip of his collarbone. Shaun's cock jerked furiously as it spurted hot cum, splattering against Stephen's stomach and chest. The warm feel of Shaun's sex made his own cock twitch wildly and he erupted with a loud grunt, spilling his own load deep inside Shaun.

Gasping for breath, he collapsed on top of Shaun, spreading Shaun's abundance of spilled spunk between their bodies. Shaun quivered beneath him, his body shaking in short rapid motions. Stephen lay there knackered, riding his lover's breaths beneath him like a wave.

"Thank you," Shaun whispered and kissed him on the cheek.

They lay there cum soaked, limbs entangled, basking in their moment of shared glory. The ocean played faintly in the background like a distant crowd cheering while the night air licked at their hot sweaty bodies with its tepid sea breeze.

Stephen could smell the perspiration—their sweat mingled together—creating their own signature scent of sex. If he could bottle it, he would, and it would be called *freedom*.

Still panting, he rolled off of Shaun and lay beside him. "Whoa," Stephen said in a heavy exhale. He planted a hand on his forehead, wiping sweat from his brow.

"That was intense," Shaun said.

Stephen nodded. "Sure was." He ran a hand down Shaun's side, resting it on his hip. "Thank you for letting me... you know?" Stephen felt like blushing.

"No, thank you," Shaun beamed.

"Are you sore?"

Shaun's eyes rolled to the side, contemplating the probing question. "A little, but I'm sure I'll live."

"Good, so I can go again then, yeah?"

Shaun laughed. "Give it a while first. It still feels like you're inside me." He buried his face into Stephen's shoulder and groaned a giggle. Stephen smiled, hearing him so happy, and kissed the back of his head.

The beautiful night had been a blessing for this. They lay side by side in all their glory, looking up at the vast mess of stars in the solar system.

"This makes me dizzy like I'm gonna fall," Stephen whispered.

Shaun grabbed an arm across Stephen's chest, hugging him tight. "If you ever feel like falling, just hold on to me," he said. "I'll catch you every time."

A shared reverence hummed between them. Stephen held Shaun's warm arm and stared at the universe lost in its infinite space, wondering if somewhere up there, Ricky sat looking down, judging him for what he had just done. Out of the blue, Stephen asked, "You believe in heaven, right?"

A pause drifted between them.

"I guess so," Shaun answered.

"Thought a bedside bible holder would answer that with a bit more conviction."

"I'm far from what you'd call an expert on such things."

"True," Stephen sighed.

Shaun leaned himself up on his elbow. "I don't know if this helps answer your question," he said, "but when I was a kid and whenever someone we knew died, Mum would always say 'well I guess they know the secret.'"

Stephen frowned. "And what's the secret?"

"You only find it out if you don't come back," Shaun said with a soft laugh. "But I always thought that was a nice way of looking at it, like it's a surprise we each get to find out no matter who you are."

Stephen was puzzled by Shaun's romanticised notion of death. "How is that nice?"

Shaun smiled. "Because it means we're all the same."

Stephen imagined what the secret could be and if Ricky now knew it. He sat up and grabbed himself a can of drink from the duffel bag, clicked the top open and gulped back a large mouthful watering his parched mouth. He looked down and saw Shaun's eyes moist like he was sad. "What's wrong?" Stephen asked worriedly.

"Nothing. I'm happy as."

"Well, could you try fucking looking it?" Stephen teased.

Shaun took a deep breath. "You've made me so happy tonight," he said, rubbing Stephen's arm. "I think if you ever broke my heart, I would probably die." He finished his admission with a nervous laugh.

Stephen put down his drink and lay atop of Shaun, kissing his heart through his beating chest. "If I ever break your heart." *Kiss.* "Then you can share mine." *Kiss.*

"Is that a promise?"

Stephen wriggled up Shaun's body 'till they were face to face. "That is a promise."

CHAPTER THIRTY-ONE — 1996

STEPHEN

Clomping around noisily in a pair of gumboots, Stephen scoured the shed, flipping over anything not nailed down, trying to find an extra pair of wire cutters. It was in complete shambles with objects scattered across the benches and the floor littered with bits of firewood and petrol canisters. The small space was riddled with cobwebs and looked more like the kind of place tools came to die than to be discovered. The longer he rummaged through all the crap, the snottier he got with himself for not being able to find what he needed. Busily swearing to himself, a tap at the window made him spin 'round.

Shaun stood at the other side of the window, pulling a face at him, looking as adorable as he did mental.

Stephen chuckled. "What are you doing, egg?"

Shaun pressed his mouth open wide against the window, blowing steam onto it and then drawing the sleeping S of his name. Stephen smiled at the gesture and walked over to the window. He pressed one of his long slim fingers against the glass and ran it through the dust, connecting his S to Shaun's. Stephen nodded his head, motioning for Shaun to come inside.

Shaun walked into the shed lugging a backpack over his shoulder, arriving all set for their trip to Auckland. Stephen had booked them into a hotel so they could stay overnight before the concert, gifting them their first proper night in a bed together.

Shaun dropped the bag on the floor then gazed across taking in the sight of Stephen wearing a flimsy singlet with his hairy legs on display in tiny black shorts. "Hey, stud." Shaun gave him a wink.

Stephen returned a flirty blink. "Thanks, you're not

looking too bad yourself."

"Aww, shucks." Shaun said, pretending to be embarrassed and hide behind his hands.

"Clown," Stephen said as he went back to hunting for the wire cutters.

Shaun nestled down on a chunk of firewood, resting his elbows on his knees, watching Stephen scour the shed aimlessly. "I'm really pumped for the concert tomorrow. It's gonna be so awesome."

"Should be," Stephen replied, only half listening as he scanned for the missing tool.

"Fuck yeah. It'll be so cool to see all of them live."

"Are you all packed yet?" Stephen asked.

"I'm not carrying this 'round just for fun," Shaun pointed to the backpack he had left at the door.

"True," Stephen said, not paying attention.

"To be honest though, I actually think I'm more excited about getting to spend the whole night with you."

"Yeah, sure," Stephen mumbled.

"Somebody's not even listening to me, are they?"

"Yep, cool."

Shaun threw a scrap of wood at Stephen's feet. Stephen twisted 'round only half-aware Shaun had thrown the piece of wood.

"Oi, ignoramus. What are you actually looking for?"

Stephen pulled at his hair, clearly frustrated. "Some fucking wire cutters. I can't see any anywhere."

"You mean these?" Shaun got up, walked straight to the bench and picked up right away what Stephen had spent so long looking for.

"How'd you bloody find those so easily?"

"Four years of being a grease monkey has taught me how to find tools, not to mention a bunch of other beneficial life skills."

"Such as?"

"Like knowing how to handle your tool, for starters." He stepped forward and grabbed Stephen's crotch, giving him a firm grope.

Stephen lolled his head back and groaned. "So, this is what you guys get up to under the cars." Stephen went to grab the wire cutters but Shaun quickly wrenched them out of his reach.

"Not so fast. Where's my finder's fee?"

"And what do you suggest that would be?"

Shaun poked his tongue against the inside of his cheek, replicating what it was he wanted to be done to him.

Stephen moved forward, lacing his arms around Shaun's neck. "We can't do that in here, fool. It's too risky," he said. "But how about I pay you back tonight in the hotel room? You can have any payment you want then." Stephen wiggled his eyebrows.

"Hmm, anything I want?"

Stephen looked down at the ground, acting his best to be coy. "Yes, *anything* you want."

Shaun raised his eyebrows. "Even…"

"Even what?"

"You'll let me… inside you?"

Stephen stood still, pretending to make his mind up on something he'd decided days ago. He nodded gently. "Even that." He tilted his face forward and kissed Shaun on the lips. Shaun smelled beautiful, all fresh and clean. To Stephen, he always smelled wonderful, even if he'd just finished a day's work, carrying a pure flavour. Stephen lowered his hands down Shaun's back to embrace him.

"STEPHEEEN," yelled a voice.

Stephen threw himself off Shaun, nearly stumbling backwards over a lump of wood. He looked out the door, thankful there was no one in line of the kissing vision, but the voice bellowed again, "STEPHEN, WHERE ARE YOU?"

Fucking Rusty.

Stephen composed himself and looked down at his pants to make sure he didn't have a visible boner. "IN THE SHED," he shouted back.

Rusty soon appeared, huffing in the doorway, bursting in, reeking of impatience. "What's the holdup? You got the wire cutters yet?" Rusty thrust his vision at Shaun, casting him a suspicious look.

"Hey Rusty," Shaun said, giving him a mock salute.

Rusty just grunted and turned back to Stephen. "So you got them?"

"Yip, here you go." Stephen held the wire cutters out.

"Ta." Rusty plucked them out his hand and stormed

off to the fence that needed urgent seeing to, apparently.

"Fuck, now that's a man on a mission." Shaun laughed

"He mustn't be feeling well 'cos it isn't like him to be in a hurry for hard work," Stephen said spitefully.

Rusty had worked for his parents now for five years, but he was a shit worker. Stephen's dad was a patient man and wouldn't fire him. Rusty rode a constant wave of second chances. If it was up to Stephen, Rusty would have been out on his arse ages ago.

Stephen went to follow after Rusty before turning to face Shaun. "We'll go up for lunch after this and then hit the road," he said. "Fancy coming to help?"

"Not really."

Stephen laughed. "Wrong answer."

Shaun got to his feet with a groan. "Fine, but I'm only helping 'cos you're my boyfriend."

Stephen felt his heart blaze at Shaun's use of the word but his worry of others ever hearing it stubbed out the thrill of it all.

∞

Once the fence was finished, they ditched Rusty and went to the house for lunch. Stephen's mum had made them ham and cheese sandwiches, all set up on their plates, waiting for them to dig in.

Shaun nattered away with Stephen's parents, hogging the conversation at the table. He spoke with such natural confidence and exaggerated interest—as he did with everyone he ever met—that he would have made an ace salesperson.

Stephen sat munching his way through lunch, letting the others at the table do the talking 'till his mother directed her voice at him, "So when are you boys going to your rock concert?"

"Big Day Out," Stephen answered.

"Yes, it will be, won't it?" she returned innocently.

Stephen rolled his eyes. "No, the concert is called the Big Day Out."

"Oh, I am so sorry, Stephen," she said sarcastically, getting a round of laughter from Shaun.

"I think we are going around two o'clock, is that right?" Shaun asked, looking at Stephen.

"Yeah, gotta be there before seven for check in."

"Make sure he drives safely," Stephen's mother said to Shaun.

Shaun smiled. "If he drives like an idiot, then I've got my imaginary pedal all ready to slow us down."

"Let's hope you don't need it." She shot Stephen a stern look.

Once they'd gobbled up what was on their plates, Stephen left Shaun to chat with his parents while he had a quick shower and packed himself an overnight bag. He raced around his room in a hurry, throwing what he needed in the bag: Rage Against the Machine T-shirt, ripped black jeans, deodorant, change of clothes, Doc Martens, rubbers, lube.

He had a near-new packet of condoms and expected to make good use of them tonight in the safety of a private room. Stephen made an effort to dress down for his less flashy companion. He got changed into a fresh pair of casual blue jeans and a plain green T-shirt. He felt naked without a label attached to any item on his body, but shrugged it off and embraced Shaun's influence.

With his bag packed he made his way out to the lounge and let Shaun know it was time to go. They chucked their gear in the boot of the car and without hesitation drove off leaving potentially prying eyes behind.

∞

The drive to Auckland was a slow one thanks to a highway plagued with slips and roadworks. The excitement of their trip kicked up a notch when they got to the top of the Bombay Hills on the southern edge of Auckland. Stephen stared down at the sprawling mass of suburbs that spread into the horizon of New Zealand's largest city. Small by international standards, the city of sails was a Kiwi New York to many folk, including Shaun whose mouth gaped open taking in its size, exclaiming how he hadn't been here since he was a kid for his birthday.

By the time they'd arrived at the hotel, with ten minutes to spare, they desperately hurried to check into the room before the 7:00 p.m. close.

A young tubby man with blonde hair and a well-trained hospitable smile showed them to their room on the tenth floor. The swanky room with its expensive furnishings and floor-to-ceiling windows looked out at the city's tall buildings, and between the gaps of the towering metal and glass structures they were offered a view of the harbour's shimmering waters. There were two beds, one double and one single, just as Stephen had requested; hiding the fact they'd only need the one.

Stephen's plan was thrown out the window when Shaun loudly declared, "Oh, we only needed the one bed. Aye, babe?"

The hotel worker's smile never faltered. "Well, I hope this room will do anyway."

Stephen felt his stomach drop and his face burn red. He ran a hand over his brow, looking bamboozled. "My mate's just joking. Thank you very much." He swiftly ushered the man out the door, a little too abruptly, keen to avoid any visual judgement for what Shaun had just outed them as.

A gay couple.

"Fuck sake, Shaun. Don't pull that shit," Stephen snapped. He stormed to the bed and dropped his bag on it, beginning to unpack even though he had no need to empty the bag.

Shaun walked over to him. "I was only taking the piss. It's not a big deal."

Stephen lifted his gaze, casting Shaun a stern frown.

"Well, yes, it's true we only need the *one* bed," Shaun said, "but it was meant as a joke to him, *babe*." He did his best to sound cheeky.

Stephen continued with the pointless emptying of his bag. "And maybe you should just remember not to make jokes about that kind of thing."

"Don't have a cow, man," Shaun scoffed.

Seriously resorting to Bart Simpson comebacks?

"Well I care, and you should care if I care," Stephen

grumbled, realising he sounded exactly like what he was, one-half of a quarrelling couple.

Shaun walked around behind him and wrapped his arms around Stephen's waist, nuzzling into his ear. "I'm sowwie," he said and kissed Stephen's neck.

Stephen ignored his greasing and continued going through his bag.

"I'm weally sowwie." Another kiss.

Stephen smiled, fighting back laughter.

"Like, weally weally weally sowwie." Stephen gave into the stupid voice and laughed out loud.

"That's better," Shaun said, slipping his hands under Stephen's shirt and rubbing his hard stomach. "How about we build our own world in here tonight, so we don't have to worry about the one out there."

Stephen looked out the window at the city's tall buildings and teams of yachts in the harbour. "That sounds good to me."

Shaun rested his head on Stephen's shoulder. "We can order in food and just stay in bed all night and pretend the floors made of lava."

Stephen laughed at the imagined scenario. It sounded perfect.

The plan pretty much went how Shaun said. They ordered up pizzas and drank beer from the mini bar. After the meal, they laid in bed watching TV channels they didn't have back home, amazed at the feeling of having more than three to choose from.

They watched the tale of The Incredibly Shrinking Man, cuddled up together in a world of their own, sneaking kisses and holding hands while they enjoyed the archaic movie. When the movie finished, once the man was invisibly minuscule, they lay there with the television on mute as it illuminated the room.

Curled up beside Shaun, a resonating peace soared within Stephen. Shaun's warm body was more than just his boyfriend or sex. He had become a home away from home. Wherever Shaun was, Stephen felt safe and he hoped he offered the same in return. He lay there charmed, listening to Shaun's soft breathing, its gentle warmth kissing his ears with a zephyr flow.

"You're so fucking special," Shaun whispered.

"Is that right, creep?"

"Huh?" Shaun responded, his body loosening and letting out a giggle when he realised what Stephen was referring to. He began belting out Radiohead, sounding horrendous like some poor creature in pain.

Stephen burst out laughing. "You know, for someone with such a sexy voice, you really can't sing for shit."

"Oi, I was trying to serenade you." Shaun said, dishing out a playful shoulder punch which Stephen returned.

"Ouch," Shaun cried out, rubbing where he had been hit.

"I barely touched you, sook," Stephen replied.

Shaun kept rubbing his arm. "That fucking hurt," he grizzled before laughing and returning to their cuddle.

Stephen waited all night for Shaun to take advantage of his body's offer, but the bliss of just laying together and cuddling won out. Stephen wasn't sure if he was disappointed or relieved about surrendering this final piece of himself, but he figured they would have plenty of nights together yet for such things.

Under the dim glow of the television screen, they fell asleep atop of the blankets where they melted into each other's arms, safe from the outside world and a floor made of lava.

∞

Stephen awoke the next morning to find Shaun fast asleep in his arms. He moved his face closer to Shaun's and gave him a tender kiss. He could smell the faint sweat of Shaun on the pillow and, maybe for the first time, he properly understood why his mother would sometimes lock herself in Ricky's room. It was amazing how a person could leave their presence in a smell; even if Shaun wasn't beside him right now, one whiff of his aroma could conjure up his image.

Stephen unhooked his arm from under Shaun's neck, trying not to wake him. Shaun stirred gently before folding up in the foetal position and continuing to sleep. Stephen made himself a coffee and gave Shaun an extra hour's sleep. Shaun's light snoring kept going, sleep having a deep hold on him. *Debbie was right. You probably could sleep through a bloody house demolition.*

After nearly two hours, Stephen gave up waiting and grabbed Shaun's arm, trying to raise him up. Shaun slowly opened his groggy eyes and begrudgingly sat up in the bed.

"What time is it?" Shaun asked as he stretched out his arms in a big yawn.

"Time you get ready, sleepy head."

Shaun sat motionless before rubbing his face. "Fuck, I'm not feeling too shit hot."

"You ain't looking too shit hot either," Stephen teased.

"Gee, thanks," Shaun said. He yawned again as he swung his feet out of the bed and leaned forward with his head in his hands.

"What you need is a shower and coffee."

"Yeah, that could liven me up," Shaun muttered.

Stephen grabbed his hand. "I'm about to go for one now. Care to join me?"

Shaun grinned. The shared-shower scenario appeared to wake him up immediately. He stood up and followed Stephen into the bathroom where they squeezed together into the shower box. Shaun laid into Stephen's chest, letting the beads of water rain on his back while Stephen soaped him thoroughly up and down with caring hands, bringing a smile to both their lips.

Once they'd dried off and got changed, they made their way through bustling cosmopolitan streets to the bus depot where they caught a ride to Ericson Stadium.

Outside the stadium gates, throngs of people lined the sides, all greedy to get in and begin the rock revelry. Shaun was buzzing, repeating how 'fucking epic' it would be. The grey skies threatening rain above did little to dampen Shaun's enthusiasm. Once inside the gates, they quickly became part of the frenzied mass, pushed around like pinballs in the entanglement of limbs all clambering for better views of the main stage.

The year before, Stephen had loved every minute of the festival and had been part of the crowd who screamed through Courtney Love giving away a blue Fender guitar to one lucky fan. Even though the bands this year were less his taste, Stephen was thriving on Shaun's excitement; it was infectious. By the time Rage Against the Machine graced the main stage, the rain was pouring in biblical proportions, turning the mosh pit into a glorious mud bath.

    Shaun was right, it was fucking epic.

CHAPTER THIRTY-TWO — 1996

STEPHEN

Shaun had barely moved from his bed all week. He was on strict orders from the doctor to rest up and take things easy. This was easier said than done with someone who couldn't keep still, even if they were sitting down. Shaun was a bundle of energy who resented stillness.

The *fucking epic* concert with its mud-soaked chaos had left Shaun with the most fucking epic flu. Within a day of being home, Shaun was crook as a dog, confined to his tiny bed in his tiny room, sweating and croaking with snotty, sickly breath.

Stephen spent every spare moment he had at Shaun's house, sitting with him, trying to keep the reluctant patient in bed. He would go visit during his lunch breaks and return in the evenings after dinner to check up on him. He took his chances of catching the same bug, the risk seeming worth it. It was a weird experience seeing Shaun so ill, bringing out a protective instinct in Stephen he didn't know he possessed. Being the youngest in his small family, he had never really had to look out for anyone else and although he loved his family, the role of protector was a foreign one. That role had always fallen to his parents or Ricky.

Despite Shaun feeling ill, Stephen enjoyed these days spent fussing over him, feeding him drinks of hot lemon juice, and rubbing him down with Vicks VapoRub. Debbie had let him be in charge of looking after Shaun whenever he would visit, something Lydia no doubt found a welcome relief, not being her brother's sole slave and having to fetch him whatever he wanted. A luxury Shaun abused more to annoy her than out of necessity.

Josie sat beside Shaun's bed like a loyal pet any chance she could, but come her bedtime, Stephen took her spot and sat there stroking Shaun's hair. Once he felt safe that no one was still awake, he would curl up alongside him in the skinny single bed, wishing him better.

On the fourth day of visiting to check up on his ill boyfriend, Stephen found Shaun had broken the sickly shackles of the bedroom and was sitting in the lounge, loudly declaring he was losing his mind with boredom.

"Come on, man. Let's go out. Anywhere, honestly, I don't care. Even if it's just to get some fucking milk." Shaun had his spark back, even if it was a frustrated one.

Stephen riled him up, insisting he couldn't take him anywhere just yet.

Shaun groaned like he was in pain and tugged at his hair.

Debbie was seated in the dining room, reading a magazine. "Stephen, you have my permission to take my darling child out of the house, far, far, far away so I don't have to hear any more of his bloody whinging." She pulled a face that told Stephen exactly how much Shaun had worn her nerves thin. "Either that, or just slap him really hard for me, would you?" She gave Stephen a cheeky smile before burying her head back behind the magazine.

"Gee, love you too, Mum," Shaun barked back.

"Come on, you. Let's take you out for that slap." Stephen dangled his keys up. The noise of their jingling lured Shaun's attention. He didn't need to be asked twice, frantically chucking on his shoes and bolting outside to Stephen's car.

Debbie called out just before Stephen could follow after him, "Oh, Stephen."

Stephen turned around to find Debbie staring at him, a soft frown marking her forehead. "Yeah?"

"Look after my boy, won't you?" Debbie answered, giving him a warm look that made Stephen feel uncomfortable.

Stephen nodded and walked outside, uneasy from her tone and stare. The words were bland and expected of a mother, but the rest of it packed the punch of something he couldn't quite put his finger on. A punch of... knowing.

She fucking knows!

He didn't know how she knew, but Stephen could

feel it in his bones that she did. They had been so careful. Hadn't they? Of course, Stephen had no proof that Debbie knew his secret, but the truth of who he really was to her son was fused in her words.

The truth of what we do together.

His stomach squirmed at the thought as he hopped in the car and backed them out the drive. Something so personal being found out about him left Stephen feeling like his clothes had been ripped from his body, completely exposing him to the ridicule and reactions he feared. Regardless of how he felt about Shaun, it didn't make the prospect of being found out any easier to cope with.

He didn't say anything to Shaun about his fear; it wasn't like Shaun could do anything about it. If anything, Stephen worried that Shaun wouldn't be worried—that he would try to convince him it was time they come clean, step out in the open and walk a new path. A path Stephen was terrified of.

"So, where you taking me?" Shaun asked excitedly.

"Where do you wanna go?"

"Anywhere private." Shaun winked.

"Okay," Stephen mumbled.

"Sheesh, don't sound too keen." Shaun laughed.

"Sorry." He gave Shaun a smile and did his best to mask his worry.

Stephen turned off on the first lonely country road he saw and parked up a couple kilometres further down on a grassy verge surrounded by trees.

Shaun grabbed Stephen's hand and gave it a possessive squeeze, bringing it over to rest on his warm and firm crotch.

"Someone must be feeling better," Stephen said smiling.

"Like you wouldn't believe," Shaun sighed, a mix of longing and exasperation coming out his vocal chords.

Stephen unclicked his seatbelt and fiddled with Shaun's shorts. Shaun raised himself off the seat so Stephen could tug them down past his knees. Unleashed and twitching, Shaun's cock stood at full attention, waiting to have its needs met. Stephen wrapped his fingers around his boyfriend's frustration.

Shaun rested his head back and closed his eyes. He groaned loudly at the feel of Stephen's frisky fingers freeing him. Stephen leaned over and crouched below the dashboard, taking Shaun in his mouth—deep, wet and firm.

You got your low blow after all.

Shaun sighed. "Yep, definitely so much fucking better."

CHAPTER THIRTY-THREE — 2016

INVER

Inver raised the blankets to discover his pale long limbs devoid of any stitch of clothing. He jerked his head up off the pillow, scanning the carpet for his clothes, but they were nowhere to be seen. A sense of dread collided with his body and his mind begged the question, *what did I do last night?* The last thing he remembered was being at the bar with Kimmy and her mate. *The one who laughed a lot.* He didn't remember how he got home or what time he left the bar. Everything was a blank. As much as he loathed not having an ounce of memory in regards to his night out and the location of his clothes, he was relieved to be missing the thrumming pain of a hangover.

He wanted to just stay in bed and let the day slip by without him, but the burning need for a pee forced him out of the warm, clammy sheets to rummage through his bag for a clean pair of briefs. On dozy toes, he slunk down the hallway in bumpy steps toward the bathroom where he came to a wobbly stop in front of the toilet. Holding himself in his hand, Inver groaned loudly as a wave of relief streamed through him while he emptied what felt like an ocean from his bladder. The cool morning air nipped at his skin just long enough to wake him up, but far from bringing him to any state capable of starting the morning with any real form of zest. Inver rubbed the sleep from his eyes and let his body lead him in its still docile daze to the kitchen in search of coffee. The kitchen tiles still draped in morning shade zapped the soles of his feet with a hideous chill. Inver flicked the kettle on and leaned back on the bench, rubbing his face awake and let rip a tired roar before scratching at his groin.

"Good morning," said a woman's voice.

Inver jumped up, knocking a coffee mug with his

elbow into the sink, clinking heavily, but thankfully not breaking. Through tired eyes, he looked across and saw a pale man with balding light hair and a well-dressed skinny brunette both in their forties sitting at the dining table with Stephen.

"Sorry. I didn't mean to startle you," the woman said.

Stephen smiled and waved for him to come over. "Inver, I want you to meet my good friends, Troy and Clare."

"More like his only friends," Troy joked. The ghostly pale man stood up from the table, so Inver took the cue and walked over and shook his hand.

"Nice morning attire," Clare teased.

Inver folded his arms across his chest, feeling stupid for being so exposed to complete strangers. "Umm, yeah, I normally don't walk around like this." Inver fought the shame that wanted to burn through on his face.

"Hey, if you got it, flaunt it," Clare replied, not helping his self-consciousness.

"This is Rusty's lad. He's staying here the week. You might remember him being about yay high." Stephen said, lowering his hand to his waist.

Inver didn't know either of these people from his days as a kid running about on the farm, but they had an aura of familiarity to them.

Troy's eyes glowed with recognition. "Wow, really? Little Inver." Troy beamed a smile filled with perfectly straight teeth before his face went straight. "Sorry to hear about your old man."

Inver gave a solemn nod. "Thanks."

"He was a good sort," Troy said.

Inver had learned this statement was an obligation probably more than a truth. It wasn't like they could turn around and say, 'Oh, yeah. He was a real prick that father of yours.'

"How's your head this morning?" Stephen smirked.

Inver rubbed his face. "Hmm, it's a little wobbly still."

"Did someone have a big night last night?" Troy asked with a grin.

"To be honest, I really don't know. I can't remember a thing." Inver answered, hugging his arms against his chest.

"Like anything?" Stephen said, staring at him with surprise.

Inver nodded. "Yep. Total blank."

Clare giggled. "Well, Inver, I think that means you probably had a very good night. If not, you won't know any better."

"Exactly," Stephen exclaimed. "What goes on tour, stays on tour, after all." He gave Inver a sly wink.

Oh god, what does he know?

Just as Inver was about to go get dressed, a loud voice came thundering through the ranch slider thwarting his quick escape, "Uncle Stephen."

Great, someone else to see me practically naked.

The carrier of the voice raced into the lounge, holding a basketball.

Fuck no!

Stephen walked down into the lounge putting a hand on the young guest's shoulder.

"Inver, this is James. Otherwise known as Trouble with a capital T." He messed up the boy's spiky brown hair.

Inver thought he was going to faint. *That face* looked back at him with a shared awkward expression.

"Hi, Inver." James hugged the basketball to his chest, his smooth pale shoulders on display in a loose blue singlet. His eyes did a quick once-over of the length of Inver's body.

Inver glared around the room. For the very first time, he noticed that amongst the Davis family photographs were snapshots of this happy family; *that face* had been with him the whole time, hanging from the walls, its eyes burning in on him.

"Hi," Inver muttered. He tried lowering his hands over his crotch discretely but still managed to make it come across all too obvious. He couldn't fight the shame off any longer, feeling his cheeks burn with a rosy glow.

More footsteps came running in from outside, these belonging to a good-looking blond boy who wrapped his arms around James's waist. *What the…*

James's eyes grew wide as he was forced into an introduction and a much overdue confession, "Inver, this is my partner, Tim." The words whacked Inver in the face and cut at his heart. Tim was the same age as James by the looks, smooth-faced and seriously cute bar a ski-jump nose that brought him down a peg or two, very much to Inver's relief.

"Nice to meet you, Inver," Tim said smiling. "Nice gruts." The words came out so mocking, Inver could almost hear Tim's eyes roll.

Young, cute, and a bitch, apparently.

Inver was flabbergasted as he stood still, resembling a clueless mime, but he knew he must maintain politeness. "Morning, Tim."

"How've you been?" James asked, his face a sickly shade of guilt.

Inver fidgeted with his feet, rubbing his heels together; desperate to disappear from James's eyes that continued to take in every detail. "I've been good," he said nodding.

"Do you two know each other?" Clare asked.

"Yeah, Mum. Inver use to work with me," James explained.

"Sure is a small world," Troy said, striking a philosophical tone.

Inver felt his body begin to shiver, but it wasn't from the cold. "Right, well I better get going. Big day of cleaning ahead." He smiled at everyone and bolted for his room, abandoning the boiling kettle. Inver groaned to himself as he raced for his bag, grabbing the first pants and top he could find, just wanting away from the house and *that face.*

A tap at the door trapped him in his room before he could get changed.

"Can I come in?" It was James.

"Umm, yep, just a sec," Inver replied. He chucked on some pants to at least cover his lower half. "Come in."

James opened the door and crept in, his hazel eyes glossed with sympathy. Inver stared at him, taking in his clear, young face.

"That was awkward," James said with a guilty grin.

Inver stood there blinking. "I guess, but it's fine."

"It's not though, is it?"

Inver didn't respond, throwing on his top, his mind craving his body to be fully-clothed.

"I wanted to tell you that I'm sorry," James whispered.

Inver grunted. "Okay." He grabbed any socks he could get his hands on and slipped them over his feet; one black and one blue.

"I know I should have told you," James's voice trailed off, "but you know how it is."

Inver's fingers reached furiously for his shoes under the bed, chucking them on hastily. "No, James. Sorry, I don't know how it is." Inver sounded like he was laughing, but he knew it was the only way he would not cry from the shame this boy was making him relive. He stepped across the room to get past James and make his way for the front door. Inver managed to get one determined foot into the hallway before James grabbed his arm, clutching it tight with his warm fingers.

"I really am sorry," James said, his kind eyes pleading with Inver's. "You must hate me."

Our first touch.

Inver looked down at the youthful hand not letting go from its grasp. "You don't have anything to be sorry for," he sighed. "And I could never *hate* you," Inver confessed.

James smiled at the words of forgiveness. "You know," he said, "I really miss Mondays now."

The words tore at Inver's heart. He pried James's fingers from his arm and darted his eyes up the end of the hallway where he saw Stephen standing with his hands buried in his pockets. Stephen didn't say a word, just stared with a curious look across his face that gave little away.

Inver swallowed the lump of emotion in his throat. He had to run away before he fainted. He cast his eyes back at James still standing in the bedroom. "James, I'm sorry but I've really gotta go," the words came out desperate like his need for fresh air. He raced outside leaving the full house to go and be alone.

For six months, Inver had been running away from *that face* which haunted his dreams; a full-time resident of his mind. Now it had returned, landing right in front of his eyes, sharing the most words they ever had. All this time he thought he had been crazy, pining after someone he thought he could never have. Well, maybe he wasn't crazy, but the damage had already been done and it didn't make him feel any less of a tremendous fool.

CHAPTER THIRTY-FOUR — 2016

INVER

The day James told him 'sorry' was the day Inver felt something break inside. Not at Stephen's, but months earlier when he thought he had found a connection. A spark of hope to burn away the loneliness. Of course, others would say he overreacted, but then they weren't in his shoes, desperate to be walking in another's.

That face

Working the phones for an insurance company was tedious and mind-numbing for most employees, but Inver focused on the good point that the days flew by with an odd speed he didn't expect. The place was filled with school leavers and graduates who treated it as an interim role 'till they found something better; at thirty-one, Inver wasn't afforded this luxury to the same extent.

At eighteen, he had entered the party scene with a great bunch of friends and crazy associates, but as the years went by, one by one his party comrades fell victim to the suburbs, careers, relationships, or just accepting maturity and getting tired of living for weekend glory. It all happened so fast, he didn't see it coming 'till he was the last man left standing on the dance floor.

In an admission of defeat, he had dropped working part-time in menial jobs whose sole objective was to gift drinking money and flexible work hours, and started work with the insurance company. Inver had taken the job with reluctant gratitude, maintaining an eye to climbing whatever ladder there was available to him. Nearly three years into the journey, he had yet to climb any rung but had certainly lost touch with former glory days of fun.

His tiny apartment, which was more a slum-like flat, had become a prison, locking him away from the outside world and any sense of inclusion. Friends were busy getting on with their lives and on the rare occasion he was invited to their homes, it was usually to be shown their 'aesthetically pleasing' kitchen tiles or something equally pain-inducing boring. They would ask about his job—'that little call centre job'—and when will he finally meet someone, 'You're too fussy Inver, far too fussy.' As much as these visits bored and infuriated him, he still envied these friends and what they had. Inver knew he would have to do his best if he ever wanted to catch up with their accomplishments.

For a long time, he craved social interaction, but eventually he became so accustomed to his own company that he actively avoided it. Inver's days were now filled with listening to many, but talking to none. Each time a promotion came up at work, he was passed over with subtle suggestions—it was his *attitude* holding him back. They were probably right. He slowly accepted that maybe he had slipped through the cracks of life and missed his moment; he wasn't going to make the slightest bit of difference.

'Till one day, completely by accident, a spark reignited hope in Inver. Hope that maybe, just maybe, good things were ahead. He had just wrapped up a phone call with a woman who had lost her husband in a head-on crash with a drunk driver. It was an emotionally-draining call that had been filled with tears from the woman and screams of frustration with the insurance company's "bullshit process."

As he took a brief break to try and conjure up his only-too-happy-to-help fake attitude, Inver noticed behind the wall of a neighbouring pod of desks, slim legs in tan pants and expensive men's dress shoes, swinging around from a chair. The fancy feet swung around excitedly, a rare sight in such a morbid space where the staff were locked in like battery hens pecking away on phones. Intrigued by this sunny view, his eyes followed the slim limbs up to a bunched crotch being sneakily adjusted by a hand wearing colourful wristbands.

The body in the chair leaned forward and caught

Inver staring. The crotch belonged to a pleasant-looking young guy with short, spiky brown hair styled to look like he'd just rolled out of bed. He gave Inver a quick, friendly smile before turning back in his chair, carrying on with his phone conversation. Inver was embarrassed for being caught perving, but relieved to see the boy mistook it for a general stare. Just as Inver was about to go back to work, he noticed the boy spun back around in his chair, looking again, but this time with curious, burning eyes. The burning eyes of a connection.

It continued for weeks, this little game of eye tag with his nameless co-worker, Inver getting a thrill each time he could feel the boy's eyes land on him. Inver knew there was more to the looks than sheer curiosity—more than a friendly glance. The boy would sometimes ditch his chair and stand up, walking around with lively body language while still connected to his phone, talking away with coolheaded charm. Inver would admire the view, taking in every detail of the stranger's well-dressed physique and self-assured strides; a moneyed confidence that told Inver this young guy didn't know the meaning of setbacks or self-doubt.

Although average-height and average-looking to most people, Inver could see the positivity in this boy's aura, the kindness in his eyes that made him extraordinary—a spark that made him truly beautiful.

With a little subtle digging through co-workers, he discovered the sexy stranger was called James. A bland name that had meant nothing to Inver, but now, any uttering of the word sent Inver flying above the clouds. He would write James's name down on bits of paper and just stare at it 'till the letters morphed from a name to a beautiful shape.

Inver began filling every spare moment thinking about James and wondering how great they would be together. It wasn't even sexual; just simple things like waiting for James to get home from work, cook him dinner, massage out his work stress as they lay together on the couch talking about each other's day. Pure intentions for a pure soul.

He found James on Facebook with relative ease, but was too scared to press the friend request button. Instead, Inver studied the information available to him—James's likes and dislikes—anything to try and get a better picture of this walking dream. He couldn't find any evidence to suggest James was gay, but then no straight guy stares that much. *Not the way he does.*

James's life was a social one of clubs, beaches and trips away, just like Inver's had been in a past life; it evoked a mix of envy and admiration for this beautiful stranger who still had the fun years ahead—unlike Inver, who was in mourning for the passing of his own. James became like some sort of fairy tale character living in a snow globe that Inver constantly stared at from the outside, dying to be trapped inside with and share in his perfect world.

Inver, who years before had lived for the weekends, found himself every Friday impatiently waiting for the start of a new working week so he could get his James-fix. When February rolled round, Inver toyed with the idea of sending James a Valentine's Day card. The problem was though, he didn't have a clue how he would get the card to James discretely, let alone what he could possibly write in it.

It was the Friday before Valentine's Day that made his mind up to send a letter, and it all stemmed from a desperate need to pee. Inver had been sitting with his legs squished together uncomfortably, trying to rush a customer off the phone so he could go to the toilet. Once he finally managed to get free, he burst out from his desk and sped off at a fast pace to the urinal, passing James's desk in a flash, unable to get a proper look.

The toilets were abandoned when he walked in, gifting him some privacy to study his face in the mirror after he'd finished peeing. Inver washed his hands before running his long fingers through his hair, trying to style it just right for when he walked back past James. Busy in his moment of vanity, he nearly missed hearing the toilet door open and the sound of shoes clopping along the linoleum floor. He dropped his hands into the basin and turned the tap back on, frantic to not be busted for striking lame poses. The footsteps got closer and closer, evident the brisk walker had bypassed the toilets and was coming straight for the mirror. Inver glanced up, ready to mumble a polite hello to whomever it was, but it wasn't a *whomever*... it was James.

The saintly James came to a stop right beside Inver, wearing a determined look, tilting his head ever-so-slightly as he gazed at their reflection.

The butterflies in Inver's stomach fluttered so hard he thought his feet would lift off the ground. He opened his mouth to speak but the words dried up before they could even leave his tongue. The cold water from the tap ran coolly over his fingers as the rest of his body burned with an intoxicating desire. Gripped in place, in time, Inver looked at the mirror watching James watch him.

James put his hands on his waist, fiddling just above his belt, proceeding to undo the bottom two buttons of his black shirt which he slowly lifted up high—almost to his nipples—exposing a flat stomach with creamy skin. James placed his hand over his taut tummy and began rubbing evocatively before grabbing hold of the waistband of his briefs, tugging at them as he adjusted himself, exposing the tip of his dark, trimmed pubes.

Oh my god. He wants me to do something.

A stinky ablution block was far from what Inver had envisioned for him and his prince. James deserved the most romantic of surroundings. But as the boy's fingers traced over his toned stomach, the moment was urging their story to go to a new page, regardless of the setting.

James's eyes pleaded with him in the mirror and just as Inver was about to extend a hand, the door burst open again followed by a new set of footsteps. Inver clumsily turned the tap off as James tucked his shirt back in, pretending like it was nothing out of the ordinary.

The move may have been thwarted, but it was a sign. The brave James had made his intentions known; now it was time for Inver to be the brave one. After work, he went to the bookstore where he bought a Valentine's Day card that he would hand over on that Monday.

Inver struggled with what to write in the card. A poem? Song lyrics? In the end, he settled on his own words. They weren't the most beautiful or romantic, but they spoke the truth of what James had done for him. How he had offered Inver redemption from a life stained with failure.

Inver was racked with nerves when Monday rolled round, sitting at his desk all morning waiting for the opportune moment, constantly shooting sly glances over at James. Just before twelve o'clock, he saw James get up from his chair and amble over to the coffee machine at the end of the floor—a spot far enough away to be safe from other workers' earshot.

Inver was in-between calls, so it was perfect timing. He opened up his desk drawer and retrieved the card tucked away in its crisp white envelope. In anxious steps, he wandered over to where James was standing and filling his cup up with caffeine. He stopped just a few feet away and inhaled the smell of rich coffee beans mixed in with James's musky cologne.

Inver took a brave breath as his heart hammered in his chest. "Hey…"

James turned around, his eyes lit up with acknowledgement. "Oh, hey man," his voice poured out sexily. Introductions weren't needed; they knew each other well enough.

Inver stepped forward and handed him the card. "This is for you," he said in a hushed tone.

James looked up at him with a confused expression. "For me?"

Inver nodded. "I was wondering if, um, maybe you'd like to get a drink with me after work tonight?"

James opened the envelope and saw it was a Valentine's card. His kind face drew a blank look. "Oh…"

"We could maybe go to the Irish pub across the street," Inver rambled.

"Cheers… but I'm not into guys. Sorry." James gave him a look of pity.

Inver was dumbfounded. Numbness hit him. *Oh my god. What have I done?*

An awkward giggle nudged Inver's ears from behind. He spun 'round and saw a young blonde girl with a hand covering her mouth, trying not to laugh. *Where the hell did she come from?*

Inver turned to James. "Yeah, no worries. All good. Sorry for bothering you." Inver rushed back to his desk, wishing the ground would swallow him whole. He looked over at the coffee machine and saw the girl gossiping with James about what she had just witnessed. She took the card

Let Me Catch You

from his hand and opened it up, reading it with greedy eyes and a mouth that slipped laughs like daggers.

Inver watched her mock his gift and its simple truth. In his mind, he repeated the words he knew it contained.

Thank you for letting me look forward to Mondays

When she saw Inver looking, she quickly handed the card back to James and stopped laughing to catch her breath. It was too late though; the damage was done.

For the first time in two months, reality fell from the sky, pummelling him like burning rocks and hot ash. He felt his palms get sweaty and the hair on the back of his neck begin to prickle. Inver thought he was going to throw up from the shock of it all. He got up from his desk and raced to the toilets where he actually did.

The rest of the week was hell. Anytime he heard the word Monday, he felt his ears burn. The boy with the name Inver could no longer speak—stopped looking. Maybe he never really had. Inver still felt eyes burning on him at work though, the eyes of others that one by one fell privy to the office gossip. The shy guy who made a point of going by unnoticed, wanting only the attention of one person, was now the focus of everyone's.

On Friday morning, Inver went to their manager and handed in his notice, effective immediately. She didn't ask questions, she appeared only too happy to accept it.

With his head hung low and his eyes aimed firmly at the ground, Inver collected his belongings from his desk drawer. One of the last things he saw as he left his soulmate behind was a pair of fancy feet swinging excitedly from a chair, happy as they ever were, unfazed by his exit. Stepping out of the insurance building for the very last time, Inver began the impossible task of finding closure for something that had never really opened.

And Inver fell for Straight Kid

*Lurgy - unwell
Melrose*

CHAPTER THIRTY-FIVE — 1996

STEPHEN

A blustery wind coming in from a temperamental Tasman Sea howled across the farm, threatening to knock Stephen's hat off. In the end, he sacrificed the hat, binning it on the back of the quad bike and continued driving along the lumpy farm track. His last chore of the day was to go check on Rusty and see how he had gotten on with his assigned task of fencing.

The plan was to quickly check on Rusty, rush home, scoff down dinner, shower and shave, then skedaddle into town and visit Shaun. He had been looking forward to the visit all day, getting to see his favourite person, a person who made Stephen feel more than wanted. He felt needed.

Of course, Shaun had argued on the phone that he was more than well enough to meet up at the reef but Stephen had tried talking sense into him, insisting he just wait a few more days till he fully recovered from his bout with the dreaded lurgy.

"Stop thinking with your cock," Stephen had teased.

Shaun had sounded sulky upon hearing this, but he accepted that Stephen come to his house, even if it did mean any action between them was unlikely with his family being around. To try and reward Shaun's patience, Stephen figured he could maybe arrange a weekend away again, just the two of them.

Horny holiday notions were cast aside when Stephen got to the fence Rusty was assigned to repair. He shook his head when his eyes locked in on the unfinished fence, and the sight of the ginger-haired worker laid on the ground napping next to the wire dispenser.

Fuck, he's useless.

Stephen got off the bike and strode towards Rusty.

"Nice day for it," Stephen said loudly and sarcastically.

Rusty shot up from his horizontal position, waking up with a huff. Seeing it was Stephen, he got to his feet and just stood there with a dumb grin spread across his face.

Stephen looked along the uncompleted fence. "Bit soon to be napping when you ain't finished, isn't it?" Stephen muttered, standing with his hands on his hips.

Rusty ignored the jab and just continued smirking.

Stephen tried his best to maintain calm despite Rusty's defiant silence rubbing him the wrong way. "This should have been finished today, mate." He glared disapprovingly at the lazy worker.

"You ain't my mate." Rusty's wide-set eyes glowed with confrontation.

"What's up your arse?" Stephen fired back.

Rusty burst out laughing. "I should be asking you that question."

Stephen stepped towards the indignant worker. "Seriously, what's with the attitude?"

Rusty ignored the question and sat back down on the ground. "I'm a have a smoke first. Then I'll get back to it."

Stephen sensed this was a losing battle. "You know what? I don't care. Just get the job done," he huffed before making his way back towards the quad bike.

"I don't care too much for taking orders from poofters," Rusty's voice carried calm and clear.

Stephen stopped in his tracks like a bucket of ice had just been poured over him. He slowly turned around. "What did you say?"

Rusty lit up a smoke and took a deep breath before answering, "I don't care much for taking orders from poofters. Or would you rather I call you a homo? See I don't know what you lot like to be called these days?"

Stephen felt his blood begin to boil. "You want to watch what you say, prick." He said the sentence as venomously as possible, hoping the tone's veracity would kill Rusty's challenge.

Rusty laughed, mocking his authority. "Ha, do I now? What you gonna do? Get your boyfriend to slap me?"

What do you fucking know?

Stephen felt this was going to go badly. He wanted to

deck him, just walk over and smash his fist into Rusty's ugly face. "What the fuck are you talking about?" Stephen asked, doing his best to sound mystified.

"You know EXACTLY what I'm talking about, Stephen." Rusty took a deep drag on his cigarette, casually blowing the smoke out like he was enjoying this game of cat and mouse. "I seen you both in the shed last week and don't pretend for a second I didn't."

Stephen did exactly what Rusty said not to. He dropped his mouth open, pretending like he didn't have a clue what Rusty was on about.

"You lads oughta be more careful if you gonna be playing hide the sausage," Rusty chuckled, his lips curled up with nasty glee as they pursed around his smoke.

Stephen shook in anger; his face burning up. "You didn't see shit!"

"Ahhh, but I did, you see. And I hear from the boy's mother down at the pub, 'you've been such a big help looking after wee Shaun while he's sick.'" Rusty did his best to impersonate Debbie's voice before bursting out with laughter.

Stephen wanted to run and kick the shit out of him. Rusty was a lightweight and Stephen knew he could take him out with one hit but he also knew he couldn't risk it. Rusty's words were like a nuclear warhead that could annihilate his entire existence.

Rusty took another drag on his smoke before casting Stephen a filthy look. "So, if you don't want me opening my trap, you'll fuck off and let me get on with my work the way I want."

Stephen was gripped between fight or flight. Fight would be a risk of Rusty opening his mouth but flight would only confirm his guilt. As much as it hurt Stephen's pride he chose flight. "You need to get your fucking eyes tested 'cos I don't know what you're talking about."

"Ain't nothing wrong with my eyesight, son. Might be with yours though if the wrong people found out about you. Not everybody round these parts will take too kindly if they found out you're an arse bandit."

Mother fucker.

"Go fuck yourself!" Stephen stormed back to the bike

and climbed on, driving off, leaving Rusty sitting there proudly like he'd won a war.

∞

Stephen wondered if he should mention anything to his parents about the run in with Rusty and insist they fire the lazy, useless prick. They probably would if they'd known the way he'd spoken to Stephen, but then Rusty's revenge would be simple. The bastard would open his big mouth, spouting off to anyone and everyone what he knew and Stephen would be found out for what he'd been up to. *For what I am.*

Stephen confined himself to his room where he fretted about what to do. His mind zinged in pain, thinking of ploys that could somehow cut the rumour off before it haemorrhaged all over town. He rang Delphi's house thinking if he could arrange another *catch up* this would protect against any leak of information. Delphi's dad answered the phone and informed him she had gone back to university a week early.

Fuck sake.

Prior to this, he had a rep for sure, one covered in the dirt of being a shallow prick that slept his way around town—but with women. If this got out, he would have no choice but to pack his bags and leave Clifton. He didn't fancy hanging around to be the all-too-easy recipient of crass jokes and nasty comments, many of which he had dished out himself through the years.

When it got to six o'clock, Stephen knew he wasn't going to Shaun's; there was no way they could be seen together for a while at least. He hid in his room, mulling over the worst possible scenarios 'till the phone rang an hour later.

"Hey man, are you still coming?" Shaun asked.

"Not tonight. Well, not for a while, actually."

"What do you mean?"

Stephen looked around to make sure no one was within earshot of the call. "Rusty saw us, Rusty fucking saw us."

"When?" Shaun asked calmly.

"At the shed last week," Stephen's voice nearly cracked. "Fuck, man, I don't know what to do. He's not said anything to anyone yet, but fuck, I can't have this shit getting out."

"Calm down, it'll be fine," Shaun urged him, "just tell him he didn't see anything."

"I did. But he knows, he fucking knows."

"Look, why don't you come 'round, we can sort it together. It's honestly not that bigger deal."

"Are you mad?" Stephen hissed. "The best thing we can do is just lay low for a while, okay?" Stephen took a deep breath. "I'm sorry, but I gotta go. I'll talk once it's died down a bit. I promise."

"Stephen, it's gonna be alright, you know," Shaun soothed.

"I hope so."

∞

Stephen avoided Rusty best he could, always opting to work a different field to the fiery farmhand. He had managed to avoid being alone with the man for the most part, but after four days, this plan went out the window when Stephen's dad asked him to help Rusty dig a trench for a new water pipe they were laying in the wonderland paddock.

As if it were a conspiracy, summer deviously served up the hottest day it had all season. Stephen worked his arse off, doing the lion's share of the work while Rusty practically sat around and watched the entire time. Stephen didn't complain though, keeping silent, letting the sound of birds in the nearby forest do the noise making in-between thuds of his shovel slicing the earth. He had hoped they could go all day without exchanging a single word, but this hope was dashed when after two hours, Rusty finally coughed up some conversation.

"It's a bloody marvellous day, ain't it, Stephen?"

Stephen grunted and kept shovelling.

"Too hot for work like this. Gets ya building up quite a sweat, dudn't it?"

Let Me Catch You

As if you'd know.

"Yep," Stephen said as his shovel dug into the ground.

"Mind you, I s'pose ya boyfriend likes seeing you all up in a sweat." Rusty flashed him a bitter smile.

"I told you. I'm not queer, so just fucking drop it." Stephen continued digging.

"No need to get stroppy," Rusty spat back, sounding very much like he was enjoying this. He took a deep breath letting Stephen know there more was to come. "Seriously though, I dunno why you'd even like that sort of thing. I guess a hole's a hole, but fuck, having something stuck up there."

Stephen spun around. "Seriously, Rusty, just fucking drop it, right?"

"Sorry, mate, didn't mean to offend," Rusty replied without an ounce of sincerity. "So tell me, do you fuck him or does he fuck you?"

"Right!" Stephen threw the shovel down and stormed over to Rusty who put his hands in the air.

"Oi, Oi, settle down, Stevie boy. I'm just joshing ya."

Stephen backed off, his breath heavy with anger. He retrieved the shovel and returned to digging.

"It's your old man I feel sorry for," Rusty said, "I'd be gutted if I had a faggot son. Just as well, I never will."

"Fuck you, Rusty," Stephen muttered.

"Sorry, sunshine, but I don't swing that way." Rusty laughed. "It ain't your fault though. I'm pickin' you was overly mothered. That's what causes it ya know."

Shovel against his face, so hard, so satisfying.

Stephen zoned out, ignoring the rest of Rusty's cruel words. The man's jealousy of Stephen had always been there, simmering below the surface. This nugget of scandal he stumbled upon must've felt like winning the lotto for the sad git. Stephen knew that he probably hadn't helped matters with his barely veiled contempt for the trashy family who helped work his family's farm, but it seemed unfair to attack and mock something that had indirectly benefited Rusty.

Being with Shaun had made Stephen try to be a nicer person and less of a snob. For so many years the warmth and kindness that had eluded his personality had begun to take hold. Now, in a survival reflex, it was about to let go, and if it did, he felt like kindness would be out of reach for good.

CHAPTER THIRTY-SIX — 1996

STEPHEN

The midnight hour was bathed in a humid air blanketing the land which made sleeping difficult. Stephen—saturated in sheets of sweat—tossed and turned, unable to drift into sleep. He lay naked, lost in his opprobrium, when a light tap ripped his attention toward the bedroom window. He sat up and plucked the bedsheet between his fingers, positioning it strategically to hide his crotch and leaned forward to open the curtain. On the other side stood Shaun, smiling back at him, a hopeful look on his face. Stephen raised a finger to his lips, signalling for Shaun to remain quiet. He dropped the modesty-providing sheet and scuttled on his knees to the window, easing open its latch.

"What are you doing here?" Stephen snarled in a surly whisper.

"I needed to see you."

Stephen sighed. "Give me a minute. I'll meet you 'round back." He picked up a ruffled pair of jeans and slipped into them commando-style, then chucked on a shirt before tiptoeing out to the lounge where he gently opened the ranch slider door and slipped outside.

The air was electric and had a heavy feeling in its warmth. Stephen crept through the garden's maze of flowers and native shrubs 'till he found Shaun waiting for him at the cliff's edge, under the pohutukawa tree. Shaun was dressed in his usual attire of shorts and a t-shirt, scuffing his feet along the patchy dirt and grass beneath the old, majestic tree. As Stephen drew closer to him, Shaun stopped his foot scrapings and greeted him with a smile.

"Hey stranger," Shaun beamed.

Stephen nodded, stopping a couple metres in front of him with a stern look. "What are you doing here?"

"I wanted to see you. It's been nearly a week."

"You shouldn't be here. I told you we have to play this cool for a while."

Shaun began fiddling with a bit of loose bark on the tree. "I've been thinking. I don't think he's going to say anything and even if he does, what's the big deal?"

"Are you retarded? Umm, the big deal is that shit sticks and I don't want people knowing what we've done. Don't you agree?"

Shaun shrugged, averting his eyes from Stephen's accusing gaze, "Look, I know what you're saying, but I just don't think it's the big deal you're making it out to be."

Shaun's quiet reasoning clashed head-on with Stephen's impending doom of the situation.

Stephen threw his arms in the air. "It's official, you are fucked in the head," he said, turning his back to Shaun.

Shaun stepped towards him. "No, I'm just not ashamed of you or what we do." He placed his hands on Stephen's shoulders, rubbing them gently.

Stephen swallowed the lump of stress in his throat. "The people I know, the ones that love me… I think they just might be more than a little ashamed," his voice wavered.

Shaun kissed the back of his neck. "But *I* love you too."

The words fired off chills through Stephen's body, his skin getting goose bumps as the hair on his arms stood up.

He said it… and he means it.

Stephen suppressed the urge to spin around and kiss him forever. He couldn't succumb to the wanting of this heart-melting moment. He knew if he did, he would crumble and be lost down a path where there would be no turning back from.

Stephen reluctantly turned around, avoiding all eye contact. "I… I can't do this," his voice trembled, "it's like everything's falling apart. I'm falling apart from all the fucking wondering what people know."

"Then let me catch you," Shaun said, his hands reaching around behind Stephen's neck, clutching at his shirt collar, begging for Stephen to hold on.

"I'm sorry, Shaun, but I think we're done."

Shaun's grip tightened. "You don't mean that."

"I do." Stephen pushed his hands on Shaun's chest, trying to separate their bodies.

"No, you don't. You're being fucking stupid, Stephen. Please don't do this," Shaun's voice trailed off, his eyes glistening with the formation of tears.

"I'm going, Shaun. Look, I'm sorry, but we're too different. This just isn't me."

"We're the same more than you want to admit it."

Stephen cast him a look of pity and began to walk away.

"FUCK YOU, Stephen Davis. You fucking coward," Shaun shouted.

Stephen marched promptly back over to Shaun. "Shut your fucking mouth or you'll wake everyone up."

"Good. I don't care. 'Cos I'm not the scared little bitch worried what they'll say."

Stephen's fists curled into balls of flesh, his voice warbling, "I'm warning you, Shaun, just keep your mouth shut."

"No, I love you and I know you love me too."

"No, I don't."

"Fucking pussy."

"What the fuck?" Stephen planted a hand to his face.

"Yeah, just a fucking PUSSY," Shaun screamed again.

Stephen put a finger to his mouth, willing Shaun to hush. "Keep it down. I told you, this just isn't who I am," he whispered.

"Well, I think it is," Shaun said indignantly.

"No, Shaun, I'm not gay. I'm not like you."

"Really? 'Cos I think you rather enjoyed having my cock in your mouth," Shaun said, sounding as crude as possible.

Stephen sizzled with rage, thrusting forward and pushing Shaun into the hard trunk of the tree, grabbing him by the throat and digging his fingers into the skin. He held his fist up in front of Shaun's face, threatening to hit him.

Shaun looked back at him, laughing, tears brewing in his eyes. "Go on then. Do it. Just fucking hit me."

Stephen's shaking fist hung in the air, so full of anger, needing to hit someone to dispose of all the pent up rage flowing through him like an infection.

But not you.

Stephen heaved out a heavy groan and dropped his fist. He mustered the nastiest tone his voice could find and looked Shaun straight in the eyes. "You were just a convenient place to put my cock. That's all, nothing more. Just like your fucking mother."

Stephen released his grip on Shaun and shoved him back into the tree.

"Fuck you, dick." Shaun sucked back on a gooby ball of spit that he hurled straight onto Stephen's face. He slid slowly down the rough trunk of the tree, crumbling to the lonely ground on a sob.

Stephen wiped the spit away and looked down at the broken Munro who was reduced to a pitiful mess, bawling into his hands. "You're pathetic." He turned and marched back through the garden, leaving Shaun behind to fester in his own tears.

The night's soft breeze catapulted heartache through the air as Shaun's pained sobs stabbed Stephen's eardrums all the way to the back porch. He shut the door behind him with a jittery hand and stood locked in shock with what had just gone down, with what he had just done. But he knew he couldn't turn back. Not now. It was best for both of them this chapter closed.

GOING HOME — 1996

SHAUN

It was as if the world had stopped moving and his chest would explode with hurt. Shaun almost wished it would and carry him away, far, far away from Stephen's damning words. He lay against the tree crying, feeling like all the love inside of him had ruptured and was now bleeding out of him in tears. He didn't know how long he was like that for but he waited plenty, praying Stephen would come back out and apologise, take back all the lies he had said—all the venom he'd spat and injected.

Shaun picked up a stick at his foot and began stabbing at the bark of the tree, trying to unleash his agony, but as his sobbing heaves settled to rolling sighs, so did his attack on the tree calm in its ferocity; he changed tact and scraped through the bark with purpose, slowly etching out *their* symbol: a reminder to Stephen that he was more than just a convenience.

When he had finished leaving his heartache's calling card, Shaun stood up, smoothed his shorts clean of twigs and dirt, and looked over the ledge to check on the tide. It was changing, high tide beginning to make its push to the shore. He would have to make the descent down the cliff, and fast, so he could avoid being trapped in its battering waters.

Shaun hoped he could stop bawling by the time he got home. He really didn't want anyone seeing him like this 'cos if they did, he would probably just let the truth tumble out of him and bare all. Even though he didn't care if they disapproved, it seemed unfair to burden them all with his bullshit.

Teetering on the edge of the vertical path, Shaun stared out at the noisy sea. The moon loomed high above, resembling a tiny hard white disk, waiting for the hands of god to snap it and offer it to the earth as communion. He lifted his leg to take a tentative step down the track, but before he could ground his foot, he was thrust forward toward the night sky.

Spiralling in slow motion through the darkness, he thought he must have jumped, but just before he hit the rocks below, he felt his shoulders burn with the imprint of angry palms.

∞

The pain of broken bones screamed throughout his body, waking Shaun from a precious escape of unconsciousness. He couldn't stand; one look at his injured legs told him they were shattered as they bent in unnatural angles. His body was wet and heavy; he looked down finding his clothes smeared in a damp blackness. It was only when he sniffed the material and recognised an almost rusty iron smell that he realised it was his own blood. The mighty sea was enormous in volume, erupting into his ears, only metres away. *How long was I knocked out for?*

He scraped and crawled his crumpled body along the craggy reef toward the path up the cliff, using every ounce of strength he had left to hoist himself onto the first steep step. He clung on precariously to the track's slippery clay edges, only managing to climb three steps before the pain outweighed his ability to move.

The water came fast and rose quickly. First lapping at his ankles, then his knees and finally his waist. Shaun tried again, climbing through unfathomable pain eating through his broken bones and ripped skin. He only got two more steps up when what felt like a bone snapping, rammed him with an agony so severe his body went into shock, his hands lost their grip, and he plunged into the cold water.

Darkness suffocated him 'till he bobbed to the surface, sucking in a deep breath of air to sustain his lungs that burned for oxygen. While floating and trying to navigate through the watery night, a large wave came in; he couldn't see it, but he heard its ferocious approach. It picked him up, raising him in its crest as it carried his broken body, slamming into the face of the cliff. Pain seared through every inch of his body, ravishing his instincts. The waves just kept coming, sucking him out with their retreat before slamming him mercilessly back against the sharp rocks, each time with greater force.

His desperate screams for help dried up as the life inside him began to drain and soon he could not tell if the darkness surrounding him was night or death. This was it. This was the end. He cried and cried—not from broken bones, but from the heartache flowing rancid in his veins. He had so little to take, but everything was being stolen from him.

Please Lord, all I want is to go home. Please!

It just didn't seem fair, but then they say such about life.

With hope abandoned and prayers unanswered, Shaun let the sea embrace him in its deep arms, closed his eyes and slept.

Shaun dead

CHAPTER THIRTY-EIGHT — 2016

INVER

The dark was locked in over the land. Looming, it was a forgotten pot of coffee—black and cold. The sea raged in the distance, fusing with the high pitched screams of the wind like a furious choir. Wandering through the sounds of nature's church, Inver used the light on his phone to guide his steps from his car to the front door.

He had spent an entire day and most of an evening aimlessly sightseeing, driving around the region's diabolical roads littered with chunks of road kill spread across the black tar seal like bits of lumpy jam. Once he felt it was safe to return, and more so at the urging of the gas light demanding the tank be fed, he drove back to Stephen's and was relieved to find James's parents silver BMW had gone.

Inver twisted the key in the door, clicking it open as gentle as he could. With only one odd-socked foot barely planted inside, a deep voice echoed down the long hallway.

"It finally returns," Stephen bellowed, standing barefoot in shorts and a t-shirt.

Inver closed the door behind him and gave Stephen a guilty wave. "Yep, like a boomerang, I always come back."

Stephen nodded and placed his hands on his hips. "Come with me. I saved you some dinner."

"You didn't have to do that."

"It's fine. I figured you'd be hungry when you got back from hiding."

"Hiding?"

"I don't know much, Inver, but I know the look of someone bolting for his life when I see it," Stephen said, cocking his head thoughtfully. "Now, come on. Come have some dinner." He disappeared toward the kitchen with Inver following in his wake. Stephen grabbed trays of Chinese food out of the fridge and a plate from the pantry.

"Dig in. Help yourself." Stephen spread the trays out over the bench, a mix of noodle, rice and meat dishes.

Inver piled his plate high, creating a dubious food pyramid. He was starving. He popped the dinner in the microwave and placed a hand over his impatiently rumbling stomach. As soon as it was cooked, he sat at the dining table, inhaling the greasy feast while Stephen chilled out in the lounge and waited for him to finish.

"Feel full now?" Stephen called out once Inver had emptied the plate.

Inver nodded, put his plate in the sink, then went and joined Stephen in the lounge. "Thank you for saving me some."

"Not a problem."

Inver just wanted to scurry off to bed, but he felt obliged to sit and talk with his host. He leaned forward in the chair, rubbing his knees. "So, how was it catching up with Troy and Clare?"

"Yeah, it was really good, aye," Stephen said. He narrowed his eyes, taking in Inver's edgy posture.

Inver waited for him to continue talking but he just kept staring like he was examining an art exhibit. The silence stretched beyond awkward.

Stephen's voice finally broke the air. "I'm sorry, but I just gotta say it."

"Say what?"

"I love James to pieces, but he was a complete dick for doing what he did."

Oh god. James told him.

"He told me what he did... the whole leading you on and the card you gave him."

Inver felt all the blood in his body rush to his face, his cheeks staining with crimson. "He told you about that?" Not only had he been outed to his host, but he had also been outed for his creepy hit on.

"Sure did," Stephen said, "I didn't give him a choice in the matter. Me and him went to get the Chinese while his folks and Tim stayed here, so I bailed him up in the car about what I saw between you two in the hallway."

Inver placed his hands over his face and groaned.

"You've got nothing to be embarrassed about," Stephen said. "He told me about the flirting and telling you he was straight. Reckons he doesn't want people at work to know he's gay was his best excuse."

"Really? But his family obviously know."

Stephen shrugged. "Guess he has his reasons, but still, it stinks with what happened with you."

"Yeah, it wasn't my finest hour."

"I told him he's lucky you didn't whack him."

Inver shook his head. "I'd never do that."

"You know what I mean. I thought you'd be angrier."

Inver looked up at the ceiling as if the answer were painted on it. "I'm just embarrassed by it all."

Stephen looked at him, sympathy radiating from his blue eyes.

Inver sighed, "I was an idiot, thinking I'd found my soulmate even though we never shared a bloody word... I don't know what it was, but I just thought he was a good person, he had such a good vibe about him you know... but yeah, turns out I'm just screwy." Inver laughed mockingly at himself.

"You're not crazy, Inver. Despite him being a little gutless shit, you didn't imagine him being a good person. That is real. Troy and Clare are lovely people and he is just like both of them," Stephen said, he tapped Inver on the leg. "It's not like it wasn't reciprocated. What you have is a case of unavailable, not uninterested."

Inver wasn't sure if this made him feel any better. It didn't make him feel any less lonely or reinstall hope for his future. "Guess I can add it to my long list of fucking regrets," Inver said, spewing the words out heatedly.

Stephen laughed out loud.

"What?" Inver asked. "How's that funny?"

"You finally said the f-word. About fucking time."

Inver gave him a crooked smile and shrugged.

"Seriously, you're too uptight, mate. You need to swear more and stop giving a toss what other people think about you. Trust me."

"I'm uptight?" Inver asked, knowing full well he was.

Stephen looked him straight in the eyes and smiled. "Yes, Little Inver, you are way too fucking uptight." He slapped Inver's leg comfortingly. "You need to loosen up, buddy. And fuck, who doesn't have regrets?"

Inver raised his eyebrows. "Lots of people."

"Nope, they're confusing being content with having no regrets," Stephen said bluntly. He leaned forward on the couch, resting his arms on his legs, clasping his hands. "We all end up taking some path at the expense of another. If we didn't, that would mean we weren't taking risks."

"I guess that's true," Inver mumbled.

"Of course it's true. I'm always right." Stephen's baby blue eyes gleamed with a cheeky glint. "Look, what you did with James… well, honestly, it's no one's fucking business but yours. You took a risk that didn't work, but good on you for trying. If we don't take risks in life, we stop evolving."

Inver felt a warmth inside him—not just from Stephen's words, but the effort attached to them to try and make him feel better. "So, do you have any paths you wished you'd taken instead?"

Stephen looked at the floor and began nodding his head. "Yeah, I do." He raised his face to match Inver's stare. "If I'm lucky, maybe I'll cross that path again one day."

The room went quiet as the talking stopped. A peaceful energy circled Inver. He relished its comfort and absorbed its peace before shattering it with a bomb. "Why did you say the underwear was from Kimmy?"

Stephen lurched back into the couch, startled by Inver's knowledge. He bit his lip with musing inspiration, taking his time to answer. "I thought I knew why, but I was wrong," he said sounding cryptic. "But you know what?" Stephen chuckled. "If I'm being completely honest with myself, then the truth is," he took a deep breath, "I wanted to see all of you." He stared at Inver, showing no sign of flinching at his openness.

Inver scratched his forehead, not sure if he had heard Stephen or something he wanted to hear. "You what?"

"You're a good-looking dude, Inver Murray," Stephen confessed, "even if you do look like a fucking hippy with that hair."

Inver shook his head, emitting a mumbled laugh and grinned ear to ear.

Stephen put a hand out, touching Inver's sandpaper-rough chin and raised his face 'till their eyes met. "You're a good person, Inver. The world needs more people like you… to make up for the ones like me."

Stephen slid down from his seat, planting his knees on the carpet and leaned forward, planting his lips on Inver's mouth to share a sticky kiss. Stephen slowly pulled his face back, a thin thread of saliva stretching like a spider's web between their lips. Stephen's nicotine breath wafted across as he tugged Inver's shirt down, tracing his fingers across Inver's chest hair.

"Shall we take a risk?" Stephen whispered, raising his eyebrows.

Inver nodded. He felt the knot in his stomach that had made its home there for so long begin to unravel. Stephen stood up and took Inver by the hand, leading him to the bedroom where their clothes fell to the floor and their paths collided.

CHAPTER THIRTY-NINE — 2016

STEPHEN

Stephen woke up feeling the wetness of lube on his behind. Inver's now limp cock slept, wedged between his cheeks. He looked on the floor seeing the purple scraps of condom wrappers and the used rubber from their first failed attempt. Stephen chose the worst guy anyone could for their first time to be fucked by; Inver was huge when erect and certainly had left Stephen more than able to lay claim to being broken in. An absolute first, having another man impale him so intrusively. It had hurt like hell, but he'd bit the pillow and grew accustomed to the pain that soon evolved into a strange, fulfilling pleasure—the kind where the hurt was a turn-on because it meant *more* than pain... it meant intimacy.

Inver's body was glued behind him, one of his long arms wrapped around Stephen's waist as he slept, breathing short shallow breaths that warmed Stephen's back. He could feel lightness in Inver. Invisible threads of burden worn for far too long had become unstitched the moment both their clothes had come off.

Stephen felt his cock twitch from the images flooding his mind of Inver riding his body only hours earlier. He was surprised by how easily he had surrendered to the dominance that roared in Inver's green eyes. The way he laid face down so willingly on the bed, ready to be taken, wanting to be taken. Stephen closed his eyes and relived the fresh memory.

He honed in on the moment when he lay face down on the bed and Inver had taken hold of his feet, spreading his legs apart with slow purpose. Stephen had lain there shaking with nerves, wondering what would come next. It was revealed when Inver gently kissed his heel, slowly running his wet tongue up the back of his leg, over his knee and thigh 'till eventually his mouth found Stephen's squished balls with a kiss. Inver had pressed his face in, tonguing at his scrotum with lashing licks. Stephen had squirmed, panting and sighing as Inver took each ball into his mouth one at a time and began sucking.

After Stephen's nuts received a thorough soaking, Inver had pulled away and let his bristly chin scrape Stephen's buttocks as he rested his head there, breathing heavily. Stephen assumed the guy had lost his lollies already and that the fun was over, but without warning Inver spread his cheeks apart and spat between them, circling a slippery finger around Stephen's hole. He gulped when he heard Inver's vigorous voice breathe over his arse, "You ready?"

After a couple false starts, Inver climbed on top and hooked his feet over Stephen's ankles, pinning him down, locking him in place. Inver's hairy chest scratched against his smooth back, a sensation teeming with virility. Inver gently guided his cock inside Stephen's arse, entering with care and precision, feeding him every wide inch he had. The green-eyed stud made sure he fucked Stephen slow but firm, invading him with a steady rhythm. Stephen felt Inver's thick throbbing dick taking ownership of more than just the moment as their bodies fused into one through held hands with fingers laced together.

As Stephen whimpered and writhed, whispering for more, Inver muttered musky words of praise into his ears before lashing his earlobes with an experienced tongue. All of a sudden, Inver thrust his cock as deep as it could go and hit a spot Stephen didn't even know he had. In that instant, Stephen cried out a vulnerable sigh, spunking a pool of sticky cum into the sheets. They'd laid there with pounding hearts, cradling one another, listening to the drizzling of the rain outside 'till they'd fallen asleep with the light still on.

Stephen kissed Inver's pale arm that was now draped over him so protectively. It had been years since he had shared a bed. Instead, he had always chased the principle of cum 'n run. Stephen had forgotten how safe it had felt, the warmth and closeness of a naked body.

The neon numbers on the bedside alarm clock glared a hideous time: 4:15 a.m. He groaned to himself knowing he didn't have time to go back to sleep. He wanted to get up and make them both breakfast—fry up some eggs, bacon, toast—and go all out, but he knew Inver needed sleep. Maybe when he got back inside from milking, he could woo Inver then. He delicately lifted Inver's arm and scooted out of bed to get changed.

After a quick shower and strong coffee, Stephen made his way outside to the frosty fields. In spritely steps, his gumboots scrunched over cold blades of grass while his breath poked the air like misty white quills. Not even the near-freezing morning could wipe the smile that Inver had spread across his face.

The field with the calves soon appeared. "Morning, you lot," Stephen chirped. He let himself in the gate, so caught up in his daydream of the naked man still in his bed he didn't notice that the usually hungry-mouthed calves hadn't rushed at his grand entrance. He scanned the paddock for any sign of movement, but there was none. Stephen lifted his torch and swept it across the field, its beam of yellow light spreading across a scene of silent chaos that made his fingers tremble. Brown and white lumps of meat littered the earth. All the calves lay dead on the ground. Stephen cringed at the sight of peaceful paddocks, forced against their will, having been morphed into killing fields.

He walked over to the nearest victim and squatted on the ground to inspect the killer blow. The animal's head had been bashed in; the curdled blood painted on its face told Stephen it had happened some hours ago.

Fucking Eddie.

Two dogs died, yes, but that couldn't justify such a savage escalation of violence. Stephen shook his head and threw the torch on the ground in a fit of anger. He took a deep breath and realised he should have never let it slide and hoped Eddie would just calm down. Now, it was time for the police to get involved, assuming Stephen could hold his temper back long enough to not walk over to the old bastard's house and smash it in with a bat. Stephen huffed his way to the torch lying on the ground, raising it up, its glowing beam dangling down to show a raw cut in the earth.

What the fuck?

Stephen shone the light over the cut line and traced its path. He gripped the torch tight in fear when he discovered he was standing in the middle of a wounded zeitgeist, the summer of 1996 beneath his feet. The ground felt like it would bleed; its dirt-skin cut deep with an infinity symbol, the circles of which stared up at him like a pair of angry eyes.

Mihi's words of tapu suddenly didn't seem so easily dismissed as he stood in what felt like the outline of a murder victim. Stephen looked around at the carnage of baby cattle, struggling to believe in ghosts and, if he could, how could one do this? Even if Eddie had been the one to kill the calves and leave an evil stench in the air, something else had swooped to earth afterward and left a mark that only two people ever knew its real meaning—one of whom was dead.

Stephen looked back at his house in the distance, seeing a glow through the trees from his bedroom light. Inside that room lay a betrayal. He scurried away from a tortured angel's reminder that he wasn't allowed happiness ever again and marched back to his house to tell Inver it would be best if he stay at Rusty's place and pretend what they did never happened.

CHAPTER FORTY — 1996

STEPHEN

Stephen's heavy eyelids opened in protest, his body shattering and running on empty, too many stressful nights having taken their toll. As he crawled his way out of bed, he felt an instant pang of regret when he remembered what he had said the night before to Shaun.
Just like your fucking mother.
The words ran on repeat, digging at his conscience. He didn't mean what he had said—of course he hadn't—but worst of all, he couldn't believe he'd made Shaun cry. Someone like that, so good and kind, was meant to have a smile on their face and never suffer from having sad eyes. Stephen did his best to shake it out of his mind and went on with his day; telling himself it was all for the best.

This approach was short-lived though, barely lasting past the morning. Stephen had come in for lunch expecting a quiet meal, but found his parents joined by Rusty and Donna, sitting and eating at the table with their annoying snot of a child, Inver. One taunting smirk from Rusty was enough to make him politely bail from the communal meal; Stephen fetched himself some of the ham and salad from the table and sat out on the back porch to eat alone.

After chewing his way through half his lunch, he threw the scraps to the sparrows and went strolling in the backyard, pacing near the scene of the previous night's dispute. Under the pohutukawa tree, he coasted over shreds of bark scattering the ground like a messy jigsaw puzzle. Stephen looked at the tree's gnarled trunk and saw *their* symbol proudly displayed; he ran his finger through its deep, splintered grooves and closed his eyes. Shaun had no intention of letting Stephen forget him that easily. He retrieved his hand and covered his face, letting out a defeated groan.

I fucked up. I've really fucked up.

Stephen marched back inside, not saying a word to anyone and grabbed the phone, shut himself in his room, sucked in a breath of courage and dialled Shaun's number. Lydia answered after the fourth ring, informing Stephen she hadn't seen her brother all day and suggested he try looking for him at the workshop in case he was working on one of his pet projects. This struck Stephen as being unlikely, but he drove down there anyway, only to find the place locked up and completely deserted.

An odd sense of unease grew in the pit of his stomach the longer the day went on without hearing from Shaun or being able to get hold of him. Something didn't feel right, and this only heightened his guilt to the point he thought he might spontaneously combust. He wanted to say sorry so badly, so fucking badly, and tell Shaun he didn't mean any of it and that maybe, just maybe, Shaun was right. *I am like you.*

The day crawled by painfully slow and by the time Stephen hopped into bed in the evening, Shaun still had made no attempt at contacting him. *He must be so angry.* With a heavy heart, Stephen went to bed listening to a summer storm lash his window, drowning out his tired brooding, and faded into sleep.

∞

The storm and its drizzly grey remnants lingered throughout the morning until the afternoon sun burnt through, delivering blue skies. The sunny disposition of the weather did little to alter the dark mood Stephen found himself in, still having not heard from Shaun. After the afternoon milking, he decided to try the only other person he could think of who would have any idea of where Shaun may be. *Megan Dombroski.*

Driving to Megan's house was tricky business thanks to the main road being fraught with debris and roadside slips left over from the storm. Megan lived just a short distance from Shaun, on a busy-for-Clifton street that led directly to the beach and holiday camp. Her house was easily spotted with two rusted out cars on its front yard—blatant white-trash beacons.

Like Shaun, she too was part of the town's small token-poverty-clique. Stephen wondered if this is why the pair gravitated to each other at any social event, finding comradery in the face of subtle mocking; their friendship tore at the egalitarian dream New Zealanders liked to sell to themselves.

Stephen pulled up on the grass verge outside Megan's house. He marched up the front yard's cracked concrete path and knocked three times at the door. Just as he was about to give up and walk off, heavy stomps came from inside the house and Megan opened the door looking ripped as fuck; her bloodshot eyes glazed with distraction. After a fumbling introduction to the topic, Megan established she hadn't heard from Shaun all week. She seemed genuinely surprised to see Stephen at her door, so if she had any knowledge of their romance, she was hiding it well through her drugged-out daze.

Stephen went back to his car, now cooking in the summer heat, his hands burning at the touch of the black steering wheel. He was about to drive home when he saw flashing lights of a police car pulling up at the end of the road. Something was going on down there, not an unusual sight during peak holiday season, but now being the first day of February, this seemed out of place. Stephen started up the car and drove towards the campground to see what the commotion was.

When he parked up, he saw an elderly man with a bag of groceries hovering at the beach's edge. Stephen got out the heat-baked vehicle and walked up to the old man, asking if he had any clue about the unfolding drama.

"Someone's saying they might've found a body. Poor soul," the man said.

Body. Stephen felt his stomach drop at the word. "You've not been down?"

"Nope, I can do without spoiling my appetite, thanks," the man said before walking on with his bags of food.

Stephen ran down the dunes to the black sand. He walked briskly along the beach 'till he reached a small crowd of people numbering about twenty. They hovered like flies, glued to something that had them intrigued, but Stephen couldn't make out through all the arses and elbows what it was they were looking at. None of the crowd looked familiar, mostly out-of-towners in fishing gear. He squinted his eyes, managing to peer through a small gap and saw a pair of sore, bloodied, bare feet.

Stephen overheard one man telling a tale of discovery. "Yip, we thought we'd caught the big one, but not at all... I don't think I'll be casting my line out here anytime soon."

Stephen approached the group and manoeuvred through the mess of limbs to get a better look. He smelled it before he saw it. A pungent aroma still light in odour, but distinctly grim, laced with the cruellest sweetness like a rank perfume.

Face up, feet pointing to the sky, death was laid out in green shorts and a ripped white t-shirt, barely held together with strained threads that exposed nasty gash marks on the side of the body. Stephen knew who owned these clothes; he knew who the grazed, battered body belonged to.

Dear god.

A synchronised gasp came from the crowd when Shaun's head flopped onto its side, his lifeless brown eyes staring straight at Stephen. A callous rip streaked across his throat where flesh had been gouged out. His face was red with burst blood vessels around his dead, vacant eye sockets.

Stephen put a hand to his mouth to stop himself from yelping in shock. He felt the strength in his body just fade away, crumbling in on itself. His lungs needed air, fresh air, not this poisonous fume. He barged back through the crowd, trying to escape the decaying corpse.

Safely away from the crowd and Shaun's hideous scent, Stephen fell to his knees heaving for air; he felt his gut churn and he threw up on the sand. He kept gagging, bringing up acidic, yellow bile that dribbled down his chin.

A woman came over and touched him on the shoulder. "You okay, love? It's not pleasant, is it?"

Bits of sick still dribbled out Stephen's mouth as he spat out, "I know him. I know him."

The woman removed her hand. "Oh my god," she whispered.

Stephen stood back up. "Cover him up. Somebody cover him up!"

The crowd stared at him in disbelief, his raw emotion briefly stealing their attention from death.

Stephen looked at the empty shell of Shaun, a body he knew every inch of. He felt the tears well in his eyes as he stormed off, sprinting fast as he could 'till he got back to his car. He threw his body inside, locking all the doors and clutching the steering wheel.

His eyes began to burn, his tear ducts moistening and his throat running dry. He heaved a tortured breath, trying to fight the storm of grief he knew was coming. A feeling like warm water rippled in his chest, like a calm before the storm. Then it hit. Sorrow so vast he had never felt anything like it for any reason. He howled with tears, consumed with loss. Stephen rocked back and forth pulling at his hair.

I'll never get to say I'm sorry.

CHAPTER FORTY-ONE — 1996

STEPHEN

Ignoring the traffic signs pleading for him to slow down on the metal road, Stephen put his foot down and raced toward an altercation. He had one hand on the steering wheel while the other wiped his snivelling nose and damp eyes. I'm gonna fucking kill him, he thought. The moment of clarity as he sat grief-stricken in the car at the beach had snapped him into action.

When he least expects it, I'll fucking be there. Luke's threat resounded with a sickening whack, stirring a rage in Stephen. Why else would Shaun end up in the fucking ocean dead? He didn't know what Luke had done, but Stephen was going to find out. The six-foot-four giant posed no challenge to Stephen in his current mind frame. Right now, he could take on an entire army.

The driveway to Luke's home came into view. His Ute was parked outside and coated in a dry flaky mud. Stephen's car juddered over the cattle grate leading into the property; he slammed his foot on the brakes, emitting a hideous screeching noise as he came to a standstill, tearing up bits of lawn.

Things could go horribly wrong, Luke could easily deck him, but Stephen felt an iron rod of courage in his back as he stepped out of the vehicle, an invisible blanket of bravery hugging his body.

A shirtless Luke stormed out the front door to see what the commotion was. He waved his hands in the air, shaking his head in disgust at the ripped up frontage.

"What the fuck did you do?" Stephen sputtered. The words had been burning like hot coal in his mouth he couldn't wait to spit out. He marched towards the front steps.

Luke didn't appear to hear him and just stared at the

state of his ripped up yard. "Oi, look what you did to my front lawn, dickhead."

"I said, what the fuck have you done, Luke?" Stephen stormed up the steps, crashing his hands into Luke's chest, sending him stumbling over and landing on his backside before hitting his head against the front door.

Luke leapt to his feet, but not fast enough before Stephen punched him in the jaw, sending him straight back down. Luke cursed in pain, grabbing his mouth where Stephen had hit him, blood pouring from his cut lip. Luke held out his hand, inspecting the gathering red droplets. He looked up at Stephen, suddenly aware how fucking crazy his mate was. Luke went to get up off the ground but Stephen stepped forward, stamping his foot, warning him to stay down.

Luke raised his hands up. "Fucking stop. What have I done?"

"You know exactly what this is about," Stephen snarled.

"No, I fucking don't. You don't just bowl on up to your best mate's house and knock them in the fucking mouth." Luke said, rubbing his still bleeding lip. "Fuck sake," he muttered and flicked the blood down on the ground, some of it plopping onto Stephen's shoes.

"Why'd ya fucking do it, Luke? Why?" Stephen's eyes shrunk in anger; his heart in overdrive.

"I don't know what you're fucking on about," Luke protested, looking again at his reddening hands. "Look what you fucking done. My lip's all busted and fucking bleeding."

"That's not the only blood you've got on your hands."

Luke shook his head like he was dismissing a child. "Well, I don't know what it is I've supposed to have done, so maybe you would like to fucking enlighten me, Chuck Norris."

"Shaun's dead."

Luke stared back dumbstruck. "What?"

"Yeah, you know. Our mate, Shaun. Shaun Munro," Stephen said, a patronizing anger rising up in his voice. "He's dead 'cos you couldn't just let go of the bullshit."

"Dead? What are you talking about?"

Stephen shook in rage. His body didn't feel like his anymore. "Shaun's dead and you fucking killed him."

Luke's mouth dropped in shock. "You're fucking crazy. I didn't kill anyone."

"All I know is I just drove from the beach where they've found his body, so don't fucking lie to me 'cos I know you had something to do with this."

Luke put a hand out cautioning Stephen to calm down. "Okay, okay, let's talk about this. Let me at least stand up."

Stephen took a step back, allowing Luke to get to his feet as he continued rubbing his jaw. "I can't believe you think I killed Shaun. What makes you think I'd kill anyone?"

"You said you'd get even. You said he'd *die* for what he did."

Luke cast Stephen a guarded stare. "What I say and what I do are two very different fucking things. Yeah, sure, I wanted to get payback on the little shit, but I didn't kill him, Stephen. You're acting fucking crazy, man." Luke scanned him up and down. "Take a look at yourself. You need to get a fucking grip."

Stephen let out a breath of disgust at Luke's denial. "You're not even sorry."

"What do you want me to say? Look, I guess it's sad he's dead, but he was never really my mate, not like you and Troy are. I'm not saying I'm glad he's dead, but you know."

"Know what?"

"I'm not exactly gonna miss him, am I? Remember?" Luke wiggled his bloody fingers in front of Stephen's face. "Anyway, how did he die?" Luke asked nonchalantly.

"You can answer that yourself. You're the one who did it."

"For fuck sake, Stephen. I told you, I didn't kill him." Luke scratched his head, clearly frustrated. "I've been away in New Plymouth all bloody week. I only got home an hour ago. So, can you please tell me what it is I'm supposed to have done from all the way down there to actually kill him?"

Luke's words punched Stephen in the heart, leaving him numb. How could Luke be away all week, yet Shaun wind up dead? His stomach churned at the answer.

He jumped... because of the things I said.

"So you only got home an hour ago?" Stephen asked, nearly choking on the question.

"Yes, that's what I'm saying. You can ask my olds if you don't believe me." Luke pointed up the road towards his parents' house. He gave Stephen a soothing glance. "Look, what's happened?"

Stephen began walking back down the stairs, scratching his head, feeling muddled. "They... they found him today on the beach... washed up. He was all hurt and..." Stephen began to tear up, rubbing his eyes, not wanting Luke to see him cry.

Luke walked down the stairs and stood beside him, putting a hand on his shoulder. "Stevie, are you okay?"

Stephen shook his head, about to let the real level of his emotions break the surface when Luke grabbed him by the scruff of his shirt.

"No, you're not fucking okay. You've fucking lost it and don't ever think you can turn up here, ruin my lawn, then punch me in the fucking face." Luke raised a hand, curled it into a fist, ready to wallop him.

Stephen tried squirming his way out of Luke's firm grip. He heaved all his weight backwards, desperate to avoid the punch. He closed his eyes, waiting for Luke's fist to bash him in the face when he heard his shirt rip open down the front of his chest.

Luke suddenly let go of him. "What the fuck?"

Stephen opened his eyes and saw Luke staring at his exposed torso.

He cast his eyes down at his ripped shirt and saw exactly what Luke was transfixed by. Faded love bites that riddled his body. The last remaining remnants of Shaun's passion, the sign of ownership that told the world who Stephen belonged to. He slowly traced his fingers over them, remembering the feel of Shaun's mouth all over him in the car parked up alongside a lonely country road.

"They're from him," Luke said in shock. "All those filthy fucking marks are from him, aren't they?" Luke shook his head, impatient for a response. "AREN'T THEY?" he yelled.

"No, they're not," Stephen's voice trembled.

Luke gazed at Stephen's damaged flesh like he was

spellbound by the numerous teeth marks. He raised his face, looking Stephen straight in the eyes as if searching his soul. Luke's mouth curled malevolently and he lowered his voice to the depths of hell. "Bullshit."

Chills, frightened chills, clawed up Stephen's back. Even though the sun was shining down bright on both of them, he knew he was standing in the shadows—shadows that lined the path of an outcast. Stephen turned away, trying to outwalk Luke's judgement, not wanting to have his mind read any further.

"Shaun gave you those," Luke demanded, "didn't he?"

Stephen glanced over his shoulder, giving Luke one last stern look before hopping in his car.

"You two were fucking," Luke laughed cruelly. "You two were actually fucking."

Stephen drove away fast as he could, knowing he had lost two friends forever in one day.

CHAPTER FORTY-TWO — 1996

STEPHEN

Shaun's funeral cast Stephen in a mood as black as his suit. It was like being an actor on a film set, a dire need to strike the appropriate balance of mourning for a lost mate, not a lover. Stephen may not have pulled it off had it not been for the dark sunglasses he wore to shield the truth.

Debbie was a complete mess as expected. Lydia wasn't much better, bawling into her mother's shoulder, soaking it with grief as Shaun's coffin was lowered. Josie seemed strangely upbeat, almost unaware of the permanence of death, and not realising her big brother who she adored was never coming back.

Stephen felt like a phoney. He knew now that he had loved Shaun. The pain he felt made him realise this all too late. He knew he shouldn't be there at a supposed celebration of Shaun's life, not the one responsible for his death. He may not have physically pushed Shaun off the cliff, but it was his words that had willed Shaun to jump. The thought haunted him. In the darkness of night, and all alone, Shaun had stepped off to another world without him.

The vicar stood at the graveside, saying a prayer and final words before the mourners each went past dropping their donations of earth and flowers into the ground. Stephen gripped his dirt offering so tight, he half expected his blood to go in the hole with it. He looked down at the coffin containing his lover who would soon become little more than jelly on bones, fed on by creatures wriggling in the earth.

Shaun would be the first of his family to taste the earth here, forever tying them to this land. This one act alone would make the Munros more local than anything they had ever done before. Shaun's freshly dug grave would sit in the front row alongside the still-remembered and recently-grieved, but like others gone before him, he too would slowly slip further back in history with each passing year as more rows propped up ahead of his own.

Just like Ricky. Stephen wished time would stop so no one ever forgot his loved ones.

There was an invite back to Debbie's after the service—no function in the community hall, just a small gathering at the Munro home. Stephen knew he should have gone, but he didn't think he could handle such an intimate gathering of grief. He lied to Debbie, telling her he had to get back to work on the farm, and how sorry he was for her loss. Debbie didn't seem to mind and must have understood. She said Shaun would have been pleased to see him as a pall bearer and as she wrapped Stephen in her arms, she whispered, "Thank you for coming today. I know how much he loved you." Debbie let go of him reluctantly, reminding him not to be a stranger and that he was welcome at her house anytime. Stephen sheepishly nodded and made a quick getaway, racing home to return to his salty pillow of tears.

∞

For the rest of the week, Stephen avoided phone calls from friends, all no doubt wanting to talk about the gossip. Someone dying in a small town was big news, especially when it was someone they all knew. Speculation was fuelled by the mystery shrouding the circumstances as to why on earth Shaun would have gone swimming in the middle of the night. Stephen knew why and his need to hide the truth kick-started a self-imposed social exile. After all, secrets come at a price.

Work on the farm felt less of a chore and more of an escape, provided he was working alone. It wasn't until the week following Shaun's funeral that he finally worked alongside Rusty. The two went about their job in uncomfortable silence, Rusty not daring to cross an invisible line, as if he could sense Stephen's fragility.

Stephen kept catching Rusty giving him strange looks. He could tell the man's mind was busy thinking of something to say, but each time Rusty would quickly drop his face and get back on with the work. After the third time he caught Rusty inspecting him like some sort of zoo animal, Stephen called out bluntly, "What?"

Rusty began stuttering out words, "Sorry to hear about your um… uh, your mate."

Stephen ignored him and went on with his work.

Rusty, it turned out, wasn't done with the subject. "But ya know, they ain't stable, those types of people, so you're better off not getting involved in stuff like that again, aye," he said with a degree of philosophical conviction.

Those types.

Stephen saw red.

He charged at Rusty, grabbing him by the throat. "There was nothing, absolutely nothing, wrong with him!" he shouted.

Rusty's face twisted in shock at Stephen's angry reaction and strangling hands.

"He was perfect. Absolutely perfect! Not one fucking thing wrong with him," Stephen preached. He let go of Rusty with a shove and began sobbing behind his hands.

Rusty keeled over, inhaling saggy gasps, trying to catch his breath. He scurried a few metres back, trying to steer clear of Stephen's meltdown. If Rusty had any doubt about what he may have seen in the shed that day, he sure as shit didn't now.

Stephen sniffled away his tears and composed himself before glaring furiously at Rusty. "If you ever tell a soul, and I mean even the faintest fucking whisper, about any of this, I will get your arse fired so fast, you won't know what hit you. You got me?"

Rusty nodded, still rubbing his freshly-throttled throat.

Stephen sized up the worried-looking farm worker and took a step towards him. "If you can keep your mouth shut, then you have a job for life if you want it." He held his hand out in good faith.

Rusty glared down at Stephen's hand, inspecting the proposition. He raised his head, looking around, inspecting the land like he was imagining his future. A soft smile appeared on his lips. "Sounds good to me," he returned, grabbing hold of Stephen's hand and shaking on it.

From that moment on, they each had a deal to uphold.

THE APPLE TREE — 1996

DEBBIE

Six lousy months—yes, six lousy months—and they say time heals. It doesn't heal. It only dulls the pain. The pain would never go away and Debbie knew this. So much for another one of her mother's old sayings: 'Time's a great healer.'

No, bitch. You're wrong again.

Debbie had thrown herself hard to the bottle since she'd lost her boy, her beautiful gentle boy. Although the booze numbed her pain, it also made her more upset, which was the most pathetic contradiction of all. Clifton and its gossip mongering didn't help. Rumours went swirling around town, vicious tales that were horrible to hear, tales of how Shaun had taken his own life.

He would never just leave us like this.

She may not have been the most present mother, but she knew her kids and she knew if they were happy or sad and her ray of sunshine had been just that. *Sunny.* He had been bright and full of life like he always was.

Hadn't he?

He had always been such a pleasure to have around and while most children would probably disown a mother as useless as she knew herself to be, he never did. Shaun accepted her, warts and all. He was such a good person and one of the few things Debbie knew she'd done right in life. If only the town had gotten to know him better, then they would have seen that.

Since the funeral, she had only really seen Megan who'd continued to visit and see how things were. Stephen Davis had been harder to spot than anyone, but Debbie knew why. This was someone who had known her son intimately; some things you can just sense.

Lydia had been brilliant and, in a weird way, naturally stepped up, taking Shaun's protective role and looked after Josie brilliantly. Debbie could see how Lydia made more of an effort with her sister than before, fearing death would snatch her away too.

Josie had asked once when Shaun was coming home and Debbie had fought for the right way to explain the finality of death to her.

"He's not coming home, bub. He's busy finding out the secret."

Her baby girl's face creased with confusion. "What's the secret?"

"One day Shaun will be able to tell us. We will visit him. Each of us will have a turn and we will sit and have fizzy drinks on a beautiful hill with him and eat lots of cake and lollies and ice cream. It'll be like the bestest party ever."

"Really? I wanna go now," Josie had said excitedly.

Debbie laughed a sad laugh. "You're not allowed to go yet and you have to be a good girl to get into heaven, so you best behave so Shaun can save us all a seat."

"Yes, Mum." Josie had hugged her and Debbie held her baby tight and wished so much she had been a good girl herself.

This town had given her nothing but grief. The plan when she'd originally come here with Mitch was to start anew, prove to everyone back in Auckland that she could make it and create a better life without them. For a long time, she thought she had done just that. Only now, aching with loss, did she realise how wrong she had been.

Debbie sat at her kitchen table looking at the half empty vodka bottle gripped between her nicotine-stained fingers. She swished it around about to pour herself another drink, stopping mid-pour, her hands shaking as she heard in her mind the sound of her mother's raspy voice. *The apple never falls far from the tree.*

The mocking words enraged her as an oscillating shiver tapped her spine. Debbie screamed and marched to the sink with the bottle where she poured its river of spirit all down the drain.

Lydia came running in. "Mum, what's wrong?"

Debbie leaned into the sink, gathering her breath

before calmly responding, "I'm fine."

Lydia stared at her like she was going crazy.

Things had to change and that was never going to happen here in Clifton. "I've decided it's time we go back to Auckland," Debbie said, forgetting Lydia had never been from there.

Lydia looked surprised, but didn't push for more information. "Umm, okay." She gave Debbie a funny smile and walked back to the lounge.

Debbie looked at the empty bottle in her hand—another king she had let rule her for too many years. Maybe this queen never needed a king. Maybe she didn't have to be like Rhonda.

It's time I chop that fucking tree down.

CHAPTER FORTY-FOUR — 2016

STEPHEN

It had been a long day. On top of everything he normally had to do on the farm, Stephen had driven to New Plymouth police station to get a trespass order for Eddie. It seemed the easiest solution to an intensifying battle that was proving all too costly.

The rain from the night before had washed away any footprints the old codger would have left behind after his killing spree. This meant no evidence to speak of and would leave them both locked in a classic case of finger pointing.

Walking out of the station, feeling empowered with a piece of paper that would achieve little more than a 'fuck you,' Stephen drove back home, stopping outside Eddie's house on the way. He grabbed an old hammer and a rusty nail from the trunk of his car and marched right on up to Eddie's front door where he took spiteful pleasure in nailing the trespass notice to the wooden frame. It took all his willpower not to succumb to a savage, retributive instinct and go around the house and break holes in every window.

When he got back inside his house, he found a message on the answerphone from Kimmy. The short message was brief and demanding.

'Stephen, I'm not well. Yes, self-inflicted, but please for the love of god, come over with some greasy food and lemonade.'

Stephen chuckled at the message which finished with a painful groan, rousing images of her wrapped in a blanket with a bucket nearby. He wasn't in the mood to go out again, but he knew if the shoe was on the other foot, Kimmy would be over in a shot. He loaded himself back in the car and drove to Kimmy's house, swinging by the takeaways to get her two burgers and the biggest bottle of lemonade they had.

Kimmy's place was a mushroom-coloured cottage near the beachfront, tucked behind pretty flower beds draped in a lavender scent. He buzzed the doorbell, alerting her to his arrival and let himself in. The front room was actually her place of work—a former sunroom she had converted into a holistic therapy oasis with numerous crystals, bamboo wall dividers and an adjustable massage bed.

Stephen passed through a rainbow beaded curtain into the hallway that led to her lounge at the rear of the cottage where he found Kimmy just as he had imagined, wrapped up in a fleecy blanket on the couch, minus the bucket. The television was on playing one of her beloved soaps, a man with a thick cockney accent appearing on the screen, rambling on about some nonsense in a dreary street.

Kimmy looked seedy for sure, dressed in pink track pants and a blue jumper, her tired face the poster child for hung over. Stephen knew from the way her blonde hair frizzed in an unruly fashion, it was safe to assume she hadn't left that spot all day.

"Hey, sicko," Stephen said, placing the burgers and drink down on the oval coffee table in front of her.

"My saviour, you're a doll," Kimmy replied. She sat up and immediately dug into the first burger.

Stephen smiled at her starving approach to the feast, under no illusion that she would down both jumbo burgers. For someone so tiny, she sure did have a large appetite.

"So, what's the story, morning glory?" he asked.

Kimmy hurriedly chewed down a chunk of the greasy burger, having no qualms about Stephen seeing her in her natural state. "Me and Mihi, against our better judgement, stupidly went out again last night."

"Thought you would have been hammered enough from the night out before. You certainly dropped Inver off legless."

"Well, you did say to give him a night he wouldn't forget."

"You did such a good job you actually failed 'cos he can't remember a fucking thing," Stephen said with a smirk.

Kimmy laughed as she wiped a hand over her mouth with a dirty sleeve. When she lowered her hand, Stephen saw on her forearm a scribbled number that brought back stomach-turning memories.

"What you got there?" he asked, knowing what it was.

Kimmy lifted her arm up, studying where his finger pointed along a line of numbers written in smeared blue ink.

"Oh shit," Kimmy blurted, "I totally forgot about that." She rolled her eyes. "That there, my dear, is too much alcohol and bad decisions which shall never be mentioned or repeated."

"Anyone I know?"

"Don't think so," she lied.

Stephen nodded. Luke's home phone number transported him back to 1996 when they had last spoke—the day Luke had read his mind and Stephen's social life in Clifton disappeared. Luke had never breathed a word about any of it as far as he was aware, but since that fateful day Stephen avoided the beach, the pub, and anywhere else the pair of them could bump into each other. Such dodging was impossible in a small town, so of course they had passed each other in the street on the odd occasion. Every time Luke eyed him like some sort of contamination, a moral leper not worthy of a cure. Stephen always crossed the road, gripped with palpitations of fear, worried if Luke would shout out his secret for everyone to hear.

"I swear I'm never drinking again," Kimmy groaned.

"Something tells me you will." Stephen laughed, jingling his keys in his pocket. "Anyway, I better head off and leave you to recuperate."

"Already?"

"Some of us have work at ridiculous hours of the morning, remember."

Kimmy nodded. "I'll come see you tomorrow. Thank you so much for bringing food over."

"No worries."

He leaned in for his obligatory hug. Kimmy was a stickler for hugs goodbye.

"Oooh, I forgot to tell you," Kimmy said, her voice perking up in dramatic excitement. "Karma does exist."

"What do you mean?" Stephen asked. He pictured the field and the etched out symbol.

"Eddie Tucker is in hospital."

"He's what?"

"I mean nothing super bad, but Sheryl at the bar was saying he had a funny turn yesterday at the pub and they had to get an ambulance to take him away."

"Is he alright?" Stephen asked concerned.

"I thought you'd want him dead?"

"I don't want anybody dead."

"That's not what I meant." Kimmy looked at him with wide eyes. "And yes, the old goat is fine. They were just gonna keep him in overnight to run some tests. Sheryl reckons they were letting him out today if it's all clear."

The karmic revelation knocked the wind out of his sails. Stephen took a short, sharp breath. "Good to know," he muttered, trying to disguise his shock. Eddie would be coming home to a rude surprise in the form of a trespass notice for something he didn't have a hand in doing.

"Say hi to Inver for me," Kimmy piped.

Stephen nodded, knowing full well he wouldn't be passing on any such message to the guy he had kicked out of his house and bed twelve hours earlier. Now, knowing that Eddie hadn't been responsible for the animals' bloodshed, he knew in his heart it had been the right thing to do.

∞

Mere seconds after Stephen walked in the door of his all too quiet home from visiting Kimmy, the weather had turned to custard and began piddling down with rain. As he had passed the fork in the driveway to Rusty's, he'd seen Inver's shit heap of a car parked outside the shit heap of a house. For a brief moment, he contemplated driving down and asking him to come back, maybe do again what they had done.

As much as he wished they could spend another night together, Stephen knew this would be a stupid idea. Besides, he doubted how well Inver would respond to being treated like a sex yoyo.

Kicking Inver out had been an arsehole move, especially the way Stephen stormed into the bedroom after finding the symbol in the dirt, barking at the still-sleeping guest how they had made a terrible mistake, repeating 'this isn't me' and that it would be best if Inver go stay at Rusty's house for the remainder of his visit.

Inver hadn't even blinked. He'd just scraped himself out of the sheets like he had half-expected a shitty outcome. With the saddest of faces and pensive eyes, Inver threw on his jeans and collected his belongings. Stephen kept saying how sorry he was as Inver got his bags from his room, not uttering a word the whole time before shutting the door behind him. He didn't even slam it, just politely closed it. This only made it worse. Why couldn't the guy just get angry? Tell Stephen to go fuck himself, any hostile reaction would have sufficed; then maybe Stephen wouldn't feel so fucking bad about booting him out.

If only I could tell him the whole story.

But Stephen knew he couldn't. Firstly, he would paint himself as even more horrible for being responsible for Shaun's suicide, and second, no sane person would believe for a split second that the symbol in the dirt was some ghost or curse haunting the farm. It all sounded too crazy, yet there was no other explanation.

What was to say that the bad things happening on the farm weren't triggered by Inver's arrival, the first man to taste Stephen in twenty years? If it wasn't Eddie that had killed the cattle, then it wasn't safe for Inver to be there. Was it even safe for himself?, Stephen wondered.

This nagging fear crept around his mind as each hour passed, not helped by a dark night sky, brewing a chaotic scene of horizontal rain thrashing against the windows.

Perfect ghost weather. The thought was ludicrous but Stephen wasn't amused by his imagination. Staring out the window, scanning a barely visible backyard thanks to sheets of rain, he imagined the cut body of a robbed life walking across the lawn, breaking inside and dragging him away kicking and screaming to wherever it was the dead go. Stephen ripped himself away from the window and nestled down on the couch, attempting to calm himself down.

BANG. Something hard and heavy attacked the side of the house; he leapt up from the couch, his heart nearly bursting from fright.

Calm down, man. It'll just be a tree branch or something. Just as he was about to sit back down and embrace his comforting lie, the ranch slider door shattered, littering the lounge carpet with bits of glass and a rock that rolled to a stop just in front of Stephen's feet.

"What the..."

Cold wind and rain burst through the gaping hole like an invading army, carrying the noise of a thunderous high tide, hell-bent on damage. Stephen tiptoed barefoot with deftly steps around the shards of glass. He curled his fingers around the ranch slider handle, pulling carefully as he did so to avoid dislodging any loose glass. He stepped outside onto the deck and put a hand above his eyes, shielding his sight from pelts of blinding rain. Stephen breathed in the rustic smell of the storm as he scanned his backyard for any sign of a rock-throwing presence.

In the distance, near the cliff's edge, a dark figure loomed—glaring back at him. He blinked his eyes, shaking them free of dripping water to be sure of what it was he was seeing. *It couldn't be?*

He cringed internally at the thought of a curse coming to his doorstep. He fought the fear and took a step forward, calling out, "Shaun?"

The figure stood there ominously. Stephen thought he heard it laugh, but the waves were too loud to make anything out. He fought the urge to run inside. If it was what he thought it was, then going inside wouldn't save him. He shook away his fear, walked forward, and made his way down the steps onto the lawn before crossing the yard, getting closer to the figure.

"Shaun is that... arrrgh," Stephen screamed, as something like monster's teeth snapped and bit his leg, sending him to the ground, writhing in pain. He felt his eyes roll back in his head as the pain pulsated through his body. Stephen reached for his leg and realised it wasn't monster's teeth, but a steel jaw trap. He looked down and saw that it had a firm grip on him, refusing to let go. It had cut deep. It had cut bad.

The mess of his leg made him queasy, his breaths coming heavy, repeating, "Fuck, fuck, fuck."

"Wash your mouth out, buddy," the figure called out before laughing.

Stephen heard its heavy-booted footsteps getting closer until they were standing right beside him. He forced himself to look up. Not a ghost at all, but a man in a dark raincoat.

You!

"Get this fucking thing off of me, Luke," Stephen screamed.

"Hold your horses," Luke said calmly. He knelt down beside Stephen. "You know, you really should be more careful, Stevie." Luke laughed.

"Just get the fucking thing off my leg already!"

Luke put his hands to the claw and with some fumbling, clicked it open. Its prising apart ripped at Stephen's leg even more, making him scream out another cry of pain. He sat up clutching above the wound, which felt cut to the bone.

"Why would you break my bloody window?" Stephen heaved through pain, "and set a fucking trap?"

Luke smiled down at him. "'Cos I felt like it." He smashed his fist into Stephen's face, sending him flat on the ground.

Stephen reached for his face and could feel his nose running red, the metallic taste of blood entering his lips. "What's your fucking problem?"

"My problem is you, cunt." Luke leaned down, staring aggressively, his eyes burning like simmering embers. "You just can't keep your fucking hands to yourself or your fucking cock in your pants, can you?"

"What the hell are you on about?"

"Gee, where to fucking begin? I dunno, any chick I've ever liked for starters, like Delphi Savage?"

"I never even touched her," Stephen said through clenched teeth. He gripped his leg tight and rocked back and forward.

"Didn't stop you from fucking trying though, did it?"

Stephen looked at the ground and the growing pool of blood from his wound. "Luke, you're being fucking crazy. Now help me up and get me inside."

Luke ignored his request and paced around him in muddy circles, looking down with a crooked smile. "And nope, that wasn't enough for you. Now you have to try and steal Kimmy."

Stephen shook his head. He couldn't believe what he was hearing. "What?"

"Me and her were seeing each other. Then she tells me she's got a new man and, oh, what a surprise. It turns out it's Stephen fucking Davis, the slut himself."

"We're not an item, me and Kimmy. We're just friends, that's all. I swear," Stephen pleaded, clutching his bleeding leg.

"BULLSHIT!" Luke screamed with black fury.

Stephen stared coldly at his old friend lost in a rage. "You've lost your touch, Luke, 'cos ya got that one soooo fucking wrong."

Luke spat in his face and kicked him in the ribs. A hot searing pain shot through Stephen's side. "No, Stephen, you're the one who is wrong for putting your cock where it ain't wanted."

"Something tells me it's wanted more than yours," Stephen said before slurping a ball of snot and spitting on Luke's leg. Luke dealt him another kick in the side, forcing Stephen to roll over.

"Mind you, you ain't too fussy where you put it, are ya?" Luke laughed. "Shaun fucking Munro! Fuck sake, Stevie. If you gonna go all homo on us, at least have some fucking class."

"Fuck you," Stephen snarled.

"Nope, I did you a favour there, mate." Luke knelt back down beside him. "Yeah, got rid of that trash for ya."

"What are you talking about?"

Luke pressed his mouth close to Stephen's ear. "Let's just say after I pushed him, it was sorta sad listening to him scream out for you," he whispered, the words so close they wet Stephen's eardrum. "He screamed out for you a lot."

Stephen lay there stunned. *You never jumped.*

Luke reeled his head back. "And I'll tell you something for nothing, Stevie boy, you wouldn't believe how freaky it sounds when someone's drowning, begging to be saved. The scariest bit, though, is when it begins to go quiet."

"FUCK YOU!" Stephen screamed. He thrust forward with a clenched fist, but Luke jumped back before he could hit him. He pressed the ground with his palms, trying to get to his feet, wanting to kill the killer. Luke laughed at his losing battle as the pain kept Stephen to the ground.

"I never thought you were like that, aye," Luke mocked. "Fuck, I'm lucky you didn't try to make the moves on me."

"As if I'd ever want to touch you, ya ugly cunt."

Luke smiled. "Sticks and stones, Stevie, sticks and stones."

"What kind of nut job fucking kills someone for sticking up for their sister?" Stephen sputtered.

"Who says I wasn't sticking up for someone myself?"

"Killing Shaun 'cos he broke your hands isn't the same fucking thing."

Luke sighed like he was getting impatient with Stephen's inability to connect the dots. "No, moron, I was sticking up for my mum."

"Huh?" Stephen was lost.

"You remember telling me how you saw my mum crying outside the shop?"

Stephen jogged his mind back through the decades. It was a blur, but he had a vague image of Luke's mum upset, running to her car.

Luke leaned closer in, his face glowering. "That was her running away from Desperate Debbie after smelling her perfume, the same perfume she'd smelled on my old man's clothes," he said, delivering the words like a detective cracking a case. "Shaun's slut of a mother was fucking my father."

You killed a woman's son for your father's adultery?

"Then you should've taken it out on your old man," Stephen said, struggling to comprehend the logic. It all seemed a convenient lie to absolve what was just cold blood on Luke's hands.

"That slut hurt my mother and Shaun had it coming for smashing my hands up. So yeah, two birds, one stone."

"You always were a fucking mummy's boy."

Luke shoved his boot in Stephen's side again, bringing out another pained yelp.

"No, Stevie boy. Maybe if you knew a thing or two about loyalty, you'd understand," Luke said. "Fuck, even dipshit Shaun had some for his maggot family."

Stephen lay clutching his throbbing side.

Luke shook his head and stared down at him like he was a parasite. He walked around and grabbed Stephen roughly by the ankles and began dragging him across the soggy lawn. The vicious grip near his injury, shot burning agony through his suffering leg; he mashed his lips together and grinded on his teeth. As he was hauled along, his shirt lifted up, exposing his back to the cold blades of wet grass. Stephen raised his chin up off the ground to see where Luke was taking him.

"No, no, no… NO!" Stephen screamed for his life. Luke was headed straight for the cliff edge. "Don't throw me off, Luke. Look, I'm sorry. Don't throw me off."

The cliff edge was getting closer and closer. Luke picked up pace, the pain in Stephen's leg taking a side seat to the impending doom. They were only a few feet from the edge; he closed his eyes and braced himself for a deadly free fall.

Luke suddenly let go of his ankles and Stephen stopped moving. He opened his eyes to find he had been planted right at the edge, his body teetering inches away from death. He scrambled up on his elbows and saw Luke walking over to the large pohutukawa tree near the cliff track. *Is he letting me go?*

It was high tide, there was no way Luke could attempt a getaway down the track. Luke stopped at the tree, his arm reaching out, grabbing something against the trunk.

A fucking gun!

"What's wrong, Stevie?" Luke taunted as he gripped the rifle in his hands. He pointed the weapon at the trunk of the tree. "See this? I been wanting to ask you what the fuck is this about?"

Luke was referring to *their* symbol. The one Shaun had carved into the tree the night he died. *The night he was killed.*

"It's none of your business," Stephen huffed.

Luke shrugged. "Ya know, I actually watched the little prick carve it into the tree after you two had ya lovers' quarrel, or whatever it is you wanna call it," he said, flashing a demonic smile. "You just a wee heartbreaker, aren't you?" Luke began walking back over to Stephen. "I had to wait fucking ages for him to finish carving that shit and stop crying so I could help him find his way down the cliff. Did you see I left it as my calling card with the dead calves?" Luke's voice oozed with cruelty.

Not a ghost. Not tapu.

"Sure did," Stephen said, trying his best to sound calm. He wanted to run, but he could barely stand, let alone outrun a bullet.

"Yeah, sorry about that and the milk vat, but you really pissed me off." Luke came to a stop in front of him, the gun at his side.

Stephen laughed at the crazy apology. "Will you be saying sorry for killing me too?" Stephen's face held firm, not wanting the prick to see how scared he was in his moment of peril.

Luke frowned at him. "What are you talking about? I'm not going to kill you."

The flood of relief that swept through Stephen's body was short-lived. *But you've just confessed to murder?*

Luke raised the gun, aiming it right at Stephen's chest. "No, Stevie, you're gonna jump."

The light grip he had on calm imploded. "Luke, please don't do this. It's not right… Come on, man. Please, we used to be best mates," he begged.

"That's right. *Used to be*, but then you lay with Munro dogs and got fleas." Luke stepped closer. "Now, Stephen, it's gonna be harder for them to believe you jumped and drowned if you got a fucking bullet in you, but I'll fill you with one if you don't do as you're told."

"So then, genius, how will you explain my fucking leg?"

An arrogant laugh escaped Luke's lips. "That's easy. The reef is sharp and who the fuck knows what's down there that'll have a good nibble on you?"

He looked at his shredded leg that was soon to be fish bait, his stomach turning at the thought. Luke, three metres away, waved his gun, letting him know to hurry up. Stephen knew there was no escape, no one nearby to hear his screams over the rain and waves; it was like water from all elements had ganged up on him. He hobbled to his feet, hissing in pain, doing his best to lean on his good leg.

Luke closed in on him like he was prey. "Over you go, mate. It's time for you to join your scum boyfriend."

Stephen teetered on the edge of the cliff, looking down into the dark abyss of thrashing cold water, turning back to face Luke. "Yes, you're right. Shaun was my boyfriend," Stephen admitted for the first and last time through choking tears. "But he wasn't scum... I loved him."

Stephen knew he had no paths left to choose. He closed his eyes, and just as the gunshot fired, he took a leap of faith, leaving the pain of this world behind.

CHAPTER FORTY-FIVE — INFINITY

STEPHEN

Stephen opened his eyes expecting death. What he saw instead was the beautiful face of an endless summer.
Shaun.
Not battered and cut from the sea, but perfect—how he had always been. His cute face framed with that long, dark-chocolate fringe falling to the side and his brown eyes, warm and soothing.

Stephen looked around and saw they were standing in Shaun's lounge. It looked how it always had, soft lumpy couches and the jungle of pot plants in this shabby happy home. "Your lounge is heaven?"

Shaun smiled at him, holding in a laugh. "Consider this the waiting room."

Stephen glanced down at his body and found no bullet hole, sore leg or mangled body from falling. "I'm not hurt," he said baffled.

"I told you, didn't I? I would catch you if you fall," Shaun said. He placed a hand on Stephen's shoulder.

Stephen felt an energy run through Shaun's fingers, one of love. He reached out with his fingers and stroked Shaun's face. "Fuck, I've missed you," he said, his eyes watering. "I never meant any of those things I said to you, none of them. I'm so sorry, so unbelievably sorry."

Shaun wiped a finger down Stephen's cheek, drying his tears. "It's okay. I've always known how sorry you were."

"You have?"

"Of course. All those times you prayed, begging for forgiveness."

"You heard those?" Stephen replied, his emotions suddenly feeling naked.

Shaun nodded. "I only wish you had heard me talk

back to you. It would have saved you a lot of heartache."

"But I was so bloody horrible to you."

"We both said things we didn't mean that night and I want you to know I'm sorry too." Shaun rubbed Stephen's shoulders as he stared sincerely into his eyes.

"You must think I'm so old and hideous," Stephen said, coughing out a pitiful laugh.

"You, Stephen Davis, could never be old or ugly." Shaun grabbed his hand and raised it up. "See?"

Stephen gasped at what he could not fathom. Instead of the weathered hands time had ravished, he saw the succulence and promise of youth.

"You need to stop robbing yourself of happiness, Stephen," Shaun said.

"I'll never be sad again. Not now that I'm here with you."

Shaun tilted his head with a thoughtful smile. "I'm sorry, but you can't stay. Not this time, anyway."

Stephen panicked. "But why?" He felt weak in the knees. "This is where I belong. Here. With you."

"You'll be back, don't worry." Shaun reassured him. "Just not yet. You have to go back, but I'll be here waiting for you. I promise."

Stephen shook his head. "No, but I'd rather be here. Nothing's been the same since you left... I'm so lonely back there." The thought of *back there* felt cold and hideous. Going back now would be like walking around in wet clothes.

"You don't have to be lonely." Shaun began rubbing Stephen's fingers. "You deserve to be happy, Stephen, just as happy as you made me. Besides, you've got more than one finger, so maybe you have more than one letter under your fingertips." Shaun raised Stephen's hands to his lips and gently kissed them.

Stephen felt his body shudder with a feeling he could only describe as truth.

Shaun breathed into his ear, "I want you to live your life with every breath." The words trickled out in a drowned whisper. He leaned forward and kissed Stephen's neck before sinking his teeth in and biting him passionately, just like he had in life.

Stephen wrapped his arms around Shaun's warm

body, pulling him in tight, never wanting to let his angel go. Two S's, hugging forever.

Shaun pecked his way up Stephen's neck 'till he found his lips and made him melt with a supplicating kiss. Energy flowed between them, pure and kind as they merged together.

Stephen was lost in a sea of emotion that slowly grew colder and colder 'till he heard a desperate yelling of his name and a calloused hand grip his arm through the fog of death.

CHAPTER FORTY-SIX — 2016

STEPHEN

The air wrapped around Stephen's saturated body like a blanket made of ice, his teeth chattering as his body shook in shivers, unable to combat nature's cold wet kiss. The rocks dug into his side like blunt nails, scratching at his rib cage, his ears deafened by the surge of a sinister tide thrashing right in front of him. He sat up, trying to gauge where he was, but his palms slipped on the slithery rock and he nearly slid back into Poseidon's realm. A rough hand snagged his arm in the nick of time.

"Whoa, settle down there, fella. I don't recommend you go for another dip. It was a bloody miracle I got you out the first time."

Stephen jerked his neck 'round and saw Eddie standing beside him. It was only then he realised they were perched on the slippery slope of the track that climbed the cliff to his backyard. Too many questions ran through his head. Like an overfilled blender, the lid popped off, and he spouted the first thing that flew out. "I was in heaven's waiting room."

Eddie nodded. "I bet you were. I'm guessing it was pretty fucking cold 'n wet."

Stephen shook his head, still disorientated. "It was warm… it was a lounge."

"Oh boy, the fall's made you nuttier than a mad woman's shit."

Numbness from the cold still owned Stephen's body. He looked down and saw his injured leg, the sight of its deep gash summoned the pain and a survival instinct kicked in, knocking him out of his daze. With wildly lucid hands, he patted his chest for any sign of a bullet wound.

"Why… why am I not shot?"

"You weren't the one that got shot, ya bleedin idiot," Eddie answered. "It was that Luke Bridgeman oaf I hit." Eddie pointed to the step behind him; leaned against its indent rested his gun.

"You shot Luke," Stephen exclaimed, trying to make sense of his survival.

"Yep, fair square right in the arse." Eddie chuckled.

Stephen looked up at his unlikely saviour. "Where is he?"

"After I threw his gun over the cliff, he pissed off like a little girl in the dark."

Stephen's eyes darted to the cliff top, amazed by the height he had fallen, astonished that he would live to tell the tale. "I should be dead," Stephen muttered in disbelief.

"Just lucky I was here then."

"Yes I am," Stephen agreed. He raised his eyebrows, puzzled by Eddie's presence. "But why are you here?"

"You'll probably know why when you see your front door," Eddie said, stepping to the side and holding a hand out to help Stephen up. "It was payback for what you did to mine with that bloody trespass notice."

Eddie's revenge had saved him from Luke's. Two wrongs didn't make a right, but they could save a life. Stephen laughed to himself at the obscure thought.

It was a long slow slog to the top with Eddie's help. All the way, Stephen wished what he had seen had been real, that heaven had been real. Even though he accepted such things didn't exist, he still felt the prophetic illusions impact as they scrambled the cliff steps. A seed of hope inside of him floating like a message in a bottle.

∞

Eddie drove Stephen to the hospital at pensioner speed, ditching him in the waiting room, insisting he couldn't spend another minute there after his own overnight stay. Stephen let him go—the guy had saved his life, so Eddie didn't owe him anything. Besides, if he stayed, Stephen figured both of them would be bored by the other's company and probably rile each other up over damaged doors.

After a long wait under all too bright hospital lights, Stephen received injections, pain meds and miles of bandages wrapped around his skin-tattered leg. If he were lucky, the scarring would be minimal but never invisible. Having a stain of such dark human behaviour seemed hideous at first, but then Stephen thought it could be seen as a good luck charm—the time he cheated death.

The police arrived shortly after he was all mended and giddy on pain relief. They questioned him about the standoff at the farm, wanting to know what exactly happened. Luke, it turned out, had driven himself to the hospital, arriving an hour earlier, insisting his injuries were from a 'misunderstanding.' Luke wouldn't be leaving in a hurry and certainly not without cuffs. Stephen knew they wouldn't be able to prove Shaun's death all those years ago had been murder, but they would certainly gather enough evidence to charge the bastard for trying to kill him.

After the police were done with their questions, a nurse let Stephen ring Kimmy to come pick him up. Being the middle of the night, she was asleep when he called, her groggy voice soon snapping alert when he told her where he was and a quick rundown of what had happened. When he got off the phone, he was allowed to lay down in one of the rooms so he could rest. He didn't get any sleep though; instead, he lay there wondering if he deserved a second chance at life, and if he did deserve one, what would he do with it?

The sound of clopping shoes an hour later disturbed him from his pondering when Kimmy stormed into the dark room and switched the light on.

"Oh my god, Stephen, are you okay?" Kimmy asked with dire urgency.

Stephen sat up from the uncomfortable bed, shielding his eyes from the harsh light. "I was fine 'till you blinded me."

"Oh shit, sorry."

She raced over to his side, planting a hand to his shoulder. "I can't tell you how sorry I am. I didn't know the crazy prick would go and pull a stunt like that."

"It's fine, you weren't to know," Stephen said. "Fuck,

I didn't even know and I was best mates with the guy once upon a time."

"Still, I feel so bad. I wish there was something I could have done or do." Kimmy bleated, her eyes looking moist like she was about to let loose water works.

"There's nothing to do. It's all taken care of. I'm okay and Luke's got himself a wee holiday coming up behind bars, so, hey, nothing to fret over." Stephen gave her a reassuring smile. "Maybe in the future, don't tell a guy you're dumping that it's 'cos of me. Even though, of course, I would be the much better catch."

Kimmy laughed. "Good to see you didn't lose any of your arrogance over the cliff." She slapped his shoulder playfully.

"Hey, hey, don't go beating up the cripple," he teased.

"Oh, I wouldn't dream of it," Kimmy replied, giving him another slap.

Stephen carefully swung his feet off the bed, lowering himself as gently as possible.

"Do these beautiful accessories belong to you?" Kimmy said, pointing to crutches against the wall.

"They do indeed."

Kimmy collected the crutches for him and as she passed them over, her eyes lit up like she had spotted scandal. She tugged at Stephen's damp shirt, exposing his collar bone. "Who gave you that, Mr.?" Kimmy grinned.

Stephen hobbled on the crutches to a small mirror on the wall; he craned his neck 'round to see his reflection wearing a very bright love bite. Stephen's body tingled as he traced his fingers over the passionate mark. *You did catch me!*

His body flooded with joy, a huge smile smearing upon his face. He knew now what to do with his second chance. He would live his life with every breath, just like Shaun had told him to. The message of hope was real, and he knew who he wanted to share it with.

"So which scarlet woman gave you that?" Kimmy asked with a giggle.

There was no way Kimmy would ever believe him if he told her, so Stephen decided to come clean with a lie. "Inver."

Kimmy looked like her mouth would drop to the

floor. "You what?"

"Inver, the guy who has been staying with me."

"Yes, I know who Inver is, fool. I just didn't know… you were gay."

"I never said I was gay."

Kimmy smiled. "No, you didn't." She stepped towards him with her arms open wide.

"Shit, do we really need to hug this one out?" Stephen said cringing.

"Give me my damn soap opera moment, Stephen," Kimmy demanded. She wrapped her arms around her friend, squeezing him a little too tight. "You know what this means, don't you?" she whispered in his ear.

"What's that?"

"No one's bloody safe from those baby blues of yours."

∞

The drive back home with Kimmy was awkward at first with nowhere to escape any prying questions that could come up, but as if she could sense his apprehension she didn't push for any. She didn't disown him, she didn't mock him, she just *accepted* him. He wondered now if Shaun had been right all those years ago. Maybe it wasn't the big deal he had built up in his mind. Sure, times had changed, but back then they would have faced the world together. Stephen knew he should have been braver back then—things could have been so different—but he also knew regret had a purpose and maybe now he had achieved it; he had evolved.

After a brief stop at a store in New Plymouth to buy Eddie a thank you gift, they got back to Clifton just after 10:00 a.m. Kimmy pulled up outside Eddie's cottage and helped Stephen bring the thank-you-for-saving-my-life gift to the old man's door.

The front door was still splintered and busted from Stephen's hammer-happy episode the day before. He knocked loudly and Eddie soon appeared in green long johns, wearing a snotty look on his face. The face of a man who had been disturbed from a nap.

"What do you lot want?" Eddie barked.

"Good morning to you too," Kimmy grumbled as she held the gift in its large cardboard box.

Stephen attempted to soothe his cranky neighbour. "Sorry to bother you, Eddie. I'm sure you're as tired as we are, but —"

"You bet your bottom dollar I'm tired after dragging your arse up out of the sea," Eddie snarled.

"Well, I got you this." Stephen pointed at the box in Kimmy's arms. "As a way to say thank you for saving me and sorry about the door."

"You don't need to be wasting your money on me," Eddie said, sounding like a martyr.

"Just open the bloody lid, Eddie," Stephen said, sighing in frustration.

Eddie looked at both of them suspiciously before leaning in and pulling up the lid. He smiled when he saw what was inside. "I'll be damned." He put his hands in and grabbed out a little fox terrier puppy that licked his dirty fingers excitedly.

"I know he ain't exactly the big breed you're used to but I'm hoping he might be a little less destructive."

Eddie lifted the puppy up to his face, eyeing the playful critter up like it was a diamond. "Ha, you just a little fur ball, aren't ya?" As if the puppy could understand the insult, it bit him on the chin. "Ough, ya little fucker." Eddie bust out a croaky laugh. "At least he's got spirit."

The puppy licked where it had just chomped on Eddie's chin. The grumpy old man seemed to warm instantly to the nipper in his hands, looking at Stephen and giving him a faint nod—the closest this man could come to saying thank you.

"So, he's a keeper?" Stephen asked, feeling glad to see Eddie happy.

"Yep, I think little Taurus here will be more than good enough company."

"That's a cool name," Kimmy said. "Taurus as in the bull?"

Eddie gave Kimmy a blank stare. "Nar, as in clitoris, I have a feeling this one could be a cunt of a dog."

CHAPTER FORTY-SEVEN — 2016

INVER

All day Inver had seen cars coming and going up the driveway to Stephen's house. Was there a celebration? Another death? What could all these people possibly want with what Inver had found to be a normally very quiet house in the nights he had stayed?

Since yesterday, and abandoning—or rather being pushed out of—Stephen's bed, he had laid low in his father's old home, scrubbing and cleaning. He wanted to just up and leave, but that wasn't possible 'till the buyer of Rusty's Ford Mondeo turned up to pay for the car.

The happy buyer had arrived just an hour earlier; he was a short and hard-looking man who introduced himself as 'Duck.' Inver had tried not to laugh at the appropriately named short arse as they shook hands. Duck's forearms were laced with green home-job tattoos, a jumble of words and badly drawn pot leaves.

Duck couldn't believe his luck at the bargain he had scored; he must have thought Inver was a fool. But Inver wasn't. Or maybe he was a fool, but he was one who was desperate for a quick sale. Now, with four-thousand dollars of freedom in his pocket, Inver felt like he had just been gifted a bit of joy and was now able to get back to Auckland. Anyone who said money doesn't buy happiness obviously never had none, Inver thought.

If Inver was being honest with himself, it wasn't just the sale of the car that kept him here the extra day; it was the faint hope that Stephen would come over and apologise for being such a dick about booting him out. However, the day and night had passed without any visit from the handsome farmer who had helped open Inver's eyes to a new way of thinking and, in some weird way, freeing him from *that face*.

Inver still couldn't think about James without feeling embarrassed, but he could now think about him without burning up in shame. There was no shame in making a mistake or taking a chance… in having regrets.

It was only that morning as he cleaned out the final belongings in his father's bedroom that Inver discovered possibly his father's own regrets. Under Rusty's manky bed, Inver had found *treasure*. It was a red cake tin with a picture of golden Labradors on the lid. The lid was jammed so tightly shut he had nearly lost a fingernail trying to prise it open.

Inside were photos of Inver as a child and one from his twenty-first birthday standing beside his dad who looked pissed as a chook. *But happy*. The makeshift time-capsule also had every single birthday and Christmas card he had ever sent his father. The father who had made no real contact with him, it turned out, had always kept him close by. Inver now suspected his father wasn't immune to other's opinions, perhaps too embarrassed to ever show his weakness that he missed someone. Looking through the memories, wishing his dad was still around, Inver felt his eyes moisten and beads of tears roll down his cheek. A happiness came from this sadness.

You did make a cheek wet with tears.

With Rusty's house now smelling like bleach and apple-scented spray 'n wipe, Inver knew he had done as much cleaning of the house as possible. He ditched his cleaning attire of a baggy red jersey and black gym shorts for a nice pair of jeans and a collared shirt. He knew if he was going back to hand over the key to Stephen and leave Clifton forever, then he would leave looking at least remotely presentable. The thought of going home to his tiny apartment depressed him, but Inver knew he wasn't wanted here, so there was no point in dragging out an inevitable departure.

No cars had gone down the drive for at least a couple of hours, Inver assumed now would be the best time to drop off the key and make his getaway, catching one last glimpse of Stephen before he left.

The walk to Stephen's was brisk in the spring afternoon breeze, the sides of the driveway dotted with their patches of daffodils flourishing with happy yellow petals. He hoped the ushering in of a new season could replicate itself with his own mood and outlook. As the driveway narrowed at the entrance of Stephen's front yard, Inver felt his stomach drop when he saw there were still several bloody cars parked up, including James's parents' car. *Oh great.*

He stopped just shy of the house, stood still and took a deep breath, trying to gather the mental bravado to face everybody. It would be unlikely they would know what happened between him and Stephen, but then what story would Stephen have told them for Inver's sudden change of abode? *It doesn't matter. I'm leaving. They can think what they like.*

Inver secretly wished they did know the sordid details of their night together, the touching, the kissing... the fucking. It was the hours after sex Inver remembered most fondly, just laying with Stephen, the feeling of being at peace for the first time in a very long time; his burdens all lay down. He thought Stephen had felt it too, but of course just like with James, he had been wrong. Jumping to the best possible conclusion was a bad habit and one he knew he would have to eradicate. It wasn't worth thinking life was giving you roses when all it delivered were pesky weeds.

He walked up to the front door and straight away wondered what the heck had happened here. The door frame was chipped and bashed like some woodpecker on steroids had taken it on. The door handle was barely attached, rendering it useless from this side at least. He shook his head and focused back on the task of delivering the key.

Here goes nothing.

Inver pressed his finger on the doorbell and waited. He heard footsteps run down the hallway and the familiar voice of Kimmy echoing, "Coming."

The door flung open and Kimmy smiled like she had just seen a long lost friend. "Inver! Come in."

Inver suddenly thought better of giving the key directly to Stephen. "I just came to give the key to Rusty's back. Would you be able to give this to Stephen for me, please?"

Kimmy cocked her head and gave him a curious look. "He's just outside on the deck. You should come in."

"Sorry, but I've really got to get going," Inver said. "It's a long drive back home, and it's best if I leave with as much daylight as possible." He extended his hand, holding out the key.

"Don't be silly," Kimmy said. She grabbed him by the wrist and hauled him down the hallway. "Stephen would be gutted if you left just like that. Shit, I'll be gutted if you don't stay for a coffee at least."

"But he has visitors. I don't want to intrude."

"You're not intruding, hun. Besides, A LOT has happened since…" Kimmy shut her mouth, not finishing what she was going to say rather flippantly.

Inver shook his wrist free just before they got to the end of the hall. "Since?" He knew she knew.

"Since you were here last," Kimmy coughed up, trying her best to sound naive. She stared at Inver, waiting for him to step forward and follow after her. He couldn't believe that Stephen would say anything; he had made Inver leave like a dirty secret, one you certainly don't share.

"Well, come on," Kimmy prodded.

Inver sighed and followed her into the kitchen where Mihi's jolly laughter filled the air. He looked down into the lounge and saw Troy and Clare on the couch. James and Tim were standing up talking with Mihi about something hilarious no doubt.

"Look who I found outside," Kimmy said.

"Son of Fanta pants, good to see you," Mihi greeted, giving him a thumbs up.

Tim cast Inver a sanctimonious stare. "Oh gosh, you've got clothes on this time."

Inver couldn't tell for sure if it was a joke or insult, but when James whacked his boyfriend's shoulder, muttering his name, something told Inver it was meant as a catty comment.

Inver smiled and came back with his own. "Yeah, I'd hate to create a puddle of drool from spectators like last time."

Mihi burst out laughing and was soon followed by everyone except Tim who blinked vacantly, unimpressed by his wit's defeat.

"His highness is outside," Kimmy said, pointing a finger to the deck. She leaned forward and whispered in Inver's ear, "I'll keep this lot in here."

Inver stepped down into the lounge, politely nodding

at the others as he passed them on his way outside. Sure enough, sitting out on the deck with his back turned, in shorts and a t-shirt, completely unequipped for the chill biting the air was Stephen busy sucking on a cigarette. His foot looked bandaged and beside him laid on the table were crutches. *What happened?*

"Hey," Inver said, sounding sheepish.

Stephen spun around, a smile spread across his lips. "Hey man, good to see you."

"What happened to you?" Inver asked.

Stephen looked down at his foot. "Long story, but it's a bloody entertaining one."

"Okay, well, I guess I can hear it another time," Inver said, knowing he never would. He walked towards Stephen and placed the key on the table. "It's all finished, and yeah, I don't think I could get that place any cleaner than it is."

"Are you leaving?" Stephen's smile faded.

"Yeah, I gotta head home. Find me a job and all that exciting adult stuff."

Stephen biffed his smoke on the lawn. He fetched the crutches from the table and worked his arms through the loops. He stood slowly, swinging forward 'till he was planted right in front of Inver. The true depth of blue in his eyes was exposed by the bright sun and accentuated by dark rings under their sockets. This was a man in desperate need of sleep. He glanced over Inver's shoulder, checking if anyone inside was listening. "You know, I'm real sorry about the other morning."

Inver stood silent, not willing to give him an ounce of emotion.

"It was a dick move and, I dunno, I just freaked out."

Inver nodded, avoiding eye contact.

Stephen bit down on his lip like he was trying to think of something better to say—something that could get a proper reaction. "You're only the second guy I've ever been with and I guess I have, or had, some issues about it, but they're gone now." Stephen gave him a smile meant to disarm Inver's hesitance. "I'd really like to tell you them, but it's pretty fucked up and I don't know if you'd believe me."

Inver relented and looked Stephen in the eyes, his frustration spilling out, "I don't need to hear your excuses,

Stephen. It's fine, I'm used to getting things wrong," he said with a faint laugh.

"They're not excuses, Inver. They're reasons."

Inver rolled his eyes. "Okay, anyway, thank you for letting me stay, but I really must get going."

Stephen grabbed hold of Inver's arm, desperate to stop him from stepping away. "Why the big rush?"

"Well, I gotta get home, find a job, sort myself out and get my life back on track."

"There's no reason you can't do that down here."

"Sorry?"

"Why don't you sort your shit out down here?"

Inver wondered what Stephen was on about. "Umm, there's nothing here for me."

"There's more than you think, Inver," Stephen said. "Besides, you told me I could do with something that's good for my health remember?"

"How on earth am I good for your health?"

Stephen looked at him and grabbed Inver's hand placing it on his chest. "Because you're good for my heart."

He waited for Stephen to bust out in a cheesy laugh but his expression held firm to sincerity. A rush of elation pumped through Inver. Did Stephen really just say that out loud?

"I think together we can help fix each other." Stephen tugged at Inver's shirt, pulling his face close in 'till their breaths rubbed each other's face.

The faint sound of gasping came from behind them. Inver turned around and saw everyone standing up in the lounge with shocked expressions.

"So what do you say, Not-So-Little-Inver?" Stephen's eyes remained solely on him. "Or are you the one who's too hung up on what everyone thinks?"

Inver turned back and looked at the guests. Most had unreadable faces, except for Kimmy who waved her arm like he should seal a deal and James who openly wore a disapproving frown.

How would everyone react if he did what he actually wanted to do? If he accepted Stephen's gift of hope? Would it go like last time? Had he learned nothing from *that face* which looked at him only a few feet away, judging him in this very moment? What about his flat, his need to find a job, start a career, wear decent clothes, buy a house, act his age and catch up in life with former friends' accomplishments?

Inver spun back 'round and grabbed his future with both hands, pulling it in for a deep kiss.

When their lips finally parted, Stephen grinned ear to ear. "So you don't care?"

Inver shook his head. "Fuck 'em all!"

EPILOGUE

Shaun opened his eyes and saw that the night had delivered him to heavenly shores. He stood on the beautiful beach he had always called home, Clifton town in the distance. He felt the warmth of god's light shine down on him, sheltering him from the storm he had just come from. He looked down at the sand and saw veins of brilliantly bright colours throbbing beneath his feet. The earth was alive; everything felt synchronised and had a purpose. All was different, but carried familiarity.

He felt pure, like some sort of spectacular spiritual energy, but no words could describe or do this feeling of merciful truth justice. He let himself ascend to the sky flying high, high, high above the lands, through celestial realms, looking down on creation. Shaun passed many souls. He knew them all. There were no strangers here. No loneliness.

From above, he could see heaven on earth—not in places, but in people. The light pouring from them when they cared, loved, gifted joy—even if unknowingly. Love, requited or not, oozed startling wonders that vibrated souls.

Of course, there was darkness too, trying to wreak its havoc, but it was no match to the light that he could tell with one flick of an invisible wrist would one day swallow sinister shadows. Down below, there were lonely hearts begging for a connection. What they didn't know was they already had one. They were never truly alone.

They just didn't understand that maybe a tender breeze enveloping their body was a father who cared more than they ever knew. An iron rod of courage or an invisible blanket of bravery; a brother who stood behind you giving you the strength you never knew you had. Oscillating shivers tapping spines; a son wanting you to be strong for his sisters. Or even hope floating like a message in a bottle; a soulmate's way of telling you he will always be there to catch you if you fall. Each was the presence of light, a sign that someone on this side cared and was right there beside them.

Shaun was free to live in fond memories or the moment. Time meant nothing here in a world of infinity; no such thing as forgotten. He would never be sad again, he knew his loved ones would share all this with him one day, and he would be sure to save them each a seat.

It made sense now, this connection they all shared; everyone he ever knew was his spirit family. If only *back there* in the storm they knew this. That when they hurt each other, they were only hurting themselves.

Shaun smiled. He was home. He knew the *secret*.

∞

ABOUT THE AUTHOR

Kent lives in New Zealand under the shadow of a mountain where it rains… a lot! Other than the pursuit of anything bad for his health, he also enjoys reading, sharing ghost stories, music, road trips and talking a wide range of excellent effluent over coffee with friends and family.